Launch to Destiny

"Now you can go kick some ass," Penny said from her seat at the command console.

"Thanks, I plan to," I said.

I stepped into the waiting capsule. It dropped, and moments later it shuddered to a halt. I triggered the suit's shock balloons and in an explosive 'ca-rumpf' they expanded out from their hidden compartments distributed around the suit. They locked me into place at the bottom of one of the largest air cannons in the world. A chill ran down my spine and my palms grew sweaty.

"Fire when ready," I radioed Penny.

"Roger, three second countdown. Three. Two. One."

It was better than the best amusement park ride. Ever.

The sound baffles flicked past and I popped out of the mouth of the cannon like a champagne cork with about as much noise. The shock balloon enveloping me collapsed and were sucked back into their hidden compartments ready to be deployed again. I rose silently into the twilight sky, the now familiar lights of my darkening neighborhood spreading out below, the distant towers of the Galacticity downtown redly reflecting the setting sun. My heart felt as if it was in my throat, rising in a crescendo of anticipation.

I triggered my jetpack, and accelerated upward on its stream of compressed air.

Dispensing Justice

Nova Genesis World #1

Fritz Freiheit

Illustrated by Matt Howarth

www.DispensingJustice.com

Liberty IV Publishing

www.FritzFreiheit.com
www.DispensingJustice.com
www.NovaGenesisWorld.com

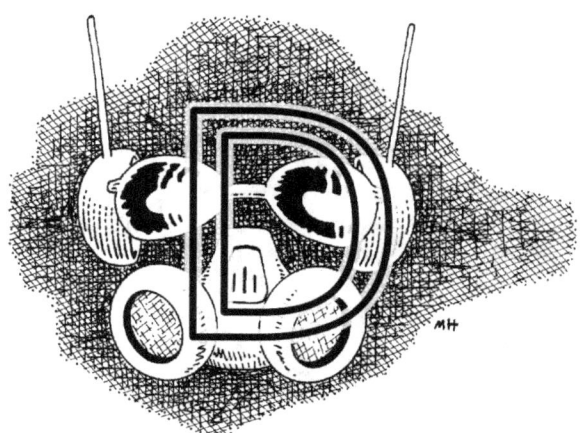

Dedication

To E.R. Burroughs, L.B. Dent, R.A. Heinlein, E.E. Smith, and H.G. Wells, whose superpowers include the ability to travel through time and inspire a sense of wonder.

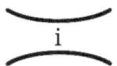

Acknowledgments

First, I'd like to give a shout out to Bill "Grandmaster of Flowers" Turnbull, Drew "Captain Justice" Hudson, Eric "Encephelon" Hall, Pat "Psion" Bills, Paul "Human Tank" Turnbull, and Theo "Major Chemical" Freiheit, who were all part of the milieu that brought about the first incarnation of the Dispenser.

To Gretchen Grey, who supported my efforts to write, as long as meals were delivered at regular intervals.

I want to express my great appreciation to John (Chris) Hocking, Joe Miller, and Lane Whittaker for their insightful, thoughtful, and beyond-the-call-of-duty attention to detail over the course of writing and bringing *Dispensing Justice* to publication.

To the Beta readers, thank you, for all your time and excellent critiques: John (Chris) Hocking, Dave Cross, Jeff Jackson, Jenny Johnson, Jessica Newberry, Joe Miller, K.M. Barrie, Lane Whittaker, Merideth Freiheit, Raghu Tadi, Skipper Hammond, and Stephanie Feldstein.

I would also like to thank the Alpha readers for their critiques and plowing through incomplete and error riddled portions of the manuscript: Adrianna Buonarroti, Bethany Neal, Courtney Conover, Patrick McHugh, Robyn Ford, and Sherlonya Turner.

To the members of the Ann Arbor Area Writers Group (AAAWG), I would like to thank them for their feedback and support during the transformation of *Dispensing Justice* from an idea for a short story into a novel: Adrianna Buonarroti, Bethany Neal, Bob Brill, Dan Gilbert, David Liu, Dave Wanty, Donnelly Hadden, Courtney Conover, Edd Tury, Elizabeth Van Ark, Jeff Jackson, Jenny Johnson, Jose Mojica, Karen Simpson, Kate Stone, Kay Posselt, Leslie McGraw, Martin Stolzenberg, Matt Bliton, Pat Tompkins, Patrick McHugh, Ray Juracek, Robyn Ford, Shelley Schanfield, Sherlonya Turner, Skipper Hammond, Stephanie Feldstein, and Sydney Bridges.

To Lisa Nichols, for her excellent copyediting, as well as Joyce Charles and Robert V. Frazier for followup corrections.

The staff at the Plymouth and Green Sweetwaters (you know who you are), for supplying me with a steady stream of iced lattes, my preferred mechanism for delivering caffeine.

And finally, to Matt Howarth, who decided to take a chance on a complete unknown. I've been a fan since 1980.

'Nuff said.

Table of Contents

Dispensing Justice

Doctor M's Robotic Hordes Attack, or Mom Interrupts the News

Friday, December 7th, 1984
(13,821 days post Supernova 1947A)

It is a well-established fact that an individual in possession of a secret subterranean laboratory is either a superhero or a supervillain. In my case, I wish it had been that unambiguous. Perhaps your opinion on the matter will differ.

My cellphone tweedled, buzzing briefly against the command-and-control console desk. My mother's disembodied voice issued forth, "Michael? Are you down *there* again?"

Before I could answer, a news-alert-filter program sounded a bell-like tone and the two goose-necked lamps illuminating the work tray in my lap blinked in sympathy. I finished inserting the o-ring and fitted the back plate into place on the tape-measure sized pump I was reassembling. Only then did I look up. As I scanned the curving bank of displays looming over me, my fingers began fitting and tightening the tiny machine screws that held the back plate in place. One of the screens was flashing like the Daily Double Jeopardy question-in-the-form-of-an-answer. Framed by a yellow-highlight border and sitting behind a Lucite slab of a desk was a masked, bronzed, and very buff anchorman.

The filter agent turned up the volume. The Super-hero News Network anchor, his too-blue eyes shining with excitement through his Lone-Ranger-esque mask, said, "We take you now to one of our news drones, hovering above the scene."

I suppressed a laugh. I don't know about you, but I find the SNN signature black domino masks and tightly tailored three-piece suits ridiculous; a cynical attempt by SNN to be 'hip' with the superhero scene. It's not as if a domino mask really conceals your identity. But then, that's almost certainly the point.

Behind the news anchor the feed from the news drone, splashed up on the SNN's studio's wall-sized bank of flat-screen monitors, was the image of a sleek black jump-jet with a red, eight-pointed starburst prominently displayed on its fuselage. I couldn't resist watching as the jet's downward-pointing fan-ducts threw up whirlwinds of dust, leaves, and litter across the plaza's dark red paving stones and between the rank upon rank of slowly advancing, mostly humanoid, robots. "A Nova League jet is even now landing in Nova Genesis Memorial Plaza to do battle against Doctor M's Robotic Horde."

The skin between my shoulder blades tingled as I thought of the suit hanging behind me in the darkened lab. The suit that I had been working on for the last six months. I had finished inserting gel padding, and the augmentation of its offensive and defensive systems had entered the second-guess-and-tweak phase. It was ready. But was I? The impulse to put it on and go join the Nova

League in their fight against the Robotic Horde was strong. But I would lose the opportunity I had been waiting for if this turned out to be the night that the Demolition Squad emerged from hiding.

The cellphone tweedled and buzzed again, this time long enough for the phone to start skittering across the desk surface. I slid the tray onto the console desk next to it. The phone stopped buzzing, halting its creeping progress when Mom said, "Michael? Are you there?"

I palmed the mute icon on the console, flipped the cellphone open and thumbed 'Talk'. "I'm here, Mom."

"What *are* you doing?"

I formulated my answer carefully. I wasn't going to give her the satisfaction that she had guessed right about my location. What was the point of a secret, subbasement lab if your mother knew about it? Okay, that wasn't fair. It wasn't exactly *my* lab, or, at least I didn't feel quite like it was. Mom had known about it from the beginning, of course, but she just didn't appreciate it the way I did. Besides, she hadn't been down here since Dad—I squashed that painful train of thought.

"I'm watching SNN, Mom." Which was true enough. The SNN news ticker at the bottom of the screen was scrolling 'Doctor M's Robotic Horde attacks the Nova League Tower' while the masked news anchor gesticulated excitedly towards the jet and the Nova Leaguers it was disgorging.

"Michael Gabriel Gurick the Third! If you're watching that channel before finishing your homework, I will *cancel* the cable subscription!"

I sighed. "Yes, Mother, I did my calculus, including the extra-credit problems, made comments on the physics forum, and wrote a history paper."

As I talked, I watched the closed caption below the masked anchorman. "The question on everyone's lips right now is," the words bubbling up read, "*Is this brazen attack by the Robotic Horde related to last summer's War-of-the-Worlds–style assault by the Demolition Squad?*" The ongoing attempts to link last July's landing of a giant metal cylinder in the middle of the plaza to every supervillain attack in Galacticity was becoming tiresome.

Sounding genuinely interested, Mom asked, "What was the history paper about?"

"The moon base," I said, scanning the bank of screens hoping to catch sight of other supervillain activity that the filter agents had missed. CNN Live was replaying the President's signing of the Supplemental Strategic Super Powers Initiative bill while First Lady Bacall looked on, but as I watched it cut away to cover the Nova League landing. CSPAN seemed completely oblivious to the events in Galacticity, continuing to show talking heads discussing the signing of the S3PI bill, then shifting to an interview with the House Minority Whip.

As I continued to scan, Mom said, "I remember the first non-superhuman moon landing. It was two years before you were born, and only six years after President Kennedy announced the initiative. We were so excited to have done it on our own! No Galactitech, just plain old Earth ingenuity."

"Yes, Mother." Damn, there was no sign of the Demolition Squad. On the other hand, the Nova League was starting to plow through the Horde.

She gave a dreamy sigh. I looked down at the phone, feeling a frown starting to form. Was she going to drift off into one of her reminiscences again? It was disconcerting. With her post-traumatic stress syndrome, I could never be sure when she would regress, slipping back to some prior state of mind. But then she continued, "You are remembering to make mistakes on your homework, aren't you, dear?"

"Yes, Mother." Good, not drifting.

"Have you finished your social studies reading assignment?"

It was the follow-up question I was expecting. "Mom, I read *The Sociological Impact of Supernova 1947A* three years ago. I can recite it by heart." Just to prove it, I shut my eyes and visualized the first page of chapter three and began to read: "'Into the impending political and racial turmoil of the 1960s, the children born under the baleful light of Supernova 1947A were beginning to manifest the powers that would become the hallmark of the first Nova Genesis generation.'"

"Isn't Professor Jane's writing marvelous?" Mom said, her voice ethereal with nostalgia. "She really captures the essence of the '60s."

"Yes, Mother." I wasn't so sure that Professor Jane's writing was really as good as Mom thought, but she had an excuse for her enthusiasm. She had met Dr. Jane Myers when she was hired to copyedit her first book, and they'd been friends ever since. I had signed copies of all the Professor's books. I'd even been interviewed, anonymously, of course, for the one she was working on now. "Can I go back to watching SNN, now?"

Friday Night in the Lab
[Watching the Superhero News Network]

"You spend too much time watching SNN," Mom said. "It's Friday night, and you're sitting down *there* alone."

"I like it down here, and it's not as if I can just ask friends over to hang out with me." Or, at least, not many of them.

Apparently stymied, she changed tactics. "Are you going out with Penny tonight?"

"Mother!"

"I just wanted to know if I needed to give you two a ride to the sophomore dance."

"I wouldn't be going to the dance with Penny, Mom. Remember? I'm dating Cleo, not Penny."

"Oh? A.J.'s daughter?"

"Yes, Sensei Fox's daughter." I didn't have the nerve to call him 'A.J.'; none of his students did.

"But she doesn't play chess."

"Not really, Mom, no." It was always a disappointment to her when she remembered that someone didn't play chess.

"Well, I don't know what she sees in you."

I heard the teasing humor in her voice, which was heartening, given her condition, and I laughed dutifully. It had been funny the first couple of times she had told that joke, Cleo being blind and all, but it was another painful reminder of Mom's continuing memory problems. Even worse than not remembering who I was dating, she would forget that I knew about the lab and fall back into the habit of acting like she didn't know I knew. And for non-professional actors, both she and Dad had been almost perfect at hiding their secret life from me, much to my irritation.

"But you are going to need a ride, though?"

"No, we won't."

"You seem awfully certain of that. Is Penny—"

"Cleo," I interjected.

"—standing you up?"

"I wouldn't put it that way." On the other hand, I wasn't sure how I would put it. Cleo had been acting strange for the past month or so, distracted and bordering on depressed. She had canceled our date for tonight with an apology and a kiss that told me in no uncertain terms that she was still interested in us. "Besides, we wouldn't need a ride, even if we were going. We have Transit passes."

"Of course you do, dear."

"But thank you for offering to drive us."

"Why not go with Penny, then? Just as friends, of course."

"She's going with someone else."

"Oh? What about Kim? Is he going to the dance? If not, you two could go to the movies. Isn't that new Eddie Murphy movie opening this weekend? *Beverly Hills Super-Detective* isn't it?"

"*Beverly Hills Super-Cop*." Not that I was particularly interested in seeing a super-detective or cop movie. I preferred films like this summer's hit *Ghostbusters*; funny, with the unreality of the supernatural. Not to mention plenty of eyeball-kicking CGI. I continued, "Kinnison—Kim told me that he wasn't feeling well. Honestly, Mom I'd rather just hang out and watch a little SNN."

She was silent for a moment, apparently running out of suggestions on how I should spend the evening. "You will tell me if you go out, though, won't you dear?"

"I'll keep you informed if I go out with anyone."

"Good. Good. Well, goodbye."

"Bye." I closed the cellphone and set it back on the command console next to the tray containing the partially assembled pump.

I reached out to tap the unmute icon, but froze when from across the lab behind me, a familiar, pleasant high alto voice said, "When are you planning on telling Liz?"

Penny Drops In

I swiveled the high-backed command chair around to face the east entrance to the lab. With the bank of monitors behind me all I needed was to shave my head and get a white cat to complete my Blofeld-in-his-lair look. Penny, completely unimpressed, was framed by the lab's eastern doorway, the tunnel corridor that ran under her house stretching out behind her. She had her hands on her hips, and was giving me that gimlet eye that Diana, her mother, had invented, patented, and been liberally applying to everyone she had an issue with since before Penny and I were born.

I suppressed the impulse to grin evilly and steeple my fingers. It didn't look like she was in the mood for my criminal mastermind schtick. Instead I watched silently as she crossed the open center of the lab, skirting the sunken and faintly glowing conference room table.

Also like Diana, Penny had copper-red hair, which she kept trimmed much shorter than her mother's. She looked relaxed in her two-sizes-too-large sweatsuit with the Roman warrior mascot of Centurion High School glaring out from her chest. While its bagginess went some way to concealing her very feminine figure, it did little to conceal her athletic grace. I'm reasonably physical. I've been playing soccer and running cross-country since middle school, and I started serious martial arts training late last spring. But Penny takes it to the next level. Or the one after that. She has gone out for, and excelled at, more sports than I bothered to keep track of. She'd be the star player on the football team if Diana would let her.

I doubt it would surprise you to find out that, as long as I've known her, she's been kicking my ass whenever she felt I'd gotten out of line, which has happened more often than I like to admit. I particularly remember the first time she gave me a bloody nose. It was not long after her family had moved in two doors down. We were both four; I had found out that her full name was Penelope Diana Riggs-Armstrong, and used it. Suffice to say, I've been calling her Penny ever since.

She stopped in front of me, a faint hint of vanilla arriving with her. I gave her my most welcoming non-evil smile. "Ah, so you got stood up, too." Which was a good thing, as far as I was concerned, given who had asked her to the dance. I wanted to say more, but as much as I disliked Dave Sweets, it was Penny's decision about who she dated. She probably had *a reason* that she wasn't sharing with me.

I hooked a backless ready-seat from under the desk with my foot and spun it out in Penny's general direction. Its wheels whirred briefly across the dense plastic of the lab's floor.

She ignored the ready-seat. "No, I stood Dave up."

I felt a cool smile of relief starting to form, but I put

a stop to it and said, "Sweets won't like that."

"Let me worry about him. Look, Michael, I know it's been a hard six months, but you have to tell Liz some time. The sooner, the better."

I sighed. I don't know why I even bothered. Distracting Penny from her chosen course was like trying to deflect a monorail. That was something else she inherited from Diana. "My mom isn't ready to talk about it yet."

"You mean *you* aren't ready." She glanced meaningfully at the chess set sitting out on the command counsel not far from the work tray. All its blue and red pieces occupied the same board positions that they had six months ago.

Feeling a coil of frustrated anger form, I stood. "Yes—No! Okay, neither of us are really ready to confront Dad's death, particularly together. It didn't help that she didn't trust me enough to give me the straight story last spring. She just played along with Agent Sellers when he showed up and oh-so-smoothly took Dad's place."

"I sympathize, Michael, I really do—"

"Yeah, I know you do." And I meant it, even if I didn't sound as if I did.

"—But you have to get over this. Sellers was just doing his job, and you know that your mom didn't want to hurt you."

"So instead, she was going to wait to tell me until after Sellers faked his own death? Making it look like my father was killed in a car crash or something? Yeah, that wouldn't have hurt."

"Be fair, Michael, it didn't end that way. Besides, do you really think she had much of a choice? Liz was co-operating with the government in order to protect the two of you from your father's enemies. It's standard operating procedure for them to—"

"—Cover up superheroes' deaths. I don't care about their S.O.P. My father deserved a hero's funeral!"

"That's not what I was going to say. And yes, he did deserve a hero's funeral."

What really hurt was that Dad hadn't shared so much of what he felt was important in his life with me. We never had a chance to talk about what it was like to hunt criminals, to bring them to justice. Now that he was gone, we never would. I guess it's one of those things that's been driving me to put his suit on; to find out what kept him going back to risk his life over and over; to experience his secret-super-life first hand.

I felt my anger with my father mutating, shifting, looking for a living target. It bubbled up as a rant, and, despite knowing full well that Dad's enemies would have come looking for Mom and me if they had discovered his secret identity, I let it happen. "They must have thought, 'Oh, he's only fourteen, he'll be easy to fool.' Well, I discovered Dad's secret when I was eight! I've been sneaking down here since then. No shape-shifting government super-agent was going to fool me into believing my father was still alive, with or without Mom's help!"

"Slow down, Michael. I'm with you on this."

"It's different for you, Penny, your family has always embraced its superness. I've had to grow up being lied to."

She held up a calming hand. "Michael. Remember? I'm on your side. I'm not the one who—" She stopped, looking up at one of the monitors. "You better take a look at that, Michael. I think tonight might be the night."

I thumped back into the command chair and whirled it. She hadn't been looking at the SNN coverage of the Nova League; instead she was pointing to one of the live web-cam feeds that had become ubiquitous in Galacticity and the Greater Metro area during the last couple of years. An armored car had driven into a pit that had somehow appeared in the middle of the road. Its rear doors were at an acute angle, while its red tail lights flashed helplessly. Several supersuited figures were assaulting it. I recognized them immediately. It took the Silhouette and Supersuit Recognition Agent program slightly longer, but before I could say anything, identification labels popped up and started following the four supervillains around the screen like comic-book word balloons.

"The Demolition Squad," I said through clenched teeth, a new flame of anger erupting to life on my already raw emotional landscape.

"All of them," Penny added. "Including Chainsaw."

I clenched my fists as the flame roared up into a momentary conflagration of hate.

"Okay, let's get you suited up," Penny said.

Zircon Man vs. the Demolition Squad

Penny's calm voice doused my anger like ice water to the face, yet I still felt a warm glow of virtuous anger smoldering somewhere deep down.

Before we could turn away from the monitor, the Demolition Squad had pried open the armored car's back door like it was a cheap tin roof. A red-and-blue supersuited figure with a golden exoskeleton and an equally golden full-face mask leapt out. He was immediately labeled Zircon Man by the system, so he must have had an active super-ID transmitter.

"That looks like a Cyber City Strong Man Mark III," Penny said, referring to Zircon Man's gold power-assist exoskeleton.

"Or an upgraded Mark II," I said.

"Could be. He doesn't stand a chance. He's not even wearing the Tough Guy armor mods."

"Definitely second string."

"He's got a cape," we said in unison.

Zircon Man was leaping about, engaging the four supervillains in a whirlwind of flying fists and kicks, his red-and-blue cape billowing up behind him.

"He won't last more than thirty seconds against the Squad."

"Unless they decide to 'play' with him."

"True. Corporate or rent-a-hero?" I asked, not bothering to look him up in the Supers Registry.

"Who cares? The League is busy dealing with the Robotic Horde at the plaza, so you've got your chance to do this without their intervention."

I palmed the lab lights icon on the console, instantly flooding the circular space with a daylight brightness. Penny wasn't discomforted by the sudden change in light levels, but I was forced to blink several times and let my eyes adjust. "I was wondering how I was going to arrange getting to the Squad before the League did."

We started moving to the north wall of the lab as I talked. Hanging six feet out from the middle of the wall there were four large, white backpacks, each with a thick silver umbilical cord arcing down from the ceiling. If you stopped and listened, you could hear the occasional heartbeat-like throb of pumps. Beyond the backpacks a half dozen suits in various states of repair were mounted on the wall. Each of them looked like a white full-bodied painter's overall, with hood, cap, goggles, and full-face rebreather mask. They each had two arcs in thick black lines inscribed on their chests, one curving up over one curving down. It was one of the standard diagrammatic symbols for a nozzle. At the mid-point of the nozzle where the curves almost touched was Dad's concession, or, perhaps, his acknowledgment of his membership in the Nova League: a red, eight-pointed starburst the diameter of a half-dollar. Looking at the suits, I felt my doubts surge up again. Was I worthy to wear any of Dad's suits? Could I ever really take his place?

Penny squeezed my shoulder with a hand that I was momentarily keenly aware was quite capable of crushing every bone therein. "You'll do him proud, Michael," she said, as if she had read my mind, which, as far as I knew, she still couldn't do.

The Suit

I stepped up to the third suit from the right, the one that I had been working on for the last six months, inserting gel padding so I would fill the suit out—Doc Styx, the oldest living Earth-born superhero, tells me that I'll be taller than Dad, not that I am dropping names or anything, because he's been treating Mom since June. All right, I admit it, I am name dropping. I stripped to my skivvies—and I wear boxer briefs, if you must know—only momentarily thinking about Penny. She had helped me suit up enough times that I was almost able to do it without thinking about how female she was.

I handed her my cellphone.

"And if Liz calls?" she said, raising an eyebrow.

I didn't think Mom would, but... "Tell her that I'm helping you with your calculus home—no, wait. Tell her that we're watching an on-demand movie or something, and if that doesn't work, patch her through."

"Of course, if you're not busy," she said, her voice

dripping with sarcasm.

"At least Diana won't be calling to check up on us tonight."

She glanced over at the monitors. The League was holding its own against Doctor M's army of robots. "Nope, she's definitely too busy to wonder what we're doing."

I stepped into the suit, gritting my teeth as the plumbing snugged into place. I kept wondering when that part of suiting up was going to get easier.

"I assume your dad is covering the attack at the plaza, but how is it that you managed to leave without the twins tagging along?" I fastened the main seam, leaving the hood and rebreather-filter mask dangling.

"I made them promise to behave."

We were moving toward the backpacks. "And that will work?"

"They've come a long way since the library incident."

I lifted the disk-shaped cold-fusion power pack from its cart. "So you really trust them now?"

"I know you went through a rough patch with them, but that was before the riots."

"Yeah, okay, we've all changed since then." I fitted the power pack into place in the backpack I'd prepped specifically to take on the Demolition Squad. The power pack was the only one I had that still worked, and while I had been studying Dad's files, I hadn't been capable of doing anything more sophisticated than general maintenance on the power pack's cold-fusion bottle. If—no, *when* I could build a new one, I'd be at least halfway to taking up Dad's role, to be more than just playing at wearing his mask. Until then, I had to make sure this one kept functioning. Without the cold-fusion bottle, the suits were just so many million-dollar Halloween costumes.

I pulled the backpack on and Penny helped me tighten it into place. I powered the suit up. The hoses locked into place with the faint whirring of servo-motors; the arms and legs stiffened, then softened, as their complement of hoses pressurized and equalized. I pulled the hood and mask up and sealed them, inhaling the slightly rubbery smell of filtered air. The internal status display appeared. Everything was green. I buckled the utility belt into place and signaled the umbilical to disconnect. I barely sagged as I took the full load of the fifty-two pound mission-ready backpack. Penny could have danced the Nutcracker while wearing it, of course. I engaged the pneumatic power-assist and the load lightened. I gave a thumbs up to Penny and braced myself.

Penny returned my thumbs up and headed for the high-backed chair at the command console. In the time it had taken to suit up, the monitor agents had identified five more trouble spots. The night was turning into a real crime wave. I spotted Electrode, Backslash, and a couple of other techno-thugs in proactive pursuit of wealth. And Penny had been right about the Demolition Squad deciding to 'play' with Zircon Man. He was still fighting, despite several obvious gaps in the golden struts of his exoskeleton, and a lurching gate.

Fear and elation fought within me, their tendrils entangling, leaving me with a muddled feeling of nausea. I tried to ignore it and started for the launch capsule door.

"Systems check." Penny's voice on the suit radio brought me up short, my non-skid soles squeaking on the seamless high-density plastic floor of the lab.

I turned back. "Roger, systems check."

"Communication links?"

"Of course the radio works. We're using it."

"This is serious, Michael."

There was no use being impatient. "Comm links. Check."

"Video link? Check," she said, answering her own question. A panoramic view of the lab centered on my head appeared in the lowest band of monitors. "Cold-fusion bottle?"

"Reading 90 kilowatts, pushing 200 kilowatts for peak output. Nominal neutron flux."

"Primary pump?" Penny queried.

"Online," I answered, its faint hum reassuring.

"Secondary pumps?"

"Online."

"Main tank pressure?"

"756 atmospheres."

"Pneumatic power-assist?"

"Check."

"All mission-specific reservoirs reading?"

"100%."

"Now you can go kick some ass."

"Thanks, I plan to." I said.

I stepped into the waiting capsule. It dropped, and moments later it shuddered to a halt. I triggered the suit's shock balloons and in an explosive 'ca-rumpf' they expanded out from their hidden compartments distributed around the suit. They locked me into place at the bottom of one of the largest air cannons in the world. A chill ran down my spine and my palms grew sweaty.

"Fire when ready," I radioed Penny.

"Roger, three second countdown. Three. Two. One."

It was better than the best amusement park ride. Ever.

The sound baffles flicked past and I popped out of the mouth of the cannon like a champagne cork with about as much noise. The shock balloons enveloping me collapsed and were sucked back into their hidden compartments ready to be deployed again. I rose silently into the twilight sky, the now familiar lights of my darkening neighborhood spreading out below, the distant towers of the Galacticity downtown redly reflecting the setting sun. Orange pinpricks of light connected by vaporous white trails created sweeping bracelets in the southeastern sky as cargo and passenger modules were boosted upward on invisible beams of ultraviolet laser light. My heart felt as if it was in my throat, rising in a crescendo of anticipation.

I triggered my jetpack, and accelerated upward on its stream of compressed air.

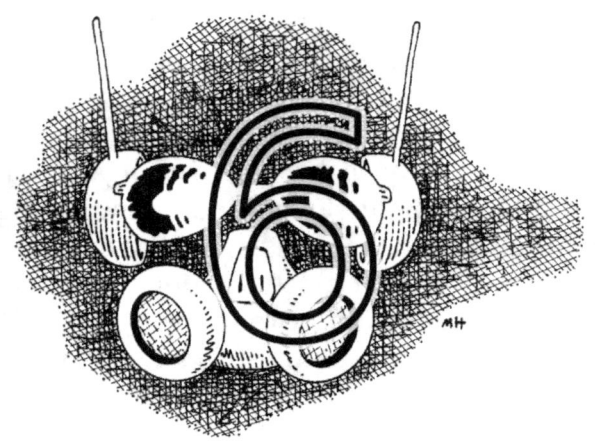

1947A

Thursday, May 3rd, 1984
(13,603 days post Supernova 1947A)

But I'm getting ahead of myself. Where should I begin? I am tempted to start with February 3rd, 1947, when the supernova wavefront first reached Earth and, if I might editorialize, the comfortable seclusion and self importance of Earth was shattered. Without the intervention of the Galactics, every major flora and fauna extant on Earth would have been wiped out. Without the least bit of prejudice. But the Galactics did intervene. What we have come to call the Shield, which was in actuality a massive array of gamma-ray and neutrino 'sterilizer' shields, worked. Mostly. But what you may not know is that complications occurred.

I am still unclear on the details of what went wrong, particularly as to the source of the Shield failure. But without Galactitech, stopping the neutrino damage would have required more than a light year of lead. With it, the Shield 'flipped' the supernova's flood of neutrinos to their sterile, non-interacting form long enough for them to pass harmlessly through the Earth. What I do know about the Shield's failure is that at least one of the Galactics' ships collided with part of the array, and a portion of the deadly melange of radiation and 'unsterilized' neutrinos slammed into Earth. The swiftness of the Galactics' response to this disaster was a clear indication that they had been prepared for the eventuality. Or perhaps it would have been necessary to drop the regenerative nanotech in the form of a cometary rain in any case.

Despite the Galactics' revealing themselves as long time observers of Earth, they have remained remarkably close-mouthed about what went wrong on February 3rd, 1947, when Supernova 1947A impinged itself on our quiet Galactic neighborhood. I should add that they have said little about what went right. As you are probably aware, if you have been paying attention in your history class—and I won't hold it against you if you haven't been, as I have trouble staying awake in Ms. LeGrange's class myself—is that not everyone, nor everything, was saved or cured by the Galactics' nanotech. Life on earth was decimated, literally. Ten percent of the human population died, as well as a similar percentage of every other species—more or less. Some species and ecosystems are more robust than others. Then there were the mutations, many of which turned out to be positive through the miracle of Galactic nanotech. Life changed. Particularly for my father's generation. Which isn't to say that those who were born before 1947A didn't personally benefit from the Galactics' intervention by more than simple survival. Many diseases were simply wiped out, and cancer has become nearly unheard of during the last thirty-seven years.

All of which is pretty much ancient history for me. Seven months earlier, May 3rd of this year to be specific, is the date of a far more significant and personal change. And for me there is a painful symmetry between February 3rd, 1947, the day of the supernova, and May 3rd, 1984, the day when my comfortable existence was terminated with prejudice.

When I came off the soccer field at the end of freshman practice that day, I was trembling, sweat soaked, and dripping gobbets of mud. Luckily the rain had stopped just before my final class of the afternoon, staying away long enough to let the scrimmage proceed as planned, returning intermittently to ensure an interesting quantity of mud. The game had been just what I needed to take my mind off the looming, monstrous event of the day. I chugged water from my formerly frozen milk jug while I watched Kinnison checking text messages on his cellphone. I had deliberately turned mine off, and despite the craving to check for texts, email, or voicemail, I was keeping it off. He looked up, noticed my stare, then looked back down at his inTouch.

"Hey, Gurick," he said, staring at the small screen and thumbing furiously away, big splattering drops of rain drawing muddy rivulets down his cheeks. "Did you hear about what the Demolition Squad did to—"

"Yes!" I said, way too forcefully, "Yes I did!"

He stopped texting and looked up at me again. "Hey, sorry man, I should have guessed you'd know. He was one of your idols, wasn't he?"

"Yeah. He was." I heard a familiar car horn from the street and turned to see the family mini-van. I turned back to Kinnison. "My ride's here."

"See you tomorrow, Gurick. And, for what it's

worth, I know what you're going through. When Turbocharger was killed, I couldn't watch the news for weeks."

But he so didn't. Which didn't mean that I didn't appreciated his lame attempt at sympathy. "Thanks, Kinnison. Tomorrow."

I Saw You Die

When I opened the door to the mini-van I almost had a heart attack of joy. Instead of finding Mom at the wheel it was, impossibly, Dad. Then the cold tendrils of reality clamped down again. How could it be him? This wasn't the comic books, where every superhero keeps coming back despite dying in four-color glory. I had watched with horror the webcast news footage shot from an SNN drone. It had gone viral just hours before, so everybody would know by now. Somehow the Demolition Squad had beaten him in the end, and the final scene was etched in my memory. A filter-masked, red goggled head being held aloft by a triumphant Chainsaw, the white suited body of my father lying at his feet. There hadn't been much blood; the suit, still trying to protect him, had sealed itself.

So who was this doppelgänger? His mimicry of my father was exact, down to the faint chemical stains on his fingers, and the platinum wedding band. I wanted a closer look at it, to see if it had the gouge that had appeared after Dad's encounter with Blowback.

"Aren't you going to get in, son?" the man who couldn't be Dad said. "Don't worry about the mud."

I continued to hesitate, absently wiping at my mud-splattered uniform. Dirtying up the interior of the van was the least of my worries. Even if I wasn't worrying about whether my dad's secret identity had been compromised, or if Mom was okay, I wouldn't have hesitated because of a little mud. But it was just like Dad to miss the fact that Mom had had the interior of the van treated with Dirt-Shield—she had been, some would say compulsively, buying the White Whirlwind's line of Super-Clean products ever since he retired from crime fighting five years ago to 'Clean Up America'. The apparent lack of concern about my muddy condition on the part of the doppelganger sitting in the van's driver seat could have been from his—its?—knowing Dad wouldn't have paid attention to a Dirt-Shield treatment in the van, or it just could have been a hole in his briefing. Which led back to the question at hand. Was this a supervillain, and was he involved with Dad's killing? The analytical part of my mind engaged, slowing the barrage of questions, prioritizing and categorizing the facts and unknowns.

After what felt like minutes, but was actually only a few seconds I managed to say, "Uh, I just have to get my bike."

As I unlocked and wheeled it around to the back of the van, my mind had shifted into analytical overdrive. Either someone had underestimated me, or they had one hell of a psych profiler, a profiler who could predict my mixture of curiosity and desire for revenge. You can guess which one of those two possibilities I preferred. I clipped the bike to the rack as I looked through the rain in the direction of the tennis courts. I expected Penny to be along soon.

Through the fabric of my backpack I fingered the high-pressure chemical sprayer that I had built into a pen, considering how I could surreptitiously get it out. It was loaded with a variation of mace that I had synthesized. Give it half a twist, and the shot of high intensity irritant would incapacitate anybody but a 'brick'. Give it a twist and a half, and it would deliver its chemical load with enough force to punch through a gas mask. Or drywall. I know. I had had to do some pretty fancy verbal footwork to explain the hole in my bedroom wall last fall.

Maybe I'd get a chance to incapacitate whoever this was and ask him some pointed questions. There were five hidden video cameras distributed about the interior of the mini-van, continuously monitored by software agents that would alert the authorities if it identified any unusual activity. Installed, so I was told, because we might be kidnapping targets, what with Dad being a VP of Energy Development at Galacticity Metro Edison and all. While the kidnapping threat was real enough, it was because of the job Dad didn't talk about, not the one he did. Of course they could have been hacked, in which case there wouldn't be a timely armed response. I'd just have to deal.

I slipped the pen from my backpack and got in next to 'Dad'. "Uh, sorry, I was just expecting Mom."

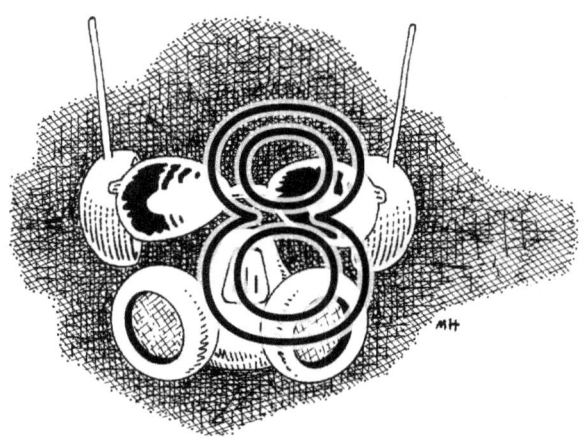

Penny Keeps Her Cool

"My afternoon meeting was canceled," 'Dad' said as I buckled my seat belt. "So I thought I would surprise you and pick you up."

I stopped myself from saying "Oh, you really surprised me, all right." Instead I said, "That Bayside fusion sub-plant installation must be going well if you could sneak away."

"The secondary heat-exchanger delivery has been delayed, and I've applied pressure with the suppliers where I can. It's all up to Fusion Dynamics now."

Damn, I thought. *He's even got the Bayside construction schedule down,*

We started to pull out of the parking lot when I spotted Penny riding her mountain bike around the edge of the soccer field, heading for home. I was torn. Should I get Penny involved? Or just take the risk myself? Penny could take care of herself, but the two of us together...

"You seem tense, Michael," 'Dad' said, "Did things not go well in school today? Or, you've already seen the news on SNN today, and—"

"There's Penny," I said, interrupting him. "Can we give Penny a ride home?" I rolled my window down and leaned out to avoid the cameras.

"Indubitably," he said, slowing the van.

Oh, crap, I thought. *This guy is even in on the family jokes!*

"Hey, Penny!" I yelled. "Want a ride?"

She waved and 'Dad' pulled the mini-van over. She stopped her bike on my side and looked in. I watched for signs of surprise.

Her eyes widened momentarily, then she said, in an admirably normal tone of voice, "Oh, hi, Mike."

I mouthed 'get in' and waggled my eyebrows.

"Hello, Penny," 'Dad' said.

"Want a ride?" I repeated with more waggling of the eyebrows.

"Sure. Thanks. Yeah, I'm pretty beat after tennis practice."

Oh, come on, I thought, rolling my eyes at her, then glancing at 'Dad', *you could play tennis all day long and then do a triathlon before dinner, just to work up a real appetite.* But 'Dad' hadn't noticed or didn't care. Penny just gave me a blank look.

She racked her bike and climbed in, taking the seat behind me. The automatic door slid shut and 'Dad' pulled out into traffic.

"So, Penny," 'Dad' said, "are you planning on going out for the football team this fall?"

Why would he ask that? Just to make conversation?

"Yes, that's the plan. That is, if I can talk Diana into letting me."

"I thought you might be, now that the school board has adopted the 'iron man' rules."

He knows about Penny! I thought. And he must know about Diana, too. Why else ask about 'iron man' football?

Penny had thought that she might talk her mother into letting her play now that NFL's 'iron man' rules had trickled down through the college football leagues to the Greater Metro high school league. I thought it was a pathetic attempt by the NFL to take back viewership it had lost to the American Supers Football League. On the other hand, you couldn't deny that average high school kids today were notably tougher now than they had been before Supernova 1947A and the Galactics' nano-tech repairs of its radiation-induced genetic damage. Whether or not they had superpowers.

I held the pen between door and seat, showing it to Penny. I made several screwdriver-like twisting motions, then jabbed it in the direction of 'Dad'.

There was a stinging pain to the back of my neck and I almost jerked around, dropping the pen in the process. I knew that Penny had flicked me with a paper pellet. One of her highly compressed paper pellets, which had been known to draw blood. I read it as a vote of no confidence in my idea of macing 'Dad'.

While I fumbled for the pen, I changed tactics, trying to make him trip up on his facts and force him to act.

"I've been thinking about interviewing Professor Jane for my sociology final project."

"Professor Jane—" he said, pausing for a fraction of a second, "—would make an excellent interviewee for your social studies project."

Smooth. If I hadn't of been looking for it, I wouldn't have caught hesitation. My fingers felt the metal barrel of the pen, and I fished it out.

"I thought so," I said. We had pulled up to a stop light. It was time to take whoever this was out, whether or not Penny liked the idea. I lifted the pen, angling it towards 'Dad's' face. I started to twist it when he said, "You just can't rely on secrecy for protection."

I froze. It was Dad's prearranged key-phrase indicating that he was okay, and not under duress. While I still didn't believe this was Dad, I was forced to conclude that the man with Dad's face and wedding ring was here with Mom's consent and foreknowledge.

It was quiet for several long heartbeats, the only sounds were the purr of the van's electric motors and the hiss of tires on rain-wet pavement as we accelerated through the intersection.

Then Penny kicked the back of my seat, hard. "Oops, sorry," she said. "Just had a muscle spasm."

Five minutes later we were pulling into Penny's driveway.

"I'll come over after dinner. I'm stuck on a calculus problem," Penny said as she slid out the back door. "I'm sure you can walk me through how to solve it." But what Penny had really said was, *You will explain what just happened to my satisfaction.*

"No problem," I said. "See you later."

We watched in silence until Penny disappeared through her front door.

"Do you want to talk about it, Michael?"

"Talk about what, 'Dad'?" Did I just say his name with quotes?

"You tell me."

We pulled into our driveway, the garage door rising in front of us. I didn't say anything.

"Well, when you are ready to talk, I am..."

It was the right thing to say. I just didn't want to hear it from him.

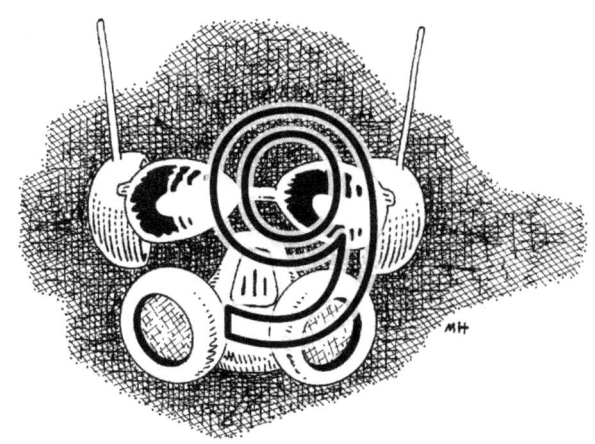

Mom Burns a Roast

When I entered the mud room, Bernoulli, our mongrel spaniel, greeted me with enthusiasm, and I wondered how he was going to react to 'Dad'; then the smell of burnt meat and a faint sobbing from the doorway to the kitchen drew my attention. I peeked through the door and saw Mom hunched over the kitchen web terminal, her black hair in disarray. Before she could turn I retreated and dumped my pack noisily to the floor and sat to remove my soccer cleats.

"Michael! Is that you?" Her voice was brittle. I heard the stool scrape against the floor.

"Yes, Mother. Just taking off my cleats."

She came to the mud room door just as 'Dad' opened the door to the garage.

"How was—Oh! Mike, thanks for picking Michael up from soccer practice." The brittleness had changed to a forced lightness. "It's just been one thing after another here. The Lansky project moved up their publication date and I'm afraid I burned dinner and—"

As Mom talked, Bernoulli's tail wagging faltered and he growled slightly, but 'Dad' put his hand out and patted Bernoulli's head without missing a beat. Bernoulli's tail went into motion again.

"It was no problem," 'Dad' said, gently interrupting her.

I focused on untying the wet shoe laces as she retreated back to the kitchen and he followed.

Abandoning the laces, I wrenched off my shoes and went after them. The state of the kitchen told me pretty much everything I needed to know. There was a White Whirlwind cleaning products order page on the web terminal, above the oven black streaks ran up the wall to spread out in a feathery delta on the ceiling. Through the oven window I glimpsed the charred carcass of a roast.

Before I could muster the resolve to say anything, 'Dad' said, "I'll order pizza." He flipped open his cellphone, but he hadn't done more than dial and say, "Yes, I'll hold," when the front doorbell rang.

Mom looked wide-eyed towards the front of the house, making me think of the Roswell sheriff in that first photo of the Galactics. I'd never known her to lose it like this. It was frightening.

"I'll get it," I said, wanting out of there.

Diana to the Rescue

I started down the hall towards the front of the house. But before I reached the foyer, the door opened, and in came Diana carrying a steaming casserole, without, I might note, the benefit of oven mitts. Even in the post 1947A Galactic cleanup world, Diana is imposing. She's standout statuesque, six foot two, and a coppery redhead like Penny. I stood aside.

She smiled encouragingly at me and said, "Hello, Michael," as she strode past. Behind her came her husband Hank, a tall, rangy man with salt-and-pepper hair, then Penny, and finally, Penny's two eleven-year-old siblings that we not-so-affectionately called the 'Terror Twins', Andy—short for Andromeda—and Achilles. Sometimes I wonder whether Diana takes her secret identity as a professor of Classical Studies at Metro U a bit too much to heart.

"I brought dinner, Liz," Diana said, leading her domestic assault squad through to the kitchen. Andy stuck out her tongue at me as she went by, and Achilles gave me a look like it was my fault he was missing an episode of the A-Team. I followed, feeling an irrational dollop of pleasure at the twins' irritation.

The parade deposited a casserole, hot rolls, steaming beans, salad, and pie on the kitchen counter.

"Set the table, Michael. You help him, Penny," Diana said, taking charge as thoroughly as she did on the battlefield, despite the absence of her form-fitting silver superwear, mask, bow, and quiver.

Mom was making weak protesting noises as Diana herded her out of the kitchen with a "You look like you need a drink, Liz."

'Dad' and Hank sized each other up like a couple of beta-males assessing their chances. The twins disappeared down the hall and into the rec room, shoving each other as they tried to go through the door simultaneously.

"Grab that end," Penny said, and we lifted, pulled, and manipulated the expansion leaf out of its hidden slot under the table without crushing so much as a single finger.

"SimOlympus!" Achilles said from the rec room.

"Galactic Bounty Hunter 4!" Andy chanted back.

"Sibs," Penny said, "Can't live with 'em, can't strangle 'em in their sleep."

"Blissfully, I wouldn't know," I said. I started shuttling plates and silverware while Penny positioned them.

As I came and went with glasses and et cetera, 'Dad' and Hank started cleaning up the remains of Mom's cooking, talking about the latest human gaffe towards a Galactic ambassador, as if they really were old friends. Hank was handling the situation like a pro. But then he was a reporter for GCTV, so he did have experience as an actor of sorts.

Diana and Mom reappeared. Diana was carrying a tray with four martini glasses filled with something bright yellow. She distributed them among the adults.

"Are these Golden Apples?" 'Dad' asked, real curiosity in his voice.

"Yes," Diana said with a wicked smile, "My sister's recipe. So good they'll make even the gods argue."

'Dad' laughed, and Mom attempted to suppress a look of shock. He even had Dad's laugh.

The rec room had gone quiet. "That's not a good sign," Penny said softly to me. Moments later, there was a crash just to prove her point.

"You'd better take care of them, Diana," Hank said.

There was another, even louder crash, and Bernoulli appeared in the doorway to the kitchen, barking, tail wagging.

The Twins Are Ejected Before Dinner

"Andromeda! Achilles!" Diana said, setting down her martini glass and stalking out of the kitchen.

Seconds later Diana reappeared, holding each of the struggling twins at the end of one of her outstretched arms without the least sign of strain. They were flailing at each other. Bernoulli danced, barking in her wake, as she crossed the kitchen, heading for the mud room and the door to the backyard.

'Dad' and Hank went in the opposite direction. Penny and I sidled up to the kitchen window to watch.

First Andy sailed into the backyard, then Achilles. Both landed in the wet grass, sliding half a dozen yards before coming to a stop in a struggling heap. Bernoulli raced out after them, barking merrily. He was a spry old dog of eighteen years, and still acting like he was eight—another unintended consequence of the 1947A nannite cleanup, one can only assume.

I'm sure that if the neighbors noticed the yelling and punching twins, they would have been thanking their lucky stars that the Riggs-Armstrongs were visiting our house and not theirs.

"You can come back in when you've cooled off," Diana said and shut the door. "I'm sorry about that. It's difficult ensuring that they get enough exercise. When they don't, well, they find other ways to blow off steam."

"Oh, I can sympathize with the poor dears," Mom said. "There are days that I don't get out of the house and it puts me into a mood, too."

'Poor dears', my ass, I thought. What they needed was a thorough thrashing. Unfortunately, other than Diana, Penny was about the only one capable of doing that these days. It was becoming difficult to resist the impulse to try out some of Dad's anesthetic gas—or, even better, his retch gas—on them.

"Didn't they go to the dojo today?" Mom was saying.

"No, Sensei Fox is on another one of his vacations," Diana said.

'Dad' and Hank came back from the rec room a short while later. "No real damage done," 'Dad' said. "They knocked over the memento cabinet, but nothing was broken."

Which was not surprising. Dad had started 'twin-proofing' over ten years ago. It had turned into an arms race: at times Dad's 'upgrades' kept the twins at bay, and at other times we cleaned up the broken glass and filled in the holes in the walls.

We seated ourselves at the kitchen table and had started loading our plates when the twins slogged back in, Bernoulli trailing, a hopeful wag-wagging to his tail. I hadn't thought they would hold out long, as food, or the lack thereof, was in question. All the Riggs-Arm-strongs—excepting Hank, of course—had metabolisms that a shrew would admire.

"Are you two ready to be civilized?"

"Yes, Diana," they said in unison from the mud room doorway.

"Then wash up and take a seat."

They did so with another pious chorus of "Yes, Diana."

I spotted only a couple of surreptitious elbow jabs between them as they came out of the bathroom. Diana had them sit on either side of her. She loaded their plates and they ate in sulky silence for five pleasant minutes.

Diana filled the conversational vacuum with retrospectives on what her grad students were working on and the political maneuvering of the other professors in the Classical Studies Department.

"Tell everyone about that incident at the Galactics' Arcology yesterday, Hank," Diana said after her fifth attempt to engage 'Dad' and Mom in a discussion was rebuffed with monosyllabic answers.

Hank smiled. "Oh, you'll love this. I was there covering the arrival of the latest group of tourists, when ten Earth-Firsters broke out their banners and started protesting the presence of the Galactics. It always gets me that the Earth-Firsters want to ban the Galactics after all they've done for us. All that would be left on Earth now would be cockroaches and bacteria if it hadn't been for their cosmic-ray shield and neutrino flipper! And what have they asked for in return? Nothing but the right to be tourists."

"And then what happened?" Diana prompted.

"The Galactics produced their own collection of placards—I have no idea where they got them from—and started marching in circles. You need to check out the video. The look on the faces of the Earth-Firsters is simply precious. The police arrived just in time to keep the Earth-Firsters from charging the

Galactics. You know, just when you think you might be starting to understand the Galactics, they go do something like this."

"Perhaps they've been watching the Olympic protests on television," I suggested.

"That's a thought," Hank said. "The Soviets have been kicking up enough of a fuss. It doesn't help that they're being held in Los Angeles."

"After the drubbing they—really pretty much everyone but the North Americans took during the last Olympics, it isn't surprising," Penny said.

"Don't you think they might have a point?" Diana added. "The drubbing in 1980, as you so eloquently put it, Penny, was a direct result of our fielding so many competitors that were, frankly, borderline supers. The screening weeds out the obvious ones, but I know for a fact that a half a dozen of the medal winners were holding back."

"On the other hand it is the way the human race has been headed," Hank said. "We didn't choose to be exposed to gamma rays or boiled in neutrino soup, and I don't see anyone at this table complaining about the effects of the Galactics' nannites. Who can seriously say that we would have done things differently if they had actually asked whether we wanted to be saved?"

Before anyone could respond, 'Dad's' cellphone tweedled. Looking at it, he said, somewhat plaintively, "It's from work..."

Diana glanced at Mom, then pursed her lips when she didn't react. It tweedled again. "Then you better take it, Mike," Diana said.

"Yes?" he said into the cellphone as he left the kitchen.

Penny's green-eyed gaze met mine. I shrugged and mouthed, "I bet he's going to be called away."

She nodded, her lips forming, "No bet."

'Dad' returned, re-holstering his cellphone. "There's a problem at the plant and I've got to fly out to Fusion Dynamics tomorrow."

"Oh," said Diana. I could hear the 'good' that didn't follow the 'Oh'.

The Vow

After the dishes had been cleared and the rest of the Riggs-Armstrong clan had gone home, Penny and I sequestered ourselves in my room on the pretense of doing calculus homework. She had turned on my old clock radio and found Rikki's Request Hour on GROQ 104.7. Gabriel's *Shock the Monkey* was playing and it seemed to sum up the current state of my mind.

"Is this Fritz Mk. III?" Penny said, looking into the gerbil cage where the animal in question was running in his wheel, which was a pretty good reflection of my thoughts about the events of the day.

"Nope, Mk. IV," I said, pulling out my desk chair but not sitting.

"'They've killed Fritz!'" Penny said, turning to look at me. "'Those dirty, stinking fairies have killed Fritz!' Does that make you one of the fairies?"

"Ha, ha. Anyways, I thought it was funny when I named the first one Fritz. And I still like *Wizards*..."

"You like *Wizards* because it was the first drive-in movie that Liz and Mike went to that you managed to spycam."

"Ah, those were the days."

"When I was your muscle, you mean."

"You had some pretty diabolical plots, too, if I remember correctly." Which I did.

"Maybe if you name one of your gerbils 'Mongo'," Penny said, redirecting the topic of conversation back into safer waters. "It would live longer."

"It's a thought."

"I talked to Diana." 'About your dad being killed today,' was the elephant she didn't have to point out.

"Ah," I said, trying to play the stoic.

"The League recovered his body before the Demolition Squad could unmask him."

"That's good." My guts were churning and I had to work at keeping the casserole down. "What about *him*?" I added, jerking my chin towards the office downstairs where the man masquerading as my father had holed up after dinner.

"He's a government agent. Diana said that they sent him to make it more difficult for your dad's enemies to track you and Liz down."

I sat. Thoughts of revenge pumping hot through my mind. I balled my hands into fists and looked up at Penny, meeting her calm, sympathetic gaze.

"You know I'll support you, Michael, whatever you decide."

"One way or another I'm going to bring Chainsaw and the rest of the Demolition Squad to justice," I said. Corny or not, having made the vow, I felt better.

Consequences of Killed in Action

Friday, May 4th, 1984
(13,604 days post Supernova 1947A)

The next day was a waking nightmare. I even went so far as to forget myself and scored 100% on my calculus test. Fortunately, it was Friday. Kinnison took the clue and didn't bring up the topic of superheroes, but he was the exception, rather than the rule. I hadn't made it general knowledge among my fellow Centurions about who it was I idolized among the supers. On the other hand, I did find out that there were a lot more fans of my father's superhero guise than I had been aware of. There were T-shirts—some using the new animated dyes, which, ironically, I didn't know at the time had been invented and patented by my father—and dozens of black armbands. Superheroes don't die in the line of duty very often, but when they do, it's a big deal. Given the two-thousand-plus student body at Centurion High, I shouldn't have been surprised.

At lunch, Penny found me in the library where I had retreated from the ebb and flow of the hallways. I was flipping through Popular Superscience, trying to take my mind off yesterday.

Looking over the magazine rack, she said in a voice low enough not to attract attention, "Formulating a plot yet?"

I said in an equally hushed voice, "Oh, hey, Penny. Not really, no."

She pulled the April 23rd issue of Superpeople off the rack—the one with the Titanium Titan showing off his new armor on the cover—then sat opposite me and began leafing through its glossy pages of hero-villain gossip. "You think too much, Michael."

"And what is that supposed to mean?"

"Sorry, that didn't come out right. What I mean is, you're brooding over you-know-what, when you should be coming up with a plan for what you're going to do about you-know-who."

A plan. Was this an attempt to distract me? Shift me away from the pits of despair that I was doing my best to wallow in? A guilty little voice reminded me: *Wallow? You haven't even cried.*

She continued, "Things are going to change when you put the suit on."

"In what way?"

"You know perfectly well what way. You're stalling."

"Okay, I admit it." I lowered my voice even more, "I *have* been thinking about taking up Dad's mask."

"Of course you have," she said, her tone of voice was matter of fact. "You haven't talked of anything but since you were eight."

I felt the blush spreading up my neck and looked

down at the cut-away infographics of the recently defeated Baron Atom's lair. "I always thought I would have more time to ease into the role."

"And you were expecting an instructional manual to come with it?"

"Well, yeah. It's in the computer 'downstairs'."

She looked exasperated. "And you think that will tell you how to be a hero?"

"No, not really."

"You either have it in you, or you—" She stopped talking, and cocked her head as if listening.

I followed Penny's gaze through the library windows. Cleo Fox, a fellow freshman, was approaching along the hall leading past the library towards the Commons, tapping her cane as she came. When Cleo was almost in front of us, she paused, and as if she were steadying herself, put her palm against the glass that separated us. I had the odd feeling that she could feel our stares. You know how people always say that being blind enhances your other senses? Cleo is living proof of it. Her gymnastics' moves are a wonder to behold. Despite the sound-proof glass separating us, I wasn't willing to risk sharing our conversation with her. So we waited, while I read her T-shirt, which said *Superfreak* in Coca-cola style cursive. After a second or two, she continued towards the Commons, and for some reason the fading click-click of her cane was strong in my imagination. The back her T-shirt read *Brickhouse Records*.

"What are you doing tonight?" I said, breaking the spell of silence.

"Max wants me to come 'round and update my character using some new rules that he's been working on. He was asking if you wanted to update yours too, but I told him that you wouldn't be in the mood and left it up in the air."

"So you can come over?"

"Sure. I'll meet you 'downstairs' at seven. I may be late if I have to ditch the twins."

"Cool. See you then."

Soccer Socks

I exited the library through the Commons door, and was heading towards the East Wing for my fourth hour Physics class, when I noticed that a group of varsity football players had surrounded Kinnison. From the look on Kinnison's face and a few of the choice words that I picked out above the hubbub of the Commons, he was being razzed for being a 'sissy soccer player'.

"Kinnison!" I yelled across the twenty or so feet that separated us. "Want some help with those goons?"

I didn't wait for his reply, but plunged through the flow of students. I'd gotten over going from being among the eldest at the Frank P. Ramsey Middle School to being the youngest at CHS. Intellectually, that is. I hate to admit it, but my emotional maturity has lagged far, far behind. Besides, I was looking for trouble.

I grabbed the first one's shoulder and gave a yank as I said, "You're brave enough when it's three against one."

He hardly budged, instead wheeling about on his own power. He was much bigger up close.

"Hey guys, there's another freshman soccer weenie," he said, grabbing at me with a hand the size of baseball mitt. It was attached to an arm that looked long enough for him to slap his own knee without bending over.

I ducked under and planted a fist just above his belt. I would have gone for the chin, if it hadn't looked like it was chiseled out of granite.

When my hand rebounded off his abs I recanted that decision. This guy was halfway to being 'brick'. The notion that a significant number of my fellow students at Centurion High are developing powers hadn't crossed my mind when I charged in.

I heard Kinnison yell, "Look out!"

I turned just in time to block a fist flung by the second, even larger, Senior. He was blond, and had a grin plastered across his face that was broad enough that I could see what was left of his lunch stuck between his gleaming teeth. Then an arm from the man-mountain-in-training behind me wrapped around my chest and the grinning one's fist slammed into my left eye. The world reeled and I saw a yelling Kinnison jump on the blond's back. Two more collisions with fists and I was down looking for a knee that I could bloody with my nose. If I'd had lunch I would have defiantly messed up their shoes.

Then things quieted and I was being helped to my feet with a "You'd better come with me, Mr. Gurick."

Through a haze I saw a pair of white slacks, then looked up to find a circle of faces, which parted as I was led along gently, but firmly, by the elbow. I heard someone say, "Pity. Not that I expected a pair of nerds to really do anything to Drumlin and his cronies."

Dr. DuQuane's Office

"We gave 'em hell, didn't we, Gurick?" Kinnison said, cradling his right hand.

We were sitting in one of the offices that was part of the principal's suite. I was holding a freezy-pack over my eye, trying to suppress the paranoid rambling of my regrets, but the hyper-kinetic energy of my swirling thoughts made the task seem Sisyphean. Of course, the adrenaline-driven thudding of my heart didn't help.

The ironic smile I tried to give Kinnison turned into a grimace. "Yeah, I'm sure they won't be tangling with us again any time soon."

He didn't seem to catch the tone of my voice; in fact there seemed to be some regret when he said, "I hope not." He looked down at the knuckles of his right hand, like he had just discovered them. He held his fist out in my direction. "Do you see anything weird?"

"Not really, no." They looked perfectly normal to me. No scrapes or redness.

"Humph. I could have sworn I hit Luther, but—"

The door to the office opened. Mr. Parker, Dr. DuQuane's personal secretary stepped lightly through the door. In his black turtleneck and white slacks he looked like he had just arrived from the Village. I half-expected him to say, "Number Two will see you, now." But instead he said, "Your turn, Mr. Gurick."

I was ushered through a door with 'Dr. Marcus DuQuane' lettered on its translucent pane of glass.

I took a seat across the desk from Dr. DuQuane, and then, feeling self-conscious, I started to lower the freezy-pack.

"Why don't you keep that on," Dr. DuQuane said. In contrast to his well-muscled henchman, Mr. Parker, Dr. DuQuane was a slim man with a shiny pate. His baldness seemed to emphasize the fact that his head was slightly too large for his body.

"Yes, sir," I said. It wasn't really a question, so I returned it to my face. I could feel my eye swelling shut.

"Well, Michael, what do you have to say for yourself?"

I ran through my options again. Stonewall? Not much hope of that—there had been enough witnesses. Tell him that I'm angry that, from his perspective, my favorite superhero was just killed? Or admit to just enough of the truth? "They were picking on Kinnison, sir."

"And you thought that attacking the boys who were bullying Kim would solve the problem?"

Boys? Had he actually *looked* at them recently? "In retrospect it doesn't seem like such a good idea, Dr. DuQuane." On the other hand, Kinnison wasn't being picked on, and Martin, Chen, and Luther were cooling their heels in another office.

"I don't understand, Michael. Your grades are quite good. In fact, you show the occasional flash of brilliance. You participate in extra-curricular activities and sports. What did you expect to gain by getting into a fight that you couldn't hope to win?"

I almost said, "Relief by way of temporary insanity," but it didn't look like he was in a humorous mood. I settled for, "Nothing, sir."

"You do know that I'm going to have to send you home?"

"Yes, sir."

Doc Styx

"Thanks for giving me a ride, Hank. I didn't want to bother my mom. She's got that Lansky project, and, well, you know the other thing."

"It's no problem Michael. I know you'll explain to Liz what happened later. I'm surprised with your chosen method of blowing off steam, but I can understand it. If I didn't know better, I would say that it was a suicide attempt."

"What can I say, Hank? I was trying out stupid, and performing masterfully at it."

He chuckled. "I'm glad you're keeping a sense of humor about you, Michael."

I smiled back, regretting it at once. I lowered the freezy-pack and looked at the mirror in the sun visor. I had a bruise the size of a grapefruit. I gently palpated the region.

"I don't think you've broken anything," Hank said. "I can usually tell."

We were pulling into my driveway.

"If you need anything, just call," he said as I got

out of his mini-van.

"I will. And thanks again, Hank. For everything."

I entered through the garage side door, being as quiet as possible and knowing that Bernoulli wouldn't betray me. I didn't really want to talk to Mom. Both because I wasn't keen on explaining why I was home early, as well as not wanting to talk to her about Dad.

But the security system ratted on me. The intercom in the garage said, "Michael. You're home early."

"Yes, Mom."

"I'm in my office. Get something to eat, then come talk to me."

"All right," I said with an entire lack of enthusiasm.

I grabbed a snack for Bernoulli from the stash in the garage in order to fulfill my end of my longstanding bargain with him not to bark when I entered the house by myself. He was patiently waiting in the mudroom. I paid him off.

After dumping my backpack in my room, I popped a burrito into the microwave, then went to attempt a postponement of my fate.

Mom was sitting at her computer, documents spread out across the screens. She swiveled towards me when I entered. "Michael! What happened to you?"

"Just a little fight, Mom."

"Little? You look like someone used you as a punching bag."

"How's the Lansky project going?" I asked, hoping against hope for the distraction to take.

"It didn't give me a black eye, that's for sure. Are you going to explain yourself?"

Okay, try straight-up honesty this time. "I was just

trying to keep Kim from being beat up. Can we talk about this later, Mom? Kim is okay, and I'm not really in trouble, I swear, and I'm sure Dr. DuQuane will be sending you an email about it."

She gave me a piercing look that softened after a moment. "Fine. We will talk about it later, though."

"Yes, Mother." And I got out of there.

It wasn't more than twenty minutes after the interview with Mom when the front door bell rang. I paused in the foyer to check the security scanner. It showed a young, clean cut man, slightly hunched, wearing a suit several sizes too large with a bundle of papers under his left arm. His image was overlaid with the uniform dim green glow of a clean scan. No energy sources—even the silver watch peeking out from his suit jacket was mechanical. I immediately labeled him as a Witness. I wasn't interested in getting another lecture, particularly one about how the Galactics were here to save our souls. I was about to turn away when he pressed the doorbell button again and I noticed that he had a cellphone clipped to his belt.

I fingered my mace pen, then opened the door. "What can I do for you?" I said through the screen.

"Are either of your parents home?" he said in a reedy voice.

"Whom may I say is calling?"

"I am John Jenkins, and I would like to bear Witness." He held up a multicolored pamphlet, waving it slightly.

"You look a little young to have been a Witness."

"Many of us were cured of all failings of the flesh during the Ice Fall, including the scourge of aging."

"Ah. Well, why don't you come in, Mr. Jenkins? My mother is home."

I opened the door and he stepped in. "I greatly appreciate your allowing me to bear Witness. May the Galactics bless you."

Without letting Mr. Jenkins out of sight, I shut the door and the security system beeped its satisfaction with the perimeter seal. "You can talk freely now, 'Mr. Jenkins'—I just swept the house for spy devices and the walls are reasonably spy-ray proof; the terahertz range in particular."

He looked puzzled. "I don't understand, young man. Is this some sort of joke?"

"Perhaps I'm wrong, but you're either Doc Styx or the Magician. Given your build I would say the odds are that you're Doc Styx."

He straightened, seeming to grow several inches and filling the suit out. Where there had been a five-ten, average-looking (if slightly hunched) man now stood a six-foot-one man who radiated charisma. "You're definitely your father's son." His voice had changed, taking on a deeper, more commanding tone that I recognized as distinctively Doc Styx's. "How did you know?"

"Your cellphone, sir. It's a prop, with no battery, I think."

"Damn," he said with wry twist of his lips. "Better you than one of the bad guys."

"Yes, sir."

"That's quite a shiner you have there."

"It's a long story, sir."

"I'd like to hear it some time."

"I doubt it would be of much interest to you, sir."

"Nonetheless. You did say your mother is here?"

"Yes, sir."

"I came to pay my respects. Your father will be missed in the League."

"I know she will appreciate it, sir. Can I ask a favor?"

"You may ask."

"She doesn't know that I know..."

"Then I won't tell her." He hunched again, seeming to shrink.

"If you'll follow me, Mr. Jenkins."

... And The Magician

Less than five minutes after I ushered Doc Styx in to see Mom, the doorbell rang again. The scanner showed another harmless-seeming young man with pamphlets. This one was rather shorter than 'Mr. Jenkins'. Either this was a real Witness or it was the Magician.

Again, I opened the door, and the conversation repeated itself. When he had entered and I'd shut the door, I said, "You really should coordinate your disguises with Doc Styx."

His eyes widened. "I don't—" His accent slipped from middle American to one that hinted at his Quebecois roots as he continued, "Why do I even bother? Sometimes I think he is deliberately trying to upstage me."

"Well, if it is any consolation, I don't think I would have guessed you were the Magician if Doc Styx hadn't just arrived in the guise of a Witness. He's in with my mother right now."

He reached into his pants pockets with both hands.

With an almost unconscious flourish, he drew two bouquets of flowers, each twice the size of his head, first one from his right pocket, then one from his left. Their heady scent filled the foyer. It was the first time I had seen the Magician demonstrate his powers in person, and I was suitably impressed.

He glanced from bouquet to bouquet. "Which one do you think your mother would prefer?"

"Uh, well, I know she likes chrysanthemums." Some of which I had spotted in the bunch in his left hand.

"Good." He pushed the one in his right hand back into his pocket, returning it to the miniature universe he had withdrawn it from. When he withdrew his hand again, it contained an expensive box of chocolates.

I gave a little cough and raised my eyebrows in the universal sign of 'Really?' What was he thinking?

"Um, I suppose not." The box disappeared again and he said, "Shall we?"

I escorted the Magician to Mom's office extracting a promise to not let her know that I knew about her and Dad and his membership in the League. At our arrival, the Magician glared at Doc Styx. I heard the Magician mutter some choice French phrases under his breath as I retreated.

To keep busy, I made dinner for Mom and me.

The Remains of a Chess Game

As I waited for Penny, I contemplated the chess-board that I had found on the command console when I came down to the lab. It was a disturbing remnant of Mom and Dad's life together.

A hiccuping sigh of air made me turn away from the chess set. Penny was stepping off what we called the 'pneumatic-pogo', a drop shaft, not unlike a high-tech version of a fireman's pole, that provided quick access to the lab from the house above. The hand-foot grip whooshed back up the pole, and I stood, putting myself between Penny and the chessboard.

"What is it?" Penny said, a look of concern on her face.

"Nothing."

She took a step to the side, spotted the chessboard and raised her eyebrows.

"Ah," she said. She came forward and looked the board over. Reaching out, she righted the blue king, then picked up a blue bishop and took the remaining red rook.

"Hey!" I said.

"What? You can easily replace the pieces where they were from memory."

"Yes, but—"

"Why did you stop playing chess with Mike?"

"I thought he was letting me win. Besides, after I found that cache of SPI wargames of his, I was more interested in them."

"But you still play chess with Liz, and you don't complain when she lets you win."

"That's different. She taught me how to play chess, and, well, it's one of those things we share."

"I know. By the way, Liz seemed rather distracted when I stopped in to see her just now."

"She had a couple of visitors before dinner."

"Oh? Who?"

"Doc Styx and the Magician. They both showed up on my doorstep disguised as Witnesses, within minutes of each other." I described Doc Styx's arrival followed by that of the Magician, concluding with, "When I brought the Magician in to Mom's office, I could have run a bank of neon lights off the tension in the room."

"Diana says that if Doc Styx has a fault, it is his persistent probing for other people's weak points. The Magician's is vanity."

"That would explain it."

The monitors burbled an alert indicating that someone with access codes had entered the tunnel complex. I scanned the monitors and found the source. The underwater locks to the tunnel at the marina on Lake Michigan had been opened and closed, and now something large, blue and silver-gray was approaching at high speed. I caught flashes of it on several more of the monitors.

"Do you know who it is?" Penny asked.

"Beyond Dad trusting them, no," I said, fumbling my way through the security interface. Mousing like a fiend, I flipped through the programs and stumbled into something labeled 'Silhouette and Supersuit Recognition Agent', just as a heavy 'ka-thoom' sounded from the corridor outside the lab's southern entrance. I swung around to face a massive metallic figure in electric blue and silver-gray, ducking through the door.

The Titanium Titan

"Titanium Titan," Penny and I said together; although I was sure I sounded awed, Penny sounded like she was announcing that the mail was here.

He paused just inside the door, every inch of his eight-foot-tall body utterly still, eye-ports crackling with tiny blue electrical arcs. After a second he took a clanging step forward and I noticed that he was carrying a bundle of what looked like white fabric.

"I wasn't expecting to find anyone here," he said. His voice boomed over an external speaker, echoing across the lab.

"Uh—" I said. The brilliance of the syllable matched my earlier moments in the CHS Commons.

"Are you here to see Liz?" Penny asked.

"Not tonight," he said.

His amplified voice was like rolling thunder, causing me to wince. Naturally, Penny was unaffected.

The lower portion of his helmet retracted, revealing a strong chin and a thin mustache perched on his

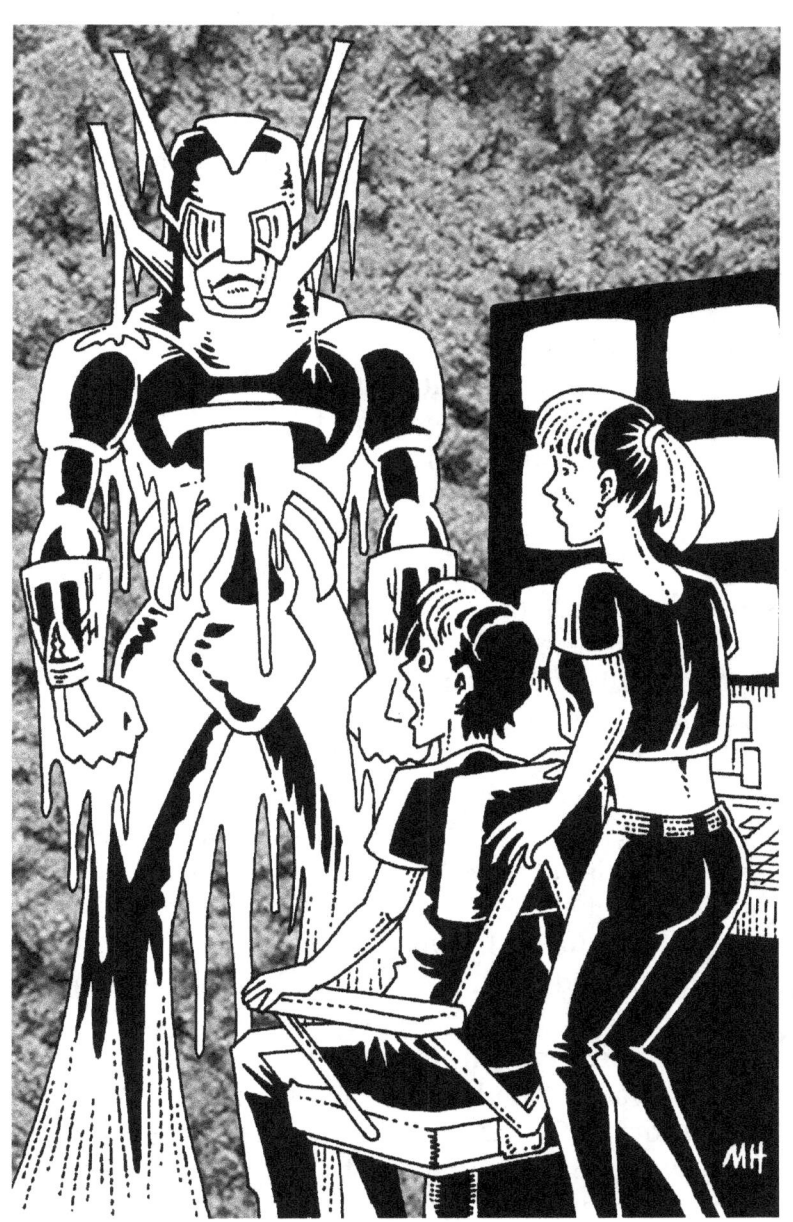

upper lip. "Sorry about that," he said, his voice normal now. "You're Penny, Diana's daughter, right? And you are Michael. You look a lot like your father."

I nodded.

Penny said, "Yes." She glanced at me, then continued, "You'll have to excuse Michael. He's a little put off by the appearance of one of his former idols."

"Penny!" I said.

"Former?" the Titanium Titan said.

Penny turned her head towards me. "You have to take these things in stride."

"Former idol?" the Titanium Titan said.

She returned her regard to the metal-suited man. "That's right, Titan, 'former'. Up until Michael discovered who his father was, you were his favorite superhero."

"Well, in that case," the Titanium Titan said, sounding mollified.

My ears were burning.

Mercifully, the Titan changed the subject. "I suppose you're wondering why I'm here?"

I had been, but with a twisting churn of my stomach I realized what the white bundle was. I swallowed. "No. You brought back my Dad's suit."

"That's right." He sounded a little surprised. "I'll put it over here." He stumped across the lab and placed it on one of the workbenches.

I swallowed again, and took a breath. When he turned back I said, "Where is his body?"

The mouth and thin mustache gave a sour grimace. "We've got him back at the League headquarters in a cryocapsule. And before you ask, I don't know when we'll be returning the body. It's up to the government agent in charge of your case."

"You mean the man who is masquerading as my

father, don't you."

I could tell he was surprised, even through all the armor. "Yes, he's the one. But I shouldn't talk about this with you, so we'll just drop that subject."

"Fine," I said. There wasn't much I could do to force the information out of him.

"Where did you get the black eye?" the Titan asked.

Why was everyone bringing that up?

"A little reminder not to go into combat without backup," Penny said.

"Or a sanity check," I said under my breath. I briefly explained my lack of self-control.

"You should have used your mace-pen," Penny said.

"Maybe I shouldn't have," I said.

Penny snapped her fingers. "You forgot it, didn't you?"

The Titanium Titan smiled. "I agree with Penny," he said. "Use a little leverage next time." He slapped himself on the chest with one gauntleted hand, the 'ka-thang' echoing through the lab. "I swear by it." He glanced at the chessboard. "Red checkmates blue in five. I'll see you kids around." Sealing his faceplate, he ducked out the way he had come. A prickly hot wash of pungent ozone from his antigravity generators marked his passing. We watched the monitors in silence until, with another burble, the system announced that he had exited through the marina locks.

I glanced over at where the Titan had deposited the remains of Dad's suit. It wasn't difficult to derail my impulse to inspect it. I looked at Penny. She was back in front of the chessboard moving pieces about. I dropped into the command chair and watched.

After a minute or so I ventured, "I think Mom and Dad played chess just before missions."

"Hmmm," Penny said.

"Probably to relieve tension."

She fingered a red rook. "Any idea who was playing blue?"

In my mind I pulled up an image of the board before Penny had started playing with it and examined the situation. "My Dad."

"That's what I think, too. Why do you think Mike was letting you win?"

"Because I was his son."

"Really? I have a better explanation. He wasn't *letting* you win at all. You were beating him because you were a better player."

"No, way! He hated to lose."

"Yet he consistently lost to your mother."

"How do you know that?"

"She told me."

Why hadn't Mom told me? Of course, she had taught Penny how to play, and they played more regularly than Mom and I did. "Why would he keep playing me until *I* stopped?"

"Because you were his son. He kept playing Liz because chess means a lot to her. You should play her more often, you know."

"Yeah, I know."

"She gave up a lot when she partnered with Mike."

Mom had been a Candidate Master before quitting organized chess. She had given up her chance at becoming a Master to become Dad's mission coordinator, his communications facilitator, allowing him to focus on the battles. But what if Mom had been more than that? What if she had been giving him tactical and strategic guidance? Applying her mastery of chess, of predicting Dad's opponents' moves eight or ten steps ahead?

"She may have given up chess competition, but I don't think she gave up pitting her tactical and strategic skills against opponents'." I explained the rest of my thought to Penny.

She nodded, unsurprised by my epiphany. "Now you're starting to think like a crime fighter."

The Brain Trust

Thursday, May 10th, 1984
(13,610 days post Supernova 1947A)

For the next week, every member of the Galacticity Nova League, and quite a few Nova Leaguers from chapters in other parts of the country, put in appearances at 3714 Proxima Drive. The only one that Dad's security system didn't record was Neutrino, but I'm sure she showed up if the rest of GC Nova League paid their respects. Between soccer practice and school—where I scrupulously avoided the varsity football gang—I kept busy, spending most of my days away from the house. 'Dad' wasn't around much, the Bayside project seeming to take up a great deal of his time. I started working on a more powerful replacement for my mace-pen; something with more punch. The white bundle left by the Titanium Titan on the workbench in the lab was an uncomfortable reminder that Dad's body was lying in a cryocapsule at the League's headquarters, making it almost impossible to work there, so I took a portable analysis-synthesis kit–a compact but fully functional lab built into an aluminum alloy suitcase–from one of the well-stocked lockers near the lab up to my bedroom. When I wasn't working on the new prototype in my room, I found myself hanging out at the Riggs-Armstrongs', despite the presence of Andy and Achilles and their exuberant and increasingly realistic superhero role-playing.

As the week wore on, the frequency of visitations dropped. Then a day passed with no Nova Leaguer or other super putting in an appearance. I assumed that the visits were at an end, so I headed for the lab. I went in through the backyard tool shed, which, in addition to storing the tools and being the recharging station for the backyard robot lawn mower, was a noise suppressor for the air cannon launch system. I climbed down a ladder to the drone magazine chamber. As I stepped out into the corridor-tunnel that stretched between the Riggs-Armstrongs' house and the equipment bay just off the lab, I heard footsteps approaching from Penny's house. I ducked back into the drone magazine, and, using the wall terminal, I punched up the corridor monitors and found the appropriate video feed. There were three men, dressed identically in brown and green jumpsuits, offset by wide silver belts with a spidery mesh of complex patterns etched into them. Each had a pair of vambraces on their forearms and circlets on their foreheads, also silver with geometrical patterns. They looked like clones or an odd mime troupe, moving abreast down the corridor with perfectly synchronized steps and swings of their arms.

I hesitated, thinking that I could let them pass and that would be the end of it. But the opportunity to talk to the most brilliant member of the Nova League, either here in Galacticity, or elsewhere, was too tempting.

I stepped out into the corridor when they were a couple of yards from the drone magazine.

They stopped moving as one, seemingly unsurprised by my sudden appearance. Three pairs of green eyes focused on me.

"Michael," the one on the left said.

"Gabriel," the one in the middle said.

"Gurick," the one on the right said.

My gaze had bounced from one to the next as they spoke.

"The Third," they said in unison.

"Brain Trust," I said, not sure which one I should focus on.

"We," they said in unison, "are here to see Elizabeth Ann Gurick."

I settled for the middle one and pretended that he was who I was having the conversation with, regardless of who spoke. "She's upstairs in her office. Would you like me to take you up?"

"We know the way," Brain Trust said. "But first, as you are conversant with your father's subterranean domain—and all that implies—we would like to ask you a few questions."

"Uh, sure, shoot," I said.

"What caused us?"

What were they, or, rather, what was he driving at? I had to be careful to not muddle my thinking. While the Brain Trust had three bodies, they had a single mind. "Supernova 1947A," I said with more confidence than I felt.

"And?"

Okay then. They wanted details. I could play that game. "Skipping over the necessary role that your parents played, I would say that it was the Galactics' nanotech-based cleanup delivered by a cometary rain, which was intended only to repair the damage caused by the 1947A's gamma ray and neutrino burst that penetrated their Shield. But it left many of your generation with mutant powers. Including a set of triplets with a single mind. Why are you asking me a question that I can't possibly hope to answer in way that will add to your knowledge?"

"We would ascertain your understanding of the events surrounding 1947A."

"What I know is pretty much textbook, augmented by what you can find on the web."

Three pairs of eyebrows went up. "Your father and mother never discussed it with you?"

Where Do Your Powers Come From?

"Sure, I've talked about 1947A with my parents. But only from the non-powered perspective of their generation. They never mentioned the super side of their lives." The bitterness in my voice was impossible to suppress.

Brain Trust ignored my tone. "You have mentioned mutants. What other classifications of the superpowered are there?"

"Aliens, of course, technological devices, cyborgs, and chimeras, created when the Galactics' nano-cleanup mixed two or more organisms into one." Like my gym teacher, Mr. Martin, who was, oddly enough, a human-gorilla chimera.

"There are other sources of powers."

A fantastic and disturbing thought struck me. "You don't mean that there is such a thing as magic!?"

"There is nothing supernatural in this world," he said, his voices coldly, calmly, reassuring. "But the Galactics' technology is sufficiently advanced that it may appear to be magical."

"As long as it's scientific," I said, a disproportionate

sense of relief flooding me at the absolute certainty in his/their voices.

"What about you, Michael Gabriel Gurick the Third? Where do your powers come from?"

"Me? I don't have powers!"

"Are you quite certain?"

"I don't have any psionic powers, and physically I'm about average for my generation, so, yes, I'm certain."

"And yet, you have a power." Maddeningly, he changed topics. "What do you know of Roswell?"

"First Contact between humans and Galactics, or, at least the first recorded contact."

"And the crashed ship?"

"I thought that was just rumors and conspiracy theory," I said. But it was strange that the Galactics had picked a remote desert town for their First Contact when they would later place their arcology-embassy in southern Lake Michigan.

"Roswell was the first well-documented intervention. There is no strong evidence that they intervened on Earth before 1947A, but since 1947A, well, it seems like they feel that they must interfere."

"Perhaps it's a 'you broke it, you bought it' sort of thing," I said.

He paused. The right-hand one stroked his chin several times; the middle one ran his fingers through his short-cropped hair; the left-hand one didn't seem to do anything at all. "That is an intriguing analogy. It would explain their social intervention of Galactic Citizenship, and participation in the Operation E.N.D. Run nuclear disarmament. We will have to pursue it." He went silent for a moment again, as if he was filing the thought away. Then his machine-gun fire of questions started up again, "What have they asked from us in exchange for this protection and repair?"

"To be tourists and art critics."

"Your knowledge is incomplete."

"And this surprises you?" I snapped back.

"The Galactics are not perfect, as they would have us believe. They made a number of grievous errors in 1947. The Shield did not function properly. Or perhaps it would have, if it hadn't been for a collision with one of their Star Wisps. We don't know for sure what happened, but we know that Earth was, possibly accidentally, seeded with military-grade nanoborg devices. The Roswell landing was a military intervention to neutralize a platoon of cyborgs created by the nanoborgs. This neutralization, like many of the others that the general public is unaware of, was not entirely effective. One of the cyborgs, a command and control unit, eluded capture."

"It's a relief to hear that the Galactics are only human," I said, "and as much as I appreciate the history lesson, I can't help but wonder why you are telling me these things."

"Perhaps if we tell you that the one that avoided reassimilation by the Galactics at Roswell is now known as Doctor M, you will begin to see the significance."

Doctor M and his spawn, the Robotic Horde, were one of the Nova League's most pernicious enemies. The fact that Doctor M was a Galactic-tech-level cyborg explained a great deal of the difficulty that the League had in putting him down and keeping him that way. "Yeees, I see your point. But I am still puzzled as to why you are telling me."

"We merely seek to illuminate the path you have chosen. You have the necessary answers. You will work out the pertinent questions in time. Now we must call on your mother."

I Express the Desire to Learn
How to Fight

Friday, May 11th, 1984
(13,611 days post Supernova 1947A)

I put my tray down next to Kinnison who was sitting across from Penny, trying to ignore the impulse to run its contents through a chemical analysis for the presence of that elusive cafeteria ingredient called 'nutrition'.

"So, Gurick, planning on showing up at a run any time soon?" Max Wright said from the other side of Kinnison. Across from Max, Lilly Henderson glanced up from her copy of the latest Heroes Weekly and gave me a wave before diving back in.

"Hey Lilly," I said. "I don't know, Max."

"Come on Gurick, we need you," Kinnison said. "And Penny. We're dyin' like henchmen! I haven't had my character resurrected so many times since running in your campaign. Max is an *evil* Architect!"

Max smirked.

"What happened to your vaunted dice luck, Kinnison?" I said. "You used to be able to wander around the dungeon all by your lonesome."

"I lost it, man," Kinnison said, a look somewhere between embarrassment and hang-dog depression on his face. He brightened and added, "Maybe you were my lucky charm? Come 'round to Max's and we can find out."

"I don't know," I said. "I've got a lot on my mind lately." It sounded lame, even to me.

"You can take time away from your chemistry set," Penny said. "When's your next run, Max?"

"Tonight." He sounded pleased. "My basement, as usual."

I sighed. "Okay, I'm in."

"Excellent!" Kinnison said.

"You'll enjoy yourself, Michael," Penny said. "A bit of hack-and-slash always cheers you up."

"That reminds me," I said, "If there's one thing I learned when I took on those three goons, it's that I have to learn how to fight."

"You need more than that," Penny said. "But yes, you could do with some hand-to-hand combat training."

"So, you have a suggestion to make?"

"Have you talked to Cleo Fox recently?"

"I was thinking more along the lines of kung fu than gymnastics."

"I'll take that as a 'no', then."

"What about where you go to work out? Don't they have martial arts instructors there?"

Penny's voice was heavy with sarcasm, "Why yes, as I recall, they do."

"What? I'm just asking."

"I've been trying to tell you. I workout at the Black

Lagoon Dojo, which is run by Cleo's dad."

"Oh," I said. "Right then. When are you going next?"

"Tomorrow afternoon. Be at my house at 2:30."

"Hey, Penny," Kinnison said, "Mind if I tag along? I got pounded, too."

"Sure, Kim," Penny said. "I don't think it will be problem."

"It's a date, then!" Kinnison said.

"Oh, I think you'll change your mind about calling it a 'date' soon enough," Penny said.

"I can't believe Jetstream is dating Magnetic Mistress," Lilly said. She looked up from the glossy spread in Heroes Weekly to find that we were all staring at her.

'Dad' and I Have a Chat

I was sitting at the table in our darkened kitchen, doing designs in my head and waiting. The only illumination was provided by the red and green glow of digital clocks and appliance ready-lights. On the table in front of me sat an empty plate with a smear of cherry pie filling and bits of crust next to a glass with milk dregs. Bernoulli had given up begging for the plate and curled up on his cushion in the corner. My encounter with Brain Trust, a little more than twenty-four hours earlier, was still fresh in my mind. His tantalizing mixture of questions and answers had gelled my resolve to add to my meager supply of facts.

I heard the garage door open, and the butterflies in my stomach took flight. Bernoulli raised his head with a barely audible 'whurfl?', then jumped up and ran into the mudroom, furiously wagging. I tracked the sound of his progress, butterflies circling. I faintly heard the car door thud shut, then the garage door closing. The mudroom door opened. A quiet "Good boy," was followed by the crunching sound of a dog treat being consumed. I waited until 'Dad' had come through to the kitchen and a kind of calm commitment enfolded me. He hadn't turned the light on. Good. "So, *Dad*, when were you planning on having *the talk* with me?"

He dropped his briefcase and whirled to face me before it thudded against the industrial rubber tile. He froze in a crouch. Halfway out from under his suit jacket his right hand was holding something darkly metallic. "Michael. You nearly gave me an aneurism."

"That would have been too convenient, 'Dad'."

He straightened, visibly relaxing as he returned the gun to an underarm holster. If I hadn't just seen it, I wouldn't have known it was there.

He reached out and flipped on the light. I looked for flaws, but he continued to be a doppelgänger of my father, perfect in every detail.

"I expected you to have come to me a bit earlier," he said. "But I wasn't going to force the issue."

Yes, why had I waited almost two weeks to have this conversation? I wasn't afraid of him, although I was coming to realize that I should respect him. I had been waiting for Mom to tell me, to trust me enough to let me into that part of her life, but she hadn't. It wasn't just my need to know; I was tired of waiting for the mask to drop. I knew this charade wasn't going to go on forever, and I wanted to bring it to an end on my terms. All of which, I decided, was beside the point. "I'm having difficulty with the fact that you look, act, even *smell* like my father."

He pulled out a chair and sat. His face rippled, then flowed like wax, his cheek bones shifting up, nose lengthening and turning slightly up. "Does this help?" His voice had shifted as well, becoming slightly nasal with a distinct New York accent.

"Is that what you really look like?" His transformation was disturbing. I knew about shape shifters, of course, but to see one change in front of you is jarring at a visceral level.

"Close enough. It takes longer for me to change the color of my skin and hair, so I'll skip them in case we're interrupted. You knew I wasn't your father, right from the get-go, didn't you?"

"Yes. And I know you are responsible for protecting my mother and me."

"That's right. And I'm truly sorry for your loss. I met with your father regularly in order to prepare for this unfortunate contingency. I admired him."

"So did I."

"Look, Michael, we got off on the wrong foot for the right reasons. Let's start over. My name is Arthur Sellers. I'm a Special Agent with the Secret Service, Family Protective Division. It's nice to meet you, Michael Gurick. I wish it had been under different circumstances." He held out his hand and gave me an encouraging smile.

I looked at it, but made no effort to reach for it. "You aren't—With Mom—I mean, Mom knows who you are, doesn't she?"

He withdrew his hand, the smile gone. "No, I'm not, and yes, she knows who I am. She's been most helpful—"

"In fooling me," I said. I made no attempt to hide the bitterness in my voice.

"Now don't blame her, Michael. We've asked for her cooperation in this operation, and she has been forthcoming with it. If we can't be friends, at least we can be partners in keeping her safe." He put his hand out again, but did not smile.

"Fine," I said, taking it. His grip was dry and firm—like Dad's—with just the right amount of pressure. No dominance games. "To keep my mom safe."

"Good, I knew we could work together."

"What's your exit strategy?" I said, "You can't just go on pretending to be my father in perpetuity."

"No, of course not. But I'm afraid I can't share my 'exit strategy' with you. Knowing what I plan to do might affect your response to it. Your mother doesn't know either."

I sat back and crossed my arms. "You're going to fake your own death." I knew that my half-guess had hit home by his momentary look of surprise.

"What makes you think—" he began to say, but at the sound of slippers in the hall he cut himself off, his face rearranging itself back into my father's. A moment later Mom appeared in the kitchen door. "I thought I heard something down here. What are you two doing at this time of night?" she said, her voice bleary with sleep.

"I found Michael in the kitchen when I got home, Liz," Sellers said in Dad's voice. "He was having a late-night snack, so I thought I would join him."

"Would you like some cherry pie and milk, Mom?" I asked, standing up and gathering my dishes. "Diana made it." I stepped around the table as I talked, letting my fork fall from the plate. I bent and picked it up, shoving the briefcase from where it lay in the middle of the floor to under the table as I did.

"No, no, thank you, Michael," Mom said, then yawned. "If everything is all right, I'll go back to bed."

I let myself yawn in sympathy, deliberately not looking at Sellers. "I'm off to bed, too. Goodnight, Dad." It was tough, but I managed to say 'Dad' without the quotes.

The Black Lagoon Dojo

Saturday, May 12th, 1984
(13,612 days post Supernova 1947A)

The next afternoon, Penny and I caught an autonomous Transit pod at the station across from the entrance to our subdivision. She gave it the destination address, and we were off. During the twenty minute ride I told her about my encounter with Agent Sellers.

"At least you know his name, now," Penny said.

"And that he's going to kill himself. Or, at least fake it."

"What makes you so certain he's going to fake his death?"

"What else can he do? Mom knows who he is, his presence simply adds to the strain, and the longer they try to keep up the charade, the more likely other people will tumble to the fact that he isn't who he says he is. The only permanent way to remove the question is for him to 'die'. Besides, he needs to be free to pretend to be some other poor schmoe's dead superhero father."

The Transit pod slowed. We were in an older industrial section of the Greater Metro area, some of the buildings looking like they predated annexation by Galacticity. When we stopped in front of an old warehouse that seemed to occupy the entire block, I said, "Here?"

"Here."

Away across the tops of the buildings I could see the skeletal outlines of container handling gantry cranes, and I heard the not-so-distant hooting of tugboat horns. I checked my cellphone's GPS map. We were only a half a mile from Lake Michigan and a major containerized cargo port.

We entered the warehouse through a small door set in a larger door above which was written 'Black Lagoon Dojo' in neon that flickered occasionally. Inside, the grime and accumulated signs of age disappeared, replaced by a tall, narrow room with a wooden balcony running around the entire circumference. Below the balcony the floor was treated and polished concrete; the central area was covered with a wooden parquet. Several doors led elsewhere, and a spiral of wooden steps occupied one corner. The other three corners had various racks of sparring weapons and exercise equipment. It smelled of sandalwood incense with a hint of the sea in the background.

"It looked a lot larger from the outside," I said.

Penny pointed at the nearest door. "You can change through there, then meet me back here in five minutes."

She disappeared through another door, and I shrugged and went through the one she had indicated. I found a small locker room and Kinnison.

"You were right, Kinnison," I said, "Your dice luck pretty much stunk like a zombie factory last night."

"Oh, hey, Gurick," Kinnison said.

For some reason I couldn't fathom, he was turning pink around the edges.

"Have you seen Cleo's father? He's one serious dude." Kinnison said, the flush ebbing.

"No, I haven't met him yet." What was it with the dice? Had he been cheating and I missed it somehow? Impossible. His run of luck had been incredible, but it hadn't mattered whose dice he used. It had even continued after we switched to the augmented ones that reported what they rolled wirelessly. But why the recent change? I had managed to swap out his dice last night at Max's, but the analysis of the stored die rolls had only validated the recent change from a streak of good luck to a streak of bad. Otherwise they were completely normal.

"I don't know, man," Kinnison said, "But he reminds me of Godzilla. And not in a guy-in-a-rubber-suit way."

"Godzilla?" I echoed, a snort of laughter escaping.

"Laugh it up, monkey-boy. I hope he picks you to demonstrate on."

When Kinnison and I exited the little locker room, Penny and Cleo were waiting. I looked around for Mr. Fox, or rather, Sensei Fox, I reminded myself, but there was no sign of him.

"Hey, Cleo," I said.

She turned her head in my direction, the gaze of her almond-shaped brown eyes boring through me, and I felt a pleasant thrill. "Hi, Michael. Penny tells me that you want to learn kung fu."

"Or something like that," I said.

"Kung fu would be cool," Kinnison said.

"We don't specialize in kung fu here," Cleo said. "Dad really has his own style, but it's primarily based on Okinawan techniques. Which, come to think of it, were historically influenced by northern Chinese kung fu styles."

"I doubt either of them could tell the difference between kung fu and karate," Penny said.

"I could, too!" Kinnison said.

"We're here," I said, "and if your martial arts moves are anything like your gymnastics, then I think we're in the right place."

Cleo gave me a broad smile while Penny shook her head. I felt an inner glow kindle with Cleo's smile.

"How do we get started?" Kinnison asked.

"You see those brooms over there?" Cleo asked, gesturing to a nearby nook.

Kinnison's smile collapsed. Penny had explained the tradition of cleaning the dojo to me, but apparently she had neglected to inform Kinnison.

The four of us joined two men and a woman already hard at work. We spent the next ten minutes or so sweeping the floor and polishing the copious brass-work in the motif of dragons, sea serpents, and lizard men. As I worked, I smelled more than the hint of the sea a couple of times. The distant sound of a gong brought the fun to an end and we returned our implements of dust destruction to their racks.

A Kick to the Head, or Is It Love?

After disposing of the cleaning utensils, we lined up along the edge of the wooden floor. We all bowed when Cleo's father strode out. Kinnison had been right. While the ground didn't quake under his footsteps, there was something about his blocky solidity that radiated power. His movements were neither fast nor slow, but simply controlled. I looked for signs of Cleo in him, and found them in his compelling brown eyes. His skin was much darker than Cleo's, and his head was completely hairless, lacking any sign of eyebrows or eyelashes.

"We have several new people with us tonight," Sensei Fox said. His voice was rough and deep with a liquid quality, like he hadn't quite managed to clear his throat after gargling. "I would like to welcome Michael and Kim to the Black Lagoon dojo. You can call me Sensei, or Sensei Fox. Because we have newcomers, I will orient the class towards introductory exercises intended to assess skill levels and physical capabilities. Let's start with some warm-up katas."

Cleo led each kata while Sensei Fox walked up and

down the line, observing and occasionally correcting the more egregious errors in stance or hand and foot placement. My prior experience in karate club in middle school and a steady diet of kung fu movies on cable TV allowed me to avoid making a complete fool of myself. When Sensei Fox stopped to adjust the spacing of my feet and the angle of my knees, I noticed a deep green, almost black pattern faintly imprinted on his skin, as if he had once had a full body dragon tattoo that had faded to near invisibility.

The little thrill returned, running up my spine when Sensei Fox split us up into pairs, and I found myself partnered with Cleo. She walked over to where I stood, easily avoiding the other sets of people, and if I hadn't known that she was blind, I wouldn't have guessed.

"I was surprised when I heard that you and Kinnison had gotten into a fight with Luther and his cronies last week," Cleo said.

"It surprised me, too," I said.

"But you started it."

"Yeah, that was the surprise."

Cleo laughed. She stepped closer, her gaze looking through me to some blind infinity. I stood very still as she rested her hand, open-palmed, on my chest. She smelled of jasmine. After several seconds, during which I focused on not letting my heart race, she took a pinch of the canvas of the jacket of my gi and said, "Where did you get your gi? Your uniform? At the Goodwill?" She gave it a quick twist and tore a small hole like it was tissue paper. She handed me the little patch of canvas.

"Uh, no, it *was* new. And I know what a gi is."

She stepped back. "Of course. Silly of me. Penny didn't tell you where to get your gi, then?" she asked.

As she spoke, I tried to tear another patch of fabric the way she had, but failed. "No, I found a shop online and picked it up this morning." I had thought I was being proactive, but apparently not.

"You'll need something tougher. Talk to Penny or me about it. Or Sensei Fox. We can give you a list of shops. It's also on our website, Black Lagoon Dojo dot org."

We bowed to each other.

"I'll do that," I said, then added, "Could I get one here?"

"Sure, but I don't want you to think that's why I tore yours."

Which left me even more in doubt about why she had ripped my gi's jacket.

"You seem to have had some experience. Karate Club, right?" she said.

"It's that obvious?"

"Trade secret," she said. "Here's the kata I'd like to practice." She demonstrated it, arms and legs striking and blocking in a precise sequence, measured and crisp. "Can you keep up?"

"I think so," I said.

"Then you attack first."

As we exchanged our first set of strike and block pairs, I asked, "May I ask how you became blind?"

"You may," Cleo said, "But don't you think you should concentrate on your form?"

"I multitask pretty well. Once I've seen it, I can carry on a conversation without it affecting the kata. Kind of like walking and talking."

"Really?" She smiled playfully before continuing, "But it might affect my concentration." It was her turn to attack, and I blocked each strike without faltering.

"You're doing better than I am. So, how did you lose your sight?"

Her strikes came faster this time, and I managed to block them. We paused, and she said, "I drowned when I was four."

I was grateful for the break. I'm pretty sure I would have screwed up if I had been in the middle of a kata when she dropped that bomb. "Drowned or almost drowned?"

"Drowned. Dad says that I was dead for the handful of minutes it took the Life-Flight to arrive. The Galactitech revived me, but the repair of my visual cortex didn't take."

"And?"

"And what?"

"And I'd like some more details."

"Maybe some other time. It's kind of complicated."

"You seem to get along quite well without seeing..."

"And you want to know how I do it?"

"I admit to some curiosity, yes."

"And I suggest that it is a rather personal question."

"Then I withdraw it," I said, trying for flippant, but afraid that it sounded forced.

She ignored my offer and continued, "It's a combination of things. Hearing, of course, but I also sense air currents and smell. You'd be surprised by how much I can tell about a person by their scent. By the way, lose the aftershave. It makes it look like you're trying too hard."

I felt my face heat up.

Cleo smiled. "You're blushing."

How could she tell? Could she perceive heat?

"Cleo, give me your best shot," I said, intending to both demonstrate that I had been paying attention and distract her.

"Okay, you asked for it."

It seem like she barely flexed and she was six feet in the air, a kick flicked out, passing through my comparatively slow and feeble block to slam into the side of my head. For a second time in two weeks I was on my knees with a tintinnabulous echoing in my skull. I got to my feet, replaying everything in my mind. "Do it again..."

"Are you sure?"

"Yes, I'm sure."

"Your headache, then." She was airborne again, but this time I saw the tell-tale movement of her leg muscles. I managed to bring my hand up, my fingers beginning to close on her foot when she changed direction, the ball of her foot pressing into my hand, her other foot snapping down on the top of my head as she pushed off, performing a back flip just as if she had been dismounting a gymnastics beam, to land lightly in front of me, her hands up and ready to block a renewed attack.

"Switch partners," Sensei Fox said before I could do anything else.

"You *were* paying attention," Cleo said as we bowed to each other. She had a little Mona Lisa smile when she straightened up.

"I try to," I said, a warm feeling bathing my insides.

Hypothesis and Confirmation

I ended up with Kinnison as my sparing partner. Apparently, he hadn't seen Cleo kick me in the head, as he immediately started talking about the latest exploits of the Nova League—in particular, how Kinethis had recently telekinetically dueled and defeated the Übermind.

While he effused about how cool the telekinetic duel had been, my thoughts were focused on Cleo, replaying our conversation, feeling the warmth it had engendered again, until Kinnison's words, like depth charges, had sunk in deep enough to explode into a theory. As the initially fantastic-seeming theory bubbled up out of my subconscious, I wondered how I might put it to the test. And then I knew how.

I opened the testing gambit with, "I borrowed your dice last night, Kinnison..."

"What? Without asking?"

"I thought you might like me to look into your recent change of luck. Better to ask forgiveness, et cetera. Besides, if you were cheating, I figured you wouldn't let me borrow them."

"I. Don't. Cheat!" he said, his punches becoming wilder and wilder as he ground out the words.

I blocked each blow, deliberately grinning.

"Oh, come on, Kinnison, everyone cheats."

"Not me!" His face had grown red and he swung his fists with abandon.

Feinting a block, I stepped back out of range, only to feel a massive blow to my chest that lifted me off my feet and sent me flying. I crashed into the floor, and felt the wind being knocked from me. I slid a dozen feet across the polished wood and came to rest gasping for breath.

The color drained from Kinnison's face.

Moments later Sensei Fox was kneeling beside me, a mixture of concern and annoyance on his face. "You seem to have a knack for taking a lickin', Michael."

I couldn't help but think he must have heard about my fight with the Football Seniors. Luckily I was prevented from further embarrassing myself by my inability to breathe, let alone speak.

Kinnison's face arrived over me, on it concern and embarrassment warring for dominance on it.

"I didn't mean to—"

"He'll be okay, Kim," Sensei Fox said. "I expect you don't really know your own strengths yet."

Strengths? I thought. *Plural. Odd turn of phrase on Sensei Fox's part. Is he thinking what I'm thinking about Kinnison?*

Kinnison gulped and nodded.

Sensei Fox checked me over, then said, "Walk it off, Michael."

Kinnison helped me up with several repetitions of "Sorry, man."

"It's okay, Kinnison, I provoked you." I leaned on him for the first few steps.

As Kinnison and I walked, Sensei Fox motioned to Penny. They talked briefly, then Sensei Fox announced, "I'm going to wrap this session up with a demonstration of the Black Lagoon combat style."

Kinnison, who had some idea of how tough Penny was, had a distinct look of anticipation on his face.

Penny took up a position with a staff that she had retrieved from one of the racks. She held it above and slightly behind her, almost like she was wielding a Samurai sword.

Sensei Fox relaxed into a neutral but ready position, held out his right hand and beckoned Penny with his fingers.

With a yell that would have frozen a Yeti's marrow, Penny attacked. It was hard to follow the flurry of blows and parries, and the air was filled with the sounds of feet slapping and sliding on the floor, intermixed with grunts, 'kia' cries and the 'thwacking' sound of the staff striking home or being deflected.

Kinnison's jaw dropped early on, and stayed in that position until the end, which came with a blindingly fast crescendo of staff blows by Penny, the cracking, splintering sound of the staff, and Sensei Fox flipping Penny over his head to slam onto her back before dropping into a pincer leg hold. She slapped the floor with her free hand and they got up, then bowed to each other as if nothing out of the ordinary had happened. Neither looked winded.

Kinnison started to clap, and I couldn't help but join in.

Sensei Fox dismissed us.

"Kim," Sensei Fox said, as Kinnison and I started

towards the little locker room.

Kinnison stopped and turned back. "Yes, Sensei?"

"Could I speak with you a moment?"

A cloud of anxiety seemed to materialize over Kinnison. "Y—yes, Sensei."

Promoted to the Advanced Class

Kinnison followed Sensei Fox to the opposite corner of the dojo while I ducked into the locker room, hoping that my little experiment in psychology hadn't gotten Kinnison into trouble. I grabbed my bag without bothering to change and came back out to find Penny and Cleo quietly talking, both still in their gis. They fell silent when I emerged.

I joined them and said, "Let's wait for Kinnison, Penny."

"That was my plan," Penny said.

"Cool. You want to share a Transit pod with us, Cleo?" I asked.

"No need, but thank you for asking," Cleo said. "We live upstairs. I'll see you in school on Monday."

I couldn't help but notice the word 'see' and I had to suppress a nervous laugh. "Yeah, I'll see you."

"My father suggested that you come back on Thursday evening. It's our next intermediate session."

"Okay," I said with a grin. At least I'd made it out of the neophyte category.

Kinnison reappeared. He was grinning ear to ear. "Sensei Fox wants me to come in for the advanced class."

"That's the one I usually take," said Penny.

"Aren't we special," I said.

Kinnison continued to grin. "Why yes, we are," he said smugly. "Apparently they appreciate something other than brains at the Black Lagoon."

"Apparently," I said, and texted a request for a Transit pod. We gathered up our gym bags and backpacks, and after saying goodbye to Cleo we headed out the door. A Transit pod was waiting at the station. When we had settled into the plastic seats, I looked down at the jacket of my gi and plucked at the hole in it. "Why was Cleo 'picking' on me?" I said.

"You really have no idea?" Penny said.

"Because you're a smartass, Gurick. When are you going to give me back my dice?"

"When you give us the details on what you and Sensei Fox talked about."

"Is that all?" Kinnison asked suspiciously.

"And you have to listen to my analysis of your dice."

He sighed theatrically. "Fine. At first, Sensei Fox wanted to know what happened when I knocked you across the room. I told him I didn't know—"

"Do you know?" I asked.

"No. Now will you let me finish? I told him that you had pissed me off and that I thought I hit you really hard. He asked me why I said 'thought' and what I had felt when I hit you." A far away look came over him and he continued. "I felt this anger building up, and a sort of coiling tension just behind my eyes. Then it 'popped' and I just lashed out, a feeling like my arm and hand were growing, stretching out and becoming really heavy. Then you were flying across the floor, and my hand felt normal again, but not at all like I had hit you with it." Kinnison stopped talking, the far away look still on his face.

"And then?" I prompted. This seemed to validate my wild theory about the source of Kinnison's dice luck. I'd have to find other, safer ways to test it.

He shook his head, then said, "Sensei Fox told me that I should come to the advanced classes. That they would better fit my needs."

"Huh," I said, looking over at Penny. She raised her eyebrows and gave me that look that told me she expected me to know what was going on and not to waste her time by asking questions that I already knew the answers to. Which I pretty much did.

"As much as it pains me, Gurick, I'm ready for your 'analysis' of the dice," Kinnison said.

"I'll keep it short and sweet, Kinnison, seeing as you've been forthcoming with your interview with Sensei Fox." I recapped my statistical analysis and summed up the big nothing that I had found. Kinnison seemed satisfied, but I expect that it was more due to my brevity than my analysis.

Kinnison's Bruises, or Double Trouble

Monday, May 14th, 1984
(13,614 days post Supernova 1947A)

Monday, the day after Kinnison's first advanced class at the Black Lagoon, he came in to first period Calculus class limping and bruised. When he sat down next to me, I was assaulted by the scent of cinnamon with a faint fishy undertone.

"How did it go?" I asked, turning up the chipper in my voice to eleven.

He groaned. "No one told me the Terror Twins were in the advanced class."

I laughed and he looked even more hurt. "Sorry, Kinnison, but seeing someone else at the focus of their attention is a rare treat for me. I assume you had the privilege of working out with one of them. Which one was it? Achilles is marginally tougher, but Andy is the meaner one."

"Both. And when it was over, Sensei Fox gave me some ointment and told me to get even next time."

"I wondered what that smell was."

"How do you cope with those two? They're quick, and even when you do land a blow, it's like punching a sandbag with gravel mixed in."

"Usually I talk my way out of any confrontation, but if they are in a particularly foul mood, I end up lying there and taking it. If you don't struggle, they quickly lose interest and wander off in search of something else they can pull the limbs off of. I recommend curling up into a fetal position to protect your vitals." It would have been misleading to say that they didn't know their own strength, and I was enjoying his discomfort a tad too much to try to explain to him how I thought the richness of the twins' imaginary landscape lent them more than the expected zeal for play of a pair of eleven-year-olds.

He harrumphed. "Can't do that, man. We're supposed to defend ourselves."

"Would you two like to share your homework solutions with the rest of the class?" Mr. Tibbits, the school's Grand Math Dictator said. "That is what I assume you're both talking about."

"Oh, thanks, Gurick," Kinnison said with a moan. "I skipped doing homework because of the advanced class."

Sellers' Advice

Saturday, June 2nd, 1984
(13,633 days post Supernova 1947A)

Dad's sedan slid into the parking lot of the Starlight Marina's Cosmic Bowling Station. I felt none of the little bumps and heard nothing of the road noise in the heavy, armored vehicle. I reminded myself that I needed to look into its capabilities. It might come in useful, if I decided to put it to the same use that I thought Dad had.

"Why are we here? Dad never took me bowling."

"To be frank," he said in his New York accented voice. "It's a little psychological trick to help separate me from your father." His face flowed and shifted and it was Agent Sellers who continued, "I wanted to have a discussion with you where you could relate to me as Arthur Sellers, not as the memory of your father."

The driver and passenger doors hissed open, pivoting upward and we got out. The sedan didn't even shift.

"Very thoughtful of you."

"My superiors at the FPD have been pressuring me to assign a telepath to surveil you."

The wing-like doors rotated down and sealed with a barely audible 'ka-thisss' followed by the chirp-chirp of the security system.

I felt my frown deepen.

"And that response is why I have resisted the suggestion. If you found out that a government agent had been mind probing you, it would negatively impact your willingness to cooperate in the future."

Damn right it would, I thought.

"I've been using a couple of the evaluations that the psych boys did on you to help make my case. Not that I needed them. In my line of work you learn how to read people."

We pushed our way through the main doors into the darker interior of the bowling alley. Some bright and cheery rock song from the late '70s was playing and I heard the pinball-machine like sound echoing up from lanes set for 'Cosmic Bowling'. There was a group of eight- or nine-year-olds loudly celebrating one of their birthdays. Lounging nearby and looking bored was Dan Sweets, a non-friend from Centurion High who happened to be in the class of 1987, too. I assumed it was a younger sib of his that was having the party.

We rented shoes and selected a lane as far away from the partiers as possible. After bowling the first frame Sellers said, "So, you see, Michael, in order to avoid a mind probe I have to ask you a few questions."

"About what?"

"What you know. What you plan on doing."

There were more pinball noises from across the lanes and I glanced over. Sweets was looking in our direction, fiddling with some sort of electronic device or hand-held game. When he saw me looking at him he slid the device into his pocket. Damn, I was hoping he wouldn't notice me. I turned back to Sellers. "Why are either of those things any business of FPD?"

Sellers ignored my response and continued, "Let me lay it out as I see it."

"Okaaay..."

"You know about your father and his extracurricular activities. You don't think your mother knows that you know, but you aren't entirely sure. You know about Diana and have a reasonably good idea about what that implies for Penny. You've been sneaking down to your dad's lab for five years—"

I practically dropped the neon-green bowling ball on my foot.

He barely paused, registering the reaction on my face, "—No, six years, now. How am I doing so far?"

"I—That is—"

"Shall I continue?" he said, but before I could answer he was on to his next point. "You've vowed to bring the Demolition Squad to justice. And you plan on taking up your father's superidentity to accomplish this."

True, and... true? The thought of putting on Dad's suit had been percolating around the back of my mind ever since I had made the vow, but it hadn't been a conscious decision. Until now. "How do you know all this? I thought you said you weren't using a telepath to spy on me."

"I'm not." He tapped his temple. "It's as I told you, I've got a pretty good psych profile on you up here."

"But why tell me this? Sure, I appreciate your not turning a telepath loose on me, but you're going to make your exit and that will be it. You'll go on to your next assignment, and I'll never see you again. The role of the FPD in my life, and more importantly, Mom's life, will be at an end."

"But the interest of the government in you will not cease. Who you become and what you do—what you *might* do—is a concern. Eventually, inevitably, you will cross paths with the PICSEA, and when you do, you don't want a cloud hanging over your head."

The Powers Investigation, Control, and Security Enforcement Agency wasn't something you messed with, and you never called one of their agents a 'pixie' to their face. Or so I was told.

"So study up on the SVA and don't give them an excuse to come down on you. You should have no problem in memorizing it."

We had read parts of the Superhero Vigilante Act in Civics. The parts we had covered had dealt with the currently voluntary powers registration—voluntary because of the backlash to the Nixon era's attempts to forcibly register and control every American super—and the civic duty of supers to use their powers for good. When I dipped into it further, I had found it to be an arcane jumble of legalese more akin to motor vehicle registration than the 27th Amendment Enhanced ERA. I'd have to go back and take a look at it again.

"I'm finished lecturing," Sellers said, handing me a business card. "Take this in case you ever need to contact me."

I looked at the card. It was unadorned, white, and had 'Arthur Sellers' printed on it. No phone number, no email, just his name. I turned it over. Blank. I shrugged and put it in my wallet. When I looked up at him again he still had a serious look on his face.

"One more bit of advice—and this could land me in

hot water if it were to get back to the Agency—be very careful what you say and do at Centurion High. Your education isn't the only concern of Dr. DuQuane and the rest of the school staff and teachers."

A scream of "Not fair!" erupted from the birthday party, followed by "He's cheating!" and a general hue and cry of thwarted nine-year-olds swelled and echoed through the long room. I looked over, catching a wicked grin on Dan Sweets' face.

Cosmic Bowling Crash

The voices of young fury filled the Cosmic Bowling Station. The lane lights indicating targets were flicking from pin to pin, cycling through the colors of the rainbow. The score boards above each alley had gone crazy. Normally they displayed player scores and bonus games, with an occasional flashy graphic for strikes, spares, and whatnot. Now they were showing fireworks and waving flags as if the 4th of July had come early. The scores were blinking, changing randomly with each blink. The bonus games had gone negative, racing downward in a tumble, only to stop on minus ninety-nine. To add to the growing cacophony, the ball returns started to groan and buzz, disgorging balls, while the gutter bumpers began to snap in and out of their hidden recesses.

Then everything went dead, every display dark, every mechanical bit locked in place.

"What now?" I said, disappointed despite myself.

"At least the lights are still on," Sellers said. "Why don't we give it a—"

He stopped. The lights on the display panels flashed, and with a clatter that ran up and down the room, the pin gathering machines activated, clearing and setting up pins while the gutter bumpers retracted into their lairs. Each alley display board showed ten free games.

"Looks like we hit the jackpot," I said, putting a healthy serving of sarcasm into my voice.

Everything seemed back to normal, so we resumed playing. Not long after, the manager came 'round and apologized, handing out coupons for free games, hoping that the 'glitch' wouldn't stop us from coming back.

As Sellers and I returned our shoes to the front desk, I saw Dan Sweets with a woman I thought might be his mom. She was arguing animatedly with the manager.

"I'm afraid I can't refund your money, Ms. Sweets," the man was saying. "But I can give vouchers for twenty five free games. That's a value of—"

"But your bowling alley, or computer system, or whatever, crashed. How do I know that won't happen again?"

"It has never happened before, Ms. Sweets. I've put a call in to the manufacturer and they have assured me that an upgrade to their latest software patches will prevent a re-occurrence. I can offer you thirty free games."

Sweets sniggered, then, unfortunately, caught sight of me. "Hey, Gurick, who sentenced you to this gulag?"

I turned to face him. "My uncle Arthur. And it isn't all that bad."

Sellers also turned. He didn't miss a beat. By the time he was facing us his features had morphed into something that wasn't Dad's, but could easily have been Dad's brother. "Who is your friend, Michael?"

"This is Dan Sweets. We're in the same physics and computer science classes at Centurion."

"Nice to meet you, Dan," Sellers said.

"Sure," Sweets said. "Nice to meet you, too, Mr. Gurick." He didn't bother to introduce his mother, who was still arguing with the manager.

"I've got to make a phone call, Michael. Why don't you come out to the car in a few minutes."

"No problem, Uncle Arthur." I was getting pretty good at calling him anything other than his real name.

"You going to the prom tonight?" Sweets said after Sellers had departed.

"Hadn't planned on it," I said, puzzled by his sudden interest in my extra-curricular activities.

"I am," he said. "Di Lopez asked me."

"Oh?" I was impressed, but there was no way I was going to let Sweets know that. Di was one of the seniors that most of the boys at Centurion High, and even a few of the girls, dreamed about going to the Prom with. And a few other things, as well.

"Yeah, I helped her out with a computer project and we hit it off real good."

He was on a bragging expedition, which would explain his sudden interest in talking to me. "Well, I'm happy for you."

He frowned, perhaps because he hadn't expected me to congratulate him. A look of calculation appeared for a moment on his face, then he said, "I expect I'll see Penny there tonight."

What? Which senior was Penny going with? And why hadn't she told me about it?

Sweets must have seen something of my reaction to his revelation. He continued, "Luther Drumlin is taking her. You remember Luther, don't you? He's on the varsity football squad. You attacked him in the Commons a month ago."

I felt my lips twitch. How could she be going to the Prom with that lout? And not tell me?

"You do remember him, then," Sweets said.

I wanted to wipe that self-satisfied smirk from his face, but I brought my boiling anger under control and said with studied nonchalance, "I remember a stomach that I bruised my knuckles on."

"Sure it wasn't your face that you pummeled him with?"

I wasn't going to give him an ounce more of satisfaction. "Could be," I said. My cellphone dinged, and thankful for the interruption I flipped it open to look at the text message. It was from Dad's phone. 'Ready when you are.'

I looked up, catching a furrowing of Sweets' brow, as if he were concentrating on listening to something. "Gotta go, Sweets. Have fun at the prom."

The little furrow disappeared. "I thought you said you were here with your uncle, Gurick."

"Yeah, he's waiting in the car for me. See you around."

"But not at the Prom." His smugness had returned in spades.

It wasn't until I was halfway to the door that I began to wonder why Sweets had just questioned who I was there with.

After the Prom

Sunday, June 3rd, 1984
(13,634 days post Supernova 1947A)

I didn't cross paths with Penny for the better part of a day. I had just arrived at the Black Lagoon Dojo for the Sunday afternoon intermediate class and she was apparently on her way out. Without preamble I said, "Why didn't you mention you were going to the prom with Luther Drumlin?"

Penny's face darkened. "Why do you care if I went to the prom with him?"

"Well, for one thing, he's one of the seniors who was picking on Kinnison."

"I'm aware of that." Her anger had sublimated and her tone was chilly.

"So how could you go with him then?"

"I had my reasons."

Despite the growing iciness in her voice I continued, "And you don't want to share them with me?"

"Not anymore."

"What does that mean?"

"It means this conversation is at an end." And she walked out without a backward glance.

My brain churned. What was up with her? Why were people—and girls in particular—so difficult to analyze? It was as if they set out to be deliberately misinterpreted.

I Am Legion's Blog

Monday, June 4th, 1984
(13,635 days post Supernova 1947A)

"Check out this blog post," Kinnison said, shoving his tablet in front of me.

It was lunch on Monday, and Penny had been giving me the 'You don't exist' treatment all morning. "Why?" I said, not feeling particularly charitable towards Kinnison's enthusiasms.

"It's an 'I Am Legion' post. You'll like it. Particularly this photo." He tapped the inTab's display meaningfully.

'I Am Legion' was a gossip blog that appeared last fall with a now-notorious post lampooning the varsity football and cheerleader squads at Centurion High. Since then, everyone had been trying to figure out who the anonymous blogger was. I had my suspicions.

"Okay," I said, taking the tablet. In among the pictures of couples caught kissing, a conga dance line being led by someone dressed up as the school's mascot, the

Centurion (including a giant foam-rubber head), and guys drinking beer trying to act drunk—something that was notably more difficult in the post-Galactic-genetic-cleanup world—there was a photo of a tricked-out red 1967 Ford Mustang on the back of a flatbed wrecker. It looked like it had been caught in a hero-villain duel. The passenger side door was twisted and hanging from one hinge. The front wheel was gone. The fender and side panel above the missing wheel was bent up and away, as if the tire had been torn off. There was a huge dent in the middle of the hood, and the front grill was missing, revealing a fist-sized hole in the radiator. The picture had been taken at 'Kissing Creek', a popular spot for parking and fogging up the interior of car windows.

I scrolled up to the top of the blog post. It was titled 'What Really Happened at the Centurion Class of 1984's Prom'.

"Don't you recognize it?"

"Recognize what? The spot?"

"No. Yeah, the spot, *and* the car."

I scrolled down again. "Is that Luther's car?"

Kinnison laughed. "Oh, yeah. That's his car all right. Looks like his date went bad. I wish I knew who he took to the Prom."

"It was Penny," I said in an almost whisper.

"Who?"

I scrolled back up, looking through the pictures. There was one where you could just make out Penny and Luther sitting at the table in the background. She was dressed in an off-the-shoulder green dress, and Luther was in a tux.

"Who did you say, Gurick?"

I turned the tablet so he could see the picture.

"That's Penny! He went with Penny?" Kinnison said.

I replayed my conversation at the dojo with Penny in my mind, and yes, her hands and forearms had a few red weals and scratches. Why hadn't I noticed them? How could I have been so angry as to not *see* the signs?

"She doesn't look like she's having much fun," Kinnison said. "Why would Penny go with Luther? He's such an asshole."

"Precisely."

"Huh? Gurick, you aren't making sense. Why would she want to go with a jerk like that?"

"Because she could count on him acting like a jerk."

"I still don't understand."

"Sorry, Kinnison, I've got to go. Thanks for cluing me in on that 'Legion' blog post."

"Sure, Gurick, anytime. You are going to explain this to me, right?"

"Yeah, but right now I've got to do something I should have done yesterday. Hope it's not too late."

I found a secluded spot and speed-dialed Penny's number. On the third ring she answered, "What?"

"Uh, hey, Penny, can you meet me in the library?"

"I'm a little busy, Michael." Her voice was cold.

'But it's lunch,' died on my lips and I thought, *Uh-oh. She is totally pissed.*

"I wanted to say this in person, Penny," I said in a rush. "I'm really sorry for not listening to you. And for jumping to stupid conclusions. I really should have trusted you."

"Yes. You should have."

"Are you sure you can't meet me in the library?"

There was a sigh on the other end. "Fine. At the usual place."

I headed for the magazine rack, my step lighter

than it had been all morning.

Penny was already there when I arrived. She was wearing a Pretenders Live at the Aqua Dome T-shirt and my mind momentarily flashed back to her in the green dress; I wasn't sure which I liked better. I shoved the thought aside, noting that this time she was flipping through the pages of Popular Super-science. For a moment I thought of getting a copy of Superpeople off the rack. It would have been satisfyingly symmetrical, but I managed to ignore the whisperings of my obsessive-compulsive fairy, and just sat down across from her. I studied her hands and forearms for a moment. The marks were almost gone now.

"Hey, Penny, I'm sorry for being such an asshole yesterday."

She paused in her page flipping and met my gaze. "That's a start."

Suppressing my desire to lay out my deductions as to what happened and why, I said, "You want to talk about it?"

She looked a little surprised. "You want me to tell you what happened?"

"Only if you want to."

"No summary analysis of what you think happened?"

I flushed. "No, I just thought you might want to talk about it with someone."

"I should ask why you think something worthy of talking about happened, but we'll forgo that little sham. Yes, Luther tried to put the moves on me, and yes, I was pretty sure he would."

I wanted to shout 'A-ha!', but I settled for "Uh, huh."

"I thought I would get a little payback for all the

freshmen Luther and his friends have terrorized. I know how attached Luther is to his car. When he asked me to the Prom a couple of months ago, I thought I might get an excuse to trash his precious Mustang. The walk back from Kissing Creek was worth every step."

"I'll add 'thank you' to the apology, then," I said.

"You're welcome, and accepted," she said.

Death at Bayside

Friday, June 15th, 1984
(13,646 days post Supernova 1947A)

Almost two weeks dragged by, increasingly punctuated by giddy behavior induced by our collective anticipation of summer break. The last day of school had arrived, and I was enjoying Ms. Spencer's traditional final day 'Chemical Shenanigans' presentation, in all its carnivalesque flash and splash, when she was interrupted by a call. She beckoned to me, her face a study in neutrality, and told me that Dr. DuQuane would like to see me in his office.

"Have a seat, Michael," DuQuane said, his bald, one-size-too-large head gleaming.

I did. I had been expecting something like this ever since my trip to the bowling alley with Agent Sellers the weekend before.

"There's been an accident at the Bayside construction site," DuQuane said. "Your father was involved. He rescued three workers, but I'm sorry to say that he was killed in the process."

It felt like I had stepped into one of Luther's boulder-sized fists, sending my thoughts into a dizzying spin. Had it been a real accident? Would Sellers have risked the lives of innocents to make Dad's death look good?

All the pent-up rage, frustration and sorrow at my father's death boiled up, and the choked-back sobs broke free. It was the second-to-last time I cried.

Mom's Cleaning Jag

When I arrived home I was greeted by the scent of pine cleaner. It wasn't a good sign.

I shut the mud room door. No Bernoulli waiting for a snack on my arrival? Another bad sign.

"Is that you, Michael?" Mom called from the kitchen.

"Yes, Mom." I had been so wound up in my own angst that I had completely forgotten about Mom and how she might react to Dad's, or rather, Sellers' death.

"Be a dear and take your shoes off."

It was nice and sunny out, and I felt a chill that wasn't the air-conditioning. "Uh, okay, Mom."

After shucking my shoes, I cautiously peered into the kitchen. I saw Bernoulli lying in the hall leading to the den. He didn't look happy. I heard the splash of water and bristles against the industrial rubber flooring of the kitchen. I found Mom on her knees vigorously scrubbing a floor that, to me, looked clean.

"If you let Bernoulli out or take him for a walk," she said by way of greeting, "make sure you put his booties on. They're next to the backdoor."

"Sure thing." The sense of unease deepened. Despite her knowing that 'Dad' wasn't Dad, she seemed to be responding as if it really had been Dad that just died. I wanted to confront her about lying to me about Dad, to yell at her that he's been dead for a month and you're just getting around to noticing it enough to be in denial? But she looked so forlorn, so brittle, scrubbing away at the spotless floor. Somebody needed to talk to her, and I didn't trust myself to do it.

I retreated to my room to make a phone call.

"Hello, Diana?"

"Yes, Michael. I heard what happened at Bayside this morning. I'm sorry."

"Thank you. We should talk about that sometime soon. But what I really called you about was Mom. I'm concerned about how she is taking the Bayside news. I think you need to come over and talk to her."

"Of course, dear. Is she doing something odd?"

"No. She's cleaning the kitchen. Again."

"Oh my. I'll be right over."

The Riggs-Armstrongs, or Home is Where the Twins Swing

"Hey," Penny said from my bedroom doorway.

"Hi, Penny. What's happening downstairs?" I was glad for the interruption to the miserable swirling of my thoughts as they circled the intractable problem of Mom.

"Diana is talking to Liz."

"Is she still scrubbing the floor?"

"Diana got her to stop by asking for coffee. But she was starting to wipe down the countertops when I came up."

"I don't know what to do. Do they have meds for this sort of thing?" I wished I had spent more time going over pharmacological drug synthesis.

"Probably."

We sat without talking for a while; the only sound was Fritz Mk. IV in his wheel—like my mind, running but going nowhere.

There was a knock at the door, and Hank said through it, "Am I interrupting anything?"

"Nope," Penny and I said at the same time. The phrase 'pity party' flashed through my mind, but I shoved it aside. Feeling sorry for myself because my mother had slipped around the bend wasn't going to do anyone any good. But before I could choke it off, a sinister little voice muttered that she deserved it for keeping secrets from me.

Hank opened the door. "Diana sent for Doc. He should be here shortly. Why don't the two of you come home with me?"

It didn't sound much like a question, and as much as I wanted to resist, there was an overwhelming part of me that didn't want to be alone. "What about Bernoulli?" I said.

"He'll be fine," Hank said. "We're just two doors down."

When we walked in the Riggs-Armstrong front door we were greeted by Tarzan cries and Achilles swinging from the front-entrance-way chandelier, brandishing a broom handle and yelling, "Taste my steel!" while Andy tried to knock him off with a hockey stick. I looked around for wreckage or other evidence of the sibs being left alone in a house, but Hank and Diana had been keeping up with the twin-proofing.

Hank skillfully disarmed Andy and coaxed Achilles down, like an experienced chimpanzee wrangler dealing with Monkey House escapees—carefully considerate of the possibility that his charges might pull his arms from their sockets, even if unintentionally. While he was engaged in this bout of superparenting, Penny and I slipped by, heading for her room.

"Too much *Three Musketeers*," Penny said on the way up the steps.

"Too much something," I said.

When I entered her room and caught sight of the chess set sitting on her desk I felt a frown break out. It was silver and black, the pieces done in a sleek and curvy '70s Modern Art style, and had been a gift from Mom on Penny's eighth birthday.

"Let's play a game of *Ragnarok City*," Penny said.

"Yeah. Okay," I replied. We hadn't played that since last summer, what with various distractions of our freshman year at Centurion High.

"Don't be so enthusiastic about it," she said, a dryness to her tone. She lifted the seat-lid of the bay window. "The card table should be in the hall closet."

I fetched the card table, checking for the presence of one of the twins before opening the hall closet door all the way, while she located her copy of the game. She spread out the map and I said, "The usual?"

"Unless you want to change."

"No, I'll take the Ragnarok Machine," I said. Penny liked playing the city defender because it was, frankly, kind of like chess, with its variety of units with which to maneuver and pounce. She had the strategic foresight and tactical finesse to give me a run for my money.

I tore a Ragnarok Machine design sheet from the pad and filled it in from my memory of the last game that Penny and I had played at the end of last summer, altering it based on a thought I had had after that game. While Penny allocated her units, I ventured, "I haven't had a chance to tell you about Sellers taking me bowling last Saturday."

She looked up from her worksheet her pencil poised and said, "Oh?"

"Should I wait until you're done picking units?"

"Are you going to play that 'Inferno Machine'

again?"

"No, I thought I'd try something different. I plan on winning this time." I had managed to incinerate a third of the city before she had immobilized my RM, resulting in a draw.

"Then I'll skip beefing up my firefighting units and use one of my tried and true setups. Go ahead and tell me about Sellers while I put the units on the map."

I filled her in on what Sellers had told me, careful to avoid any speculation.

I hesitated when I came to Dan Sweets being there, but decided not to leave anything out. She finished her deployment before I reached the conversation with Sweets. Her piercing green gaze went contemplative as I wound up my narrative.

"That explains your behavior on Sunday."

I flushed. "Should I apologize again for—"

She held up a hand. "No, once will do. Your move."

Who's Afraid of the Ragnarok Machine?

I glanced over Penny's unit deployment and put the chit representing the Ragnarok Machine down on the map's northwest entry point.

"Went for speed, eh?" Penny said as I advanced the RM chit. "Do you think what happened at Bayside this morning was faked?"

"I'm not really sure. I can't help but wonder whether the people Sellers saved were really in danger. If the news reports are accurate, it wouldn't have been difficult for an expert to hack the computer controls into inducing a power surge through the containment magnets and cause the transformer to explode. Sellers helped three workers to escape the smoke and fire in the control room, but when he went in a second time he didn't come out. The firefighters found his body, and they're reporting death by smoke inhalation and not decapitation, so it wasn't Dad's body that they found."

I had moved the RM through the hinterlands, not bothering to engage any of her units except the ones directly in my path.

"No long-range weapons, either? Where did you put your points? Anti-infantry and armor?"

"And treads."

"Treads? Oh, I see what you're doing, now." She started shifting her main battle and hover tanks.

Penny, being an experienced *Ragnarok City* player, knew that a key defensive strategy was to sacrifice some of your units to maximize damage against the RM's treads, slowing it down enough to swarm it with your remaining units.

"Hank told me that there's some speculation among the reporters about why he went back into the control room. According to the workers, they told him they were pretty sure no one else was left inside."

"No hint that the three workers were in on it, then?"

"Not that I've heard. Do you think Sellers is actually dead?"

I had moved the RM into the outskirts of the city, careful to avoid the subway stations and tunnels, a frequent point of ambush for mole tanks. Unfortunately, but not unexpectedly, her long-range artillery was starting to take a toll.

"No. Not really. But I can't be certain. We don't even know if it was Sellers' body that was recovered."

"Any thoughts on how you are going to find out if he is alive?"

"Um, well, I can't exactly phone up the FPD and ask for Sellers, and what would you search for on the net? I can try, but I assume the FPD has been pretty thorough in purging any connections between its agents' past and their current activities."

"There is that card he gave you. Have you examined it yet?"

"Yeah, that's an idea. But I'll need the lab to do that."

I was nearing the heart of the nameless city, where she had positioned her Command and Control unit. She had been throwing power-armored infantry at the RM, which had been chewing through them, but like army ants; if there were enough of them they could take down a behemoth like the Ragnarok Machine. Just a few more hexes and—

I glanced out the bay window, spotting three figures coming down the sidewalk towards the house.

"Maybe its simpler than that. Have you tried—?" Penny was saying, as I forgot about her C&C unit and came to my feet.

"What is it?" Penny asked, looking up from the board.

"Your mom, and a man I assume is the doctor that she called, are bringing Mom here."

There was something familiar about the doctor, but my interest in him was swept aside by concern for Mom. She moved slowly, as if in a daze. I felt a sinking feeling. Were my fears confirmed?

"It looks like they gave her a sedative," Penny said.

"I'm going to go lend a hand," I said.

I hurried down the steps, dodging a Spungi-a-rang thrown by Achilles and out the front door.

"Here's Michael," Diana said as I trotted up.

"Oh? Michael? Why aren't you in school, dear? And, Penny, too."

"Summer vacation started today, Mom."

"It was a half day," Penny said from just behind me.

"Oh, that's nice," Mom said.

"Here, Michael, why don't you take my side," the doctor said.

His voice was familiar, too. "Doc Styx?" I asked.

"Doctor who?" Mom said.

"No, Doctor Styx," Diana said.

"I can't slip anything by you, Michael, can I?" Doc Styx said. "You can manage?"

"Yes," I said, taking Mom's arm.

"I'm going to talk to Hank, Diana," Doc Styx said.

"Manage what?" Mom said.

"Never mind, Mom," I said. *She's really out of it,* I thought. "Let's go in so you can rest."

"But the downstairs bathroom needs cleaning. And the kitchen is a disaster area."

It felt like a lump of ice had formed in my gut. "It's fine, Mom. I'll make sure everything at home gets taken care of."

We maneuvered Mom through the front door. In the foyer Doc Styx was telling Hank, "Make sure she gets plenty of rest. I'll be back tomorrow to run a full battery of tests."

"Doc Styx?" I said.

"Yes?"

"What's your prognosis on my mother?"

"I'd rather run her through a battery of tests before I make a diagnosis."

"Please, sir. I need to know."

After a long, nerve wracking pause he took mercy on me. "I'd say she is suffering from post-traumatic stress obsessive-compulsive disorder. And before you ask the next question, it should be treatable with cognitive therapy and medication. The particulars of which are dependent on a more definitive diagnosis."

"Thank you, sir." At least there was a path forward, even if only tentative steps could be taken along it.

The Ninja Twins Attack

Sunday, June 17th, 1984
(13,648 days post Supernova 1947A)

Penny and I turned on to Tau Ceti Street, Bernoulli in the lead, snuffling along, nose to the ground, tail wagging. I glanced over at Penny, but she only nodded. It seemed like a rather encouraging nod, so I took the plunge. "I can't stay here with those two, Penny. It's like being Inspector Clouseau with *two* Catos trying to sneak up and kill me when I least expect it. The start of it was chilling enough. I woke up to find Andy and Achilles looming over my bed, looking all serious. They announced that, as ninjas in training, they were going to 'hunt' me. When I tried to talk them out of the idea, starting with 'Oh, I'm too weak to be worthy prey' then escalating up to 'I'll just lay there and take it', they said that it was Sensei Fox's idea, and that it is a formal duel with my 'honor' at stake. 'My wits against their ninja powers.' You've been in the advanced classes at Black Lagoon—has Sensei Fox ever told you to do something like that?"

Penny hesitated. "Well, you could interpret some of the things he's said that way."

"And the Terror Twins would twist it that way."

"Yeah, they would. So your 'honor' is at stake, eh?" There was a hint of a smile on her lips.

"It's not funny. I don't feel a lot of honor accruing from battling a couple of eleven-year-old wanna-be ninjas. Even if they are capable of turning me into monkey stew. It's going to escalate until I lose a limb or something."

"They wouldn't intentionally do that."

We stopped while Bernoulli carefully marked his third bush. "Maimed is maimed. I don't really care if they feel bad about it afterward or not."

"So, what have they done?"

"In the past twenty-four hours they've attacked me with Spungi-swords—"

"That won't maim you."

"—and a net—"

"No risk of limb loss, either."

"—and while I was in the bathroom!"

"Which means you might have died of embarrassment?"

"Har, har. Maybe a little more detail will give you a better impression of what's going on."

"Okay. I'm truly curious."

"First time: I was in the kitchen making Mom a sandwich when they came at me from either side, screaming their martial arts screams. I managed to fling the refrigerator door open into Andy as I sprayed mustard into Achilles' eyes. They slammed into each other and I beat a hasty retreat."

Penny chuckled. "Did you save the sandwich?"

"Yes." I snorted a laugh, then stifled it. "Okay, so

that one might actually have been funny. The second time was less fun. After the kitchen incident, I put together a dispenser belt of a few things, which turned out to save my ass when Andy dropped a weighted net—"

"I thought Diana and Hank had confiscated that."

"Well, apparently not. Anyways, I was walking through the foyer, and—"

"You didn't check the balcony before going in?"

"Yes, I checked the balcony, and they weren't on it. Andy had climbed up on the window ledge on the exterior wall across from the balcony, where I didn't look. The net slammed down on me, but I managed to trigger a smoke grenade—"

"Ah, that explains the smoke alarm. You never can tell with the twins."

"—and I rolled out of the way, dragging the net with me. They both tried to jump on me, Andy from her ledge and Achilles running out from his position in the upstairs hall. I heard a crash and jingling noise as one of them, probably Achilles, hit the chandelier on the way down. By the time they stopped bashing on each other I'd cut a hole in the net and escaped. If they had landed on me..."

"Okay, that might have really hurt you."

"Finally, I was—well, I was on the—I was in the bathroom, and Achilles must have climbed up the outside wall. It's brick—"

"I know."

"Right. So of course it would have been easy enough for him. Luckily, I saw his shadow as he wrenched open the window behind me. I'm glad he didn't just smash through the glass—"

"Couldn't have. It's bulletproof."

"I'll have to remember to thank Hank for that little

favor. After I complain about his homicidal children, that is." I paused, opened my mouth to continue, then shut it. How could I put this without sounding like I was whining?

"Spit it out, Michael."

"You'd think the little brutes would cut me a break. I mean, even with their stunted empathy they should see how much it sucks to have your father die and your mom drugged to her gills."

"Have you considered that they might actually be aware of that? And that this has all been an attempt, albeit warped, to distract you? Maybe even cheer you up?"

I hadn't considered that at all. "Hunh. Okay. Maybe I'm misjudging the little monsters. Still, you have to admit that I have room for complaint."

"Speaking of which, why haven't you said something to Hank or Diana about the Terrible Twins?"

"I'm just grateful for them looking after Mom. I don't want them to think I'm unappreciative of their hospitality and all." And, come to think about it, the twins had been very solicitous towards Mom, fetching her drinks and pillows. They even managed to sit still long enough to read with her a couple of times. Their selection of Doc Savage novels was questionable, but Mom didn't complain.

"They're not going to think that."

"Still, I feel awkward about it. I need to go home where I can get some sleep without fear of waking up to find one of the Twins standing over me with an ax. Spungi or otherwise."

"Yeah, I can understand that. But I don't think Diana's going to let you go home by yourself."

I had already thought of that, and I knew arguing with Diana wouldn't work. "What about the Kinnisons? If they'd take me, do you think Diana would agree?"

"I think she'll go for it. So how did you escape Achilles the last time?"

"I'd rather not say."

"Oh, come on Michael, how bad could it be?"

"I'll just say that he slipped on wet tile."

Safe Harbor at the Kinnisons'

"Oh, Michael, I'm so sorry," Dr. Kinnison said as I threw my overnight bag into the back of her mini-van and took a seat next to Kinnison.

"Mom!" Kinnison said, as if she were violating diplomatic protocol.

"Thanks, Dr. Kinnison. I really appreciate this."

"It's no problem, Michael," Dr. Kinnison said, the van's electric motors quietly accelerating us down Proxima Drive. She caught Kinnison's gaze in the rear-view mirror. "We discussed this, Kimball. We can't pretend that nothing happened to Michael's father." She shifted her gaze to me. "Under the circumstances, it's the least Sam and I can do. Besides, we always like having you around."

I mumbled some more thank-yous.

"Now you know what I've been putting up with at the Black Lagoon," Kinnison said.

"I've always known," I said. "It just got to be more than I wanted to deal with right now."

"Andy and Achilles can be a handful," Dr. Kinnison

said. "But they mean well."

"They've got Mom snowed, too," Kinnison said sotto voce.

"Their cunning knows no bounds when it comes to masking their sinister nature. At least to adults." In reality, I was beginning to think I was wrong about that, but there was a distinct entertainment value to stringing Kinnison along on this point.

Dr. Kinnison gave me an encouraging grin in the rear-view mirror.

Kinnison's Dice Luck Explained

It was late on the first night after my escape from the Twins' gentle attentions, and we had finished a bit of web surfing to watch online trailers—the one for the new *Terminator* movie due out that fall had been particularly cool—and we were both feeling a bit keyed up.

"Too bad Max isn't around. I could go for a dungeon crawl right about now," Kinnison said. "I have it, why don't we play *Android Assassins vs. Kung Fu Clones*?"

"That's not a bad idea. You want to play the Central Computer or the Kung Fu Clones?"

"I'll take the Clones."

We set the board up while the radio belted out the synthpop catchiness of 'Safety Dance' and started in. He was onto his third clone in less than ten minutes when I said, "Kinnison, you've got to do something about your dice luck. It's not much fun when you keep dying within three rooms of the entrance."

"I can't help it!"

I looked at him shrewdly. "You really believe that don't you? You are so afraid of cheating that you do the opposite."

He bristled. "What do you mean, Gurick? I thought you'd gotten over the whole cheating thing."

"I have, but I don't think you have." I held up a calming hand. "Look, I'm not trying to accuse you of anything underhanded. I just think you aren't being fair to yourself."

"What? By rolling really crappy?"

"Yes. Precisely. Let's try a little experiment. Think of something happy, something cool or that you really want. Like you're going up against an army of Terminators and you're the one that's going to kick their ass and save the world."

"Okaaay," he said, looking puzzled.

I fished two ten-sided die out of his box of dice. "Close your eyes. Now, if you roll double-aught, you kill one." He closed his eyes and I picked up his hand, pushing the dice into them. "Roll."

He did. Two zeroes. "See?"

He opened his eyes. One of the dice trembled and rolled to a nine, as if he had bumped the table, but I knew he hadn't.

"What happened?" he said in a hushed voice.

"Close your eyes again, and don't open them until I tell you, too. Now focus and roll again... Again... Again..." Each time he rolled double aughts. Each time I scooped the dice up and put them back in his hand.

I held each die, to make sure he couldn't tip them away from zeros again and said, "Open your eyes."

I felt the dice press against my fingers, trying to rotate when he looked at them. "What's going on, Gurick? Are you playing some sort of trick?" He sounded hesitant in his accusation.

"No, you're doing it, Kinnison. You're telekinetic."

"No way!"

"You've been so afraid that you've been cheating that you've been sabotaging your own die rolls."

"If I'm telekinetic, then no one is going to want to play with me!" he said, a note of rising panic in his voice.

"We'll just keep it a secret."

Righteous conviction returned. "That would be lying."

I sighed. "In a way, but you're going to have to reconcile yourself to that kind of lie."

His face fell. "I just realized something. It doesn't matter if I keep it a secret or not. Someone else already knows."

I was surprised. "What do you mean? Wait, I think I know who you are talking about. Sensei Fox, right?"

It was his turn to be surprised. "Yeah, but—"

"Why else would he put you in the advanced class with Penny and the Twins? You can blame me for that, Kinnison."

The radio filled the ensuing silence with, "You're listening to one-oh-four-point-seven Geee-Roq! The station that knows what Galacticity wants to hear!"

"You thought I was telekinetic back then?" Kinnison said.

"It was a theory of mine, yes."

He picked up one of the ten-sided dice and held it in the palm of his hand, looking at it intently. Then he took his hand away. The die floated between us for several seconds before it dropped with a clatter to the table.

"Looks like another one of your wild-ass theories was right," he said.

Dad's Memorial

Tuesday, June 19th, 1984
(13,650 days post Supernova 1947A)

"Who have you spotted?" I asked Penny. Despite the fact it was the memorial service for Dad, I couldn't help scanning for Nova League members in their secret identities. Doc Styx was sitting with Mom—something I was most appreciative of. There were at least a handful of other men around who were in the right ranges of height and weight to be a disguised Magician.

"Who are you looking for?" Cleo's voice came from behind me. I jerked my head around.

"Cleo," Penny said, also turning, "You could sneak up on Argus."

"I'm looking for work colleagues of my dad. What brings you to the memorial service?" I asked.

"Apparently my dad knows your parents from back in the day. Before he retired, mostly."

There was a lingering sense of 'and you know what that means' in her voice. I turned back and caught sight of Sensei Fox. He was talking to Mom and, much to my relief, she was smiling, and more animated than I had seen her since the day of the accident. I also noticed a man approaching Mom in an expensive-looking three-piece suit and a thin mustache, that reminded me more than a little of the one under the Titanium Titan's faceplate. "Is that who I think it is?"

"The mustache looks familiar," Penny said.

"The man with the expensive shoes?" Cleo asked.

"That's the one." Penny said.

Cleo cocked her head. "Then, yes, I think it's who you think it is."

People were taking their seats as Robert Stack, a short, roundish, bespectacled man in his fifties and the CEO of Galacticity Metro Edison, took his place in front of the podium. It looked like the eulogy was about to start.

In retrospect, I really had to hand it to Sellers. As cold and calculating as it sounds, he really planned his 'death'—Dad's public death—to the tee. At the time I didn't know for sure, but strongly suspected that Sellers hadn't actually died at the Bayside reactor site. My talks with the three people whom Sellers had res-cued led me to conclude that their lives had actually been at risk. Not that it really mattered; the news re-ports ate it up, and Dad was getting some small measure of the hero's memorial he deserved. More importantly, after a month and a half of pretending that Dad wasn't dead, Mom could finally grieve pub-licly. It would have been easier if she had cried. The need to clean and clean again was painful to see. I won't dwell on the details of the funeral. It was closed casket. The Riggs-Armstrongs were there, as well as Doc Styx, the Magician, and a handful of other Nova League members in their civilian identities.

"Did I miss anything?" Kinnison said, sliding in next to me.

"Not really," I said. "Some old friends of my Dad are talking with my mom."

"Sensei Fox knew your parents?"

"Who would have guessed?" I said.

From the podium Robert Stack said, "In this day and age of super-powered heroes it is heartening to find heroes without powers. Michael Gabriel Gurick, Jr., was such a hero."

It was difficult to focus on what Mr. Stack was saying. I wasn't ready for this, and I let myself go back to scanning the attendees, knowing I could retrieve the eulogy from my memory later. I glanced back at Cleo. Uncannily, she gave me a supportive smile, even as her gaze looked through me. I smiled back.

"Michael Gurick's quick action and selfless sacrifice saved the lives of Robert Hui, Betsy McAllen, and Troy Speigle."

I had spent some time talking with each of them, and they seemed genuinely grateful that the man whom they thought was my father had saved them.

"Very few of you know," Mr. Stack said, "But Michael Gurick had fifty percent of the profits accrued from a dozen patents that he jointly owned with GME regularly transferred to charity."

On the surface, my life had been pretty much like our house: similar to that of every other kid on Proxima Drive. We lived a middle class life in a middle class neighborhood established in the mid-'50s during the early suburban boom set off by the Galactics dropping their Arcology in southern Lake Michigan. But very few people knew that Dad had made a few modifications, such as the subbasement lab and control center. Like the profits from the patents he shared with GME and contributed to charity, he invested the money from the royalties on hundreds of other patents, and used it to build extensive underground facilities as well as the tools and weapons he used in his crusade against crime. Those patents range from self-cooling beverage cans and self-heating soup cups you enjoy everyday, to the Crash-Foam that protects you in your car, to the spray-on ablative coatings that protect the now-retired shuttle as well as suborbital passenger and freight modules during re-entry. Of course, these patents are held by dozens of shell companies which channel their profits into trusts that, as I noted, supported Dad's crime fighting.

Which means Dad will keep on having a positive impact on the quality of your life. And that, despite almost no one knowing it, is better than any eulogy.

A Visit to the Lab

It was the afternoon after the memorial service, and despite the intermittent rain, Kinnison and I were out walking Bernoulli. You would have thought Kinnison would take a pass on ambling about in an early summer shower. I had tried to discourage him from 'wasting his time' with me—and not entirely altruistically, I might add. But every time I tried to sneak out, Kinnison was there, insisting on tagging along. It was uncanny. I had begun to entertain the idea that he was developing some other power in addition to the telekinesis. Which, in another context, would have been good news to add to the fact that Mom was starting to recover. Doc Styx had recommended that she be kept away from the house and its temptation to clean until he could work out an appropriate drug regimen and start her on cognitive therapy.

Seeing her confused and helpless after Sellers' apparent death re-ignited my anger with the still-at-large Demolition Squad. A feeling that justice delayed was justice denied began to make me itch to put on Dad's mask. But in order to do that I needed to get back down to the lab and start work on analyzing Dad's suits, not to mention looking for a user's manual.

Unfortunately, Kinnison wasn't cooperating with my plans. He had even accompanied me to visit Mom, despite the threat of the twins and their overactive imaginations—a problem compounded exponentially by their brick-in-development physical capabilities. Don't get me wrong. I was appreciative of Kinnison and his presence, not the least of which was because having a target-rich environment tended to confuse the twins' hunting impulses. Of course, it might have helped if I had actually shared my plans with Kinnison, but, at the time, it didn't seem like the right thing to do. It was hard to break the habit of telling no one about what lay under my house. No one except Penny, of course.

Kinnison's voice broke in on my thoughts. "There's something you're not telling me."

"What makes you say that?"

"I don't know. I get this feeling you've been preoccupied with something. Something you need to do. Are planning to do."

Which was too close for comfort. I tried to deflect him with the obvious. "Like taking care of my mom?"

"Yes, naturally that. There's something deeper, though." His gaze grew distant, and he almost tripped over a crack in the sidewalk. "Something to do with your dad."

He *was* developing another power. Telepathy? Empathy? Precognition? I tried to swat the curiosity bug, but it bit me. If I couldn't ditch Kinnison, then I'd just have to bring him along.

"I think we should run some tests on you. Let's go to the lab, Kinnison."

"You're not getting me into the medical lab!" He shuddered. "The smell of formaldehyde makes me want to puke."

"Not the medical lab—"

"School's closed for the summer. Or are there summer classes?"

"Not one of the school labs. I've got access to something better."

"At the U?"

"Nope. Even better. It's something my dad set up. Come on, we'll take Bernoulli home and I'll show you."

I led Kinnison into our backyard with the intent of entering the lab through the shed, but when I took Bernoulli in the mud room and started to clean him up, his yip of displeasure and big brown eyes persuaded me that he needed more outdoor time. I opened the door to the backyard and he bolted out to take up his longstanding argument with the squirrels, leaving Kinnison and me standing there watching.

"So where are you hiding this lab?" Kinnison said. "It can't be obvious. I've been here too many times for that."

I opened the broom closet and hung up Bernoulli's leash. Then, suppressing a smile, I said, "In here."

Kinnison's face darkened on seeing the cleaning supplies and old boots. "Oh, that *is* funny, Gurick."

I took a long sidestep and punched a code into the security pad next to the door to the garage as he continued, "You drag me over here with the promises of a secret—"

The contents of the closet rotated out of sight to be replaced by a dimly lit shaft. He started to lean over to look, and I restrained him with a hand on his shoulder. "Wait."

"For wha—" he started to ask. Then the pneumatic-pogo popped up with a 'pa-thisss'.

"Don't want to brain you on your first visit," I said.

"When did you find this? How did you figure out

how to open it?"

"This was the first entrance to my Dad's lab that I discovered. I was eight. I would hear Dad park his car in the garage, but then he wouldn't appear and I'd go looking for him, only to find him in the study later, or coming out of the mud room as we were sitting down to dinner. I couldn't make sense of his—or, to a lesser extent, Mom's—movements in my own house. I set up a few mini-vid spycams to record what was happening. I had to reposition the camera to get the code." I waved at the pogo where it hung in the center of the shaft. Two horizontal struts swept out to disappear into a channel in the far wall. "We call this a 'pneumatic-pogo'. I'll go first. Watch what I do, and follow me when the pogo comes back, okay?"

"Got it."

I gripped the handles, then stepped onto the foot bars. The pogo dropped, giving me that tickling sensation in my stomach. It came to rest with a little hiccuping sigh of air. I stepped off and gave it an upward jerk. It whooshed back up.

I heard an "Excellent!" echo down the shaft as it returned with Kinnison. After a moment Kinnison put out a hesitant foot, then quickly dismounted and turned. He was grinning and his face was flushed. "You should sell tickets! How deep are we?"

"Eighty feet below the mud room floor."

"Wow!"

We were in the ready room between the lab and the main vehicle silo. The silo side of the ready room had floor-to-ceiling windows through which light poured. In the corner was a transparent cylindrical airlock, currently rotated to allow unimpeded passage to and from the silo.

Moments later Kinnison was practically pressing his

face against the armored glass. "It's like the Batcave!"

Should have come through the backyard shed, I thought. It would have been less distracting. *But then,* a sly little voice reminded me, *you wouldn't have gotten this reaction out of Kinnison.*

The windows looked out onto the main silo floor, forty feet below. The space doubled as a garage and fabrication bay. Arrayed around the outer wall were a dozen vehicles, ranging in size from the battery-powered utility carts to a tanker trailer that carried a mole machine disguised as its tank. Each vehicle faced the center of the chamber floor, which was a massive turntable. At the points of the compass there were four airlocks big enough to accommodate the tanker, each currently irised shut. At the very top of the silo, right under the garage, were a series of four car-sized shelves on tracks. Three of the shelves held a sedan that looked like the one in which Sellers had driven me to the bowling alley.

"Who was your father?" Kinnison said, his breath briefly fogging the glass.

And a Submarine

"You remember what happened the day before we got in the fight with Luther and friends?" I said.

Kinnison dragged himself away from the view, turning to look at me. "Your dad was the Dis—?"

I cut him off, "Yes."

"Oh. I understand," he said, channeling, or using whatever his new power was. "You don't want me to get in the habit of using his superhero name. No wonder he was your favorite. You found this place when you were eight, right? Wasn't that when the Titanium Titan became your second-favorite?"

His empathy or whatever was working overtime.

He didn't wait for an answer; already grokking or reading it from me, he turned back to the silo. "Where did all the dirt go?"

"One of the exits is through a gravel pit."

"Your dad built all of this?"

"With the help of my mom, yes." You can accomplish a lot in fifteen years. Particularly when you have millions of dollars at your disposal.

"Your mom's a super, too? Who is she?"

"No, she's not a super. She was born before 1947A."

"Oh." He seemed disappointed for a moment; then his empathy kicked in again. "She helped your dad in his fight against crime, though, didn't she?"

I've got to get him hooked up to the psi-scope, I thought, then said, "That's right."

His gaze roamed the cylindrical space. "It's fantastic!" After a couple of seconds, he was pointing down and to the right of us towards a paneled van and read off its side, "'Acme Pest Control'." He chuckled. "What's that one for?"

"Mobile Command Center."

"You mean like what the SWAT use? Why would a superhero need something like that?"

"It's a little complicated to explain. Why don't you come look at the command center in the lab? It'll give you a better idea of what the MCC is used for." *And I can sit you down and use the psi-scope on you.* I started across the ready room.

"Okay. But I have one more question for you."

I stopped and turned to face him. "Shoot."

"Where are the aircraft?"

"In a warehouse on the shore of Lake Michigan."

"Really? There are planes? I was joking!"

"Joke's on you, then."

"Boats and hydrofoils, too?"

"And a submarine."

"Coool!"

I opened the door to the lab and passed through into the heart of my father's domain. I stopped and turned to watch Kinnison's face as he entered. It did not disappoint.

"Why is everything curved?" Kinnison said, looking around the cylindrical room, then at the domed ceiling that arced upward into dimness.

"Construction technique. Nearly all of this complex was hollowed out using what might be described as balloons and high-pressure water. There are some pretty interesting videos of the process stored in the lab's computer systems. I'll have to show them to you sometime."

"That would be cool, Gurick."

Directly across from us was the command-and-control area, with its banks of flat-screen monitors, semi-circular desk, and high-backed command chair. The screens were all on, showing live news feeds, and public webcams from around Galacticity. The workbenches, suit racks, backpacks, and assorted lab gear were unlit and shrouded in shadow.

Kinnison, catching sight of the bank of monitors, stared, his jaw working. "Okay, I understand why you need a command center."

"I thought you might."

"But why a mobile one?"

"Sometimes you need to be close to the action. And it has a compact lab, repair facilities, recharge reservoirs, and medical supplies." I waved at the chair directly in front of us. "Have a seat."

In the center of the room was a sunken area, three steps down, in the middle of which sat a round conference table, its blue-white surface lit from within, making it appear to be a milky pool glowing with an internal light. The chair I indicated was one of the ten arrayed around the table.

Kinnison's eyes widened. "It's like the Nova League Action Center!"

"Only smaller," I said. "I'll get the psi-scope."

Under the Psi-scope

I left Kinnison playing with the conference table's display surface. I located the aluminum case in the storage locker where I'd found it on one of my 'fishing expeditions'. I slid it onto the table and opened it. It was old, probably built in the early '70s as part of the response to the wave of anti-telepath fervor in the wake of Watergate. It had a serious retro feel, with enough gauges, dials and knobs to send an old-time radio ham operator into a swoon of nerdish delight. There was a roll of thermal sensitive paper to record the psi-scope output running in a band below the dials.

I unclipped the headband and pulled it out of the lid. There was a tube of neural gel, too. It looked straightforward enough. Besides, I'd seen enough spy movies to know how it should work. I applied the gel to the six nickel-sized sensors and said, "This is the psi-scope brain sensor."

"Looks like something from one of those Agent Psmith movies."

"It does, doesn't it? Hold still for a minute," I said, slipping it down onto his forehead and giving the knob at the back a handful of twists to snug it into place. "How does that feel?"

"Cold and gooey."

"I'll use less gel next time. The psi-scope will record your psionic activity and give us an idea about what kind of powers you have." I attached the leads and flipped the main switch. The needles snapped into the red, withdrew, jiggled and trembled into a near steady state, while the roll of thermal paper started to scroll out, jittering lines of data appearing on it.

"It tickles," Kinnison said, waving his fingers near his temples like he was brushing something away. "It goes zzzz, zzzz."

I fiddled with some of the dials. Kinnison yelped and ripped the headset off. "Sorry about that. I think I'd better look at the manual."

It was labeled 'Property of PsiCorp', and 'Top Secret'. I flipped through a couple of pages, but it was written in dense techno-bureaucratise that expected you to have at least a Master's in psionics. I put it aside. "Let's try it again, okay?"

"Okay." His voice had lost all enthusiasm.

I reset the dials from memory, then let the device ping along without touching them. Kinnison's look of discomfort slowly grew.

"Are you okay? What does it feel like?" I said.

He groaned. "I don't know if I'm okay or not. It feels like something is pressing down on my head, but from the inside. Then there are the bees."

"The bees?"

"A buzzing. It comes and goes. Changes spots. Can we stop yet?"

"Yeah, we can stop." I flipped the main power

switch. "I don't understand how to read the output, but I've got enough data. I'll go through the manual and I expect I'll figure it out."

He sighed, then pulled the headband off with a wince. "I've got a mondo headache. Here."

I took the headband. "Why don't you go wipe off the goop. There's a bathroom over there, and you should find some aspirin in the cabinet behind the mirror."

While he was gone I cleaned up the headset and looked over the curled roll of thermal paper, comparing it to the samples in the manual. The telekinetic line was easy to see, as it stood out from the rest, but there were several other significant-looking lines that I didn't know how to read.

When Kinnison returned, he said, "Well? What have you figured out?"

"Oddly enough, that you're telekinetic." I pointed to the strong line above the rest.

"And we needed the psi-scope to figure that out?"

"Nope. It's the other stuff you're doing that I want to get a handle on. Unfortunately, I'm baffled by the rest of the chart." I indicated the rising and falling lines that muddled along the lower portion of the paper strip. It occurred to me that Professor Jane might be able to help me make sense of this—anonymously, of course.

"What now, oh great brain?" Kinnison said.

"I guess that's up to you. Are you going to be a superhero? Or go the government route? I suppose you could apply your talents in the civilian realm. Go to work for Hollywood as a special effects man or something."

He looked surprised. "I didn't think there was any question of that. Superhero, of course. I always dreamed about finding an Orb and becoming an Astral Agent, which would be like getting a Lens from the Arisians, maybe even better than getting a Lens, but now that I know that I have powers without an Artifact, well..."

"Hmmm, yes, I think you've mentioned that fantasy before." Not that I blamed him for having it. It was something that a lot of kids dreamed about. Who wouldn't want an Orb? "But if you're going to be a superhero, you need a name." And I needed a reason to get Penny involved.

Of Names and Supersuits

"I was thinking of calling myself the Lensman," Kinnison said.

"I know you love Doc Smith's space operas, but I think you need something that won't get you in copyright or trademark trouble. Remember what happened to 'Spider-Guy'?"

"But all the good names are taken!"

"Why don't we ask Penny? Remember all the great names she comes up with for her characters?"

"Yeah. But—Wait, she already knows about your dad, then?"

"Yup."

"That is so unfair! Her being in on it all this time!"

Did he even realize he was guessing about Penny? Filling in information he shouldn't know? "There's a reason."

"And that is?"

"I'll explain, but first I need to make a call."

"How do you get reception down here?"

"Repeaters," I said, flipping open my cellphone and

speed dialing. "In for a pound, in for a Penny."

"Isn't that the other way around?"

"Hey, Penny, I was wondering if you might come 'round and join Kinnison and me in the lab."

"Okay, I get it now," Kinnison said.

"What have you dragged Kim into?" Penny said, her voice slightly distorted by the cellphone.

"Just running a few tests—"

"And he's letting you?"

"—psionic tests, that is."

"Very unpleasant," Kinnison said in a loud voice.

"It doesn't involve opening his skull up does it? 'Cause I wouldn't put—"

"No, course not. Why don't you come over and make sure that I don't open his head up or anything."

"You want me to come over and babysit him."

"What do you mean, 'open his head up'?" Kinnison said.

I waved a shushing hand at him. "I wouldn't put it that way, but, fair enough. I've got to get to work on the suit, figure out how not to die in it, and—"

"Fine. But you're not going to leave distracting Kim entirely up to me."

"Deal. See you in a few."

During the five minutes it would take Penny to arrive I started to fill Kinnison in on Penny and her family. At first Kinnison's empathy seemed to desert him, and he thought that Hank was the super one, but I told him to think about what he was saying. While I really should have left it up to Penny to tell him, I knew that with his burgeoning telepathy-empathy, or whatever power it was, he was going to find out about the Riggs-Armstrongs sooner rather than later.

"I think Diana and Hank moved in down the street from us because she was already partnering with my dad and mom. A lot of the arrows she uses are gadgets. Spycams, gas, bombs, and other stuff."

"It's easy for me to believe that Diana is the Silver Ar—"

"You have to stop doing that," I said.

"Oh, sorry."

"Stop doing what?" Penny said from the east entrance to the lab.

"Using the superhero names of people we know in conversation."

"I said I was sorry," Kinnison said.

Penny crossed to the conference room table. "I understand, Kim. It's hard to get used to, but—"

"—it's safer that way," he finished. "I get it. But what I don't understand is why all this paranoia right now? Aren't we in your dad's lab, Gurick? I'd think this is about as secure as any place in Galacticity."

"It is, but I want you to get in the habit of not mixing superhero and secret identity names. For instance, I never use Dad's superhero identity if I can help it. It's a matter of being hyper-aware of when and how one uses names."

He rubbed his chin for a few seconds. "Okay, that makes sense."

"Good. Why don't we talk about your ideas for a superhero name, then. Just to bring you up to date, Penny, Kinnison was thinking about calling himself the Lensman."

"An obscure reference. How about something a bit modern?" Penny said.

"But you've heard it. How bad could it be?"

"I've already mentioned that Doc Smith might object," I said.

"But he might not."

"Let's not take the chance. And there is the unfortunate

linkage with your name."

"How about combining the 'lens' part with something else that Smith wrote?" Penny said.

Kinnison pursed his lips in concentration. "Arisians? Skylark? Duquense? No, he's a villain."

"Skylark," Penny said. "Sky. Lark. How about lensark?"

"Lensark? Lensark," he rolled the sound around in his mouth. "Lensark. Yeah, I like the sound of that."

While Kinnison was trying out the new name, I typed it into the lab computer system. When the search came back empty, I announced, "Nobody's registered Lensark with any of the super-ID systems."

"Good," Kinnison said. "So that's settled. Now I was thinking about a suit, too..."

I sighed. It was never take it slow with Kinnison. He had to always keep moving forward. "What colors? And remember, only two, maybe three. Four at the absolute max, and only if you use two of them for highlighting."

"Um, okay, let me think about it. Only two?"

"Michael is right, Kim," Penny said. "Keep it simple. Remember Arcobaleno Rex's supersuit? Or 'costume' would be more appropriate."

I stood. "While you ponder that, let me take your measurements. I'll be right back."

I pulled a forty-inch-diameter steel hoop out of a utility closet. It reminded me of a hula hoop. I returned to the conference table, idly rocking it back and forth.

I leaned over, placed one end on the floor next to Kinnison and dropped the other end. It made a thring-thring-thringing noise as it came to rest. "Okay, step into the hoop, Kinnison."

"Is it going to hurt?"

"No, of course not."

"You didn't think the psi-scope would hurt, either."

"This is different."

"Really?"

Penny heaved a sigh and stepped into the hoop. "Scan me first."

"Right," I said. "Relax and hold as still as possible." I pressed the activation button on the hoop. Four handles snapped out and red lights came on around the interior of the hoop. I gripped two of the handles and raised the loop slowly up over her head.

"See?" Penny said. "Nothing to it."

"Yeah, and you're a brick."

"Come on, Kinnison, you won't feel a thing. I promise."

He took a step towards the hoop. Paused. "Fine," he said, stepping in.

I bent to take the hoop handles and Kinnison's hands darted towards his groin, and hovered there, twitching for a moment.

"Now what?" I said.

"It won't—I mean—"

I stifled a laugh. "No, Kinnison, it uses terra-hertz, not X-rays."

He sighed and relaxed, his hands falling to his sides. "Okay. Do it."

Almost a Date

Sunday, July 1st, 1984
(13,662 days post Supernova 1947A)

"Are you coming or not?" Kinnison asked, stuffing his gi into his backpack.

Part of me wanted to go to the lab and work on the suit, but another, more insistent part wanted to see Cleo. And then there was watching Kinnison apply his new powers. I had made progress with adapting the suit to fit me, so it could wait, I rationalized.

"I'll go," I said.

"Cool," he said. "I always seem to do better when you're there."

"Not sure why you think that."

"Yeah. Odd. Sensei Fox thinks it might be that I'm picking up something of your mental state, your calm planning or something."

"Huh. Sensei Fox seems to know a great deal about psionics. Not what you would expect from any old martial arts trainer."

Kinnison shrugged. "I only get a faint buzzing when I try to focus on him."

"Are you saying he's psionic?"

Kinnison shrugged again. "I don't know what I'm saying. This telepathy thing is new to me."

We met up with Penny and the twins, who chattered about their latest video game exploits during the entire Transit ride to the dojo. Kinnison, Penny and I talked about *Karate Kid*, the latest summer blockbuster, and how realistic its depiction of learning how to use superpowers was—the dissection of which lasted through the cleaning and up until the start of class gong rang, when Penny and Kinnison went to line up with the rest of the class. I made myself comfortable on a bench along the wall and watched. As Kinnison's fear of injury at the hands of the twins had receded, his telekinetic powers had grown. Or perhaps it was the other way around. He had progressed so far that he was fighting and holding his own against both the twins. Blindfolded. This new confidence had even extended beyond the walls of the dojo. Thankfully, his die rolling was back to normal, or at least average.

After the session, while I waited for Kinnison to change, I worked up my nerve and went to talk to Cleo.

"Uh, hey Cleo," I said. She was wearing a Eurythmics T-shirt under her gi.

"Hi, Michael. I'm glad you've been coming along with Kim."

"Yeah, he said something about his abilities working better when I was here, but that seems, well, I don't know, weird."

"Not as 'weird' as you might think. What do you think about when you watch Kim spar?"

"Pretty much what I think about when I watch anyone

spar. I try to predict what people will do, how the fight will progress—Ah. Okay."

She smiled.

"So you think Kim is reading my mind? Leveraging my analysis of his opponents and what I would do next in his place?"

"Seems like a reasonable explanation."

"Yeah. It does."

The conversation seemed to trail off into the ether for a few moments, and I almost managed to blurt out my question when Cleo said, "Are you doing anything special over the 4th?"

"Diana and Hank are hosting a barbeque, and I'm bringing the fireworks..." I trailed off, memories of my father lighting off his homemade fireworks rising unbidden.

Thankfully, Cleo stepped into the breach. "Oh, I expect the twins are excited about that."

"That would be an understatement. They're writing up detailed requests for colors, sequences of explosions, and anything else they can think of."

Cleo laughed, and I almost forgot to miss Dad.

"Would you and Sensei Fox like to come to the barbeque? Diana and Hank said I could invite anyone I wanted."

"I'm sorry, but Father and I already have plans. Can I take a rain check?"

"Absolutely." Okay, on to Plan B. "Um, what are you doing this Friday night?"

"Funny you should ask."

Confusion set in. I had expected her to say she was busy or something. "Funny?"

She noted my discomfort. "Not funny, in a 'ha-ha' way, Michael. Rather, it's peculiar. Sensei Fox—Father would like you and Kim to come to dinner on Friday night."

"Come to dinner?" I said. Stupid. Why was I repeating the obvious?

"Yes. I'll let him explain. He prefers it that way."

"We'll have to check with Mr. and Dr. Kinnison, of course."

"Of course."

It wasn't until Kinnison and I were boarding the Transit pod that I remembered why I had started the conversation with Cleo. Damn.

Kinnison and I Dine with the Foxes

Friday, July 6th, 1984
(13,667 days post Supernova 1947A)

Permission from Kinnison's parents was readily given and Kinnison and I presented ourselves at the dojo at six sharp that Friday. Speculation, at least on Kinnison's part, had run rampant. It ranged from 'we're going to get kicked out (but why did we get invited to dinner for that?)' to 'he's going to ask us to join a super-secret advanced class'. I tended to think that I had been invited because of my apparent 'positive influence' on his fighting abilities. Which was fine by me. It gave me another chance to ask Cleo out.

We arrived at the little door under the flickering neon of 'Black Lagoon Dojo' promptly at six. We knocked on the door and it swung inward to reveal Cleo. She was wearing a gray silk kimono with two huge orange and white carp embroidered on it. I felt seriously underdressed in my slacks and white dress shirt.

I gulped.

She bowed and said in a formal voice, "Welcome." But when her blind gaze stared through me, she gave me a little smile that made me feel simultaneously hot and cold. I mumbled a greeting and Kinnison said, "Cool kimono, Cleo."

"Thank you, Kim. It was my mother's."

Except for a pool of light around the entrance and the stairs leading up to the living quarters, the rest of the dojo was in darkness.

"It's quiet," Kinnison said, adding with a grin, "Too quiet."

"Would you rather have the twins in attendance?" I asked.

"They'll grow up," Cleo said in a way that dismissed them as a non-interesting topic of conversation. She led the way up the stairs, her wooden geta clonking rhythmically with each step, making me think how much she looked like Mariko from the mini-series Shōgun. A hint of jasmine trailed her, mingling with the familiar dojo smells of polished wood and brass with a trace of the sea spray.

It was my first visit to the Fox's living quarters at the dojo. I had been expecting tatamis and the shoji screens of paper walls. Instead it was modern middle-class American, something that you might find in any of the houses along Proxima Drive. Feeling that my expectations had been skewed, I suppressed my disappointment.

We ended up in the kitchen dining area, rather than in the more formal dining room we passed along the way. Sensei Fox greeted us with a broad smile and rock solid handshakes. "Please, sit."

We sat down at the table. An electric skillet sat in the center, with platters of vegetables, tofu, and thinly sliced beef arrayed around it.

"Have either of you ever had sukiyaki?" Sensei asked.

"No, Sensei," I said.

"Me neither, Sensei," Kinnison said.

"I think you'll like it. Sukiyaki was a 'traditional' peasant meal in Japan. A sort of 'stone soup', cooked over a fire in a shovel. Or at least that's what I've been told." He picked up the platter of beef and, using long chopsticks, he slid a small pile of fat and a round disk of bone into the hot skillet. It sizzled, filling the room with a rich scent that started my stomach to rumbling.

While Sensei Fox gradually prepared the meal by adding the meat, then vegetables, tofu, and broth, sprinkling on soy sauce and sugar before letting it all simmer, he asked us how we felt we were coming along in our training, and what we wanted to get out of it. Cleo served green tea and bowls of rice, with an occasional insightful comment on our progress. When the sukiyaki was ready, we all served ourselves from the skillet, Cleo and Sensei Fox using chopsticks, and Kinnison and myself using forks thoughtfully provided. As we ate, Sensei Fox added more beef to the skillet and started the process again.

When we had eaten our fill, which took half a dozen rounds of cooking, each one more flavorful than the last, Sensei Fox asked Kinnison to join him, and the two left the kitchen table for a tête-à-tête in another room.

"Can you show me how to use chopsticks?" I asked Cleo.

"Sure," she said. She held out her right hand, one chopstick in it. "You hold the lower one pressed between your thumb and finger like this. Then you hold the upper one sort of like a pencil." She waggled the upper one deftly.

I copied her, moving them together awkwardly. Her hand gently closed on mine, feeling the motion of the sticks.

"Good. But more like this." She adjusted my grip, her fingers warm and nimble. Part of me concentrated on the chopsticks. A lot more of me didn't. The part that was working the sticks decided that it was almost easy when you got them into the right position.

"Weren't you going to ask me something?" she said.

I was keenly aware that she hadn't let go of my hand. It was difficult to focus. "Uh, oh, yeah. I was wondering if you'd like to go see Depeche Mode with me next week. They're playing at the Aqua Dome." I started to second guess myself and added, "Or is that too big? We could go see the Cape and Banter Improv. Their stand up is really good, and—"

She interrupted my panic-babble. "Are you asking me on a date, Michael?"

"Yes—No—Only if you want."

"Then, yes. I do want. I'd love to see Depeche Mode, but tickets for the Dome are kind of steep, so why don't we make it the Cape and Banter."

"I—" I started to say, wanting to tell her that money wasn't a concern, but Kinnison reappeared with Sensei Fox behind him. I reluctantly pulled my hand out from under Cleo's. It was my turn for a private talk with Sensei Fox. She gave me an encouraging smile as I followed her father. The warm glow was a pleasant distraction from the potential self-critical-speculation of why Sensei Fox wanted to talk to me.

"Michael," Sensei Fox said after we had settled down in his den in front of a large, silent flat-screen TV, "I'd like you to join the advanced class."

For a second I didn't know what to say. One voice was repeating 'I am not worthy', then the more practical thought *I'll get pounded to a pulp* presented itself. Cautious to not contradict Sensei Fox, I said, "I don't understand, Sensei. I'm honored that you—"

He waved a big hand dismissively. "Let's cut through the crap, Michael. I'd be surprised if you weren't reluctant to start the advanced course. You will be at a distinct physical disadvantage."

"Yes, Sensei. But I'm willing to try." *It's not like I'm a stranger to having the snot kicked out of me.*

"I know. On the other hand, unarmed and unarmored styles are not the sole focus of my training. Not by a long shot. What would you say if I allowed, even encouraged you to use weapons and body armor?"

"That would help."

"How about weapons of your own design? As long as I vet them first, of course."

"I—Yes." That *would* be worth taking a beating for. I'd been wondering when I might get a chance to try out the 'gas-slammer'.

"Good. You can start this Sunday. Bring along whatever you'd like to try out half an hour early so you can demonstrate it for me."

"How did you know I had my own weapons, Sensei?"

He gave me a I-have-my-secrets-and-you-have-yours look. "Let's save that question for another day, shall we?"

Tsunami and Lady Lightning

Saturday, July 7th, 1984
(13,668 days post Supernova 1947A)

Sensei Fox's refusal to answer my question on how he knew about Dad's weapons redirected my curiosity. A number of peculiar things about Sensei Fox and the Black Lagoon Dojo had been lurking in the back of my mind, attempting to get together and make the happy 'Ah-ha!' dance. I pulled out my laptop and established a secure VPN connection to the lab's servers. Ten minutes later I was humming along with "Burning Down the House" on the radio as the facts twirled in my head.

"Are you humming because you got a date with Cleo?" Kinnison asked as he flopped down on his lower bunk.

I turned away from my laptop, which was sitting on a small area of his desk that I had managed to clear of paperbacks, comics, action figures and other fanboy detritus. "No—Are you poking around in my brain,

Kinnison?"

"Of course, not! I just assumed that's why you were happy. I wouldn't probe you."

"Not consciously, anyways," I said.

He looked sheepish. "Okay, yeah, it's possible I picked up something by accident. I can tell you've been thinking about Cleo a lot. Or as much as you let yourself think about her."

"I was researching Sensei Fox," I said, attempting to change the subject.

"So you do have a date with Cleo."

"Yes."

"But you'd rather talk about Sensei Fox? Fine. What have you found out?"

I pulled out a bug scanner. Its rippling green lights assured me that we weren't being eavesdropped on. At least electronically. I was still researching a portable psi-scope. "I think Sensei Fox is Tsunami."

Kinnison sat up. "I always thought Tsunami was Japanese."

"Good misdirection on his part. I found this old publicity shot of the Aegis Team after they foiled the Kingfisher's plot to blow up the Galactics' arcology. Take a look." I pulled up the old photo on the laptop. It was of Dad in his all-white suit, the Silver Archer, Lady Lightning, and Tsunami. It showed the four of them on the deck of the captured Kingfisher's submarine amid a forest of pylons that supported the underbelly of the Galactics' arcology. "He has the right build. His supersuit and mask make it impossible to see anything else, so you can't tell whether he is Japanese or not. This was taken in 1973, right before Tsunami retired from superheroing."

"Why is that significant? The Black Lagoon Dojo was established in 1971."

"When did Cleo have her accident?"

"When she was four... That was 1973."

I tapped the image of the woman in a black and orange superwear floating inches above the metal deck. "What do you know about Lady Lightning?"

"She was Chinese—"

"Japanese."

"Oh? Sorry, but I was four when Lady Lightning was killed by Iodine. I only vaguely remember the funeral. Didn't her death and the retirement of Tsunami cause the Aegis Team to break up?"

"Losing half your team members can do that, but yes, that's the way I understand it. Silver Archer joined the Nova League and Dad went solo for a couple of years before he joined the League, too. When did Cleo's mom die?"

"1973. Wait. You're telling me that Lady Lightning is Cleo's mother? Both her parents were supers!?"

"Obvious, when you think about it."

"Maybe for you."

Doc Styx Makes a Request

Monday, July 9th, 1984
(13,670 days post Supernova 1947A)

I had suit number two laid out on a workbench and was adjusting the gel padding so I wouldn't slide around inside it when my cellphone burbled. I looked at the caller ID. Restricted. I almost ignored it. But it was restricted, not unknown, which wasn't the same thing.

It burbled again, and I thumbed it on. "Yes?" The phone gave a small, yet confident beep, telling me that the connection was secure.

"Michael," a deep, familiar voice said.

"Doc Styx!" I hoped he wasn't calling with bad news about Mom. She had seemed to be responding nicely to the meds.

"The one and the same. I'd like to drop by for a chat."

"A chat?" I said stupidly, dread burbling up. I mastered my fear and continued, "This isn't about my mother, is it?"

"No, it isn't. Can we meet in your lab? If it's convenient for you, of course."

"Of course it's convenient. Now?" Relief mixed with a little thrill at his use of 'your lab'.

"I'm on my way. I'll be entering your complex via the eastern entrance off I-94 in ten minutes."

"I'll see you in a few, then." Now what did Doc Styx want? Ah, well, best not to speculate. I had been thinking about calling him anyway, as I had a few things that were bothering me that he might be able to illuminate.

I went back to molding and padding.

The security system beeped an alert. The entrance at the road maintenance depot off I-94 had been used. I got up and went through the ready room overlooking the vehicle silo to await Doc Styx's arrival on the silo's balcony. I brought along a video tablet in order to watch his nearly silent progress through the tunnels. He was riding one of his signature vehicles, which you could call a motorcycle, if you allow for motorcycles that have four-foot diameter wheels that are almost as wide as they are tall, and superconducting electrical motors at their hubs. Oh, and seats that suspend their drivers between the wheels, their backs mere inches from the road-bed. With all the streamlined panels and molding, Doc Styx's 'bike' resembled a stubby torpedo more than a motorcycle.

I triggered the silo's western tunnel door. It had almost finished irising open when the bike, decelerating almost fast enough to leave yard-wide skid marks, raced over its rapidly disappearing edge with a 'ba-dump' that would have been teeth jarring in a lesser vehicle. It came to a stop on the edge of the vehicle turntable nearest the ready room. Doc Styx sat up and dismounted, pulling off his skull-like helmet. Not a lick of his short silver-gray hair was out of place. Leaving his helmet, black gloves, and armored jacket on the seat, he gave me a wave and walked to the open-platform elevator up to the balcony.

I watched him during the handful of seconds that it took for the platform to rise to the level of the balcony. His clothes and knee-high boots were mostly black with silver accoutrements, many in a subtle Styxian skull motif. His collarless tunic was reminiscent of a priest's, but without the white tab at the throat. If you looked close you could see the seams of its many and multifarious pockets.

He put out his right hand. He was subtly intimidating, despite his six-foot, one-hundred-and-ninety-pound frame, having the smooth poise I associated with Fred Astaire. Or, perhaps, because of it. "Michael," he said in a baritone. "You are looking well."

I shook the hand he'd extended. His grip was easy, almost casual. "Thank you, sir. How do you think Mom is doing?"

"She's responding well to the medications, and I'm seeing continuing gradual improvement. But post-traumatic stress doesn't clear up overnight."

"I know, sir. And I've noticed her improvement, too."

He met my gaze, his eyes were a mild, almost colorless hazel. "Could we forgo the 'sirs', Michael?"

"Yes, all right. Why don't you come on in to the Command Center?"

I led the way. Not that it was necessary. Doc Styx had the demeanor of someone who had visited many times before.

When we had seated ourselves at the conference room table he said, "Looks like you are settling in down here. Have you been able to access much of your father's computer system?"

"Some."

He smiled. "I understand your reluctance to talk about it. But I ask because I need you to do something that Mike—something your father used to do for me."

"Oh?"

"Yes. To be blunt, your father used to supply me with drugs. But before you get the wrong idea, I should explain."

At the word 'drugs' I had quirked my eyebrow up at him in my best Spock imitation.

"You and your mother aren't my only patients. Many of the supers in the greater Galacticity area, both active and inactive, see me. One of the reasons is that I can provide them with drugs to control or mitigate the negative components of their powers, as well as enhance the positives. Your father was my primary pharmacist—both because he had the ability to manufacture almost any drug that I might prescribe and because I could rely on his discretion."

This revelation opened up a completely new dimension of my father's secret life.

I leaned forward in my chair, resting my elbows on the faintly glowing surface of the conference room table. "So you think I can synthesize drugs for you?"

"For my patients. Yes, I'm confident that you can. You have the facilities." He waved a hand, indicating the darkened lab around us. "The formulas, synthesis instructions, quantities, all you need to know is in your father's computer system. But in case you haven't come across this information yet, I have a copy here." He removed a data stick from one of the many pockets of his tunic and placed it on the table between us.

I picked it up, rotating the slim cylinder of high density ceramics between my fingers, its metal connector glinting in the light of the conference room table. "But I've only been able to access a fraction of the system! And it's vast. Petaflops of computing power combined with exabytes of data. I haven't found anything like a pharmaceutical formulary, but, again, I'm not surprised that I missed it."

"I've got an account on the system that I used to help your father maintain and add new formulas, but it's dual passkey protected, so I can only access it with the permission of one of the root accounts. Your father's, Liz's, or, I suspect, yours."

"My account doesn't have root access. I think."

"But you do have an account."

"Yes." Interestingly, it was the same account as the one on the house network. I held out the tablet to him. "Let's give your account a try."

He didn't take it, but gestured at the command-and-control console. "We'll have to use one of those terminals. They have the iris scanners."

He logged in and had his iris scanned, and then a voice eerily reminiscent of my mother's said, "Root account verification required." There was a pause as I started to put my eye to the scanner; then the voice continued, and I pulled back. "All root accounts have been inactivated due to lack of activity. Please reverify identity."

I hadn't been asked for anything like this before. There were layers to Dad's system that I knew nothing about.

The iris scanner was blinking.

"We're going to have to get Liz to come down. Or the Brain Trust—they helped your father install the system."

"No, let me try." I pressed my eye up to the reader.

There was an almost painful flash of light and the voice said, "Probationary status to Michael Gabriel Gurick the Third granted. Please submit tissue sample for genetic confirmation."

A slot opened next to the iris scanner. I put my finger into it. There was a prick and I resisted the impulse to jerk my finger out.

"Genetic confirmation in ten minutes," it said as I removed my finger from its clutches. A drop of blood slowly welled up on my fingertip.

A Question of Powers

"I have some questions for you while we wait," I said to the leather-clad figure of Doc Styx. We were back at the conference room table, and he was intimidating even sitting down. "You know when you visited Mom right after Dad died?"

Doc Styx leaned forward, entwining the fingers of his big hands. "Yes. I also remember telling you that I was available to talk if you wanted."

"This isn't about Dad, or Mom. Well, in a way, it is. Anyways, Brain Trust also came around to see Mom almost a week after you and the Magician. We had a bit of a conversation. More of an interrogation, actually."

"Ah. Where social niceties are in play, Brain Trust is, well, 'challenged' is the polite word that comes to mind. The other word that I associate with their behavior is 'enigmatic'."

"Um, yeah, that." It was reassuring to know, given Doc Styx's use of 'their', that he struggled with pronouns for the Brain Trust, too. "One thing he asked me was 'Where do your powers come from?' I told him I didn't have any powers, but he disagreed and changed the subject."

"Are you so certain you don't have powers?"

"I'm starting to have some doubts."

"What do you think my powers are?" Doc Styx said.

"I'd have to say that Bad-Assery is the one that comes to mind first."

He gave a throaty chuckle. "I certainly cultivate that, but I wouldn't call it a power."

"And you don't use Galactitech."

"Not quite correct. I have a Galactitech ID."

Of course he would have a G.I.D.. Nearly every superhero, and even some supervillains, carried one of the biometric unspoofable, incorruptible Galactic identifiers. There was the government-run PICSID, but only naïve newbies used that superidentity system, preferring JASON, the Joint Authentication Superidentification Open Net protocol, available through Doc Styx's company Orpheus Information Systems, among others. Why use two super-ID systems? While each G.I.D. was viewable from any other G.I.D., they were invisible to normal Earth tech unless physically jacked into an Earth-tech device, thus necessitating either PICSID or JASON to be seen by law enforcement regulars, reporters, et cetera.

"Okay. Then I am forced to say that you don't have any powers. While you are rumored to be superhuman, I have no evidence that you are. What I have seen or heard from reliable sources falls within human norms, 99th percentile plus, but human nonetheless. No offense intended."

Doc Styx nodded. "None taken. And you are quite correct. Physically, I am all too human. Mentally, well, that is arguably another matter. Since 1947 the average IQ has risen significantly. While the mean has gone up, it's the upper-end IQs that have really surged. We used to have only one or two Einsteins a generation. Now they number in the hundreds, with the trans-Einsteinian intellects in the tens. Which brings us back to you."

Was I being amazingly dense? Or just in denial? Because when I admitted to myself that brains were a power, was I admitting that I had a responsibility to use that power for the good of society? And it wasn't as if I hadn't been aware of the Unified Powers Classification System. Not that 'Brains' was ever listed as a power, but the UPCS had plenty of categories in which intellect played a critical or defining role, when you thought about it. The classifications Master Mind, Tool Master, and, to a lesser extent, Gadgeteer came immediately to mind. Not surprising that the UPCS didn't classify brains that way. It's not like anyone actually was thinking people directly to death. Okay, there was Mindspike, but that was psionics, which wasn't the same as being smart by any stretch. And if you happened to think of Pscreamer just now, then you know exactly what I'm talking about.

"Like your father was for his generation," Doc Styx said, "You are developing into one of the great minds of your generation."

"I am still struggling with the idea that 'intellect' is a 'power'," I said, then gave him a crooked smile and continued, "Intellectually, I see your point, but emotionally, well, I've been told by my parents to disguise my intelligence, to deliberately make mistakes and not draw attention to myself by demonstrating anything more than a moderately above average IQ. All, as it turns out, in order to protect my family from being discovered. Sometimes it seems like it would be so much easier to be a brick like the Silver Archer, or psionic. Or a normal."

"I understand where you're coming from, Michael, I really do. But I am one of the few people you will ever meet that has been on both sides of the brain-vs-brawn debate. I would, did in fact, choose mind over matter."

"Oh?" I prompted.

"I suppose it is only fair I fill you in," he mused, "I've known you since you were a gleam in your father's eye and a smile on your mother's face. I compiled your first genetic profile and counseled your parents. Genetic counseling, particularly for the powered, was the smart thing to do. Still is." He met my gaze and solemnly continued, "You know that."

Was he making some oblique reference to me and Cleo? I felt the heat of a blush creep onto my face.

He made a barely perceptible nod, his point apparently made. "But you want to know about me. My pre-1947A life, while interesting to me, is not particularly pertinent."

My eyes widened in surprise. "You were born on Earth, though?"

"Oh, yes, I'm as human as you are. Not always, mind you, but quite human now. I was at Roswell, and became part of the first wave of supers because of it. I spent ten years fighting crime as the nanoborg-enhanced Cyberion, and more importantly, capturing the rogue cyborgs created as a result of the Roswell crash and elsewhere."

I knew about Cyberion, of course. So that had been Doc Styx, eh? That went some way towards explaining the ongoing conflict between Doctor M and the Nova League, Doc Styx being one of the founding members. "The Brain Trust told me that Doctor M was created—augmented?—at Roswell."

"Ah. Doctor M. Yes, he was there, too. Would that he hadn't been. In any case, I allowed myself to be 'decommissioned' in 1957 when the U.S. government decided that the rogue cyborg threat had been dealt with. The process wasn't entirely reversible, though. Despite my brain augmentations being dissolved and literally pissed away, I remained nearly as intelligent as I had been with the nanoborgs in my system. Not that I was a stupid man before 1947A—my father saw to that. But the brain augmentation was like being led from a theater into the light of day after growing up sitting in the dark watching scratchy newsreels. I re-emerged with the first Nova Genesis generation in the wake of Kill Switch's assassination of Kennedy with a renewed sense of youthful purpose, despite entering my sixth decade. My life since then is a matter of public record."

Public indeed. He had been a pioneer in so many ways. As a superhero without a secret identity, he had led the way by giving up his U.S. citizenship and becoming a Galactic Citizen, in a defiant demonstration of independence from the increasingly draconian attempts by the Nixon administration, with or without the help of Congress, to collar and domesticate that first generation of U.S. supers. The U.S. government could do little but collectively grit its teeth as Styx Enterprises, with all its critical subdivisions, such as Cerberus Defense Systems and Charon Aerospace, reincorporated under Galactic law. It helped, of course, that Cyril T. Mayhew, one of the greatest legal minds alive, turned out to be a close friend of Dr. Lamont C. Styx, M.D., Ph.D., D.S., D.M.A., et cetera, et cetera.

I felt a thrill of inspiration. Like Doc Styx and Dad, I knew I was going to use my 'power' to not only fight crime directly, but to fight it indirectly. My thoughts were interrupted by almost-Mom's voice. "Genetic identity verified, root access granted."

"Excellent," Doc Styx said, standing up. "Let me show you that formulary."

Secrets and Lies

Doc Styx completed logging in to the lab's computer system, and we were surfing a huge database of drug formulations, annotated for synthesis, patient reactions, delivery schedules, and more. When Doc Styx was satisfied that I knew my way around, we logged off.

"Would you like something to drink?" I said as Doc Styx settled back into his seat at the conference table.

"I'll take a Dr. Pepper, please. If you've got one, that is."

I told him that I remembered seeing some in the cupboard and went to fetch a couple of them. *Dr. Pepper, eh?* I thought. *Unexpectedly appropriate.*

When the cans were cooling on the table Doc Styx said, "I talked to A.J.—" I must have looked confused, because he added, "Sensei Fox, at the Black Lagoon..."

I nodded. "Sorry, but I've only ever known him as Sensei Fox." I had found out his full name was Arthur James Fox when I had done the research into his background, but hadn't connected it to A.J. "Well, Cleo calls him Father sometimes, but..." I felt a tinge of heat creep into my ears as I trailed off.

He ignored my discomfort. "He tells me that he has invited you to join his advanced class. I have every confidence you will find Sensei Fox's tutelage enlightening. You can trust him."

"Because he's Tsunami?"

He gave me an appraising look. "Now that's what I'm talking about, Michael. Your mind is your power."

This time my ears were really burning.

"I assume you know who Cleo's mother is, then."

"Yes. And that Cleo is psionic, too."

"Well, actually, she's not."

Not psionic? Then what was she? I thought. "But she is powered. I'm certain she has some form of super-senses." Then I added, before I could restrain myself, "Can her vision be repaired?"

"Certainly. With Galactitech."

"Then why hasn't she...?"

"I'm afraid I can't say much more without breaking patient-doctor confidentiality."

"I see." He hadn't told me anything I wouldn't have figured out eventually.

"What are you trying out at the Black Lagoon?"

"This." I handed him a dense plastic object about the shape and size of a set of brass knuckles. "I call it the 'slammer'."

He took it. "Compressed gas?"

"And quite effective against Andy or Achilles, if only temporarily."

"Amazing rates of recovery run in that family. Oh," Doc Styx said, unfastening and reaching into another one of his many pockets. "Before I forget, there is another reason I wanted to see you today." He removed a package about the size and shape of a paperback wrapped in glossy red paper quartered by a thin yellow ribbon. "Happy birthday."

I took the package.

"I find it interesting that you are down here working on your birthday, rather than out celebrating with your friends."

"I—" I started to say, but stopped. Why wasn't I up there with my friends celebrating my fifteenth birthday? The harsh truth was I didn't want to celebrate. Dad was dead and Mom was taking drugs so she wouldn't clean everything that didn't move.

"It's okay," Doc Styx said. "We can talk when you're ready. Go ahead and open it."

I looked down at the package I had momentarily forgotten I was holding, as my mind had skittered off making up excuses. I unwrapped it. It was a very recent model Orpheus IS cellphone with a clam-shell triple-folding screen.

"Thank you."

"You are more than welcome." He handed me a sim card with the Tantalus Microdevices logo. "This has the latest encryption algorithms. Check it for backdoors and such."

"But I trust you."

"Nonetheless. For a man with your responsibilities, you shouldn't take anything on faith."

Did he just call me a man? "So you are saying 'Trust but verify'?"

"That's an oxymoron. Where did you hear that?"

"It was in a speech by one of the California Congressional Representatives I saw on C-SPAN."

He looked over at where one of Dad's suit's was splayed out on a workbench under spotlights. "When do you find time to watch?"

"I don't. I mostly listen while I work. Speaking of government representatives, I'd like to show you something."

I went to the evidence lockers, punched in the security code on one of them, and retrieved the small envelope it contained. I slipped the card out and handed it to Doc Styx.

"Arthur Sellers," he read. "And an 888 number for Heroic Relations, a PR firm here in Galacticity."

He handed the card back.

I returned it to the envelope. "The phone number appeared sometime between when Sellers gave it to me and Dad's memorial. Thorough testing has revealed nothing else of interest about it."

"I presume you called the number."

"Yes. The extension leads to a John Smith's voicemail message that states he is currently unavailable and to contact a Jonah Jones at a different extension."

"And this Jonah Jones... ?"

"Is a real person, but he claims to know nothing of Arthur Sellers. It seems to be a dead end."

"Are you trying to get a hold of Agent Sellers, or are you just curious?"

"It's mostly curiosity right now, but he gave me the card for a reason."

"Yes, I suspect he did. I'll make one observation that might help. 888 is one of the new U.S. government domain IPs."

"Ah. Yes, that does help."

An Outing to the Galacticity Library

Wednesday, July 18th, 1984
(13,679 days post Supernova 1947A)

"Where are the little spazzes?" Kinnison said, looking around the atrium, examining with exaggerated care the Calder mobile with its swooping rounded triangles hanging thirty feet above us.

"They dragged Diana into the gift shop," Penny said, "whining about needing T-shirts or some such thing to help them remember the exhibit."

"They are pretty determined to leave with something," I said. "They've been more than their usual handful. I had to intervene twice." Only made possible, I reminded myself, by the last couple of weeks of advanced classes. While they didn't exactly respect me—who could say if they respected anyone—but they had developed a healthy wariness now that I was armed. "They were particularly unhappy when I stopped them from re-arranging the mannequins in the martial arts exhibit into 'more realistic' poses."

We had 'volunteered' to accompany Diana and the twins to the Chinese cultural exhibit and film festival which the Galacticity Nova Genesis Memorial Library had been putting on all July.

"Speak of the little devils," Kinnison said, his voice a study in nonchalance.

Andy and Achilles were strolling across the atrium floor in our direction, carrying plastic bags from the gift shop. They each wore jeans and black T-shirts. Andy's had a big red Gothic-looking 'A', and Achilles had a blocky serif '1' that was as plain as the 'A' was ornate. Above the 'A' and '1' each had a printed 'Thing'.

"Where's Diana?" Penny said at their arrival.

"She's talking to the exhibit curator," Andy said.

"We got bored," Achilles said.

Andy held up her bag and shook it. "And we have T-shirts." The 'neener-neener' was implied.

Achilles struck a one-legged crane pose. "Let's go see the martial arts exhibit again." He hopped in the air and kicked and chopped at Andy, who easily blocked him.

"This isn't the dojo," Penny said.

While the twins harangued Penny, I turned my back on them and looked out the four-story glass wall of the atrium at the Nova Genesis Memorial Plaza. The afternoon sun caused waves of heat to ripple the air above the dark red paving stones. Two solitary figures hurried between the air-conditioned buildings that surrounded the plaza. At the opposite side, out across the flat blue waters of Lake Michigan, the glittering towers of the Galactics' Arcology reached impossibly far into the sky.

I became aware of a whistling sound, like a bomb

dropping, that rapidly grew. A gray-haired man who was crossing the atrium yelled "Incoming!" as he threw himself to the floor.

Kinnison, who was facing in the other direction, and despite not even seeing the gray-haired man, mirrored his actions. Looks of surprise and fear struggled for dominance on his face.

Reflected in the glass, I saw Penny lunge at the twins, bringing them down in a protesting jumble of limbs.

I stood frozen as a shadow swelled on the plaza stones and the sound reached an ear-splitting screech. Something huge and darkly metallic impacted with a thunderous roar that threw up shattered paving stones and sandy dirt. I took several steps back as the wave of debris smashed into the glass wall with a crackling, spreading spider web of fractures. Amazingly, the wall held.

Swirling dust filled the plaza.

A pseudo-silence followed. In the space that had been filled by the voices of people, a low grumbling and grinding of settling building reigned. Gratitude for modern supers-inspired building codes flashed through my mind.

From above, an ominous creaking and clattering sound filtered down for a moment until it was drowned out by the querulous, echoing voices of library patrons as they picked themselves up and started to re-orient.

I looked up. The mobile was swaying. "Guys," I said, "we'd better move."

Kinnison got to his feet. "What just happened?"

Achilles brushed Penny's arm off. "What was that for?"

"You made me drop my bag!" Andy said.

"You're welcome," Penny said, also rising. "Honestly, you two have the survival instincts of flatworms," Penny said. "And you're no better, Michael, with your nose practically pressed against the atrium wall."

"Uh. I couldn't help myself, I just had to—"

"—watch," she interrupted. "It's a bad habit of yours. And it's going to get you into real trouble."

I pointed up. "We need to move. Now."

Their gazes followed my finger, then everyone shifted out from under the half a ton of swaying blade-shaped metal and moved towards the spidery cracked front wall of the atrium. The recriminations the twins were visiting on Penny restarted.

Outside there was a rumbling, grinding noise, and I turned back to look. At first, I could see nothing moving in the plaza except swirling dust. The cracks in the glass wall and clouds of dust beyond made it difficult to see what was going on. I stepped up to the wall. Thirty yards away, the hazy ridgeline that must have been the rim of a crater began to resolve. Rising up at a shallow angle was a dark cylindrical shape twenty feet in diameter. Beyond was the statue of the Unknown Hero, his arm, due to its new precariously tilted position, pointing directly skyward.

Is It Aliens?

Kinnison joined me at the atrium wall. "That thing's gotta be at least forty feet long."

"More. A good chunk of it's buried."

A buzzing sound and flicker of movement between the buildings announced the arrival of a news drone. It began circling the plaza. Within seconds two more had joined it.

Color was seeping back into Kinnison's face. "There's four people alive on that thing. How did they—?"

"—survive?" I did a quick mental calculation based on the size of the crater. "Without Galactitech, no one but a super could have."

"Shut up you two," Penny said behind me, her voice cutting through the twins' excited chatter about alien invaders. "Stick close to me and Michael."

"Why should we?" the twins said in unison. "Where's Diana?" Achilles added. "She'd know what to do!"

"Until Diana gets back, I'm responsible for your

safety," Penny said.

Insectile mechanical legs were emerging from the cylinder, pushing it rapidly upright.

"Do you think it's alien invaders?" Achilles said.

"I hope it's alien invaders," Andy said.

"Of course it's not aliens." I watched the cylinder shudder to a halt at a forty-five or so degree angle. It looked like one of the four legs was jammed. "This isn't Galactitech."

"I'm picking up three, no, four minds on board," Kinnison said. "They're groggy, but definitely human."

Three of the legs adjusted their positions, and the cylinder continued its movement towards vertical.

"Can you get anything else? What are they planning?" I said.

"To steal something."

"Probably girls," Achilles said. "Aliens always want to steal Earth girls."

"Not our boys," Andy said. "Who would want you, Achilles?"

The cylinder was fully upright now. A rod with a ball at the end rose from the top.

"Why are we—" Penny started to say.

There was a bright flash from the ball, then the top half of the cylinder broke open to reveal racks containing dozens of spheres.

"—standing—"

Another flash, this one accompanied by a concussive blast that threw the spheres violently outward from the cylinder. Two landed with 'ker-thumps' on the glass wall above us and started to open, their surfaces peeling outward like metallic flower petals.

"—here?"

The twins jerked free of Penny's grip and rushed forward to take up positions just to my right, their hands pressed against the cracked glass.

"Are those bombs?" Andy asked.

"No—" I started to say, but stopped to listen to Kinnison.

He had his eyes closed in concentration as he murmured, "They're fully awake now... They're getting ready now, anticipating something..."

The lower half of the cylinder split open.

The Cylinder's Contents Revealed

Four supersuited figures emerged from the darkly metallic, glowing interior of the cylinder. A flame of unreasoning anger stabbed through me, and Kinnison's forehead crinkled in apparent pain. He turned to look at me wild-eyed. Did I look like that?

"Hey!" said Achilles.

"That's the—" said Andy.

"—Demolition Squad!" the twins said together.

I struggled to suppress a surge of hatred while Penny stopped trying to get the twins to back off from the atrium wall, and just stood there staring with the rest of us.

I focused on my analytical side, watching intently as the Squad came up and over the crater wall. The biggest of them was Wreckingbar, armored in matte purple and silver-gray, twirling his signature seven-foot-long bar of composite titanium. Following behind him came the blue-and-silver Dragline, her two cables whirling blurs in her hands; then Bang Galore, her armor patterned in harlequin-esque red and silver-white with a belt of red and white devices; finally Chainsaw, the man who killed my father, bringing up the rear, his armor a Tonka-Truck yellow and his right arm a toothed blade from the elbow down.

At the Squad's appearance, my hand had snapped down to the dispenser belt under my T-shirt. I had put it on this morning in anticipation that I might have to use it against the twins, but now I had an entirely different set of targets. But, no, there was no way that I was going to tangle with the Squad with just the contents of the belt.

A Galacticity squad car raced into the plaza, trailing a plume of dust; its siren, unlike the whirr of its electric motors, was audible through the glass. The dark blossoms attached to the walls of the buildings in its path erupted with an orange flame and the chatter of machine-gun fire. Everything but the central armored core of the car disintegrated in the barrage of bullets. They weren't going to be any help.

"Where's the Nova League?" Kinnison said, apparently having recovered from his unexpected exposure to my raw emotions. "This is basically their front yard."

As if to emphasize their lack of intervention, the Nova League Tower's silhouette became visible through the settling dust. It stood on the opposite side of the plaza next to the UN building, relocated to Galacticity ten years ago after Graviton hijacked it by floating it up to low-Earth orbit. The Nova League had foiled Graviton's plans—rescuing the hostages, and even managing to return the building from orbit, landing it intact a hundred yards from where I stood now.

"Where *is* Diana? She needs to see this," I said, flipping open my cellphone. There was no signal. But the digital video recorder still worked.

My heart raced as I held the phone up, filming the Demolition Squad as it moved with surprising speed, seeming to charge directly towards where I stood. A moment later it became clear that its actual target was the building just to my right, and I relaxed a little. It was the First Bank of Terra, rather than the library—a target which made more sense.

I heard the twins whispering back and forth, but I didn't pay any attention to what they were saying.

"And what do you think you two are doing?" Penny said.

I looked up. The twins were in the process of tying their new T-shirts around their heads, leaving only their eyes exposed.

"Cool ninja-masks," Kinnison said.

"Do *not* encourage them, Kim," Penny said.

While Penny was momentarily fixed on Kinnison, the twins started sidling towards the door to the plaza, looking at the Demolition Squad like a cat watching a mouse run for its hole.

"Stop right there," Penny said, returning her regard to the twins.

"If you aren't going to do anything, we are," Andy said, drawing a rope with metal weights at each end out of her T-shirt arm hole.

"We're not going to stand by while the Squad robs a bank," Achilles said.

"But I think you are going to do just that," Penny said, taking a step in their direction.

"You can't stop us," Achilles said, moving away from Andy and pulling a pair of nunchaku from the small of his back.

"Not both of us," Andy agreed, putting more distance between herself and Achilles.

I felt like joining the twins, but knew that that was a recipe for disaster. No plan. No preparation. No chance. Instead, I fingered the canister of sleep gas clipped to my utility belt, as I edged along the glass wall intent on flanking them.

The Silver Archer

"Wreckingbar just smashed the doors to the bank," Kinnison said in a hushed voice, as if he was trying not to attract the Demolition Squad's attention.

When the twins turned to look, I put myself between them and the atrium's entrance. Then, like an angel in silver, Diana appeared striding across the floor, moving fast but not appearing to do so. She was dressed in her tight fitting superwear that glittered with the silver iridescence of fish scales, on her fore-head a slim circlet of silver with its red Nova League starburst. Where she had gotten the bow and quiver of arrows was unclear. Perhaps she had a set stashed in the family mini-van that we had left in the parking structure.

"You two can stand down, now," I told the twins, continuing to shoot video. "The Silver Archer is here." They knew who the Archer was, and I hoped they wouldn't try to help their mom out.

They turned and watched her with envy in their eyes.

The Demolition Squad had vanished into the bank by the time the Silver Archer reached the atrium doors. When she pushed on them, they shattered. She stepped through their remains and sprinted across the plaza. The machine-gun spheres came to life again and began firing with a chattering roar that echoed and boomed from the buildings. The Silver Archer didn't falter as the automatic guns zeroed in, cracking the pavement around her. I couldn't tell if she was hit or was just dodging, but she made it to the bank door and, without slacking her pace, plunged into the dark interior.

When I turned back, the twins were looking a little green around the gills.

"Something is happening down there," Kinnison said, pointing towards the center of the library.

"What do you mean?" I said.

"It's like little earthquakes. Or explosions."

What was really going on? The ballistic cylinder was more of a crash-lander than a vehicle. The Demolition Squad didn't have a mastermind who would plot out a sophisticated attack. They were more of the smash and grab types. Were they, and the crash-lander, a noisy distraction for what was really going on? And who would be behind such an elaborate ruse?

The bank shook, then collapsed in on itself. A gush of white dust rose from the center of the slumping pile that had once been a three story building.

"Is the Silver Archer—?" I said.

"She's still alive," Kinnison said. "And so are the Demolition Squad."

An electric blue and silver-gray figure dropped from the sky, and the interdiction drones opened fire. The Titanium Titan landed next to the pile of rubble that had been the bank, and, ignoring the rain of bullets, he began pulling up slabs of concrete and I-beams and tossing them out into the plaza like they were made of cardboard.

If the bank wasn't the only target, then what? Something in the adjacent buildings? The one on the other side of the bank contained only offices, with no concentration of valuables that I was aware of. And I was pretty sure I would know about anything transient, as I had made good progress in reading Dad's summary reports of potential crime hot spots.

What was in the library's subbasements? The Rare Volumes Vault. Kept sealed in nitrogen and only accessible by permission and with an escort. That must be it. "Where is the Demolition Squad now? Are they coming this way? Underground, right?"

Kinnison concentrated. "Yes... I think so. How did you know that, Gurick?"

I quickly sketched my theory of what the real target was for him, then raised my voice so I could be heard over the twins' chatter about how the Silver Archer was going take down the Squad. They had taken a building falling on their mom with the same concern that would have greeted seeing her caught out in the rain. "Penny?"

"What?"

I motioned her over. I explained my theory and Kinnison's 'empathic' sensing. While I did so, we watched the twins.

"What are you proposing we do about it?" Penny asked.

"We should go down and look."

"What about the twins?" Penny said.

The twins were looking at a grate in the floor. They made several surreptitious glances in our direction.

"What's going on there?" I called over to them.

They ignored me.

"Ready?" Achilles said as he bent towards the grate.

"Ready," Andy replied as she knelt next to it.

"Hey!" I said. "Don't—"

Achilles ripped the grate up and Andy snapped her hands down and pulled up a black cable. It jerked back, almost pulling Andy into the duct. She braced herself and gave an even harder tug, and it snapped off.

"Follow it!" Achilles said.

Andy dove into the duct.

"Get back here!" Penny roared, attempting to jump on Achilles, but he was too fast, sliding into the duct after his sister.

I picked up the few feet of severed black cable, cursing myself for not tagging the little monsters with tracers before coming on this what-could-possibly-go-wrong outing. The cable dripped hydraulic fluid from the broken end and had a camera lens on the other. "I don't think we have any choice now."

Gathering Intelligence

"What—Rather, *who* can you detect now?" I said.

"It's getting muddled, but it feels like Di—Silver Archer is following—stalking—the Squad somewhere down there." Kinnison pointed down and between the library and the bank. "The twins are below us. Still close and intent on pursuing that robotic tentacle."

"We have to follow them," Penny said.

"I don't—" I started to say.

Penny overrode my objection, "Or at least try to intercept them."

"I wasn't going to suggest that we leave them to their own devices. We all know where that can lead."

"I think I can track them," Kinnison said.

I knew the basic layout of the Galacticity Library, but hadn't been able to get the full architectural schema in the time that I had allotted to the task. Something I regretted now. I looked at the guard station. The man and woman in dark blue uniforms with white and red shield patches looked like they were hunkering down for a siege. They'd know the layout of the vault area, but I didn't think they would hand out the info to a bunch of kids. On the other hand, they just had to think about it. "Kinnison."

"What?" he said, his arm still pointing downward, slowly tracking the progress of the twins.

"Come on, I need you to try some more of your Lensman mind tricks."

"Like what?"

"Like how to get down to the vault."

"I thought we were going after the twins."

I lowered my voice. "Where do you think they're headed? Try to focus on what those guards are thinking when I ask my questions."

We had arrived at the security desk and the two guards were looking like they wanted to pull their guns out and tell us to back off.

"Uh, hi there," I said in my most calm and helpless voice, "We're looking for my mom. She went down to the Rare Collections Vault and I'm worried about her."

"Sorry kid, you're just going to have to wait for the police to get here in force," said the one with 'Vance' on his ID card.

"Can you at least tell me how to get to the vault, sir?" I glanced out the corner of my eye at Kinnison. He gave a little shrug.

"Of course not," Vance said.

"Is it through there?" I asked, indicating a secure looking door a couple of yards down from where we where standing. It had a discreet brass sign with 'Authorized Personnel' engraved on it.

"I'm sure your mother is safer than we are," the other guard said, trying to look reassuring while her eyes nervously strayed to the dust-filled plaza beyond the cracked windows. "Why don't you wait over there?" She pointed at a cluster of library patrons gathering outside of the cafeteria.

I let some of the anxiety drain away, trying to look reassured. "Okay, sure, we can wait over there." I waved at Kinnison. "Come on, we shouldn't be bothering them."

"What'd you get?" I asked as we strolled back across the floor, the faint crunch of tiny bits of debris under our feet.

"The first door came through clearly, but I picked up a lot of impressions of what's behind it."

"Only the first door?"

"Hey, I'm trying. This isn't like telepathy in books."

"Okay, we'll just have to wing it."

Following Achilles and Andromeda

When we got back to Penny, the look on her face was even more ominous than when we had left. The storm clouds of her frustration were now towering up into a truly scary looking thunderhead of anger. "I'm glad we didn't take you along, Penny, you would have just scared the guards."

"I'll kill the little—" She stopped. With a visible effort she wiped away most of the emotion from her face. Anger, along with other uncontrolled emotions, has always been her bane. When you can crush stone and bend steel you have to be careful to not let your emotions carry you away. Penny, in one of her more vulnerable moments, had confessed to me that killing someone was one of her worst nightmares.

"The door we want is the one next to the guard station," Kinnison said.

Penny started striding towards the door. "Let's go," she threw over her shoulder.

The two guards were now occupied with an older couple, the woman of which was gesticulating, pointing at the collapsed bank and jabbing her finger at the guards.

I hurried to catch up with Penny. "Let Kinnison deal with the door."

She glanced at me. "That will take too long."

"Are you going to disable the guards, too?"

"You can seal it, then?"

"Of course."

"Fine. Kim!"

"Yes?" Kinnison called from behind us.

"Deal with the door."

"I—" He started to say something, but must have thought better of his reply. "Right, Penny."

We arrived at the door, and Penny turned to face the guard station, crossed her arms and waited. The elderly couple seemed to be making as much progress with the guards as Kinnison and I had. I tried the door, just in case, but it was locked. Kinnison gave me a desperate look. "You can do it. Just like you've been practicing."

"What are you kids doing?" Vance-the-guard said, leaving his partner to deal with the irate older patrons.

"Nothing," Penny said. "Just waiting for my mom."

Kinnison had laid his hand on the lock, a look of concentration on his face. I pulled out the can of spray adhesive foam from my utility belt.

"Clear away from that door!" Vance said.

"But this is where my mother told us to meet her," Penny said.

Kinnison's lips were moving, and a bit of his tongue stuck out like he was meshing a particularly fine-toothed set of gears. There was a click, and the door swung inward to reveal a corridor dimly lit by emergency lights.

"Hey!" cried Vance, beginning to move around the desk. He was pulling out his taser.

"Don't get involved," Penny said, abandoning her

attempt at appeasement. "I don't want to hurt you."

I pushed Kinnison through the door. "Come on!"

Penny moved. Vance must have been startled by her speed because there was a 'crack' from his taser and the darts skittered off the wall outside the door well after she was through it.

I sprayed the adhesive foam down the inner-door frame and slammed it shut, then leaned against it. "A little help here, Penny."

She leaned into the door with me and there was a buzz of the lock, then a thud against the door. Kinnison picked himself up off the floor and looked around. "I can see where we are," he said in a hushed voice.

"Oh?" I said, as there was another thud against the door.

"Yeah, I can 'see' it in Vance's mind."

"The door should hold now." Penny said.

I checked my mental timer. "Yup. Where to next, Kinnison?"

He pointed down the hall. "Along here. I think there's a service elevator and stairs."

A Slammer in Hand is Worth Twins in the Ducts

We jogged down the corridor with Kinnison in the lead, passing through pools of emergency lighting and ignoring the mostly open doors. Twice from darkened offices people yelled at us to stop.

"Pick up the pace," Penny said from the rear.

Kinnison reached an intersecting corridor and turned left without hesitation. He stopped in front of a closed metal double door. The sign next to it read 'Service Personnel Only'. "Through here."

Penny gripped the handle and gave it a twist. It came off in her hand. She dropped it, and it thudded against the carpet. She drew her arm back, her hand curling into a fist.

"Hold up, Penny," I said. "That's going to make too much noise." She stepped back and I pulled my slammer from my belt, inserted its nozzle into the crack above the lock, and triggered it. There was a quiet 'fwump' as the slammer foam expanded, then crumbled to dust, revealing a gap in the crumpled metal that a dead bolt still spanned.

"Nice!" Kinnison said. "That has more uses than busting the twins' chops."

"And why didn't you do that on the first door?" Penny said, pushing her hand into the gap.

"Remember? We wanted to glue that one shut."

"Ah." She yanked. The door opened with a 'ping' of snapping metal. The room beyond was floored in concrete. More yellow emergency lights cast odd shadows as we entered. The closed doors to a large freight elevator occupied most of one wall. Opposite the elevator doors was a steel fire door. Next to it was a '1 F' sign.

"Down the stairs," Kinnison said, pushing the steel door open.

As he did, there was a whooshing sound and I felt a breeze carrying an epoxy-like chemical scent blow out from the crack between the elevator doors. "Hang on a minute, Kinnison." I gestured at the elevator doors. "If you wouldn't mind, Penny."

She must have felt the breeze, too, as she didn't argue, but simply wedged her fingers into the rubber of the horizontal gap and pulled the doors open a foot or so. The breeze intensified, the epoxy-like smell even stronger. In the darkness beyond the horizontal slit I glimpsed movement. Then a sensor tentacle slid out.

Penny released the doors and they clam-shelled shut. The tentacle didn't seem to notice, pushing more of itself through the rubber seal.

"I got it," Penny said, her hand whipping out in an almost invisible blur, snatching it from the air. She pulled, smashing the camera end of it against the wall. There was a tinkle of glass.

"Tie it to the door handle," I said.

"Right," Penny said. It writhed as she did.

Penny pried the elevator doors open again. I carefully peered in. I counted eight tentacles stretching upward in the gloom. I risked putting in my head.

"Hey!" Kinnison said behind me.

I yanked my head back. "What?"

"Isn't that dangerous?" Kinnison said.

"I don't know," I replied. "You tell me."

"Uh, I don't know either. Did you see anything?"

"There's a light at the bottom of the shaft. I think it was the bottom. I didn't get much of a chance to look."

"Are we done here?" Penny said.

"Yeah, I guess."

She let the door close. "Let's move, then. Are the twins nearby?"

"Still moving. Still in ventilation ducts below us," Kinnison said, looking relieved at the change of subject.

Into the Bowels of the Library

Penny started down the concrete and steel steps, taking them three at a time. I followed and Kinnison brought up the rear.

"How far down was the light, Michael?" Penny asked as she rounded the first landing, her voice echoing off the poured concrete walls.

"Forty or fifty feet. Probably only two floors."

"Good."

Sure enough, four flights down the stairs ended in a concrete landing and another steel door. The smell of epoxy strengthened. Penny paused for a moment and I gave her a shrug. She pushed through the door.

A bright, almost painful blue-white light greeted us. It was reflecting off the opposite wall, where the elevator doors stood open. The tentacle cables ran across the floor and up the shaft. The room that they emerged from was the source of the blue-white light, and at least seventy-five feet across and a good twenty-five feet high. The doors that had once sealed the room were steel and six inches thick. Now they were bent and crumpled, as if they had been pried open. Across from us, ten feet off the vault's floor, were a series of rooms with floor-to-ceiling windows looking out onto the larger room. Each of these rooms contained a desk and chairs, probably for viewing documents.

"Welcome to the Rare Documents Vault," I said.

"You were right," Kinnison said. "It was a diversion."

Penny met my gaze. "Don't let it go to your head. Kim, where are the twins now?" Penny said to Kinnison.

"Above us now," Kinnison said. "Over there." He was pointing towards the end opposite the light source. As he did, a large, brown and green flatbed vehicle with the letters IBS marked on its side whirred past the opening to the room, heading towards the source of the light, its electric motors loud in the otherwise silent vault. We all flinched back at its sudden appearance. I realized after it was gone that it had no driver's compartment or cab, only a large, man-high metal cask with hundreds of panels circling it that reminded me of safety deposit box doors.

We moved forward as one. The vault was a hundred feet wide, with the windows of more reading rooms around the walls. At one end sat the snout of a massive mole-machine, two bright blue-white lights jutting up from it like eyes on stalks. Beneath the 'eyes' the conical drill head was split open like the beak of a monstrous bird. The flatbed truck disappeared through this dim red maw, like it was being swallowed whole. Opposite the mole machine sat three casks and a brown and green unmanned forklift. Dozens of tentacles crisscrossed the floor, running past us, up and through the broken reading room windows.

"Now what? No twins. No villains," Kinnison said. "Maybe we should disable that forklift—"

Kinnison stopped as another truck appeared. It was empty, and raced down the ramp, heading across the room towards us. It passed us decelerating, its destination the three remaining casks and the brown and green forklift that was even now starting to lift a cask from the floor. It drove over some of the sensor tentacles that were splayed out across the vault's floor, running from the mole-machine to the smashed windows of four or five reading rooms. The flatbed came to stop next to the fork lift, which began maneuvering its burden onto its bed.

"The twins. They're moving—" Kinnison began. With a crash and rain of debris Achilles—no, the red Gothic 'A' pegged the ninja-masked acrobat as Andy—burst through the roof of a reading room just beyond the robotic fork lift. Achilles followed, and the two slid down sensor tentacles towards the floor and the flatbed truck.

"You two are in big trouble!" Penny roared, echoes reverberating across the nearly empty vault.

The sensor tentacles near us twitched.

"Penny," I said.

The fork lift finished positioning the cask on the flatbed. The twins hopped up behind it. The flatbed accelerated.

"Stop this nonsense now!" Penny yelled.

"Penny," I tried again. "You need to keep it down."

The tentacles lurched off the floor, swarming around Penny as she tried to move forward to intercept the flatbed, tangling her feet, sending her sprawling as the flatbed sped past. The twins, their eyes almost glowing with excitement, waved at us from their perch behind the cask as the flatbed climbed the ramp and was swallowed by the mole-machine's maw. I'd have bet the lab's gas chromatography-mass spectrometer that they were grinning like demons under those masks.

A Ride Into the Dark

Penny rolled, gripped a handful of metal tentacles as they looped and coiled around her legs. She gave them a sharp jerk, and they tore with a squishy squeal, spurting hydraulic fluid.

Dodging the flailing tentacles, I grabbed Kinnison and pulled him towards the remaining two casks. "Come on."

"What about Penny?" Kinnison said.

"She could deal with a giant squid. Those things will only slow her down a bit. We've got to be ready to catch the next ride."

I sprinted towards the forklift, keeping the wall to my left, the whirring of electric motors and the 'ba-drump-drump' of rubber tires running over sensor tentacles behind me.

The flatbed brushed past, missing me by only a couple of feet and causing my untucked T-shirt to swirl up, briefly cooling me in the hot ozone laden air of the vault. It braked to a stop a dozen feet in front of me, positioned perfectly for the forklift to lower the

second-to-last steel cask onto its metallic bed. It thonked down in a way that made me think a large electromagnet was involved.

I put on a last burst of speed and managed to scramble up onto the bed. The truck's acceleration pushed me back, and I would have slipped off if I hadn't slid into the cask. I rolled and caught sight of Kinnison starting to dodge out of the way of the flatbed. "Grab on!" I called, leaning out over the edge of the bed towards him.

Our hands slapped together, and with a wrench I pulled him aboard. Ahead, broken tentacles waved while unmoving segments lay curled and dead at Penny's feet.

"Help hold me, Kinnison," I said. He grabbed me around the waist and, with one hand gripping the gap between cask and flatbed, I leaned, stretching my other hand towards Penny. "Come on!" I yelled.

She leapt free of the tentacles and we gripped each other's wrists, but her hand was slick with hydraulic fluid and I knew I was going to lose her.

The look in her green eyes told me she knew it, too. "No, I'll—"

"Hold on!" I said, and heaved, feeling something pop in my shoulder. I spun her up towards the trailing end of the bed even as her hand slipped from mine.

"—crush your—!" she continued as she landed mostly on the bed just beyond the cask, sliding along its flat, slightly ridged surface, her legs dangling over the side. Abandoning what she was trying to say, she dug her fingers in, the aluminum of the bed screeched, and her legs collided with the rear wheel, almost dragging her under. There was a 'squeee' of rubber and a puff of smoke; then she was pulling herself free of the tire like she was coming up out of a swamp. She flopped up onto the flatbed's deck, leaving six-inch-long gouges in its metal.

I breathed out. I hadn't realized that I had been holding my breath. I also became aware of a deep, burning pain in my right shoulder where I had felt the pop.

A second later she had to dig her fingers into the deck again as, with a jolt that sent another stab of pain through my shoulder, the truck climbed the ramp beneath the glowing spot-light eyes of the mole-machine. Then we were passing through a long metal tube that was its interior. I forgot the pain for a moment. There was something odd about this. Where was the machine's power source? Control systems?

"You okay, Penny?" Kinnison called around the cask.

"Yeah, just peachy," she said. "You?"

"I'm good."

There was another bump, and the flat whirr of rubber on metal turned into a more muted moan, and then we were in a bare tunnel, the walls blurring past nearly invisible in the truck's running lights.

I put my good hand out, feeling the smooth epoxy-coated walls sliding past under my fingers. We were accelerating, and I had to snatch my hand back after a few seconds when the friction started to burn the tips of my fingers. Someone had gone to a great deal of trouble to create this back entrance to the Rare Documents Vault. The vibration caused by the impact of the cylinder containing the Demolition Squad had disguised the creation of the final segment of tunnel that had breached the vault. While everyone had been focused on the Squad and the bank, a robotic fork lift and fleet of trucks had been making off with millions of dollars' worth of first edition books, hand-illustrated maps, pulp magazines, and comic books. The whole thing stank of Doctor M.

The hot wind in my face grew stronger as we headed downward, picking up speed. It smelled of ozone and epoxy. Far ahead there was a faint gleam of reflected red lights.

"Let's move to the back, Kinnison," I called over the rushing air stream. It felt like we were doing at least sixty now.

Penny was sitting with her back against the cask. I pulled a mini-mag flashlight out and played its blue-white LED light over her. Penny's left pant leg was blackened and shredded. I could smell the burnt rubber. And her left shoe and sock were missing. I braced myself and knelt next to her, giving her shoulder a squeeze with my left hand. "I didn't think you were going to make it there for a second."

"No problem, o ye of little faith," she said.

"Your arm," Kinnison said. "It feels like—"

"It's okay, Kinnison," I said.

"No, it's—"

"Drop it, Kinnison. I'll live."

Penny shook her head. "That was stupid, Michael. I could have crushed your wrist or taken your arm off."

"I trusted that you wouldn't."

Discussing Strategy and Tactics
[Mind If I Call You 'Pots'?]

I settled down, my back against the cold steel of the cask, putting my flashlight away. No point in raising the chances that we might be spotted. "I don't know how much time we have," I said. "So let's get our act together before we arrive, wherever we're headed." I stopped and grabbed onto the lip of the cask as the truck bed swayed to the left, running slightly up the side of the tubular tunnel, then drove back down, crossed the center line, and climbed even higher on the right side of the tunnel. I instinctively ducked as a truck heading in the opposite direction passed us halfway up the opposite wall, its empty metal bed close enough that we could have reached out and touched it if we had been standing.

"Our biggest problem, other than keeping up with the twins," Penny said after several seconds of watching the receding lights of the empty flatbed, "will be if we run into the Demolition Squad."

"Right," I said. "There's no way we can take them."

"Which means we have to keep the twins from engaging them at all costs," she said.

Kinnison was looking back and forth between us, like he was watching a tennis match.

"Which means distract, trip, or otherwise disable the twins as necessary," I said.

"That could be fun," Kinnison said, unfortunately echoing my mood.

Penny gave him the look. "Otherwise, we evade the Squad."

Kinnison looked meaningfully at my shoulder. "And if we have to fight them?"

I ignored the throbbing pain. "We know their tactics."

"We do?" Kinnison said.

"Being underground and in tight quarters will be our best advantage," Penny said.

"Unless you are dealing with Chainsaw," I said.

"Keep your distance from him," Penny said.

"Bang Galore won't risk using serious explosives underground," I said.

"You hope," Penny said.

"We all hope," I said.

"Wreckingbar and Dragline both have weapons that are more effective in open spaces," Penny said.

"And—" I started to say, but paused as the truck made another left then right climb-and-dodge maneuver to avoid another flatbed heading towards the vault.

"That should be the last one," I said.

"Why do you say that?" Kinnison asked. "Oh, right, one cask left."

"As I was saying," I said. "Wreckingbar and Dragline's weapons are much less effective at close quarters."

"But don't let it come to that," Penny said. "They're heavily armed and armored cyborgs with Galactitech V-tap power sources."

Kinnison squirmed excitedly, bumping me in my shoulder. A hot lance of pain made me grimace.

"This is just like prepping for a crawl in Max's Dungeon Inglorious," he proclaimed. "What do you think, 'Pots'?"

'Pots' was the name of my alchemist-thief in Max's world. "You may have a point, 'Lando'. We just might be able use our game names in a fight and expect to respond to them. Then again, maybe not. Just keep in mind that you aren't really an elven martial artist."

"It's worth a try. And I know I'm not an elf, but if anyone is like their character, it's Penny. You could pass for a real version of a barbarian thief, Penny. You could kick Conan's butt up and down the Elephant's Tower. Right, 'Cinder'?"

"I think you're losing your marbles, Kim."

We sat in silence for a couple of minutes, my shoulder throbbing. At some level, what Kinnison was saying was that, as 'Lando', 'Cinder', and 'Pots' we had been going into tight situations and acting, arguably under pressure, as a team. While it was impossible to know how any of us would react when push came to shove and our lives were on the line, there was some value in holding the optimistic view we would perform as we assumed we would.

The tunnel briefly leveled out, then we were heading upward.

"Halfway point," I said. The air was noticeably cooler now. I stood and looked around the cask, but all was darkness ahead. After what seemed like an interminable time in the dark, but was actually only about six minutes, we could see a light ahead. And like the proverbial light at the end of the tunnel, I was hoping it wouldn't turn out to be the train-wrecks-in-training, Andy and Achilles, taking on the Demolition Squad.

Kinnison, who had been trying to get a signal on his inTouch for the last few minutes, said, "I've got a couple of bars now!"

"I'd say we're about five miles from the library," I said. "Southshore district, right?"

"Just about bang on, Gurick." He held up his phone, the pulsing map cross hairs confirming my guess.

"Don't look so smug, Michael," Penny said as we emerged from the tunnel. "Now, where are the miscreants?"

"Man! Now I've got zero bars," Kinnison said.

The Twins Run to Ground

We emerged from the tunnel, and were moving across the concrete floor of a large room. It was even bigger than the vault, and looked like a cross between a warehouse and a containerized shipping port. As we exited the tunnel, I counted seven parked flatbeds. Opposite us, and our apparent destination, was the room's most notable feature. It looked like a giant canon breach. A dozen sleek rectangular, modular shipping containers were arrayed across the floor next to it, with dozens more stacked along the two walls to either side. Each container had a brown and green stylized IBS logo emblazoned on its side. Under the 'IBS', in smaller letters, it read '90 minutes is all it takes'. The flatbed truck slowed and stopped next to the container closest to the breach mechanism. Another unmanned brown and green forklift moved forward, gripped the cask and lifted it off the flat bed as we jumped down. Inside the open container that the forklift was headed for was another cask from the vault.

"This is an automated loading system for a ballistic linear accelerator!" Kinnison said, as a crane mounted on tracks in the ceiling lowered monstrous grippers and picked up the container and its load of casks. "I've always wanted to see the inside of one of these."

"He did a report in seventh grade on these things. Even built a scale model," I said to Penny as the crane whirred towards the breach mechanism, then lowered its burden into it.

"I remember."

"You have to admit," I said. "Using International Ballistic Shipping to deliver the loot to yourself is rather clever."

"I suppose," Penny said, then called out, "Andy! Achilles!"

One of the twins' ninja-masked heads appeared in the open door of the third container down. "What kept you?" Andy said.

From within came Achilles' disappointed voice, "Oh, man. Now we'll never catch up with the Squad!"

Andy jumped down from the container, Achilles close on her heels. They stopped to watch the crane lower the container into the breach mechanism.

"What's going on?" Andy asked.

There was a loud 'ka-klunk' before it disappeared within.

"It's going to launch a container," Kinnison said.

"You mean like a catapult? Or a cannon?" Achilles asked, a gleam coming into his eyes.

"Catapult, I guess," Kinnison said. "It uses a linear accelerator."

Penny was looking around. "So how do we get

out of here? I don't see any doors."

"It's an automated facility," Kinnison said.

"They have to get in here to service—" Penny said.

"Where are your masks?" Andy interrupted.

Does Everyone Have a Mask?

"We don't have time for masks, Andy," Penny said.

Andy put her hands on her hips. "You have to protect your identities!"

"She has a point, you know," I said. "They could arrive any time now."

"All the more reason to find the exit," Penny said.

Kinnison's head was turning right and left, searching the room. "But we've already been scanned by security cameras."

"I'm not worried about the security cameras," I said. "It's not as if they're going to end up on WatchMe."

"We have spare masks," Andy said, as if being caught without one was a serious faux pas. She produced a pair of stockings from some pocket.

"Those had better not be mine," Penny said.

"Mom's," Andy said. "Yours were too small."

"You can keep living, then," Penny said, taking the proffered stocking.

"Well, I'm not wearing one of those," I said.

"You could cut holes in your T-shirt and pull it up over your head," Kinnison said.

"Easier said than done. I'll just wear my gas mask, if need be. What about you?"

He looked embarrassed.

"Don't tell me you brought a mask, too?"

He nodded, pulling out a gray cloth with two holes neatly cut in it.

I shook my head in disgust. Half because he had a mask, and half because he was under the impression that covering up the upper part of his face was an effective disguise. I turned towards the container that the twins had just vacated. It had four huge crash seats arranged in a line, one after the other, facing the blank wall of the far end. "Looks like we got here before the Demolition Squad," I said, climbing in.

"They're headed this way?" Achilles asked, a hungry keenness in his voice.

"Yup," I said, but I was more focused on the contents of the container, only barely registering the swish-swish of his nunchuks and Penny's attempts to squash the twins' renewed outbreak of enthusiasm.

Not only was the loot being sent via sub-orbital delivery—so were the villains. I brought out the slammer from my utility belt and went to the lead couch, sabotage in my heart. I glued it to the base of the struts so the tip of it was right up against the bottom plate and floor. I glued the spare slammer cartridge to the trigger. When the container was launched, the acceleration would trigger the slammer and the gas would be discharged between the plate and floor, which, combined with the acceleration, should rip the first crash-couch free, making physics do the dirty work. Then it would hit the next couch and the chain reaction would be unstoppable.

Penny's voice penetrated my consciousness. "Michael! What *are* you doing?"

"Something devious," Kinnison said.

I returned to the exit. "Dropping a wooden shoe."

"Saay what?" Achilles said.

"Sabotage," Penny translated. "You know, he read an entire dictionary when he was five."

"You're never going to let me live that down, are you?" I said as I positioned one of my spy webcams in the corner above the door. "Crap."

"Crap, what?" Kinnison said.

"I just remembered that the next flatbed should have arrived with its load by now." I quickly exited. Staying focused around the twins was hard. It was as if one of their powers was to induce chaos. "Has anyone located a way out yet?"

Trapped in an International Ballistic Shipping Facility

"Nope, we're still trapped," Andy said in a tone of voice reserved for "I'll have two scoops with sprinkles."

Kinnison's eyes glazed over for a moment. "They're here."

I rotated the lens of my second webcam to fish-eye and attached it to the underside of the next container over.

Moments later I heard the whirr of electrical motors and the second-to-last flatbed zipped out of the tunnel. Behind the Rare Documents Vault-cask rode the Demolition Squad.

"Damn," I said under my breath. Then out loud, "Mask up, everybody."

Penny stiffened momentarily, saying something under her breath that sounded like "Sit!"

At the rubbery purr of tires on concrete Kinnison and the twins whirled to face the oncoming flatbed. "All right!" they all said in unison, sounding like

Christmas was early.

Was Kinnison channeling the twins? I elbowed him. Hard.

"Hey—" he started to say, but stopped as the Squad, each carrying a man-sized duffel bag, jumped off the slowing flatbed, landing with a nearly soundless agility that caused the bottom to fall out of my stomach. The flatbed passed us, still decelerating.

A little less than ten yards of empty concrete floor separated us, and for one long Spaghetti Western moment we stood frozen, staring at the Demolition Squad while they stared back at us. It must have been sheer, stunned amazement on their part, running into five punk-ass kids in a motley collection of masks—two of whom must have seemed to be barely out of diapers—in a sealed underground automated facility which should have been completely devoid of human life. For our part, we were confronted with four cyborgs, more killing machines than human parts, the smallest of whom was the six-foot-two Bang Galore in her red-and-silver-white-harlequin-patterned armor. They looked as if they had just come from battle—and I didn't know whether to interpret this as a positive or negative thing—the sooty smudges and the scarred and dented armor were indications of having seen some serious action against the Silver Archer.

What happened next was a chaotic stutter of events that I was only able to parse out and put into a cohesive order later. Even so, it stands out as a starkly vivid memory.

The Demolition Squad all pitched their duffel bags aside. Most of my attention was locked on Chainsaw. Beneath the visored upper half of his face, a grin of almost childish glee twisted his scarred visage, and he powered up the saw blades spiraling along his arms and legs, as well as those circling his torso. At first their hissing whirr was faint, but it grew louder as they picked up speed, the individual cutting edges disappearing into a blue-gray blur against the enamel Tonka-Truck yellow of his armor.

"Get behind me," Penny said, grasping the twins' T-shirts and pulling them back. The super-tough fabric stretched but held as the twins strained forward.

I went for a couple of smoke grenades.

"What are you waiting for, Dragline?" Wreckingbar said. His battle-scarred matte purple armor seemed more ominous at this range. "They're only kids."

As Wreckingbar spoke, Dragline threw both her arms forward in a silver-and-blue blur, like she was bowling with both hands, the sharply pointed ends of her cables darting out across the gap between us, one directly towards my head, the other for Kinnison's.

One analytical part of me was cursing, convinced that my hands darting under my T-shirt were what had attracted Dragline's attention.

I started to duck, then Penny was slamming into my right side, sending me staggering. A spike of pain pierced my shoulder and "Aaah!" escaped my lips. As I staggered left, almost tripping on the lip of an empty container, I saw Kinnison fling up both his arms and duck. Dragline's cable seemed to hit an invisible barrier, bouncing up and away with a spring-like 'ke-spang'.

Penny had lost her grip on the twins. Andy snapped out an end of her weighted rope surujin. It wrapped around the cable that Dragline had just missed me with. Dragline power-reeled the cable back almost as fast as it had gone out. Andy braced herself, but it jerked her off her feet, flying at chest height towards Dragline. She neatly twisted in mid-flight, slamming both feet into Dragline's visored face. She performed an elegant backflip to land in front of Dragline, spinning the ends of her weighted rope in both hands.

"So the wittle zz-heroes want to pway," Dragline said in a cloying coo.

Achilles, with Penny no longer holding him back, charged the Squad with his nunchuks swinging, letting rip with his best "Kiaaaaah!"

The Twins' Fury

I felt useless watching the twins rushing into battle with Dragline. I had no offensive weapons left, unless I wanted to go back for the slammer. It was reasonably effective against the twins, but not so much against the weaponized cyborgs of the Squad. I mentally reviewed the contents of my utility belt, but, barring the smoke grenades, nothing presented itself as immediately useful in the situation, so I was forced to continue to helplessly watch the unfolding events.

Chainsaw, his six-foot-ten armored bulk now humming with blades, moved to intercept Achilles.

"Chainsaw! Leave them to Dragline," Wreckingbar said.

Chainsaw stopped. His grin disappeared and he turned wordlessly, following Wreckingbar and Bang Galore towards the tunnel entrance.

They're expecting Silver Archer, I thought.

Achilles had only managed to close half the distance when Dragline, a cruel smile twisted onto her face, whipped her left-hand cable, forming a loop that rippled out in a blink of an eye to snap down on Achilles neck. Dragline wrenched. Achilles' attack cry ended abruptly with a sickening 'crack'. He spasmed, and went limp, his nunchuks spinning away from his paralyzed grip. Dragline gave a yanking twirl and his body flew, crashing into the side of a container with a hollow boom, then sliding to the floor. I brutally squashed the impulse to run, reminding myself that Kinnison would be infected by any fear on my part.

Kinnison, with a look that was a mixture of fear and fury, lunged, punching the air in the direction of Dragline. Her head rocked back with the force of his telekinetic strike.

One of the metal weights at the end of Andy's su-rujin caught Dragline in the chin with a force that should have shattered her jaw. The other end wrapped around Dragline's left wrist.

Dragline lashed out with her right-hand cable, its pointed tip whistling towards Kinnison, who barely managed another telekinetic deflection.

As the cable rebounded off Kinnison's invisible TK shield, Penny grabbed it. Through the stocking, I could see a look of concentrated fury on her squash-nosed face. Bracing herself, she gave the cable a two-handed yank up, then down, sending a hump-wave down it, lifting Dragline off her feet and sending her crashing to the concrete. Rolling, Dragline yanked back, and Penny was pulled from her feet in turn, then dragged towards the cyborg.

I stowed my smoke grenades and edged my way out and around the few yards to where Achilles' body lay crumpled. A wild whirl of Dragline's cable snapped overhead and into the container with a 'ka-crack-boom', and I ducked and grabbed Achilles, dragging him back behind Kinnison.

With a trip-hammer sound of metal against ceramic-metal armor, Andy pummeled Dragline with whirling overhand blows. Then Dragline punched out. Her fist connected with a meaty 'thwack' and Andy's limp body flew back out. Penny, releasing the cable, bounded to her feet and snagged her sister, one-handed, from the air.

Oblivious to the events around it, the forklift whirred past me with its cask, sliding its burden into the open empty container next to me. I felt for Achilles' pulse, finding it reedy and thin.

"Pots, she's almost here," Kinnison said, managing to remember to use my role-playing name.

I went for the two smoke grenades again, but hesitated, unsure what benefit they would have at this point. "The Silver Archer?"

Kinnison, his face scrunched in concentration, said, "Yes."

Wreckingbar took up a position just outside the tunnel mouth and a little to the side, with Chainsaw a half-dozen steps behind him.

I had to warn the Archer. I flicked out a flare, igniting it as I threw. Wreckingbar was bringing up his bar two-handed in an easy stance, like a baseball batter calmly facing a pitcher. Bang Galore plucked several cylinders from her half-empty belt and tossed them down the tunnel.

The flair bounced past Dragline and came to rest a few yards from the tunnel entrance, leaving burning after-images on my retinas.

Wreckingbar glanced back at the flare. Beyond the burning light I saw a flash of movement in the tunnel and an arrow with a silver egg-shaped tip zipped out, slewing in apparent defiance of physics to strike Wreckingbar with a 'crack-bang' and a burst of light that burned a streak across my vision. He went over backward with a crash and the flatbed hurtled out of the tunnel mouth. Chainsaw aborted a swing of his saw-arm when he found no target riding behind the cask.

Bang Galore stepped out of the way of the truck, and a 'ka-bang-bang-bang' followed. The tunnel entrance collapsed with a 'fwump' and gout of billowing dust.

Take Down

Dragline swept a cable at us, Kinnison blocking it again with a telekinetically augmented punch.

"Lando, slow the cable!" Penny yelled, making another grab for it.

Kinnison's forehead was furrowed with the strain. "I'm trying, Cinder, I'm trying!"

Something big and silver dropped from the slowing truck's undercarriage. The Silver Archer, using her momentum, bounced and rolled towards where the Wreckingbar's weapon lay. She snatched it up as she came to her feet, and swung it hard. There was a tinny 'ker-clang' as it connected with Bang Galore's head. She crumpled.

Penny was in a pitched tug of war with Dragline, gripping one of her cables with both hands, her bare left foot leading, while Kinnison tried to deflect the whipping probes of Dragline's other cable. Twice it penetrated his defenses, cracking into Penny, tearing cloth and leaving red, bleeding welts on her arm and side.

Chainsaw leapt at Silver Archer, his blades now buzzing like a swarm of bees. The Archer brought the bar up and blocked Chainsaw's arm-blade. In a blur that I could barely make out, she brought the bar around to crack into the side of Chainsaw's head. He pin-wheeled away, crashed spread-eagle into the side of a container, where the blades dug into its tough carbon-composite, keeping him upright long enough for the Silver Archer to charge across the distance, the bar held two-handed like a spear. The Silver Archer's run terminated in a thrust that hit Chainsaw in the abdomen just below where his ribs would be, her shoulder muscles bunching as she punched the sharp tip of the bar through his armor, pushing the entire stack of containers back several feet. A coruscating flash of lighting ripped through the Silver Archer, causing the muscles on her arms to spasm, and bunch. Chainsaw's chin dropped and the whirring blades ground to a halt. Silver Archer yanked the bar free in a screech of metal, then dropped it with a clang. Two discolored areas on the bar showed where she'd left cooked skin behind. Something the color and consistency of honey was leaking from the hole in Chainsaw's chest.

Now we just have to deal with Dragline, I thought, allowing a sense of relief to creep in.

Dragline, sensing that her comrades were down, turned and lashed out at the Archer's back with her free cable. "Look out!" I cried, my voice muffled by my gas mask.

Silver Archer turned. Sidestepping, she threw up a silver-armored arm and the cable wrapped around it.

There was a snapping, grinding noise and a spattering of concrete dust from Dragline's armored boots as they sent anchors into the floor. The cable snapped taut. Dragline whirled out her other cable, as the Silver Archer wrenched with a sharply exhaled grunt. Dragline's boot-anchors gave with a sharp pop-popping noise like gunfire, and she was flying across the room. The Archer swung her other fist, connecting in an uppercut with Dragline's chin as she flew towards her.

Dragline's body bounced off the ceiling before coming to rest in a heap on the floor, dozens of yards of limp cable strewn about her.

It looked like it was all over, except for the application of restraints and calling in the Supers Crime Unit.

Reboot

Wreckingbar's armored limbs twitched, the fingers of his armored gauntlet curled into fists. He sat up and reached his hand out towards where his seven-foot-long bar lay. It gave a static electricity crackle, and the dust puffed up around it; then it skittered across the floor for a few feet, bounced and flew into Wreckingbar's outstretched hand with a resounding 'thwang'. As the bar pulled him upright, Bang Galore groaned and rolled over and Chainsaw's blades began to grind into motion again.

Was everyone rebooting at once? I thought, my relief suddenly gone like a mainsail in a hurricane.

Chainsaw wrenched himself free from the container wall, and he took a couple of tottering steps towards the Silver Archer.

I saw a twinkle of movement, like a red-and-silver-white hummingbird darting between flowers, and something like a mechanical beetle landed on the Silver Archer, right between her shoulder blades. For a half-second the deck-of-cards-sized beetle clung there. Then a flash and 'ba-bam' threw the Archer across the room to slam into a stack of containers. They tottered, then slowly fell over, burying her still form.

The forklift was maneuvering to lift the cask off the last flatbed, and I knew what our exit strategy had to be.

I pitched the two smoke grenades clattering across the cement floor between us and Dragline. Gray, greasy-looking clouds erupted and engulfed her, expanding to form a screen between us and the squad.

"Switch to IR," Wreckingbar said from the depths of the cloud as it roiled and rolled in our direction.

Like Dad hadn't thought of that, I thought.

I whistled and waved to catch Penny and Kinnison's attention, then pointed at the open container. "Lando! Cinder! That's our ticket out of here."

"What about Silver—?" Kinnison started to say, but stopped as Penny, still holding Andy's unconscious body, bent, and gripped Achilles' T-shirt.

Kinnison put out a hand as if to stop her. "But his neck is broken! You shouldn't move him, should you?"

"He'll get over it," Penny said, throwing his rag-doll limp body over her shoulder. "He has before."

She leaped through the open door of the half empty container, Andy and Achilles flopping over her shoulders. Kinnison followed.

Seconds ahead of the forklift, I jumped into the container. Everyone crowded to the back as it deposited the final cask. The Silver Archer's eight-foot bow was attached to the smooth steel top of it by a magnet.

The door slammed shut, sealing off the smoke that was wisping in and cutting off the sounds of the Squad.

I pulled out my cellphone and punched in the P2P code for the fish-eye webcam as Penny laid the twins out on the floor between the casks. No response.

She straightened. "Now what?"

Kinnison watched me for a moment, then whipped out his phone, punching 9-1-1. "Crap. I'm still not getting any bars, are you?"

"Nope." I put the phone away.

"I repeat," Penny said, "Now what?"

"We wait until we've been loaded into the launcher."

"And then?"

"You break us out of here."

"Good. I'm glad that our plans finally converged."

Kinnison was looking like he was going to burst. Or that he had to make a pit stop. "What is it, Kinnison?"

"Well, once we are inside the linear accelerator launch system we can climb up the engineering access ladders. Unfortunately, we'll only have about thirty seconds or so between loading and launching to bust out."

"You can find the way?" I asked.

"It'll be obvious. I think," Kinnison said, slumping back against the side of the container and massaging his temples. "By the way, what was it with the theme from *The Good, the Bad, and the Ugly*, Gurick?"

"You were channeling—" The container rocked, throwing my right shoulder against the nearest cask and I groaned. Kinnison grimaced with me. I reached out to steady myself and hit the Silver Archer's bow. It slid off the top of the cask and clattered to the floor as we began to rise.

"Battery's dead," Kinnison said, echoing my thought.

The container dropped, then there was jarring 'k-ka-thunk', then forward motion, and foam began gushing from nozzles in the ceiling of the container.

Kinnison thrust himself away from the wall. "Acceleration foam!"

"Can we breathe it?" Penny asked.

"No, not if it's just for shipping," I said. "It's time to get out of here. Penny, if you would?"

Penny moved to the door, opened her hand like she was going to karate chop it, and drove her fingers into the seam between the two carbon-composite doors. It didn't seem to have much effect.

The container jolted as if we had run into something. "That's the nose-cone—we have about fifteen seconds," Kinnison said.

The Automated Shipping Blues

I grabbed the bow up off the floor. It was heavier than I expected, but it had sharp steel ends. "Here, try wedging this into the crack."

Penny took it. "Thanks."

I turned back. "Kinnison, help me get the twins."

Kinnison heaved Achilles up.

"Put him over my left shoulder."

The foam was thigh high and rising fast by the time we made it to the doors. A gun-like crack announced Penny's progress, and she jammed a hand into the gap, planted her bare foot against a door and heaved. The locking mechanism shattered, and the left-hand door flew open. We tumbled out into another dimly lit tunnel, this one filled with servo-mechanisms and a container-wide track running along the floor.

A second later, as the container continued its motion along the track, the servo-mechanisms lowered a large hemisphere and attached it to the end, sealing the doors shut again in a hardening splash of foam.

"Re-entry shield and drogue chute," Kinnison said,

shifting awkwardly under Andy's weight. I sympathized. Achilles was at least as heavy as I was.

I looked around. There was a maintenance hatch not far along the tunnel.

The container was sucked through a circular set of doors, which sealed shut behind it. I heard the distinctive sound of vacuum pumps.

Penny had spotted the maintenance hatch, too, and was advancing on it with purpose. Holding the bow in her left hand she twisted the handle. The bolts slid back, and she pushed it open easily. "After you," she said, waving Kinnison and me through.

The door clanged shut behind us. We were in an engineering access corridor. Concrete, cables, and the distant thudding of vacuum pumps greeted us. To our left it turned upward at an angle sharp enough to require stairs. To our right, it ended in a floor-to-ceiling double door beyond which could only be the smoke-filled launch facility.

Kinnison waved towards the stairs. "It parallels the launch rail. I think we can get out that way. Can I put Andy down now? She's worse than a bag of cement. At least the cement isn't bony."

Penny leaned the bow against the wall. "Here, I'll take her." She lifted Andy's limp body like she was the large stuffed panda Penny had won at the carnival when she was nine after dropping a hoop over a milk can a quarter of an inch narrower. "How about you, Michael? You want me to take Achilles?"

I almost laughed at her squashed nose under the impromptu stocking mask, but instead said, "Sure, I wouldn't mind."

While Penny laid the twins out, Achilles lying down, and Andy slumped against the wall, I checked my cellphone again. The fish-eye webcam was still offline, as was the one in the container with the couches. "How long will it be before the next launch, Kinnison?"

"It can launch a container every sixty seconds."

"Are you still picking up their vibes?" I asked Kinnison.

He closed his eyes, a brow furrow appearing. "Yeah. They're waiting for something to happen."

I put my ear against the door to the launch tunnel. I heard the faint sounds of whirring servo-mechanisms and chittering machinery. It grew louder, then faded. There was a final ka-thunk, and the pump vibration ramped up.

"They're gone now," Kinnison said.

My cellphone dinged. *Finally.*

Dispersing the Cloud

I flipped open my cellphone. There was a text from the fish-eye spycam I had attached to the bottom of the container, telling me that its buffer was 20% full and it was ready to start uploading.

"Ah, now we can see what happened." I held up my cellphone, unfolding the screen to its largest size so he and Penny could watch with me. Not that there was much to see.

Kinnison squinted at it. "But it's just smoke."

"When I say 'see', I mean that in a general sense. Listen." There was the tramp of steel-shod boots. They weren't bothering with being stealthy.

"Where are the brats?" Wreckingbar said.

"In the shipping container," Dragline replied.

"But they're in with *his* loot," Chainsaw said.

"We'll let the Doctor sort them out at the other end." Wreckingbar said. "Bang, help me with *our* loot. Dragline, make sure those kids don't get out. Chainsaw, watch and see if Silver Archer moves. You are *not* to go in looking for her."

"Looks like they're going to—did ignore Diana—Silver Archer," I said, trying to sound as hopeful as possible.

There was the heavy thumping sounds of duffels being tossed into the container with the crash-couches, followed by the hollow tread of metal-shod boots on the container's composite floor, then the faint twanging of bungee cords. I mentally crossed my fingers, hoping that they hadn't discovered my spycam or the slammer. I heard the door thunk shut, and then the crane whirred overhead, growing louder. I checked the timestamp in the lower right-hand corner of the screen. Five minutes ago. Four minutes had passed since it had been launched.

"Let's go back and see if we can help the Silver Archer," I said.

The double door at the end of the tunnel gave way to a combination of Kinnison's telekinesis and a hefty kick from Penny.

"Can you do something about this smoke?" Kinnison said, as its oily blackness rolled through the open door.

"Yeah, hold on." I removed another canister from my belt and threw it into the room. It clattered to a stop and began to hiss. A moment later the smoke began to clear, precipitating out of the air as a black, greasy dust.

The door let out into a part of the room that had been hidden from us by a wall of shipping containers. A whirring grinding noise came from the top of the wall, and a gap appeared as the ceiling crane took a box away.

"Leave the door open; I think the twins will be okay where they are. Let's see if Silver Archer is hurt, or—"

"She's alive," Kinnison said.

"Good, that's a relief." I cupped my left hand and braced myself. "Come on, we can climb over. And watch the dust. It can be slippery on smooth surfaces."

Wake-me-up

The launch chamber was as we left it, except for the new, thin layer of grime. The jumble of containers beneath which the Archer had disappeared seemed to teeter precariously.

I took a moment to recover and disable the remaining spycam.

Penny jumped up onto the bottom-most container of the jumble.

"Just a minute," I said, consulting my scanner. There was no indication that we were under video surveillance. "I'm pretty sure that the Squad disabled the security monitors. Go ahead, Penny."

She gripped a container, braced herself and lifted with a grunt. The one she was on creaked ominously as she swung the container around and let it down with a hollow 'booom'. Two containers later we were kneeling next to the still body of Diana. Or the nearly still body; her Olympian-proportioned, silver-micro-mail-clad chest was rising and falling in a regular manner.

"What is that smell?" Kinnison said.

"Mostly burned flesh," I replied. But there was a chemical hint to it. Some sort of pinkish, sticky fluid wet the concrete under her.

I gripped her left arm and tried to roll her. Even with the expectation of increased mass, I could barely shift her.

"Here, let me," Penny said.

"Are you sure that's a good idea?" Kinnison said.

"I want to see how much damage Bang Galore's flying bomb did," I said.

"But what can you do?"

"I'm not completely useless in a fight, you know," I said. "Or when its over. Just like Pots."

The silver micro-mail of her suit had been split and shredded by the force of the explosion. Its remains had been smashed into her flesh, which was oozing the pinkish fluid. It looked like someone had been pounding an aluminum-foil-clad steak with a meat tenderizing hammer.

I glanced at Penny, but her face was a stoic mask. I pulled out a canister.

"This is going to sting a little," I said under my breath.

"What is that?" Kinnison said.

"Spray-on syntheskin." The canister hissed and Diana jerked.

"It stops the bleeding," Penny said, holding her mother as still as she could.

As I moved it carefully back and forth across her broad back, a translucent layer formed, sealing in the oozing fluids.

"Did your dad invent that, too?"

"Yup. Okay, you can lay her down again."

"What about the bits of metal?" Kinnison said.

"We'll worry about those later."

"Should we try and get her mask off?" Kinnison asked.

"You have to know how to take it off. It's a Smart-mask. It doesn't just come off," I said. "Besides, it isn't like its interfering with her breathing."

"You have some of that wake-me-up?" Penny asked.

"Sure. Do you want—?"

"Yes."

"Fine." I pulled out a small ampule.

"Will that penetrate her skin?" Kinnison said.

"It's a spray." I handed it to Penny. "You do the honors. I want to be out of her reach when she comes around." I pulled Kinnison back with me, saying, "So do you."

Penny snapped the end off the ampule and squeezed it up Diana's nose. She snorted violently and sat up with a snap, knocking Penny back, despite her obvious preparation.

"Wha—?!" Diana said. "I hate it when you do that Disp—" She stopped, looked around, then continued, "I should ask what you three are doing here."

"Don't these masks work?" Kinnison said, sounding disappointed as he removed his mask and stuffed it in a pocket.

"Well, we haven't changed clothes since we left the library..." I pulled the gas mask down with relief; I was beginning to feel like Karth Adder, the evil overlord from Mars Wars.

I yanked the gas mask off and stuffed it into my back pocket. That was the last time I was going to be caught without a proper mask and nose plugs.

"We followed the twins," Penny said, also unmask-ing. "They're a little worse for the wear, but they'll recover."

"And the Squad escaped," Silver Archer said, obviously disappointed. "With the money and rare documents."

"We tried to stop them!" Kinnison said.

"You shouldn't have," Silver Archer said, but it sounded perfunctory. And was there a hint of pride in her voice that we had survived our encounter with the Demolition Squad?

"We didn't have much choice," I said, "We were right in the middle of their escape route."

"We looked for a way out—"

"But the Squad arrived—"

"And the twins attacked them—"

"Then you showed up—"

"Whoa, you're making my head spin," Silver Archer said. "Can just one of you talk?"

We looked at each other. Then Penny quickly filled her in on what had happened since the cylinder had landed, but taking care to leave out, misdirect, or otherwise obscure Kinnison's telepathy, mostly by inflating the value of my guesses about the true target of the heist.

"You did the right thing," Silver Archer said when Penny had finished. "I'll have to have a little chat with Achilles and Andromeda."

Somehow I didn't think a 'talk' would have much of an impact on the twins.

Breakup on Launch

"Hey!" Kinnison whispered. He had stopped next to a door marked 'CC-0102' which had been left ajar.

"What?" I said, pausing. Not that I had much choice. Kinnison had Andy's legs and I had her shoulders, and they were still attached. On the other hand, I was grateful for the breather after trudging up the half-mile or so of tunnel stairs. I had even started to regret the decision to not use the wake-me-up on her, despite the logic behind waiting for Doc Styx to examine the twins before administering anything.

"The control room is behind this door. Listen."

"What have you got?" a frantic voice said through the gap.

"It just broke up!"

"What altitude?"

"All sensors and telemetry from the container were dead from the get-go. The external camera's recorded the container starting to disintegrate before it left the rails."

Telemetry dead? And the spycam in the Squad's container never came online, never uploaded. It wasn't because they had found it. It was because it was jammed. That must be it. The Squad had some sort of built-in active jammers.

"Why did it launch at all?"

"Who knows. Luckily the debris is splashing down in Lake Michigan."

Which was perversely pleasing. While I could only hope that the Squad had been seriously damaged by this, it was too much to assume, based on what I knew about them, that they had been killed.

There were footsteps, and before we had time to do more than step back from the door, it opened, and a man wearing a brown short-sleeved shirt with green trim and an IBS logo and holding a tablet stepped through. He stiffened when he saw us, smeared as we were with the black greasy remains of the smoke and our limp burden. "What are you two doing?" He fumbled with the cellphone clipped to his belt.

"We were just—" I started to say.

Diana's voice, still commanding, despite the bur of weariness it contained, echoed up the hall, cutting off what would have been a feeble explanation, at best. "They're with me."

The three of us turned our heads to look. The man dropped his stylus. Silver Archer stood there, the hallway lights gleaming off her mask and armor despite its obvious battle scarring. Penny had stopped a half-pace behind her, Achilles' unconscious body casually slung over her shoulder, looking as if she were ready to catch her mother if she staggered.

The Silver Archer continued, her voice gaining strength as she spoke, "I need to talk to your facility manager. Your launch systems have been compromised."

"Uh, right. Absolutely." He successfully detached his cellphone this time. It tweedled as he pushed the P2P send. "Sarah, things just got more complicated."

I heard a faint response; then he said, "Right. We're on our way." Then to us, "Follow me, please. Ms. Khan, the manager, told me to tell you that she is at your disposal."

"Tell me again why we didn't use some wake-me-up on Andy?" Kinnison said, shifting his burden as we set off.

High Speed Rails

Sunday, August 19th, 1984
(13,711 days post Supernova 1947A)

I hardly noted the passing of the summer Olympics, which was a pretty good trick, considering the overwhelming medals sweep by the U.S., Canada, and Mexico, and the subsequent outraged television coverage of the Olympic Committee's nullification of the results and announcement that supers and near-supers would be strictly banned, to be enforced by genetic testing and body scans. I did notice when the riots protesting the O.C.'s decision arrived in Galacticity after starting in L.A., then leaping to New York, Detroit, and Mexico City. It gave the crime-monitoring software agents in the command center fits. By the time it died down, every major city in the U.S. and Mexico had burned and trampled the Olympic Flag. Twice. Somehow the Canadians resisted the urge to take to the street in anger, a fact which did wonders to reinforce their standing as the Nice Guys of the world.

All of which led to my being on a shuttle train with the entire contingent of the Riggs-Armstrongs and two-thirds of the Kinnisons. A shuttle that would be delivering us to a high-speed train which was even now speeding towards Washington D.C. at over two hundred miles per hour.

I was still a little uncomfortable in leaving Mom behind, but Doc Styx had assured me that the drug regime he had worked out for her was effective, and that she was fine to return home. Besides, he would be seeing her daily. When you added in that both the Magician and Mr. Kinnison had volunteered to spend time with her, I should have, logically, been satisfied that she would be looked after.

The twins, after serious haranguing and a solemn promise to behave, had managed to take the seat next to the driver's compartment. Hank, Diana, and Dr. Kinnison took the seats behind the twins, while Penny, Kinnison and I had gone for the rear-most seats in the nearly empty shuttle.

"I still can't believe they want to talk to my mom," Kinnison said for the fourth time in less than an hour.

I sighed. "Why do you keep saying that, Kinnison? It's not like you didn't know she was an expert in transgenetic studies." But then, I doubt Kinnison read any of the literature, such as *Transgenetica* or *Genetics, Transgenetics, and Molecular Research*, where he would have found the name Dr. Erin Kinnison as lead investigator on three articles in the past year alone.

"But why would the Senate want to talk—"

"Depose," I said.

"—to her? I understand why they want to talk—depose the Silver Archer. She is the current president of the Galacticity branch—the *main* branch of the League, after all."

"Please be seated and fasten your seat belts," a pleasant male voice on the intercom announced. The shuttle, which was about the size and shape of a bus, had filled up with other D.C.-bound passengers as we talked, and was almost full now.

A young man in an Amtrak uniform emerged from the driver's compartment and made his way down the central aisle, inspecting each passenger's seat belt. He reminded me of an amusement-ride attendant.

"We'll be docking with the Zephyr in ten minutes. Please remain seated at all times," the pleasant voice said.

The shuttle eased out of the station, then rapidly accelerated, pushing us back into our seats—not quite as good as the British Ballistics launch, but respectable nonetheless. We exited the station and were speeding through the suburban sprawl that spread out from Galacticity to the east on this side of the Lake.

It would take a little under three hours for the trip to Washington D.C., including the connecting shuttles at both ends. The Zephyr was one of the high-speed looping trains that only stopped for weekly maintenance. After the simultaneous hijacking—which everyone just referred to as the Hijacking—of every major commercial aircraft in the world by Doctor M in 1970, demand for commercial flights had fallen off dramatically, and rail transport, with help of large government subsidies or outright ownership, had expanded to replace it. Automobile travel had remained popular here in the U.S., but even it was losing ground to mass transit locally, and high-speed rail for intra-continental travel. Intercontinental travel had been replaced by either ships, if you weren't in a hurry, or by ballistic and semi-ballistic unpowered flight designed to minimize the possibility of hijacking, robotic or otherwise.

In the U.S., the modern high-speed rail system was based on a series of trains continually running in regional large loops at two-hundred-plus miles per hour. During the past five years the double-wide raised or stilt chassis model had come into primary use. This style of train ran on two mag-lev tracks separated by dual normal-gage tracks, thus allowing two old-style trains to simultaneously pass beneath the raised body of the double-wide.

Other than taking about half the time on longer trips, I had difficulty imagining why anyone would want to travel by commercial aircraft. When compared to the comparatively capacious seating, and always being able to get up and walk around or visit the restrooms, vending machines, and, for the older crowd, full service bars, not to mention the sleeper cabins, it was mind boggling that anyone flew. Well, except for the hobbyist fliers, and the military, of course. Should I mention that even on the upper decks one is a mere forty feet off the ground? Of course, intercontinental ballistic travel is still basically like traveling in a large box with small round windows. While quite exciting—and just that much more so, as I was ten when our European vacation was cut short and Dad booked us on a British Ballistics launch out of Heathrow, just prior to the resolution of the Iranian hostage situation by the Nova League—it does make you think about the quality of engineering that goes into each ballistic module. Oh, and if you're wondering what the best part was, it's a toss-up between the freefall apogee, with its view of Earth curving away beneath you, and the splashdown in Lake Michigan as the module sways under its enormous parachutes.

Penny and I listened while Kinnison regaled us with his most recent run in Max's dungeon, while ahead the high-speed train straddling the tracks, forming an ever-moving tunnel, drew slowly closer. When the shuttle finally caught up and eased under the last car, the shuttle lurched and we were docked. After a moment the passenger section of the shuttle was lifted up, then slid to the middle of the reception lounge, coming to rest with a gentle thunking. It was all uncomfortably reminiscent of the brief container ride in the IBS shipping facility last month, if you didn't regard the fact that it wasn't dark or three hundred feet underground.

The reception lounge, which surrounded the shuttle, was walled in glass on both sides, the green foliage of trees through the lounge windows rushing past at 200-plus miles per hour. Half the walls of the shuttle slid aside like chrome and glass shoji, leaving every row of seats open to the lounge. At the very rear of the shuttle lounge was a windowed area with a snack bar, vending machines, etc. In the distance, slowly dwindling, were the skyscrapers of the western end of Galacticity. To the west of these rose the much, much taller spires of the Arcology. Gentle thumping noises came from below as luggage modules were exchanged.

We all hefted our carry-ons, and the twins bolted, responding with a "We know!" when Diana and Hank yelled our seat numbers at their backs. The rest of us made our way forward to B lounge in a more leisurely manner, passing through the tourist class seating area. The business class section was divided up into smaller semi-private clusters of seats separated by floor-to-ceiling privacy panels. Andy and Achilles were already ensconced in the window seats when we arrived.

Kinnison made a disgusted noise, and dumped his bag in the locker reserved for this cluster of seats. Penny and I followed suit. Kinnison was glaring at Achilles, who had his legs up, sprawling across several seats.

I nudged him. "Why don't we go back to the rear

observation deck. You can see the shuttles come and go right under your feet."

"Be back here by one to get your carry-on," Hank said. "The shuttle drop for the D.C. terminal is at 1:15."

We chorused our understanding.

"Everyone have money for lunch and snacks?"

We made more assenting noises and scooted out of there.

We paused in the rear observation lounge to buy cans of pop from the vending machine, then descended the spiral stairway to the observation deck, the self-cooling cans chilling in our hands.

A Conversation on the Train, or What Did You Do During the Riots?

Kinnison settled onto the couch with a sigh. "So what's the latest twinscapade?"

Penny sat and crossed her legs. "You remember how the crowd turned nasty in L.A. after the O.C. Ruling?"

"Yeah."

"Well, the twins were watching the live news coverage of it and talking about how, if they lived in L.A., they would don their masks and go down to Memorial Plaza and help with the crowd control."

Kinnison "Why? It's not like dealing with rioters is a ninja thing."

"Who knows what passes for logic in their minds," I said.

"I can see where this is going," Kinnison said.

"I should have—" Penny paused. I looked up to see what had interrupted her to find Cleo making her way down the spiral stairs, red-tipped cane probing ahead of her.

I came up out of the chair, partly in surprise, and

partly, I told myself, because I wanted to help Cleo maintain the appearance of having difficulty navigating the stairs. While that was true, I would be lying to you if I didn't also say that there was a desire to be chivalrous, too.

"Here, watch your step," I said, reaching up to take her right arm.

She gave me one of her radiant look-through-to-your-soul smiles. "Thank you, Michael."

And that's the other reason, I thought.

After settling Cleo into the seat next to where I was sitting, I said, "So. Sensei Fox has been summoned by the Senate, too? That makes four people we know."

"Are you surprised?" Cleo said. "The riots must have made the Senate feel like they weren't in control. Not that they are, but I'm sure they like to think so."

"It's disgraceful," Penny said. "The Olympic Committee had every right to strip us and Canada of our medals. Not one gold medal went to anyone else."

"Don't forget Mexico," Cleo said.

"And Mexico," Penny echoed.

"It's not our fault," Kinnison said, "that we have more supers than anyone else. They might as well blame the supernova. Or the Galactics. And its not like we were the only ones with superpowered athletes competing. Everyone was fielding them."

"The Olympic Committee was going to ban supers from competition sooner or later," I said.

"Anyways," Penny said. "The twins had been bugging Diana for a souvenir from the War-of-the-Worlds lander that the Squad used."

"Oh, yeah," Kinnison said, "I went down and bought one for myself. If I'd known I would have gotten some for the little monsters."

"Well, thank you for the thought, Kim, but as I was

saying, they were merciless in their pursuit, but as Diana was preoccupied with actually hunting down the Demolition Squad, she was putting them off and putting them off. It got so bad that you couldn't go anywhere in the house without seeing a yellow sticky note, or something scrawled on the bathroom mirrors in lipstick declaring their 'needs'. The last straw was when I booted up the family PC and had to watch a ten-minute slide presentation about the advantages of owning a chunk of the lander. So I volunteered to take them, after making them swear that they would stick with me and follow orders."

"Did they?" Kinnison asked.

"Just wait. So we took a Transit pod down to Nova Genesis Plaza. By this time they had the lander dismembered and trucked out of there and were working on replacing the paving stones. There was a crowd in front of the UN building, marching back and forth and carrying placards protesting the O.C.'s decision. The twins stopped and watched the picketing with looks reminiscent of Bernoulli watching the squirrels in Michael's backyard. I reminded them of why we were there, and for once they went quietly, at least as far as the Library souvenir shop, where they proceeded to argue over which iron-hull segment was better, as they picked over every one in the bin and—"

"Did you get one for yourself?"

Penny gave Kinnison the look.

"Okay, it doesn't matter—Oh, you did buy one for yourself."

"Yes I did. The money is going to the repair of the plaza. May I continue?"

"By all means."

"By the time we left the Library, the crowd had doubled, maybe even tripled in size, with more pouring into the plaza every minute. The police were now out in force, and with the majority of the Nova League responding to riots elsewhere in Galacticity, Chicago and Detroit, they must have been thinking—"

"Or not thinking," I interjected.

"—that no one was going to stop them. When someone noticed that the paving stones at the edges of the crater repair could simply be picked up, it became a mob." She stopped speaking, a far-away, haunted look closing her face off.

Kinnison opened his mouth and I elbowed him.

"Hey—"

"Just give her time," I said in an undertone. "She'll tell it when she wants to."

Kinnison nodded.

After several more seconds Penny shook her head. "I never thought I would say this, but it was Andromeda's and Achilles' restraint that pulled the three of us through without our having to..."

As she trailed off I heard Kinnison whisper, "Kill anyone."

"Anyone feel like a game of Hearts?" I said to fill the awkward gap. I pulled out a pack of cards that, conveniently, had braille embossing.

Penny met my gaze and gave me a little smile. "Sure."

"Sounds like fun," Cleo said.

"Don't forget to take down Michael first," Kinnison said.

I started to shuffle.

Arrival in D.C.

When we exited the shuttle we found a line of uniformed limo drivers holding placards announcing which party they were to shepherd. There was one for the Foxes, one for the Kinnisons, and one for the Riggs-Armstrongs.

Diana must have seen the look on my face and she said, "You're with us, Michael. Not that it really matters. We're all staying at the Star Ambassador."

"That's a relief," I said, eying the twins.

"The twins will be staying with Hank and me. You, Kim, and A.J. are in one side of a double suite, while Penny, Cleo, and Erin are in the other side."

"Oh? That sounds great, Diana!" I was rather intrigued by the idea of living in close proximity to Sensei Fox.

She smiled. "Now you sound relieved. I know the twins are quite a handful, but A.J. tells me that you are handling them on your own now. With a little material help, of course."

"Oh, its not that, Diana. I know that Andy and

Achilles don't mean to be destructive—well, they mean to a little, but things get going and they have a hard time figuring out when to stop."

She smiled at me. "You're a trooper. So very much like Mike."

Before I could respond, the woman carrying the Riggs-Armstrong placard came forward, and Diana exclaimed, "Georgi!" and strode to meet her. "So good to see a friendly face on arrival." She was a petite woman in a blue limo driver's uniform, and someone who could handle herself, as she showed no discomfort or attempt to dodge out of the way as Diana's six-foot-two frame bore down on her. Perhaps it was because she was wearing a discreet exoskeleton. But then, from what I could see, so were many of the other limo drivers.

"Welcome back to D.C., Diana," Georgi said, taking her out-thrust hand and shaking it. "Good to see you, too."

"Does Diana know everyone?" Kinnison said.

"You'd be surprised," Penny said.

"Didn't she guest lecture at West Point? Greek and Roman military history, right?"

"But that isn't in D.C."

"True. But maybe Georgi went there."

We all trooped down to the luggage recovery area. It wasn't long before the conveyor started up and the twins had to be dragged off of it.

"You don't travel light, do you?" Kinnison said, as I recovered my third and final bag.

"I would have brought more, if I thought I could have gotten it through security," I said. "But this isn't all for me." I glanced around, noting that the twins were thoroughly occupied with trying to get the limo driver to demonstrate her exoskeleton. I patted the large suitcase. "I brought a few things to keep Achilles and Andy distracted, and, more importantly, to track where they are."

Happy Birthday to Us!

As I was unpacking, the twins wandered into our suite, looking for their next source of amusement. I decided to oblige them.

"Happy birthday!" I said by way of greeting.

"But it isn't until tomorrow," they said together.

"I know," I said, conspiratorially. "Want your presents now?"

"Presents?" Achilles said.

"You have presents for us?" Andy said, her voice tinted with suspicion.

Achilles ignored her objection and grinned, rubbing his hands together theatrically. "Happy birthday to us!"

I opened the large suitcase and pulled out two unmarked boxes. "Here they are. Sorry about not wrapping them. I knew they would want to inspect them before I got on the train."

"Oh, that's okay," Achilles said. "Wrapping paper is for sissies."

"I like it. Am I a sissy?"

Achilles eyed Andy's ready stance. "I meant wrapping paper *with ribbons* is for sissies."

"Ribbons are—"

I interrupted, thrusting out the boxes. "Come on, open them."

Each took one of the shoe-box–sized packages and opened them. Inside were tough plastic cases labeled 'Supertech Heli-drones—Just the like SNN uses!' I thought the labels were a nice touch. It made it look like I had purchased them rather than fabricating them in the lab. Fabricated not because I couldn't afford to buy them, but because it was faster and I was sure that they had been built to my specifications.

"Excellent!" Achilles said.

"Awesome!" Andy said.

In moments they had the miniature heli-drones out of their contoured foam hollows and were eagerly inspecting them.

I went to the room mini-bar and pulled out a couple of bottles of vodka.

"Diana told us not to."

"Don't worry, I'll take responsibility for it. The heli-drones have fuel cells that will run on alcohol. Here, let me see that." Andy handed hers over and watched as I poured one of the vodkas into its tank. "Get the controller, Andy."

The heli-drone's four sets of blades spun up, the only sound the hum of electric motors and the rotors cutting the air. It lifted off, and I had to duck as Andy manipulated the controller joysticks and it swooped in my direction.

"Watch it!" Achilles called as it banked and headed in his direction, skimmed over his head, and buzzed directly towards the wall.

"Cool!" Andy yelled, as, instead of crashing, it

pulled up short and hovered for a moment less than an inch from the wall.

"Anti-collision sensors," I said. *Which makes them a whole lot harder to break,* I thought. And I needed one functioning if I was going to plant the relay. Speaking of which, "I've got something else for the two of you."

"More?"

"Yup." I dug out the two masks that I had also fabricated in the lab. "I have one more thing for each of you. But you have to promise you won't tell anyone where you got them."

"We promise!" they said.

I handed them the microcircuit embedded, servo-muscle emulating, full-face masks.

"Coooool!" Achilles whispered.

"Yeah!" Andy said.

"You won't have to wrap your T-shirts over your heads like ninja masks now," I said. "When you put the masks on, they'll stick to your skin. And there's a trick to taking the masks off. You have to pry them off with both hands. You can set the pry points, but right now they are at the corners of the eyes."

Andy looked up from studying her mask. "Oh, they're Smartmasks, then."

"That's right. Now that you have real superhero masks, I want you two to start acting with more maturity and constraint. I know that you are capable of it. Penny told me about what happened during the riot at the Nova Genesis Memorial Plaza. Okay?"

They grinned, then looked at each other and became solemn-faced, placing their hands over their hearts. "We swear on the Nova League charter to try and grow up."

"Good." That would have to do.

I hung around with the twins for half an hour,

watching them maneuver the heli-drones in a not-so-mock dogfight. The anti-collision sensors worked like a charm. Eventually they got restless enough for me to talk them into lending me their controllers. First, I showed them some of the pre-programmed flight maneuvers; then when their appetites were whetted, I let them borrow a tablet with animations of the flight stunts and showed them how to select the corresponding programs on a controller. While they viewed and tried these out on one of the drones, I used the other one to drop off a radio relay on the communication tower of a nearby hotel. With the relay in place, I could safely track the transponders embedded in their masks anywhere in D.C. Satisfied, I turned the controller and drone over to the twins and went to hang out with Kinnison in the lounge area of the suite.

"Where have you been?" Kinnison said, looking up from the TV. He had found MTV and was checking his email on his inTouch while he watched zombies line dance.

I sat down on the couch next to him. "Giving the twins their birthday presents."

"Crap, I forgot to get them anything."

"No problem. I gave them enough loot to distract them."

"Oh? Good."

I got out my cellphone, and we both spent the next ten minutes or so self-absorbed.

"I can't believe you actually gave them masks!" Penny said from the door to the suite.

I looked up from my cellphone where I had been checking up on the lab. Penny looked like she had just been calved from a glacier: cold and ready to send the Titanic to an icy grave. "Shhh. Not so loud. There's a reason."

"And what, pray tell, is that?" Despite still sounding irritated, she had lowered her voice.

"I put remotely activated radio beacons into them."

"Oh, really?" The irritation had left her voice, being replaced by a more thoughtful tone. "That's a good idea. You can trace them?"

"And you can, too. I hacked together a cellphone app to track them."

"How do I get it?"

"Here, give me your phone. It won't take but a moment to transfer it from mine."

"What about me?" Kinnison said.

"Give me yours, too."

After I had installed the apps and demonstrated how to get into them, activate the beacons via the relay, and track the twins, Penny said, "I just hope we don't have to use it."

The Senate Hearings of the Powers Oversight Committee

Monday, August 20th, 1984
(13,712 days post Supernova 1947A)

"Well, this is an interesting lifestyle statement on your part, Michael," Hank said from the door of the suite.

I turned, considered for a moment sweeping the five mini-bottles of vodka sitting in a row on the edge of the desk into the trash, then rejected it. "I swear, Hank, that we only used the vodka to power the model drones."

Hank winked and laughed. "I'm sure you could get all the booze you wanted, Michael. Or make it, for that matter. I was pretty wild myself before I met Diana."

An awkward chuckle escaped me. "Uh, yeah, but really, Hank, I used it in the twins' new heli-drones." *I'm going to have to pump him for details about that, sometime,* I thought.

"Fine, fine. But I'll pick up a bottle of rubbing alcohol

at the pharmacy. That will work, won't it?"

"Oh, sure. Much better than the vodka. And a lot cheaper, too." I had already run up a twenty-dollar tab on the mini-bar.

"Good. Oh, yes, I came in to tell you that we are planning on leaving for the Senate hearings in half an hour. Are you going to be ready to go?"

"Absolutely." *Time to make sure Kinnison has taken his pill,* I thought.

I found Kinnison staring at the innocuous-looking blue capsule lying on his open palm. He grimaced when he caught sight of me. "I don't understand why I have to take this. It's not like I'm going to be *using* my powers to steal state secrets or anything. I can control it."

"First," I said, "You don't always have control over your telepathy." I held up a hand to preempt the flow of objections. "Second, it is a very bad idea for you to walk in to the Senate gallery broadcasting the fact that you are a telepath. I am forced to remind you that Watergate is still a bad memory. Third, if Doc Styx recommends something, you think twice before disregarding it."

"I have thought about it, and I think I don't like the idea."

"Remember what Sensei Fox said," Penny put in from the door, her voice turning into a credible, if not bass, imitation of his voice. "'The nail that sticks up gets pounded down.'"

I focused my thoughts on a single phrase and watched as Kinnison, looking dumbfounded, blurted out, *"Deru kui wa utareru."* He clapped his empty hand to his mouth, then mumbled through his fingers. "But I don't know Japanese."

I gave him a wolfish grin. "And that proves my

point."

Penny shook her head. "You walked into that one, Kim."

He glared at me. "When did you start learning Japanese, Gurick? When you started dating Cleo?"

"Nope."

"So, when did you start studying Japanese?" Cleo said from behind Penny, then added in Japanese, "<When were you planning on telling me?>"

I sighed. "Sorry, Cleo, I was planning on telling you when I got a little better at it. As to when I started learning it, it was shortly after I began attending the Black Lagoon Dojo." I turned back to Kinnison and gestured at the blue capsule. "Anytime now."

"Suck-up. Fine. I'll take the damn pill."

The four of us joined Hank and the twins in the lobby. Sensei Fox and Diana had already left, leaving him to wrangle us because he wasn't scheduled to testify today. The subway ride to the Capitol went smoothly; the twins, each with a backpack and wearing their Chinese exhibit T-shirts, seemed to be on their best behavior. At the entrance we had to run the gauntlet of metal detectors that also must have operated as psionic detectors, as I spotted a discreet version of the PsiCorp's glowing eye logo. I had assumed that the security would be tight, so had left the slammer and the rest of the metal-bearing gear back at the hotel. We threaded our way through the long halls to the observation gallery overlooking the largest committee room in the building. When we arrived we found the gallery nearly full, managing, with the enthusiastic help of the twins, to find a spot with enough seats to accommodate us together. As we worked our way through the crowd, I noted the number of teenagers, and had to assume that many of the people testifying had brought their families.

I looked around the committee chamber where the various superheroes waited in their colorful super-wear, making a mental note of who was there and who wasn't. One thing that stood out to me was the distinct lack of Galactic-sponsored heroes or anyone with a Galactic Citizenship. There was no sign of the Galactic Sentinel, or even one of the Astral Agents.

While the parade of supers was impressive, including Captain Fusion, and Jetstream—which made me wonder if Magnetic Mistress was going to put in an appearance, but I didn't see her—it was all rather mundane, even pedestrian to see superheroes sitting (and in some cases standing, because no chair there would accommodate them) and talking. I suppose this was because my expectations of how they should act had been formed by watching them on the news in combat with their enemies. It was all a bit of a let-down–that is, until Mind Fire arrived with his shock of red hair sticking up like a small brush fire. A simultaneous chirp from what I had taken for fire detectors around the room and gallery had preceded his entrance, leading me to think that the innocuous-looking beige devices also included more PsiCorp gear. As Mind Fire approached the table to take his seat in front of the Powers Oversight Committee, he passed a knot of men and women in what I mentally dubbed Men-in-Black chic: thin ties, white shirts, black jackets. As he went by he gave them a look like Mom finding something Bernoulli left after not being let out in a timely manner. What struck me about this little incident was that I hadn't noticed the Men-in-Black contingent until Mind Fire gave them that look.

"When did they come in?" I said to Penny, nodding in the direction of the Men in Black.

"Haven't they been here all along?"

"I don't think so. Which agency do you think they work for?"

The fire-and-psi detectors chirped again.

"FBI? PICSEA? Secret Service? Who knows. Why do you care?"

"I saw Mind Fire give them a look that could have fried eggs."

"Well, that is one of his powers. If minds were eggs, that is."

"I think you're missing my point. What got him mad at them? They're not villains. Not here, not now. I'm—"

"Intrigued? Insane? Irritating?"

"I'd agree with two of those."

I looked over at Kinnison, wondering why he had been silent for so long. His face was blank and he was staring into the middle distance. Was he having some sort of adverse reaction to the telepathy blocker? I snapped my fingers in front of his eyes. "Kinnison? You okay?"

The detectors chirp-chirped, like their batteries were going.

"What's up with Kim?" Penny asked.

He blinked, but continued to stare.

"I don't know. He looks like he's in some sort of trance. Is he leaking psi? Those detectors keep going off." *I'm going to have to build a portable one of those,* I thought.

"Yeah, I was noticing them, too."

I snapped my fingers in front of Kinnison again. "Earth to Kinnison. Come in Kinnison."

He blinked again, then mumbled, "Wha—?"

"His eyes look normal. Is it the blocker?"

I pressed a couple of fingers to his neck. "Pulse

seems normal. Should I slap him?"

"Try a pinch first."

Another chirp-chirp.

I did.

"Hey! What was that for?" he said, rubbing his arm where I had gripped and twisted.

"Welcome back, Kinnison."

"You zoned out, Kim."

"I did? I don't remember doing that. Do you think it was the blocker?"

"That's been suggested. But I think you would have reacted before now. It's been a good hour since you took it."

"Hmmph. My head does feel funny."

The psionic detectors continued their occasional chirruping until Mind Fire finished his testimony and left with another, even dirtier look at the Men in Black.

The Silver Archer Respectfully Disagrees

We all perked up when the Silver Archer took her place at the witness table, had her identity verified and was sworn in.

"Silver Archer," Teddy Williamson, the Senator from Tennessee and the chairman of the Powers Oversight Committee began. "I would like to thank you for taking the time to come to Washington and give us your perspective on recent events. I understand you are also here as the official representative of the Nova League as well, and I look forward to your advice from that role as well."

Senator Williamson was acting like he had no issues with the Nova League. Obviously he wasn't going to bring up his prior attempts to resurrect the Power Registration Act.

"You are more than welcome, Senator Williamson. And yes, as the current Galacticity President and National Deputy of the Nova League I will attempt to address your questions."

"Given that Doc Styx is the current national president of the League," I said. "It's no surprise that Silver Archer is here representing them."

"Because Doc Styx is a Galactic Citizen?" Kinnison asked.

I nodded. "Not just any Galactic Citizen. The first superhero to become one. Which is why the Power Registration Act failed."

"There was no way Senator Williamson would have allowed Doc Styx in front of *his* committee," Penny said. "Too much bad blood between them."

"You are a First Generation super, are you not, Silver Archer?" Senator Williamson asked.

"Yes, Senator. I was born in 1947."

"And you think it is appropriate for supers to compete in the Olympics?"

"Only against other supers, Senator. Given that a significant majority of us were born in North America, it isn't surprising that the Olympic Committee did what it did."

"But you must agree that the United States of America should use its superpowered resources to promote liberty, deter aggression, and defend itself."

"With all due respect, Senator Williamson, power, whether super or not, can't be used to impose freedom. If Vietnam taught us anything, it taught us that."

A shadow of anger flicked across Senator Williamson's face, but he maintained the overall equanimity so important to a politician. Which was probably another reason they frowned on telepaths in Washington.

Hypernauts Can Be Politicians Too

During the exchange between Senator Williamson and Silver Archer, I had kept an eye on Clarke Prescott, the junior member of the Powers Oversight Committee from Massachusetts, a Bostonian Brahmin, Vietnam war hero when he was only few years older than me, and the first super to be elected to the Senate. Or at least the first one to have taken off his mask and publicly announce that he was a super. He was already gray-haired at the age of thirty-three, with prominent wrinkles around the corners of his eyes and mouth, making him look like he was around Senator Williamson's age. It was rumored to be the result of premature aging, and given that he was a hypernaut with a sped-up metabolism, there was probably more than a little truth to that rumor. I was interested in his response to Senator Williamson and Silver Archer, as he was, in addition to being in the minority party in the Senate, outspoken in his opposition to the Power Registration Act, and a proponent of closer ties with the Galactics—thus an opponent to Senator Williamson at a number of levels.

"If I may, Senator Williamson?" Senator Prescott said.

"You may," Williamson said, all politeness. It was a testament to how anxious he was for this committee to be seen to be supporting supers that he yielded the limelight to Senator Prescott.

"Thank you, Senator Williamson. Silver Archer, as we all know, much of the rest of world resents the abundance of supers that are Americans. This is simply a quirk of fate. If the wavefront from the 1947A supernova had arrived twelve hours earlier or later, then Europe and the Soviet Union would have borne the brunt of the cosmic rays and lost twenty percent of their populations, and consequently been gifted with a majority of the powered. But it did not happen that way. Do you have any suggestions as to how we might mitigate this misunderstanding? How we can make ourselves into a beacon of freedom, so that the rest of the world wants to emulate us, rather than hate us?"

Ah, a very good question indeed.

"First and foremost, Senator Prescott," Silver Archer said. "The United States government should only use supers defensively, and it must ensure that those supers operating as government agents are doing so voluntarily."

"So you wouldn't object to supers operating in clandestine missions as long as they are doing so of their own free will?"

"And following U.S. law."

"Of course. What about 'civilian' supers? If I may be allowed to use a potential oxymoron."

"I think that depends on the nature of their powers and how they are using them. Certainly, supers engaging in law enforcement or any other activities that would fall under the Superhero Vigilante Act must use superidentities, whether or not they have secret identities. Superidentities are crucial in verifying that a super is who she or he appears to be."

"Could you elaborate on that, Silver Archer?"

"Superidentities were established in the decade following 1947A by what we now call the Zero-Generation of superheroes, a majority of which were directly or indirectly sponsored by the Galactics. While people in some quarters find it objectionable to acknowledge this, it is an obvious fact that the Galactics have gone out of their way to protect the Earth and its indigenous cultures. What is less obvious is that the protections extended by the Galactics consisted of more than the radiation shield deployed against the 1947A wavefront and the subsequent nanotech intervention to repair the damage incurred during the brief failure of that shield. The world would have lost more than the two hundred and thirty-six million people that it did without their intervention. That's one of the reasons that everyone commemorates Nova Day and celebrates Ice Fall."

"You mean the social engineering, the meddling in Earth cultures," Senator Williamson interjected.

"That is one way of putting it, yes. Another way of looking at it is that they prepared us for our super-selves, primed our sensibilities of how and when superpowers should be used. Showed us that it was the responsibility and duty of those with power to not abuse power but to protect those with less power from exploitation by those with more, and, when possible, give power to the power-less."

The Senators spent the next few minutes airing their disagreement, with the Silver Archer siding with Prescott. Williamson managed to keep a lid on his growing frustration until he put a stop to the argument by calling the next witness.

Penny Volunteers

It wasn't long after Silver Archer had concluded her testimony that Andy said, "We're bored."

"Yeah, now that we've seen Silver Archer talk. We want to do something else," Achilles said.

Hank sighed. "What do you suggest?"

Andy started undoing her backpack. "We brought our heli-drones."

Something I had encouraged them to do.

"Well, you can't fly them in here."

"Of course not," Achilles said. "There's a park across the street. We saw it when we got off the Metro."

"Pleeeease," they said together making woeful puppy-dog faces.

"I'll take them," Penny said.

I squinted at Penny's face. "Where's Penny?"

"Are you sure?" Hank said.

"Yes. I'm sure."

"All right. Anyone else volunteering to go?"

Kinnison and I looked at each other.

Cleo shook her head. "Sorry, but my father hasn't testified yet, and I was—"

"Hey, really, it's no problem guys," Penny said.

"If you're sure," I said, feeling guilty about feeling happy to stay.

"We'll come out and join you later," Kinnison said, sounding as if he meant it. He probably did.

I welcomed the break when it came, half an hour later. Kinnison was looking uncomfortable, too, but Cleo seemed as fresh as she was when we left the hotel.

"Come on," Hank said, leading the way from the gallery. "They've set up a lounge for visitors. We can get something to drink and a snack, I think."

We followed him to the visitors lounge, which, as predicted, was laid out with refreshments. The lounge was milling with people from the gallery, and I recognized some of those who had testified as well.

After collecting our cookies and cans of pop, Kinnison, Cleo and I positioned ourselves for a little people watching. We took turns describing and speculating about various members of the throng to Cleo.

"Over there," Kinnison said. "Check it out."

I looked in the direction his finger indicated. It looked like an Astral Agent had shown up after all. I glanced at Cleo, and her blank gaze was also directed towards where Kinnison was pointing. I described the Agent, whom I recognized as Vermillion, to Cleo, detailing how her Astral Orb was slowly circling her head while she stood talking to another super, Light Fantastic. They both seemed oblivious to the stares and whispers of many of the teens, and even some of the adults around them.

"Have I ever told you I really wanted to be an Astral Agent when I was a kid?" Kinnison said.

"Many times, Kinnison."

"How smart do you think Vermillion's Orb is?"

"Pretty smart."

"As smart as you?"

"Smarter. Remember it's linked into the Galactics' StarNet. And they solved the AI problem a long time ago. Which brings up an interesting question. Which is the master, and which is the pet?"

"Well, duh, the Agent is the master," Kinnison said.

"I'm not so sure," I said.

Mind Fire Confronts the Man in Black

As Cleo, Kinnison, and I scanned the crowd for more supers—each in our own special way—I noticed one of the Men in Black standing off to the side and observing. His face was impassive under mirrored glasses. For some reason I had the feeling that he was scanning the packed room for something.

"Hey!" A voice filled with anger rose above the rumble of conversation, and suddenly Mind Fire was bearing down on the Man in Black, the crowd parting in front of him.

"Mind Fire's back, and he looks even more pissed," I said to Cleo. I continued to commentate as Mind Fire stopped in front of the Man in Black, his sunglasses-shrouded features remaining calm and impassive.

Mind Fire grabbed the lapels of the Man in Black's coat. "If you ever do that again, *Agent* Thrush, I will break you."

Vermillion's Orb flicked across the room, coming to rest afloat in the six-inch gap that separated the two men's faces. "Is there a problem, gentleman?" it said in a calm, soothing voice reminiscent of HAL from 2001.

Mind Fire released Thrush's lapels and backed away. "This is between me and Thrush, Vermillion."

"Not if you insist on doing whatever it is you're doing in public."

Mind Fire did not respond to the Orb. Instead he said, "You've been warned, Thrush." He turned and strode out of the room, the now-silent crowd parting for him. Throughout the exchange, if one could call it that, Thrush had remained silent and unmoved.

"What was all that about?" I said.

"Do you think Vermillion could have stopped Mind Fire?" Cleo said.

"Depends. Physically stopped, I have no doubt. Mentally—psionically stopped Mind Fire from brain blasting him? I don't know."

While we talked, a cluster of people, many of them teens, had formed around Vermillion.

"It looks like Vermillion has expanded her fan base," I said.

"Oh?" Cleo said.

"They're lining up, and, yes, she's giving out autographs. I don't think Senator Williamson would approve." I shot a glance over towards Thrush—it took me a moment to locate him, as he had been joined by two more Men in Black and was moving towards one of the exits—but it was still impossible to gauge what he was thinking.

"Where's Kim going?" Cleo said, reeling my attention back.

I turned, catching sight of Kinnison's short-cropped blonde head disappearing into the crowd. "I don't know. He didn't say anything to me."

"Bathroom break?"

"He usually says something. You know how he is."

"Yeah. Odd. Follow?"

I was already moving. "Absolutely."

Before I could do more than take two steps, Cleo thwicked my wrist with her cane. "Sorry," I said, and gripped its red tip, leading the way through the crowd. When we had finally pushed our way through the throng and out into the hall, I spotted Kinnison disappearing around the corner.

"Come on," I said, picking up my pace.

"You can go faster, Michael. I can keep up. Just don't let go of the cane."

"Cool."

But when we turned the corner, there was no sign of Kinnison.

"Gone," I said.

"No, wait. There's an elevator through those doors. And it's running."

I pushed through the doors. They were marked 'Service Personnel Only'. "I'm starting to develop a bad feeling about this, Cleo."

"You can let go of the cane, now. We're alone."

"Right." I dropped it. "Lets take—"

But she was already moving. "—the stairs? We should be able to catch up if we hurry."

We pounded down the stairs, pausing once while Cleo listened at a door. She shook her head and we pushed on. Three flights down we exited the stairwell. We found ourselves on a loading dock, which was empty except for a large brown and green IBS delivery truck backed up against the dock. Seconds later the freight elevator doors to our right opened and Kinnison and two other teenagers I recognized from the gallery stepped out.

"Kinnison, what *are* you doing?" I said.

He ignored me and started walking towards the delivery van. The other two followed him. One was a girl of about our age, with dark, shoulder-length hair and dressed in jeans and a JFK High School jersey, which made me assume she was from Galacticity, too. The other was a boy who looked to be the same age as the twins, with brown curly hair. He might have been the girl's younger sib. None of them spoke, gestured, or did anything but walk towards the van.

"Okay, this is creepy, Kinnison," I said, moving quickly to catch up with him and take his arm. He jerked free without looking at me or otherwise acknowledging my presence.

I was thinking about tripping him, when Cleo shouted, "Look out!"

The doors of the van swung open and two Men-in-Black agents I hadn't seen before stepped out. I caught a glimpse of the dimly lit interior; there were no packages, at least not of the normal kind that IBS delivers. What I saw looked like a couple of bodies strapped to stretchers, and I felt the cold thrill of adventure breathe down my neck. I yelled, "Trap!" and lunged towards Kinnison.

Even as the word left my lips, I became aware of a hissing spray, and Kinnison, who had been the closest to the two Men in Black, was tumbling to the concrete. Then the girl and boy followed him down, falling bonelessly to the hard surface of the loading dock. Cleo, who had leapt back as the doors opened, had turned and started to run back towards the stairs before collapsing.

I felt light-headed, and, despite the precaution of my nose plugs, I knew I was going down. I clawed at my neck just below the collar of my shirt. I felt my fingernails rake through the dermal patch I had placed there when I put the nose plugs in that morning. An analytical part of me was cataloging the physiological effects of the gas. I had isolated it down to three nerve toxin candidates that were absorbed through the skin when my head thunked against the concrete next to Kinnison's and I blacked out.

Kamikaze Homing Pigeon

I jerked awake. The wake-me-up in the patch I had clawed open was raging through me. I felt hot; my head was spinning and I had difficulty remaining still. My heart was pounding in my chest, feeling as if it was going to tear itself free. *Too much wake-me-up,* I thought. Keeping my eyes shut, I took a second to assess my situation. I felt a cold metal floor beneath me. It was in motion, and at an angle that indicated that the vehicle—the IBS delivery van, I had to assume—was being driven up some sort of ramp. I guessed that I hadn't been out for very long if we were just exiting the building. I cracked my lids open and found Kinnison flopped out on the floor beside me, his head lolling back and forth with the motion of the van. Beyond him was one of the bodies I had seen, still strapped to a stretcher. It looked like another kid about our age.

The van bumped over something, and I felt my gorge rise. The pounding of my heart had grown worse. It was amazing to me that no one else seemed to hear it. Or maybe they had, because I felt someone grip my wrists. I forced myself to relax, remaining limp as they pulled my hands behind my back, leaving me on my stomach, face pressed into the cool, diamond-patterned aluminum floor. I heard a 'ziiip' sound, and felt the cold plastic of disposable handcuffs being snugged down on my wrists. Damn. That would complicate things. A voice above me said, "What's this kid got on under his shirt?" and I felt a cold chill. It would be all over if they found my vest and put two and two together.

As the man straddling me began to fumble with the pockets of my vest, the truck took another turn and I rolled as hard as I could with its motion into his leg. He went down with a shout of "Code X-ray!"

I kicked him as hard as I could in the stomach. "Pandora!" I said.

I felt my cellphone vibrate its acknowledgment as it entered voice command mode.

The Man in Black lay sprawled on top of Kinnison, gasping for breath.

I never felt more grateful for Sensei Fox's insistence on practice, practice, practice than I did in that moment, when I rolled on my side, arched my back, and pulled my cuffed wrists over my feet, as I clearly articulated, "Kamikaze Homing Pigeon. Execute."

My cellphone vibrated its acknowledgment again.

Another voice, calm and controlled said, "I've got him."

I rolled onto my back, my gaze locking with that of the second Man in Black. Then he fired his taser.

The dart thwicked into my chest just above my heart and the back of the van filled with the rapid 'ti-ti-ti-tick' of the high-voltage discharge.

I faked a spasm as my vest grounded the taser, and rolled into the Man in Black still lying on Kinnison. He screamed, his muscles spasming for real.

"Subject Six seems immune to tasers," the second Man in Black calmly said, dropping the taser and drawing what looked like an air-gun.

Damn these cuffs, I thought, as I fumbled momentarily with my shirt, trying to get at my vest pockets.

"I want him neutralized," a voice said with cold authority over the intercom. "I'm coming through."

I rolled as he fired, the gun making a quiet 'thwifp', and the dart skittered off the aluminum floor. I scrabbled backward as he methodically reloaded and the door leading to the forward part of the van slid open. A man stepped through, and it slid shut behind him. I recognized the Man in Black whom Mind Fire had confronted in the break room: Agent Thrush, still neat in his black suit, white shirt, thin black tie—like he was still living in 1951 or something—and, despite the dim light in the back of the van, the Man-in-Black signature mirrored sun glasses.

"I'll deal with him, Benson," Agent Thrush said.

I felt a very odd sensation. It was like I was remembering something, but something old and dim, a memory of an uncle whom I was terribly fond of, and didn't want to disappoint by being willful and disobedient. And I realized that this uncle was standing in front of me, dressed in black and wearing the sunglasses that I always remembered him wearing. All of this was completely novel to me. I never had difficulty remembering anything. When I wanted it, it was there, crisp and clear. "You're not my uncle," I said.

Agent Thrush looked surprised. Which was the first time I had seen any emotion on his face. Then I heard a faint bang from the driver's compartment, the truck swayed right, then left as a raspy voice on the intercom said, "What the fu—?!"

There was another bang, and a second voice on the

intercom said, "What was that?"

The alien memories seemed to be draining away.

"A couple of drones just crashed into the wind-shield," the raspy voice replied.

"I want you to—" the first voice began, but finished with a yell of "—look out!"

The driver slammed on his brakes. A second later there was a 'fwham' that shook the truck, and it swerved hard this time. There was a metallic crunch that jarred me through the floor. Then the truck was accelerating.

"*What* is going on?" Thrush said.

"It's a couple of kids. We hit one, he's clinging to the—"

Just a couple of kids? If you only knew, I thought.

"Boarding countermeasures, full power!" Thrush said.

The lights dimmed.

So you do have a clue, I thought.

The driver slammed on the brakes again, and the truck swerved, tires screeching. There were two more metallic crump-bangs, and with a crashing crescendo, the interior of the truck rotated ninety degrees, and everyone in the rear compartment who wasn't strapped down was thrown forward. I pivoted as I plunged towards the bulkhead, aiming both feet for the head of Agent Thrush. The soles of my shoes were less than a foot from his face, and I could see the knobbly pattern on their soles growing larger in his mirrored sunglasses, when he vanished with a collapsing pop of air, and I slammed into the aluminum wall behind him with enough force to jar me up to my teeth. A second later the screeching-scraping sound of the truck sliding across pavement stopped.

I rolled over and sat up. The two remaining agents

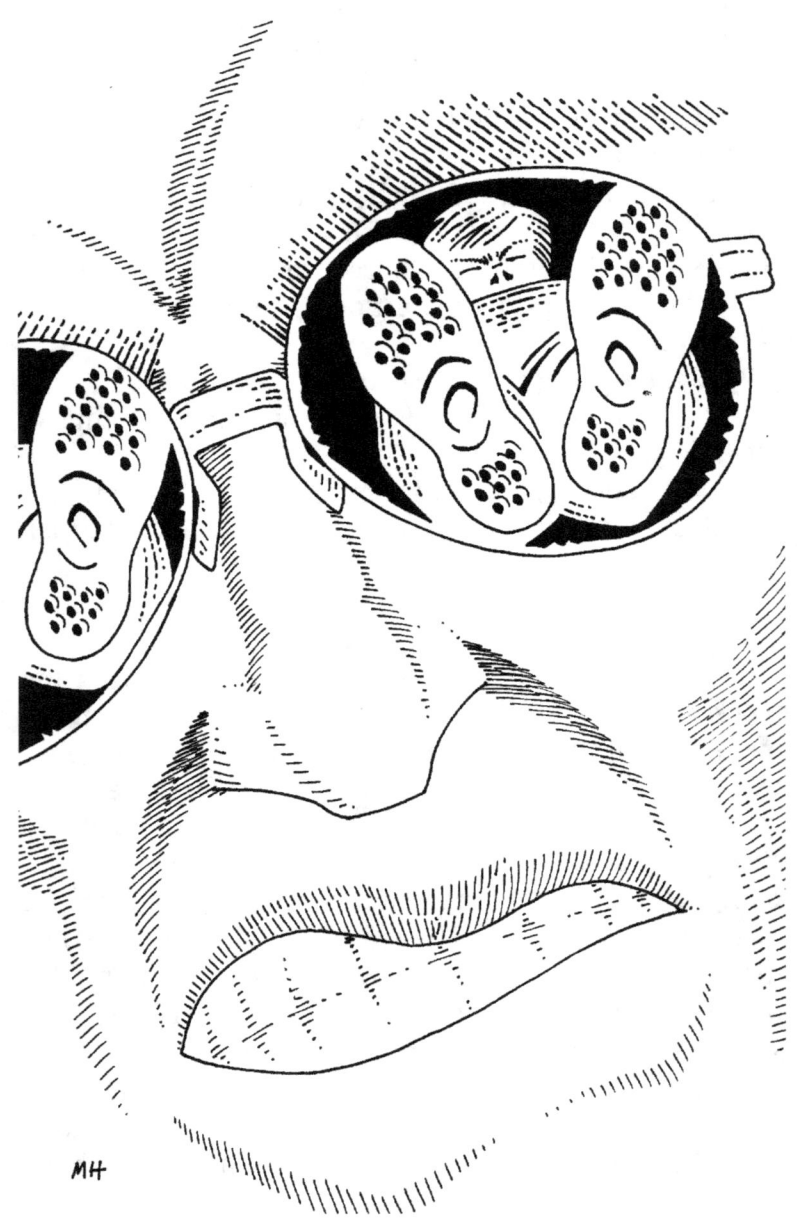

weakly groaned. I quickly went through the tasered one's pockets. I found a handful of plastic cuff ties, and a pocket knife. I cut my cuffs off and used fresh ones to zip the two agents' wrists together, with their arms interlocking.

I was finishing up when a banging started on the van's back door, causing me to practically swallow my tongue. Fist-sized dents starting to appear in it.

I pulled out my cellphone and speeddialed Penny.

"Penny!" I yelled over the banging.

"What? Michael, are you *inside* that IBS van?"

"Yes—" I started to reply.

"Achilles, stop! Michael's inside."

The banging stopped.

"Okay, that's better. Make sure you and the twins are clear of the rear door."

"Who's in there with you?"

"No time. I'll explain later." I closed the phone, and pulled out a coil of thermite putty. I had a bad feeling that Agent Thrush wasn't lying on a beach somewhere congratulating himself on his escape. Thirty seconds later I was kicking the dented rear door off its hinges and looking out through the drifting smoke to find Andy and Achilles' grinning faces—apparently more interested in another adventure than the recent destruction of their new heli-drones. I had to admit to myself that at that moment I was never so happy to see the two of them.

Homeward Bound

Saturday, August 25th, 1984
(13,717 days post Supernova 1947A)

The rear observation deck of the Galacticity-bound
high-speed double-wide train was deserted. Penny, Kinnison, Cleo and I settled in and watched the tracks blur
out into the distance for several long, silent minutes as
we waited for the security sensor strapped to my wrist to
complete its sweep. When the faux-wristwatch burbled
its satisfaction, I said, "I'm beginning to think we can't go
anywhere without some superpowered interruption."
What I wanted to do was rant about how, no matter how
much I prepped, speculated, and counter-plotted, it
never seemed like quite the right combination of things
to deal with the threats that inevitably popped up. And
while I knew I would get sympathy, I didn't want to deal
with an inexorable variation on a "No plan survives
contact with the enemy" statement—delivered in a dry,
you-already-know-that tone of voice by Penny—so I kept
my own counsel and said, "How's the head, Kinnison?"

"I hate those telepathy blockers. It makes it feel like I'm holding my head underwater."

"And the headache?"

"Still lurking."

"Sorry to hear it."

"I still think I would have been able to resist the mind control if I hadn't been drugged up to the gills."

"I'll say it again, Kinnison. You don't know that. And, furthermore, you don't know whether you would have been *more* vulnerable without it."

"Michael has a point," Cleo said. "You were the only one of us affected, and you're the only one with psionic-based powers."

"Okay, yeah, but what—"

He fell silent as the elevator dinged. We all turned and all watched as the doors opened to reveal a stooped, nearly hunch-backed older woman. Her gray hair was bound up in a bun, and she was carrying a carpet bag in which you could have smuggled a baby elephant through Customs. She shuffled off, stopping to peer myopically about the observation deck. "Oh, such a nicely turned-out set of young gentlemen and ladies," she said in a voice that quavered ever so slightly. "I do hope I'm not interrupting anything."

"Oh, no, of course not, ma'am," Kinnison said, coming smartly to his feet. He had never been a boy scout, but you wouldn't know that by looking at him now.

She let Kinnison take her arm and guide her to the spot on the couch that he had vacated. "Why thank you, young man. It is so unusual to find such good manners in young people these days."

As she settled back into the cushions something was nagging at me. Something about the way that she was sitting wasn't quite right.

She reached into the carpet bag at her feet and pulled

out a round tin decorated with a basketful of beagle puppies. "Would anyone like some homemade chocolate chip cookies? I baked them this morning."

"Yes, please!" Kinnison said.

Penny looked at him as if he was taking an apple brought to the cottage door by an old crone. Cleo was holding her cane across her lap in a semi-defensive posture.

"Do you—" I started to say to Kinnison, but stopped when she popped the lid, and the rich, warm smell of freshly-baked chocolate chip cookies permeated the lounge. I started to salivate despite myself. *Would a supervillain actually bake cookies?* I thought. *A very clever one would,* I answered myself, *but are the four of us a likely target?* I relaxed a little, still wondering what it was about her that had left my obsessive-compulsive fairy poking me with its wand.

"Yes, I'd like one, too." I caught Penny's eye and gave her little nod, while I reached out and gave Cleo's hand a squeeze saying in the barest whisper, "I think it's safe."

Cleo squeezed my hand in return.

The old woman handed the tin to Kinnison. "Why don't you hand that around, young man."

"Thank you, ma'am," I said, when Kinnison shoved the tin under my nose.

I bit into the cookie, and the old woman gave me a crinkly smile, and I clued in to what had been bothering me about her. The cushions on the couch where she was sitting were depressed far further than I would have expected for an older woman of her apparent height and build. My mind leapt back to the first Witness who had visited my house back in May, and I knew who this woman really was.

"Doc Styx!" I said, as quietly as I could manage in my incredulity.

The Old Lady's Debrief

I surreptitiously rechecked my security sensors. They were still clean. How had Kinnison missed this? Lingering effects of the telepathy blockers? Or did Doc Styx have some sort of mind shield? And what about Cleo? I glanced over at her but she was looking as surprised as I felt. Somehow her hypersenses were being spoofed.

The old woman's lips curled up in another crinkled smile, then Doc Styx's voice emerged from those lips. "I heard about your run in with PICSEA."

The impulse to put my face in my palm was strong. "Yeah, about that—"

Doc Styx held up a wrinkled and liver-spotted hand. "I'm not here to criticize. Critique, yes, but the fact that you are here now, riding back to Galacticity without implanted tracker chips, is enough for me to say that you avoided PICSEA's 'tag and release' program without too much difficulty."

"How did you find out? Did Diana tell you?" Penny said.

"I did hear about it from Diana, but that wasn't my first source of information. Why don't you tell me about it, and then I'll share how I found out?"

I did most of the talking, and as I relayed the events, my anger grew. Cleo filled in a few details leading up to the loading dock, and Kinnison's only contribution was to confirm, multiple times, that he had taken the telepathy blockers. Penny hadn't noticed anything until the twins bolted in pursuit of their suddenly unresponsive heli-drones. Then it had been a mad chase for her, cursing the two of them for breaking their promise. She had had no idea that Cleo, Kinnison and I had been kidnapped until I had called her cellphone to stop the twins from using the van as a punching bag.

"The wake-me-up patches that I had slapped on Kinnison and Cleo got them moving—I was reluctant to use them on the four other kids in the back of the van, not knowing anything about their metabolisms or medical histories—and the six of us managed to carry the unconscious four with us into the Metro before the police or more agents arrived."

"Yeah, it was lucky the station was right there," Kinnison said.

"What was lucky," Penny said, "was the fact that the PICSEA van was driving *towards* the twins and me when Michael put 'Kamikaze Homing Pigeon' into play."

I nodded, then continued, "Our first problem was what to do with the four unconscious kids. It's not like you can pretend they're drunk or anything. Then I remembered Agent Sellers' card and the supposed phone number. You were right, Doc—it was a government IP address disguised as a phone number. I opened it up as a web page and got a chat widget, but it wasn't Sellers on the other side. When I asked for him, they said he was unavailable. I told them that I didn't have time to mess around and that I had four unconscious kids whose mom or dad was some unknown super, and that much of Protective Services thus didn't apply. Anyways, they agreed to send an agent. A couple of minutes later, Georgi, the limo driver who met us at the train station the day before, showed up and took the four of them off our hands.

"Meanwhile, Penny had called Hank, and boy was he pissed, wanting to know where we had all wandered off to. But when she briefly explained what had happened, his journalistic instinct kicked in and he said he'd meet us back at the hotel. He interviewed us, saying that he's planning on writing an investigative article about it. He's sure this isn't the first time that kids have been kidnapped, and I'm in entire agreement."

I noticed that my fists had clenched, and I forced myself to relax, as I continued. "So this Man in Black, Agent Thrush, he seemed to be in charge of the operation. What you said about this being a 'tag-and-release' seems to imply that PICSEA is cataloging supers."

"I'm afraid you encountered one of the more ethically challenged government agents. Agent Thrush believes that the ends justify the means, and because supers are a potential threat to the government, they must be monitored, and if possible, controlled. Which is one of the not-so-hidden mandates of the PICSEA."

"And, ironically, Agent Thrush is a super himself," I said, anger still burning, the hypocrisy of it adding fuel to the fire.

"Yes. That is where the ethical thicket becomes the thorniest for Agent Thrush. Apparently he can copy some of the powers of other supers. The evidence suggests that this copying is limited to psionic powers, and that he maintains a psionic link with those he has copied from. When he uses a power, the psionic link is activated and the super knows that their power is being duplicated."

"He's going around looking for supers to copy from? And that's why he went after Kim?" Penny said, her indignation was palpable.

"It would seem so."

"That would explain Mind Fire's confrontation with Thrush," I said. "Thrush was using Mind Fire's mind control on Kinnison."

"Are Agent Thrush's actions sanctioned by the U.S. government?" Penny said, her voice scathing.

"Yes and no. His superiors in PICSEA turn a blind eye in his direction. They'd rather not know details about his 'tag and release' program, but they find it useful, so he isn't reigned in."

"Do you mind if I discuss this with Hank?" I said. "I'd like to see Thrush prosecuted."

"Yes. Prosecuted," Penny echoed.

"Go ahead. I will rely on your discretion."

"Of course."

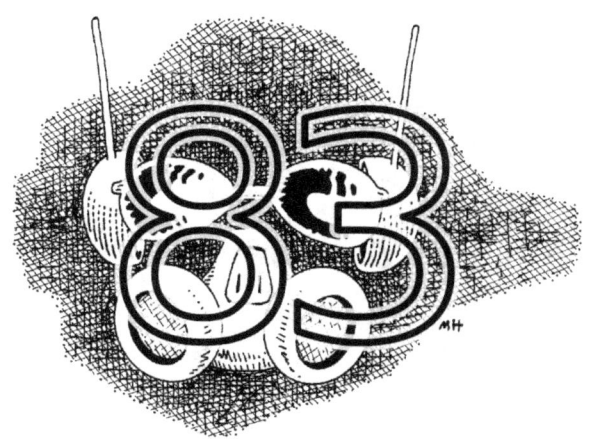

Penny Loafing

Monday, September 3rd, 1984
(13,726 days post Supernova 1947A)

"I thought I'd find you down here."

I swiveled the high back command chair and found Penny crossing the room with her usual purposeful stride, a large bag slung over her shoulder. "Hi," I said. "It's been rather hectic recently, and I haven't—"

"It's always hectic with you, Michael."

"Yeah, but ever since I agreed to be Doc Styx's pharmacist, I've started to feel like the Red Queen, running to stay in place. Not that I really begrudge the time away from working on the suit—it's wearable now, and I'm pretty far along in weapons development—but—"

She waved her hand, cutting me off. "It's understandable that you feel resentful about all the pulls on your time. What's important is that you don't let it stop you from getting the things you need to get done

done."

"But I can't just *not* synthesize the drugs for Doc! People's lives depend on them." I was starting to sound whiny, and I didn't like it.

"I know. I'm not saying you should stop. You make time to walk Bernoulli, right?"

"Yeah. And I was thinking about building a robot to take that over, but I couldn't figure out how to disguise it, given the time constraints."

"You can't solve all your problems with technology. You need to balance your life. Which is the reason I'm here. You need to spend some time not thinking about Doc Styx's patients, your father, or how you are going to bring the Squad to justice."

"I don't—"

"How about a movie? *The Adventures of Buckaroo Banzai* is showing at the multi-plex. In 3D. I know you haven't seen it yet. I'd like to see it, and while it isn't going to take your mind away from superscientists, it will be a fun distraction from all this." She swept her arm at the darkened expanse of the lab.

Could I say that I had been planning on taking Cleo to *Buckaroo Banzai*? Another part of me answered the question: *She's just going to say 'Why don't you then?'*

"I can't. I've got to monitor this new batch of drugs for Doc Styx, " I said, trying to suppress the frustration in my voice. I wanted to spend time with my friends, I really did. I waved at the bank of monitors and the ever-shifting news feeds, webcams, and traffic cameras. "Besides, I want to be here if—when the Demolition Squad rear their heads."

"You know you can neglect your friends, and being real friends, they're going to let it slide. Or not. I'm here for the not part. So, in anticipation of you having a legitimate reason for not leaving the lab, I brought these along." She held up the shoulder bag. "How about a game?" She pulled out each sealed game bag and put them on the control counsel next to the chess set as she said, "I've got *Ragnarok City, Android Assassins vs. Kung Fu Clones, Nexus War,* and the ever-popular *The Things in the Saucer Tomb.*"

I hadn't played a board game since before the D.C. trip. "Okay, but I have to be able to keep monitoring the drug synthesis."

"That shouldn't be a problem. Which one?"

"Something on the lighter side."

"*The Things in the Saucer Tomb* it is. Arctic Archeologists or Saucer Things?"

"I'll take the scientists."

She swept the other games back into the bag. "You don't want to shake things up a little and play the Things?"

"I'm stressed out enough as it is." I opened the bag and pulled out the map, then dumped the smaller bags of counters onto the conference room table.

"True enough. At least you aren't blowing off Sensei Fox. We need a chit cup."

"The training is too important." I got up, heading for the infirmary. "Besides, even with the backpack and extra weights that he makes me wear, it's fun," I said over my shoulder.

"Like your friends aren't?" was her retort.

When I got back with the bed pan, Penny had the map of the saucer set up and Thing tokens distributed across its rooms.

"Oh, come on, Michael," Penny said, eying the white enameled bed pan that I plunked down on the table.

"What?" I said, trying to sound as innocent as I could.

"You know 'what'."

"It's clean. In fact, I doubt anyone has ever used it."

"Fine. It'll work."

We started in, and my exploratory team of adventurer archeologists made good progress, discovering that the Things were vulnerable to fire almost immediately. Which is almost always helpful for the explorers.

"I understand that you haven't brought Cleo into your inner clique."

I looked up from the map, my finger poised over the archeologists chit that I was about to move into the saucer's Power Room. "I'm not sure our relationship is ready for that. And, come to think of it, how do you know that?"

"Cleo and I talk. It's something that friends do, you know."

"Yeah. It happens sometimes." I pushed the explorer chit into the Power Room and Penny flipped over the Thing counter there. It was the Gelatinous Mass.

"She knows about the lab. She knows about your father."

"I had guessed as much." My explorer failed his escape roll and was subsumed by the Mass.

"Yet you don't talk about it. I've told her that she should bring it up, but she demurs, saying that it's up to you to broach the subject. That it would be impolite and intrusive if she did." She put down a new Gelatinous Mass counter in the hallway outside the Power Room.

"She is half-Japanese." I moved another explorer into the corridor. She was wielding the Grease Gun, but when I drew the effect chit from the bedpan, it turned out that the Things found the grease nourishing. Penny put another Gelatinous Mass token in the corridor as my archeologist successfully retreated.

"Irrelevant. She grew up in Galacticity just like you and I did. You need to bring her into the loop. It's not just a matter of trust, or your feelings. You're planning on putting your life at risk and she deserves to know that."

"But I'm—" I brought up the explorer with the Molotov Cocktails and bombed the Power Room corridor, clearing the Gelatinous Mass.

"—afraid that she'll get scared? Reject you because you're going to put on a supersuit and fight crime? You told me who you think Cleo's father and mother are, and you still think she's going to bail on you?"

"Honestly?"

"That would be nice."

"Yes. I am afraid of just that, and more. And how do I tell her that I'm going after four cyborgs wearing the suit that my father was killed in? By those very same cyborgs?"

"I think you underestimate Cleo."

"And I think there are things that *we* don't know about Cleo."

"What makes you say that?"

"I've been doing some research. In my copious spare time, of course, and there is some serious weirdness in the Tsunami–Lady Lightning–Iodine triangle."

"Triangle? You mean a love triangle? Is that why Iodine killed Lady Lightning?"

"I don't know, but that's one explanation. Iodine's civilian identity, according to the trial reporting, is Yvette Fox. I'm guessing that Cleo hasn't mentioned this to you."

"Noooo. She hasn't. I'm going to have think about

this."

"Yes. Do. I would very much like another vantage point on this." But a little Clue fairy was whispering, *Penny hasn't lost a parent. She has no idea what it's like.*

By this time I managed to get an archeologist into the Power Room and successfully shut down the Saucer's generators. It didn't win me the game, but it sure put a crimp in the ability of the Things to regenerate.

Sophomore Year Begins

Monday, September 10th, 1984
(13,733 days post Supernova 1947A)

Kinnison and I took seats at the same table in Ms. Pertwell's English class, our first class of the first day of sophomore year.

"Why aren't you in AP English with Penny and Cleo?" Kinnison said.

"You know why. Besides, how much English do you need to write a lab report? It's not like you need project management skills to write."

Ms. Pertwell, smelling of coffee and cigarette smoke, said as she walked past on her way to the blackboard, "You might be surprised by what it takes to write well, Michael."

I flushed and Kinnison said, "Whoops!"

Ms. Pertwell took up station in front of the blackboard. "Welcome back to Centurion High, everyone. Some of you were in my freshman English class and will be familiar with my first day traditions, while the rest of you have probably heard rumors. Given the rather eventful summer, I expect you will have no trouble with the first assignment, an essay entitled 'What I Did This Summer'."

There were moans from a number of my fellow students.

She began passing out blank essay books.

"The dreaded summer vacation essay," Kinnison said, following up his moan with a dramatic sigh. Then he perked up. "And what a summer it was. So much to write about."

I wrote in the title to the essay and waited for the next bump in Kinnison's road to enlightenment, thinking about how, if I'd wanted to be even remotely accurate, I should have been writing: 'I watched my mother have a breakdown, did chemistry in my secret lab, worked out at a dojo for up-and-coming super-heroes, rebuilt my father's supersuit, did some more chemistry, started dating a blind girl who sees better than anyone I know, ran into a sealed room with the four supervillains that killed my father but managed to escape with a little help from my friends, foiled a kidnapping, and did I mention the chemistry? I like chemistry.'

Meanwhile, Kinnison's pencil hovered over his page, darting down only to retreat several times before "This sucks!" erupted with the realization that everything he wanted to put in the essay, he couldn't. "What are you writing about, Gurick?"

"Mostly about going to see movies like *Red Dawn* and *Revenge of the Nerds*, oh, and about how inform-ative my visit to the Senate hearings by the Powers Oversight Committee was."

"That sounds like something I can write about, too."

"Feel free, Kinnison."

"What about *Heavy Metal 2*? That Post Brothers segment was awesome, but, you know..."

"It was rated R? Sure, but it was an animated R. I think it'll be okay to mention it."

"Am I going to have to separate you two?" Ms. Pertwell said.

I looked up to find her standing in front of our table. She wasn't tapping her foot, but she might as well have been. "No, Ms. Pertwell."

"Sorry, Ms. Pertwell," Kinnison said.

I put my head down and started working on the fluff that I was passing off as my essay, hoping that this wasn't some sort of harbinger for the year.

Unfortunately, it was. If it hadn't been for the irritating discovery that Dave Sweets was in my second hour gym class, I would have greeted with pleasure the return to the gentle ministrations of the gorilla-chimera Mr. Martin with my new-found confidence in my physical capabilities, and a 'thank you' to everyone at the Black Lagoon Dojo. Instead, it turned out to be the beginning of an all-out Sweets sweep. His smirking face was in my calculus, chemistry, and computer applications classes. Lest you think the day was a complete downer, Penny, Kinnison, and Cleo had schedules that overlapped at least two classes with mine.

By the end of my first day back at Centurion High all I could think about was going home to the lab and getting something useful done. At least cross country didn't start for a couple more days. *With my luck,* I thought, *Sweets will be joining the team this year.* Thankfully, he didn't.

As the semester wore on, I began to notice a disturbing pattern of malfunctions all too reminiscent of the Cosmic Bowling Station incident. At first I couldn't figure the pattern, until I realized Sweets was the common presence. Calculators would give wrong answers, particularly during tests, computers would mysteriously lose homework files, etc. I had no real evidence. But the obsessive-compulsive fairy insisted that it was Sweets behind it all. And the fairy would know; it was the one that kept track of everything, whether or not I wanted it to.

Crystals for Kinnison

Saturday, October 6th, 1984
(13,759 days post Supernova 1947A)

"What do you think?" I said. "It's psionotropic."

Kinnison and I were sitting at the conference room table in the lab, the gentle light from its surface casting odd shadows up his face.

Kinnison turned the crystal disk over and over, his fingers leaving ripples on its dimly glowing surface. "Psiono-what?" he said in a distracted voice.

"Tropic. It reacts to your psionic energies. Levitate it."

He held the crystal in his open hand and as it rose off his palm the glow intensified. "Cooool," he breathed.

"I've taken the liberty of adding a few crystals to your supersuit. For the awesome factor. You can turn them on and off when you want."

"With my mind?"

"Yup. Try thinking 'off' at it."

"Right," he muttered. The glow snapped out, but the

crystal continued to drift lazily an inch above his out-stretched palm. He smiled.

"Now 'on'."

Glow returned.

"How fast...?" The floating crystal started to blink on and off.

"I think you've got the hang of it."

"But how—"

"—did I figure this out? I had a little help from Doc Styx. Apparently they're doing some pretty cool research into thought-based psionic interfaces at Orpheus IS." As I spoke, I slipped a plastic box a little larger than a deck of cards from my pocket and slid it towards him. "Here."

He picked up the case and snapped it open, then set it back down, like it smelled bad. "Dice? Are you testing me or something?"

"No. They're kind of an apology. Try 'em out."

"An apology? You don't need to apologize, Gurick. I'm getting used to you being a jerk." Despite the words, his tone had a smile to it. He pulled the icosohedron and rolled it clattering across the dense plastic of the table surface. It flashed red and came to a stop with a twenty on its uppermost triangular surface. The red glow faded.

He raised his eyebrows. "What's with the red glow? Oh. It's psiono-whatever, too."

"Psionotropic. Yup."

He picked it up and rolled again. This time it didn't glow red and came to a stop showing a five.

"You didn't use your telekinesis that time. I made a full set of polyhedral dice for you, so you can play games and know that you aren't subconsciously manipulating the dice."

"Excellent!" he said. "I take it back, Gurick, you aren't a jerk."

"At least not all the time." I pulled out the plastic carrying case I had stowed the Lensark suit in out from under the conference room table and put it down in front of me.

"What's that? A new game?" Kinnison said.

"Amusing thought," I said. "But no." I thumbed the locks and flipped the case open to reveal the upper torso of the Lincoln green micro-mesh cloth with its gold Lensark symbol. The symbol was done in gold lines, forming an eye-inside-a-triangle-inside-a-circle.

"Cool," he breathed.

I rotated it towards him. "It's mostly to your specs."

"Mostly?"

"Oh, I put in a few enhancements. Commo-gear, IFF, that sort of thing. Not quite strong enough to stop a bullet, or any kind of blunt weapon for that matter, but it's tough enough to turn anything under a molecular-edged weapon."

He fingered the green and gold fabric—thankfully he hadn't picked the CHS blue and white—then pulled it out and laid it on the table. He touched the left wrist's psionic crystal. It flared, then faded. "But the Arisians only gave a Lensman one lens."

"Look, you're Lensark, not a Lensman. I thought it would look better with psionotropic crystals on each wrist, rather than just one. There's also one in the middle of the mask's forehead. I can take them off if you like, but..."

"No. No. It's just not what I was thinking of. Shall I try it on?"

But What If I Have to Take a Leak?

"By all means, try it on. You know where the locker room is?"

He frowned in concentration. "I do now."

Ah, to be a telepath, I thought. *I'm going to have to work on that.* "Then use whichever locker doesn't have a name on it. Here, let me show you something." I flopped the suit over on its front. "The main seam is in the back. But—"

"Why did you make it that way? I'm going to need help—"

"But," I said, interrupting him. "You touch this pad at the base of the seam and it will 'zip' up automatically. It'll be baggy until you do that, but then the fabric will snug down to your skin. You can wear something light under it without it showing, but anything with seams or significant bulk will show through."

"What if I have to take a leak?"

I flipped it back over. "Front seam here, or you can just pee."

"Pee in the suit? How—?"

"I'll get to that in a moment. The hood will snug down to your skin, too."

"And to get out?"

"Pinch here and here." I demonstrated the locations on the front of the collar just below the chin, splitting the fabric in a long line down the back. "As to the peeing, the suit will absorb and recycle your sweat and urine, with a distributed storage of about a quart. After that it will 'sweat' the water out through its surface. It uses the same technology that my father developed for NASA. As for taking a crap, well, I could install a high-tech diaper like the astronauts—"

"No. No, that's okay, I think I can deal with that the usual way."

"I thought you would feel that way. Finally, we have the *pièce de résistance*," I said in my best faux-French accent as I raised the full-face mask out of the carrying case. "A Smartmask."

"Wow," he said. "I have been *so* jealous ever since you gave Smartmasks to the twins." He took the mask; then, almost reverently, using both hands, he pressed it to his face. There was a faint sucking sound as it molded itself to the contours of his face, and the crystal above the bridge of his nose pulsed with light.

"How's it feel?"

"Like I'm not even wearing it." His voice had been lowered by the mask's built-in vocoder. He smiled; the mask, detecting and mimicking the movements of his face, smiled too. "Is that my voice? Testing. Testing. Wow! Does it do reverb, too? 'Cause that would be awesome!"

"It seems to be working," I said, a dryness creeping into my voice. "Let's turn off the voice disguise." I reached out and pinched the hidden switch on the side of mask. "And yes, it can do other effects. Why don't you look at it yourself in the mirror?"

He did, making faces and watching the mask duplicate the grimaces, smiles, and frowns. "Spiffin'!" he finally announced.

After this had gone on for a half minute or so, I said, "Blink twice."

"Like this—? Whoa! What's all this stuff?" He waved his hands in front of his face.

"That's the HUD. The mask projects icons indicating the current state of the suit directly into your eyes. They should be more or less self-explanatory. Battery level—"

"Battery level? Why do I need electricity?"

"Of course you need electricity. How do you think the vocoder is powered? Or the HUD?"

"HUD, huh? I think you should call it the H.C.I.T.D., the How-Cool-Is-That-Display. That's much better than 'Heads Up'." He looked down, patting himself around his waist, then tried to look around at his butt. "Where do I plug it in?"

"You don't. It has a network of micro-generators that recharge the batteries from your motion. There's also a heat differential array in the surface of your mask and hood that generates electricity by taking advantage of the difference between the ambient temperature and your head's. Oh, there's one more thing. I need to show you how to get the mask off. It takes two hands. A Smartmask won't come off unless you started peeling it at specific spots while pressing your thumbs down in others. Or, at least, it won't come off without taking the skin with it."

I show him where to grip and pull. It came away with a faint sucking sound.

"Why don't you suit up and I'll see if there are any adjustments to make?"

He did, and there were. When he returned from changing back into his civvies, he had a hang-dog look.

"What's wrong? Is it the wrong colors?"

"No, the colors are great. I was just wondering how long it's going to take to make the adjustments? Should I wait?"

I chuckled, and his look grew even more pathetic. "Sorry, I didn't mean to look like I was making fun of you. I just realized you want to take the suit home with you."

"Yeah. I do."

"I'll see what I can do to expedite the mods. Can you come back tomorrow? I should be done with it by then."

"Promise?"

"I promise to try."

He nodded and started for the door.

"Hold up, Kinnison," I said, holding the mask out. "Take it. It's ready to go."

He practically glowed. The crystals definitely did. "Hey, thanks!"

He hummed something that sounded like the tune from "She Blinded Me With Science" as he headed for the eastern exit.

Rock-Paper-Scissors

Sunday, October 7th, 1984
(13,760 days post Supernova 1947A)

"I'm in here," I called out to Kinnison when he entered the lab.

"Is it ready?" were the first words out of his mouth as he came through the doorway to the firing range.

"Absolutely. It's hanging in the closet next to the eastern entrance. Suit up and rejoin me."

I followed him back out to the main lab and waited while he got into the suit. It didn't take long, and when he emerged from the bathroom I said, "Looking good, Lensark. How does it feel?"

"Feels like I've been shrinkwrapped in thin rubber," he said, his voice pitched lower by the mask's vocoder. "Kind of what I imagine wearing a wetsuit would feel like, only freer, more flexible."

"Good. Do some deep knee bends, then jumping jacks."

He did so.

"Any chafing? Binding?"

He flung out his upper arms and did some upper body rotations. "Nope," he said in his now manly voice.

His vocoder lowered voice was beginning to wear thin on me. "Turn off the vocoder, would you?"

"Sure." He pinched the edge of his mask. "How's this?" His voice back to normal.

"Much better. I want you to wear it around the lab, get used to moving in it. While you're doing that I'll show you some of the stuff that I've been working on."

I had a table laid out with five of the items that I had been working on. I picked up the small flashlight-like one first.

"That looks like a taser," Kinnison said. "Is it?"

I pointed it down range at a three inch diameter alloy steel post. "Watch." I fired. There was a whistling sound and whirling blur of motion with tiny blue flames that briefly formed a blue line in the air as it whipped towards the target. It wrapped itself around the post with a faint clink.

"Is that it?"

"Not quite. Let's go take a look at it."

We walked down to the post.

"I still don't see anything."

I placed my palm against the top of the post and pushed. Six inches of steel toppled over and struck the floor with a heavy thud. The two weights, connected by a very thin, almost invisible wire, clattered after it.

"Oh. What was that?"

"I call it 'angel-wire', after something similar that they used to fire from cannons in the Age of Sail."

"Ah, anti-rigging shot. It has rockets on either end of a mono-filament wire?"

"Right."

"Impressive. What else have you got cooking down

here?"

I went through the handful of other things I had laid out, Kinnison enthusiastically helping me set up targets and clearing away the aftermath. Even the less-than-perfect performance, and outright failure of another, was met with lively interest on his part.

A number of responses to the demonstrations that ran like this:

"What do you call this one?" Kinnison said.

"The Gum Up and Immobilize grenade, or 'Gooey' grenade," I said.

"Not bad, but I think 'Booger Bomb' would be better. It's the right color of green, you know."

He suggested a few other names, including 'Rust Never Sleeps' and 'Dragon's Teeth' for another, making me think that he had been studying up on his Greek mythology, as it was the same name that Penny had suggested.

"I don't want you to think I'm bragging or any-thing—"

"No, no, Gurick, this is the *coolest* gadgetry I've seen outside of TV or the movies. Bondian cool. Stuff that Q would have been proud to invent."

"I'm not just building it be cool. There is—"

"—a plan? Sure, I get that. You have to be prepared to take on the Demolition Squad."

"I'm not sure you entirely grok the situation. Why don't we get a drink? I want to elaborate on a corollary to being prepared."

"All right."

I opened the cupboard in the kitchenette next to the clinic off the main lab. "Coke?"

"Sure." He took the can I proffered and pulled the tab. Holding the can he watched the moisture condense on its surface as it cooled itself. "Are these gloves insulated? I'm not feeling it get colder."

"Yup. Just like the rest of the suit."

I took a swig of mine as he raised the can to his lips, then stopped. I could see his frown echoed by the mask. He put the can on the counter and started to pull his mask off.

"You can leave the mask on. I've got straws."

We went out to the conference room table and took a pair of seats.

Kinnison squirmed a little after sitting. "It feels like I'm in my underwear."

"I think you'll get used to it."

"What's it like to wear your dad's suit?"

"Not the same, I imagine. Dad's suit is bulkier, and even without the backpack, weighs more than twenty pounds. While it isn't a tin can like the Titanium Titan's power armor, it has more in common with the Titan's than it does with your suit."

For once, he waited patiently, sucking on his straw.

"Here's my point, Kinnison," I said, drawing circles in the condensation left on the conference room table by my pop can. "And just in case it isn't painfully obvious, I'll spell it out so it doesn't become obviously painful. Or worse. There will always be a power or set of powers that will defeat you."

"And by 'you', you don't just mean me."

"Right. It's like rock-paper-scissors to the nth degree. In the superpowered world there is always some combination of powers, abilities, or even tools and sufficient planning, to defeat you. If you have ice powers, you will end up fighting someone who controls or generates heat; if your weapon is a laser, then your opponent will have the ability to absorb or reflect light. No one is omnipotent. No one can think of every contingency."

"That's why people team up," Kinnison said.

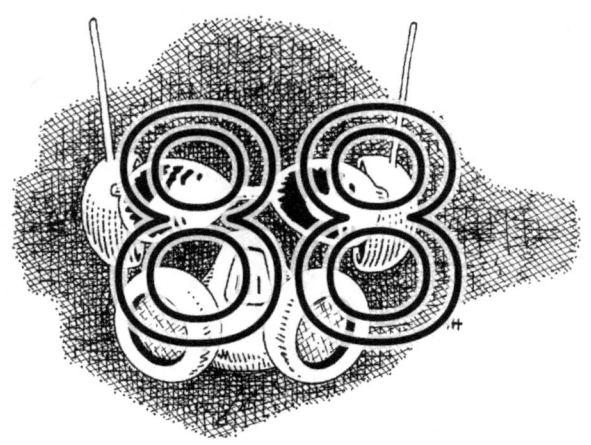

Bad-Good Grades

Wednesday, October 17th, 1984
(13,770 days post Supernova 1947A)

I couldn't believe it. How had I screwed up so badly as to score 100% on, not one, not two, but *three* of my midterms? Okay, that was a rhetorical question. I knew full well what had happened. I had been spending way too much time in the lab. Going on a fifteen minute cat-nap every four hours—and hey, if Tesla and Edison could do it, I thought, then I can—so I'd ended up in a daze, running on autopilot. And bang! Perfect scores when I should have been paying attention and only scoring my usual ninety to ninety-fives. I'd have to focus and climb back down into my A-minus hole. *Or,* I thought, *I suppose I could hack into the school computer and lower my grades.*

"What are you all depressed about, Tesla-boy?"

I jerked at the sound of Cleo's voice, and folded my tests and slid them into my backpack. I was going to have to build a Cleo detector. I felt a bit of my mind spin off down that track and I said, "Oh, hey, Kitsune-chan. I didn't get the grades I was hoping for."

She quirked an eyebrow at me. "*That* is one of the things I love about you, Michael. You have your own standards and the rest of the world can go fry an egg."

"Ah. I like to think of it as being in the same vein as your cane."

She laughed. "Touché!"

"Are we on for tonight? You're sure your dad doesn't object to not having you around for your birthday dinner?"

"He's cool with it. We decided to have the celebratory dinner at the Milkyway on Saturday after our shopping expedition to Star Arcades."

"I'm jealous. The Galactics' Arcology has always been one of my favorite places."

"Well, it's not all fun and games. I'm getting my biannual checkup, too."

"Oh? Let me guess, your family doctor is..."

"The same as the one who is treating Liz. Yes."

"Ah. I thought so." Could I tell her that I was the one responsible for synthesizing whatever specialty drugs Doc Styx had her on? Later. Not on her birthday. *That's just an excuse,* part of me whispered. *You're going to have to tell her sometime.*

"Now I feel a little inadequate," I said. "Merely taking you to Atomic Jack's. It's pretty much a theme-driven hole-in-the-wall compared to the Milkyway. Entirely lacking in fine linen, haute cuisine, and enough silverware to bankroll a small mercenary army."

"Yet it doesn't have roller skating waitroids. Or you."

"How am I supposed to argue with that?"

"You aren't. I'll be ready by seven. Make sure you leave enough time to talk to Father."

"Of course. See you at seven."

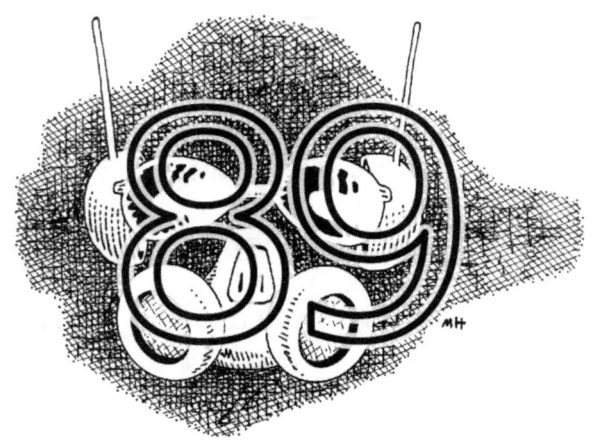

Caught with My Hand in the Cookie Jar

Tuesday, October 23rd, 1984
(13,776 days post Supernova 1947A)

It took almost a week, but I finally found myself alone in the computer lab after school. I pushed my specially prepared data stick into one of the workstations closest to the computer lab's door and started in on my homework as the programs on the stick began to worm their way into the school's servers. Ten minutes after I had jacked in, I was watching the visual tell-tales masquerading as a spreadsheet of world population figures track the program's progress through the student records database, systematically lowering my grades. As I was about to commit the changes, all around the lab I could hear the computers powering up, and I stopped typing, pushing my chair back. After a moment, the spreadsheet disappeared. I hit the control key a couple of times, but the workstation was frozen.

The room filled with light as every other computer monitor lit up at once, scrolling in letters almost as tall as each screen, "Your hand was in the cookie jar, Michael Gurick."

Was it some sort of computer virus from the servers? My program wouldn't have just shut down like it did unless it had detected an assault on its integrity.

I pulled the data stick out and stood. I thumbed the biometric surface of the stick as I shrugged into my backpack, waiting for the increase in heat from the stick that would assure me the memory chip had been destroyed. I took the couple of steps towards the door. Each monitor was now displaying, "Dr. DuQuane has been informed," over and over, like the opening to Mars Wars, scrolling up and away towards infinity against a star scape that Phobos and Deimos were slowly transiting.

I paused at the door, the data stick still cool against my thumb, thinking, *Don't panic.* Out of the corner of my eye, I saw a message scrolling across the screen. "Your little self-destruct on that data stick won't work. I control it now."

Several less than helpful thoughts rose up. *Now it's time to panic!* beat counterpoint to *How is he doing that?*

I suppressed both. No time to think about how this was happening. I twisted the data stick and felt rather than heard the tiny snaps as the chip split. This time I felt it heat up, ensuring me that the compromising programs and data were gone as the memory fused. In the old days, spies could just eat their secret messages. I'd have to work on an edible memory chip.

The words continued to scroll, responding to the destruction of the data stick. "Or maybe not. You're still—"

I tried to turn the door knob, but it didn't budge. I turned, my back against the door when the computers all beeped.

"—trapped, Gurick. I control the door's lock," scrolled across screen to my right, running smoothly around the room, jumping from screen to screen. "Have a seat. DuQuane will be here soon. He's bringing the police. You'll be enjoying the hospitality of a police interrogation room soon."

I couldn't afford to draw attention to myself, have the house searched, the lab discovered. I derailed that train of thought and the chill of fear it prompted. Now was not the time to speculate about what would happen if I was caught. Now was the time to not get caught.

I checked my cellphone, but it was dead, too. Which wasn't surprising. It would have automatically powered down when it had detected a breach of its firewall or loss of computational integrity. Thank you, Doc Styx.

"You have some interesting toys, Gurick. I particularly like what I saw on your cellphone before it went into panic mode. Why all the security? You don't just call mom for a ride with it. What do you really use it for?"

So whoever—or whatever—this was, it was capable of detecting and hacking into my devices, despite military-grade firewalls.

I looked around the computer room trying to look as calm and innocent as I could manage, taking inventory. There were the workstations on every desk, each system with its webcam transmitting-light a steady red. An archaic punch card machine in the corner. And standing next to it, the old-fashioned pop vending machine that several generations of Centurion computer students had hacked, adding such things as an elaborate scrolling LED bar, an Ethernet network card, a web server, and, most recently, a webcam.

A plan began to take shape.

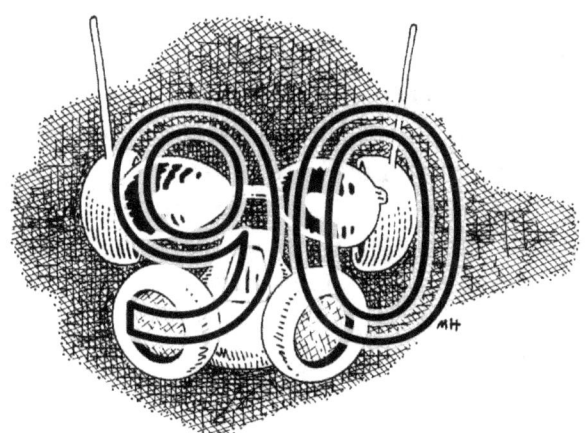

Vending Release Depending on Good Behavior, or Houdini in a Can

I knew that I was being videoed, and if my mysterious hacker-voice could be believed, the CHS Principal and a band of police were on their way. While the situation seemed desperate, I hadn't actually done anything more than hack into the school database. But I didn't want to compound this by doing something physical, such as melting the door off its hinges, blowing a hole in the wall, or even smashing one of the windows.

Start with negotiation. I doubted it would lead to anything, but it might serve to distract my captor. Careful to keep any sign of mockery from my voice, I said, "So, wizard controlling the souls of these machines, what is it you want?" Would he—or was it a she? Or an it? No, for some reason I was pretty sure it was a he. Would *he* take it as flattery?

"Gurick, Gurick, Gurick. You have nothing that I want."

I walked over to the pop machine. "Then why are you doing this? Have I offended you in some way?"

"You have trespassed on MY domain, Gurick."

I almost asked, "You mean the *school's* computers?" but swallowed the question and my pride and said, "I'm sorry, I didn't know." I made no attempt to cover up the lens of the webcam, but fed the vending machine a dollar bill and pressed the Coca-Cola button.

"I'm in here, too," scrolled across the red LED bar above the coin feed. "No pop for you."

"Surely I can have something to drink while I wait for Dr. DuQuane."

"Nope."

I pulled out a handful of change. The machine was old enough that the coin handler was completely mechanical. I slotted in three quarters. The machine rattled and a can of Coke dropped into receptacle. I fished it out. It was room temperature, of course. They had turned off the refrigeration almost a decade ago when they had converted over to the self-cooling cans. Invented by Dad. Thank you, Dad.

I fed it two more quarters, a couple dimes, and a nickel. The LED bar responded with, "Two cans?"

"I'm thirsty."

I went back to the computer desk next to the door, set one can of pop on the table and felt around under the desk locating a projecting bolt head. "You know," I said, "I haven't done anything wrong." Which was, more or less, true. While I had hacked into the system, I hadn't actually changed my grades. Apparently, mysterious hacker had been in too much of a hurry to trap me.

"What are you talking about, Gurick? You were hacking into the database and altering your grades."

I pressed the pop can against the bolt, creating a dent that I knew would mangle the cooling surfaces inside the can. "But I didn't. I've just been working on homework. That's what the videos will show. You could modify them, of course."

"You did—I have the logs of you breaking in."

I put the dented can on the desk, right under the fire detector, and set my cellphone next to it. "But you don't. Unless *you* modified the logs or changed the database, of course."

"You're lying, Gurick!"

I popped the can open, triggering the endothermic chemical reaction that would cool its contents. "And you're an anonymous informant. Who are they going to believe?"

There was no reply.

"So why don't you unlock the door, and I'll just walk out of here and we can call it a draw."

"They're almost here, Gurick. You're going to go down for this."

The can began to vibrate and there was a faint whistling noise of escaping reaction gas. I picked up my cellphone and looked at it as if I was checking a message.

The can blew, spraying a geyser of slushy pop straight up. The fire alarm went off. Fire-suppressant foam began to spray everywhere.

I snatched up the other can, shaking it vigorously as I stood, shoving the chair back to clatter across the floor. I bent and popped the can, spraying its contents into the wall outlet. The circuit breaker blew, taking down every machine in the room. Unobserved, I took the two steps to the door, hoping that my remote friend hadn't thought of overriding the fire system's automatic unlocking of the door. I twisted the knob, and for one heart pounding moment it failed to turn, but then I was out, moving down the hall at a fast walk. If I encountered Dr. DuQuane or the police now, I had nothing on me that would be really incriminating, with the possible exception of my phone, which might be a bit difficult to explain, unless I brought Doc Styx into it. But I would leap that chasm when I came to it. Otherwise, it was my word against his anonymous one, and unless he was very good indeed, any alterations to the videos would be noticeable.

I did encounter Dr. DuQuane, who said that he had received a message saying that someone was hacking into the school database from the computer lab. He hadn't called the police, being unsure if it was a prank message or not. I explained that the fire alarm had been set off by an exploding can of pop, something that had been known to happen, and reassured him that I had been alone in the lab. I finished with, other than there being some sort of glitch in the network causing the lab's computers to all remote boot, I hadn't seen anything. I asked him if he would like me to investigate the attempted hacking, and he said that wouldn't be necessary. He had already informed Mr. Alexander, the school network admin, about the breach and that he would investigate. After reassuring him that I would be happy to answer any questions he let me go.

Riding the Transit pod home, I pulled up the suit's control schematics in my mind and reviewed how vulnerable the systems were to electronic intrusion. It wasn't good. The oldest—and consequently the core—suit systems seemed to have been based on pneumatic controllers, but nearly all of the later functionality was based on electronic computers. When I got back to the lab I emailed Doc Styx about the micro-mechanical computers that Tantalus Microdevices was rumored to be working on. I figured it was an I-scratch-your-back-you-scratch-mine situation.

Then there the was the matter of anonymity that this incident brought up. Or rather, the need to ensure that no one would mistake or spoof my identity. It was time to visit the Galactics' Arcology and have Dad's super-identity-G.I.D. transferred to me.

Later, as I was dropping off to sleep, I remembered the incident at Cosmic Bowling and Sweets' smug face. The theatrics of the two events had a lot in common.

Kinnison's Tale
[An Adventure at the Cowl]

Friday, November 9th, 1984
(13,793 days post Supernova 1947A)

"Where's Cleo?" Kinnison asked, watching Bernoulli sniff his way through the shrubs along the walk up to the Riggs-Armstrongs' front door.

"She said she wasn't feeling like hanging out tonight," I said. Kinnison and I were standing on Penny's porch waiting for her to finish getting ready so that we could head over to Max's to take another run at Dungeon Inglorious.

"It's Friday," Kinnison said, as if Cleo was blowing off Christmas Eve to attend an anti-gift-giving rally. "And that's the third time she's bailed on us in the last couple of weeks. Is there something going on? Are you two fighting?"

"Not as far as I know. We had a great time on her birthday at Atomic Jack's. The Cape and Banter Improv troupe was so good we couldn't stop laughing most of the way home. But we haven't done anything much together since her visit to the Arcology." The timing had been bothering me. I couldn't help but wonder if Doc Styx had found something wrong during her checkup. She wasn't talking about it, and there was no way I was going to ask Doc about her health.

Penny opened the door and joined us on the porch. The catchy tune and sharply satirical lyrics of Frank Zappa's "Galacticity Girl" thundered out briefly before being cut off by the shutting door. She heaved a sigh of apparent relief. "If I hear *that* song again, I won't be responsible for my actions."

"The twins?" I said as Bernoulli bounded up the walk, the leash cord buzzing back into its reel as he came. They were the other half of the reason we had chosen to wait outside.

Penny bent and gave Bernoulli a good dose of behind-the-ear rubbing. "Yeah. I left them playing SimOlympus and listening to "Galacticity Girl" for the umpteenth time in a row. It was a major struggle to get them to agree on what game to play; then they both wanted to play Zeus. All done now, Bernoulli, you're a good boy."

We set off for Max's. Bernoulli went ahead, sniffing and peeing.

"I don't think President Bogart's re-election mandate will get much traction in the new Democratic-controlled congress," I said, picking up the theme that Penny and I had been hashing over since the election on Tuesday.

"Doc Styx on a pogo!" Kim exclaimed. "Enough about the election! It's all I heard about at dinner tonight."

"Fine. No more politics for the evening. If that's okay with you Penny."

"It's fine by me. You were starting to repeat yourself, anyways. Two days ago."

"Sorry. My ob-comp. By the way, where did you learn that one about Doc on a pogo?" I asked.

"At the Cowl."

Intrigued, I said, "How did you get in?" The Cowl was a well-known (or I should say, notorious?) bar a couple of miles from the Black Lagoon Dojo that catered to wanna-be supers and low-life villains who either weren't powerful enough, or couldn't get their acts together enough to rise much above the level of minor threat.

"They don't card you there if you're wearing a supersuit. Not that it would have done any good. There aren't any pockets in mine."

"Ah. That makes—"

"More importantly," Penny said with a quelling glance in my direction. "What were you doing there? You know you shouldn't be going anywhere in your Lensark guise without a G.I.D."

"His new suit was probably talking to him," I said.

"That—" Kinnison began to say, but Penny cut him off.

"Literally? What did you put into it, Michael?"

"No—" Kinnison tried again.

"Of course not literally. I meant that it was probably lying there, and he started to think—"

"Can I tell this story?" Kinnison said.

"Sure, no problem."

"So, yes, Gurick is right. I began thinking about putting it on and taking it for a spin, so to speak. It's weird, you know, where *is* all the good crime going on in this city? But I couldn't figure out where to patrol."

"Which is a *good* thing," Penny said.

"But I remembered seeing that bar, the Cowl, from the Transit. You remember, that night when it started to glow?"

"Of course," I said.

"So I put on the Lensark suit and my dad's old trench coat and fedora, and took a Transit pod over."

We had turned on to Centaurus Way.

"You'd better hurry this story along, Kinnison, we're almost there."

"I can see that. Okay. I hand my coat and hat over to the coat-and-weapon check—the guy running it was a classic brick, bigger than Silver Archer, with sick yellow, knobbly looking skin. He looked like he could crush rocks with his bare hands. I made my way to the bar and bought a beer."

"I thought you said you didn't have pockets."

"But the trench coat did."

"So you did have your ID."

"No. That would have been stupid. I left it at home. I had to carry my money around in my hand. You've got to put pockets in my suit, Gurick."

We stopped at the end of Max's driveway. "Okay. So you bought a beer. And then?"

"Yeah, it was kind of embarrassing. The bartender, who was some sort of lizard chimera with scales and a snake's eyes, gave me this look when I picked up the beer and hesitated with it halfway to my mouth, remembering my mask. After a couple of seconds he pulled out a straw and slid it across the bar without saying anything, which was pretty cool on his part."

Bernoulli sat, patiently staring at Max's front door.

"When I turned around to get a better look at who was there, this guy with a big hammer on his chest and red cape caught my eye, grinned and gestured me over to join him and his friends. What the hell, I thought, so I went over and pulled up a chair, feeling a little dorky that I was drinking through a straw, until I noticed a number of the other masked supers were too."

"Was this the guy you learned that charming slang from?" Penny said.

"Yup. A real friendly sort. Not. He went by the name of Mallet. It was pretty obvious I was a newbie and I'm sure he thought he would have a little fun at my expense."

"Naturally, you were reading this off him," I said.

"Naturally. When I sat down the Mallet snickered and said I was just a cape-tugging purple pisser—"

"A what?" I said.

"Purple pisser. It means someone who has a worthless power. I'd never heard that before either, but I got the gist of it from the Mallet's head without even trying, he was thinking so loud. So, of course I had to prove myself, so I TK-levitated him, chair and all, until he was floating above the table. Then I asked him who was pissing purple, which got a laugh from the room and broke the tension."

Lilly opened the front door, and the lyrics "Relax! Don't do it!" backed by high powered synth and drum machines rolled down the front walk. Bernoulli gave a happy yip at the sight of her. I pressed the button that released his collar hook as he bounded up the walk. "Are you guys going to stand there and yack all night? Or are you coming in?"

Bernoulli reached the porch and sat politely in front of Lilly, his tail swishing back and forth across the cement. Lilly murmured something to him, and fished a treat out of her pocket.

"We're coming," Penny called. "You're lucky you made it out in one piece, Kim. Not everybody that patronizes the Cowl is a 'purple pisser', as you so colorfully put it."

I could not resist adding, "No pun intended."

Flight to Destiny

Friday, December 7th, 1984
(13,821 days post Supernova 1947A)

Almost an entire month passed with no new sign of the Demolition Squad and I was beginning to think that all my preparations were going to go to waste. I found myself sitting in the command chair watching the monitors after school and on into the night. I knew I was beginning to put a strain on my friendships, but I couldn't help myself. Then came the attack on Nova Genesis Plaza, and Penny, sensing that this was the night the Squad was going to re-emerge, came down to the lab, helped me suit up, and, more importantly, took up the role of tactical adviser and communication coordinator.

I launched from the largest compressed air cannon in the world. Below me Galacticity spread out, the stretches between the street lamps illuminated by the nearly full moon halfway up the eastern sky behind me. A city that was filled with mostly normal people, going about their mostly normal lives, mostly oblivious to what was above them.

Despite the confrontation ahead of me, I felt a sense of freedom that I hadn't felt for far too long. I don't know if you've ever flown a jetpack before, but there is a sense of empowerment, of elation, to feel the roar of the thrusters at your back; the wind whistling past your mask. It's not like antigravity, which is entirely silent, or even a microlight with its looming wing and enclosing struts. When you're flying a jetpack you are embedded in a vibrant, vibrating sky.

"I've launched the tactical support drone," Penny said, bringing me out of reverie. "It should arrive shortly after you do."

"Roger that. Have the Squad finished with the armored car?"

"Not quite, they're moving crates into a van—"

She broke off.

"What?" I said.

"A police cruiser just pulled up. You have the feed?"

"Yes." I watched as Dragline put a cable through it. I checked my gauges, but I was already pushing max speed and still climbing. I hoped that the patrol car's armored passenger compartment held up long enough for me to get there.

The airspeed telemetry displayed 120 mph when I reached the apogee of my arc and began to descend towards the streets of Galacticity. My target was conveniently highlighted in the goggles' HUD. I zoomed in on the armored car nose down in a pit, reading the 'Wolverine Dispatch and Security Services' and, in smaller print under it, on the side facing me, 'All Our Supers Bonded'. The caped super Zircon Man lay sprawled in the street like a broken and discarded red, blue, and gold doll, while the Squad was busy unloading long flat crates that might contain paintings. Apparently, they had developed an interest in fine art since the Galacticity Library–First Bank of Terra job.

Around the stranded armored car the infrared overlay showed large puddles of darkness that had to be more pits, each disguised to appear as normal asphalt. Beyond, in the middle distance, high-rise buildings loomed in downtown Galacticity. Flashes reflecting off the building faces marked the location of the battle raging in Nova Genesis Memorial Plaza.

"Can you give me an update on the Nova League?" I radioed. "Still battling the Robotic Horde?"

"Fully engaged. Silver Archer is up to her hips in dismembered robots, and the Titanium Titan is toe-to-toeing it with one of those Megabots. There's a Leviathan-bot half out of the water, and using its water canon against the League headquarters. I'm going to go out on a limb here and say that the League won't be showing up to deal with the Demolition Squad any time soon."

"Good."

"Let's hope you don't change your mind about that. You have less than thirty seconds of flight time left before you have to recharge."

"Roger that." I picked a landing site at the raw edge of my tank's capacity. "I'm going to land on the building with those two round and white air conditioning units." I blinked the targeting cross-hairs into position.

"Copy. Twenty-five seconds remaining."

Dial It Up to H

I touched down on the roof just as the jetpack ran dry. The backpack's pumps immediately throbbed into life, starting to refill the main air tank.

"—loosing—" Penny said, static rising and falling. "—breaking up. Laun—"

I pulled the transceiver mini-drone off my utility belt, flicked its wings open and threw it over the side of the building. It flitted up and away to take up station, circling me a couple hundred yards up, keeping its multi-channel, spread spectrum sensor array focused on my backpack. It would take more than the normal Demolition Squad jamming to cut me off from Penny.

"How's that?"

"All com-channels back online."

I drew in a deep breath of recycled air. "Show time," I said over the now clear laser-relayed com-channel.

"Dial it up to H," Penny said.

"Oh, I will." I stepped over to the edge of the building. Chainsaw, having only one hand, was standing guard while Wreckingbar, Bang Galore, and Dragline were finishing loading the crates into a large truck. The wreckage of the police car was a block away, its wheels torn off, its windshields opaque with the white webbing of shattered but still extant armored glass. I couldn't tell if the police inside were still alive.

I adjusted the targeting spread on the mortars attached to either side of the backpack.

"Well, well, if it isn't my old buddies, the Demolition Squad," I said, my voice echoing off the buildings, amplified and distorted by the vocoder built into the mask, trying to keep the ice in my gut from spreading.

They all froze.

"What was that?" Chainsaw said, looking around.

"Too much distortion," Penny said.

"Oops," I said over the com-link. I adjusted the vocoder and repeated, "Well, well, if it isn't my old buddies, the Demolition Squad."

Chainsaw looked up and caught sight me. "But the Dispenser is dead!"

"And you killed me," I replied. "I got better."

Friday Night's All Right for a Fight

"It doesn't matter whether or not he was dead," Wreckingbar said, pointing his titanium bar in my direction. "Kill him now!"

I triggered the mortars attached to the outside of the backpack, and four gas canisters arched upward with muffled thumping-bangs.

Bang Galore swung her arm up and gestured like she was drawing a line along the face of the building below where I stood. As she did, the end of her arm made a rapid 'fwip-fwip-fwip' sound as she launched a dozen or more bomblets.

Bang Galore's bomblets spattered across the facade of the building below me. As they began to detonate with a 'crump-crump-crump' I jumped—shards of glass and stonework peppered my back as I fell.

Four gas canisters landed, clattering and bouncing between and around the overturned armored car and the yellow rental van, one making a drum-like sound as it bounced off the cover of a disguised pit. I didn't have time to evaluate their effect, as my jetpack was currently useless, the compressed air tanks still recharging with a heavy throbbing at my back. As gravity had her way with me, I sprayed the pavement below with a liberal dose of concrete-foam sans-solidifier catalyst, rather than the more obvious choice of impact-foam. The timing would be tricky. Just before I hit, I gave the expanding white dome a shot of solidifier. It was turning tacky as I hit. By time the foam closed over my head it had stiffened to the consistency of styrofoam. I never reached the ground, coming to an abrupt halt, trapped like a fly in opaque amber. But unlike the fly, I had an out.

The dome trembled with explosions as Bang Galore spit her fury.

"How long is that going to last?" Penny said.

"Long enough." I took a moment to gauge the positions of each member of the Demolition Squad using the HUD overlay camera feed. The gas canisters were spewing their contents, which included a colorless, but extremely odoriferous, retch gas. "How is the gas doing?" I asked Penny as I sprayed solvent. The foam began to crumble in front of me and I lofted a fine stream of alcohol and magnesium-sodium slurry towards Bang Galore. Triggering it, I stepped out under the cover of the orange-white fireball that sent Bang Galore stumbling back.

"It caught Bang Galore and Wreckingbar off guard—looks like they had Italian for dinner—but the other two switched to their internal oxygen supplies before they were affected. The truck with the loot just started its engine."

I turned and unclipped a balloon-grenade from my belt. I couldn't see the van's driver, but it wasn't one of the Squad. "Who's driving?" I thumbed the grenade to magnetic proximity.

"They're silver, so either a robot or costumed minion," Penny said. "Windows are up, so I can't tell if they're affected by the gas."

I made a snap judgment. Hardly anybody ever henched for the Demolition Squad. Too many work-related casualties. I sidearm pitched the hockey-puck-shaped grenade at the front chassis as the truck accelerated. It skipped across the road-bed, and blew with a muffled 'ka-fwump'. A six-foot diameter balloon violently expanded, throwing the truck up onto two wheels. It wobbled along for dozen yards before crashing into a parked car and crunching down on its side.

As the truck headed for its rendezvous with the parked car, Wreckingbar managed to to yell between coughing gags, "Take him down!"

"I've got 'im," Dragline said, her cables snapping out to wrap around the armored car, her titanium-steel boot anchors driving down into the asphalt.

"Bang, finish your job," Wreckingbar said.

"But—" she started to reply.

Wreckingbar cut her off. "Now!"

Dragline heaved, pivoting, bringing the armored car up and into a two hundred and seventy degree arc, hurtling around towards where I stood.

Need a Hand With These Miscreants?

I kept my position, despite the electric buzz of fear that ran down my spine, as the armored truck whipped around towards me. I could have easily dodged it, but the horror on the faces of the two guards visible through the cracked and starred windshield made me stand my ground. I brought up both arms, selecting impact-absorbing foam as I did, and sprayed, feeling the throb of the pump in my backpack and fluid coursing down the arm hoses, the dark streams leaving the nozzles projecting over my wrist, expanding, first, into a snowy foam, then merging into a full, blinding blizzard of white. The van hit the wall of foam with an almost delicate 'thwiiipthhh'. I continued to spray, taking several steps backward as the gray shape visible through the wall grew larger, slowing, then settling towards the ground.

Dragline yanked the armored car back, but the foam clung to it, causing the truck to noisily scrape and bump along the ground. Dragline jerked her cables, releasing the truck. As they reeled in, gobs of foam spewed away from her hands, sheared off as the cables disappeared back into the ports at her wrists.

I heard the whirr of blades, and Penny said over the com-channel, "On your right. Chainsaw closing fast."

I pivoted and switched my right arm to what Kinnison had dubbed 'silly webbing' and gave Chainsaw a full-on blast of it, then stepped and continued my pivot, avoiding his rush, spaying all the while.

Chainsaw staggered, his blades stuttering momentarily, chewing through the webbing. He swung his right arm chainsaw towards where I had been.

Penny said, "Wreckingbar is throwing—"

I pivoted half a turn more, stopped spraying and drew the rocket pack I had prepped just for this purpose. I had one chance to deal with "—his bar," Penny finished saying.

The bar was pinwheeling down on me, and I pitched myself over backwards. Just as the bar whirled over my head I threw the rocket pack up and into its path. Half a dozen cords snapped out as the pack spun, entangling with one end of the bar, wrapping around it. As the bar curved up away to boomeranging back towards Wreckingbar, the rocket pack thrusters began their random stutter, throwing the bar off course.

"We have incoming," Penny said.

I fired the jetpack, and bounced up ten feet on a blast of compressed air. "Friend or Foe? I've got nothing on my G.I.D." Dragline's cables rippled and snapped through the spot I vacated a moment ago.

"Unknown. No G.I.D.? Then either they've deliberately turned off their JASON or PICSID transponders, or they're a complete neo."

The jetpack died two feet from landing, and I came down in a bone-jarring stagger, pumps throbbing at my back.

"Looks like you need a hand with these miscreants," said a deep, yet familiar voice.

I looked from the bar, wobbling in its course, back to Wreckingbar to see Kinnison—strike that—to see *Lensark* standing on the roof of a parked car. His green and gold suit, with its glowing forehead and wrist crystals, looked quite impressive, if I do say so myself. Luckily the Smartmask would already be filtering the air for him. Unfortunately, I wasn't exactly thrilled to see him, but I suppressed that thought. I couldn't let him know that. "Welcome to the party, Lensark," I said through my vocoder.

"Is he ready for this?" Penny said.

"Obviously he thinks so," I said. "Try to hook him in to one of the com-channels. His suit is equipped with the necessary transponders."

"What about the retch gas?"

"He already knows about it."

"Really?"

"I'll explain later. Make sure he knows about the pits."

Lensark leaped off the top of the car and swung his arm overhanded as if he was playing whack-a-mole, his TK-strike slammed into Wreckingbar's head, driving him to his knees.

"Deal with the newbie, Dragline," Wreckingbar said. "I'm going to grind the Dispenser to dust. No one touches my bar."

Lensark landed, whirled, and with TK-slap sent the bar spinning away from Wreckingbar. "Now I've touched it, too!" he said, taking a TK-powered leap out of the path of Dragline's whipping cables, which punched through both the car's windows and into the building behind it.

Lights Out

Lensark's next TK-punch caught Dragline off guard, breaking her free from her anchors and lifting her up, her cables flailing. Lensark followed up by TK-throwing her into Bang Galore. The two went down.

The antigrav powered bar swooped around, wobbling as it came, and Wreckingbar crouched and leaped, snatching the bar from the air a good thirty feet up. Taking it in a two-handed grip as he fell, he landed and slammed its titanium tip downward, as if he were planting a flag pole; the purple flare of its force field erupted in a wide arc around its tip when it struck the asphalt. The rocket pack split and spluttered, falling away as he thrust the bar deep. He levered it back, the purple coruscating into violet as a chunk of the road two or three times the size of an SUV came up with a rippling groan—which went a long way towards explaining where the holes had come from.

"That didn't work out as well I had hoped," I said, throwing myself out of the way of the hurtling asphalt and concrete boulder. It bounced and rolled, smashing its way into the ground floor of a now dark and empty Toyota sales room.

"No, not one of your best efforts," Penny said.

"But points for trying," Lensark said over the laser-relayed com-channel, his voice undistorted by the vocoder.

"And welcome to the party-line, Lensark," I said over the com-channel, "I suggest a round-robin."

"Right," Lensark replied, and TK-punched Wrecking-bar from behind, slamming him into the crater he had so conveniently created.

I turned my attention to Dragline and Bang Galore. I unclipped a canister-grenade from my belt and heaved it towards where the two cyborgs were untangling themselves. It clattered to a stop in front of Dragline as she was reeling in her cables and detonated with a wet 'ker-fwumph', splattering sticky green globules in a five-yard radius that included Dragline's cables.

"Booger-bomb! Sweet!" Lensark said, TK-levitating Chainsaw and throwing him into the crater after Wreck-ingbar. "Pitch another one in this direction."

I obliged, and Lensark caught it with his TK and threw it in after Chainsaw. There was another wet 'krumpf'. I switched back to flamethrower mode, this time mixing in a gelatinous slurry that would stick to nearly any surface, and fanned it in the direction of Dragline and Bang Galore, sending Bang diving for cover. Dragline stood her ground, lashing out with her cables through the wall of flame, one spike tip punching into my right chest with enough force to crack ribs, even through the shock-absorbing gel of the suit. I grunted with pain and staggered; only the suit's stabilizers prevented me from going down.

I had caught a good look at the cable before it retracted. There were tiny gray-white spots on it, like a dusting of frost.

The road bed shook with a series of underground explosions, causing the tarpaulin sheets disguising the holes in the road to jump skyward. A building down the block collapsed in on itself, and all the street and building lights went out.

"What was that?" Kinnison said over the com-channel.

"The lights are failing all the way to downtown," Penny said.

"I think that explains what Bang Galore has been up to. That was a major power relay-transmission substation that just collapsed."

"But why—" Kinnison started to ask.

"Can't discuss it now," I said as Chainsaw climbed out of the crater, his blades stuttering on and off, running slower and slower, wisps of smoke puffing out. The gooey-grenade's frictive gunk was taking its toll on his cyber-workings. Wreckingbar's bar flew up out of the crater, followed by its master. Like a missile, it flew straight towards Lensark's heart.

I nearly hit the panic switch, but Lensark swung both arms out, bringing his hands together in a clap, and the bar simply stopped in mid-air, like it had been caught between Lensark's palms.

Rust Never Sleeps

"Behind you!" Penny said.

Her alert came in time for me to turn and see a coil of Dragline's cable whistling towards me. I fired a stream of web-glue, but instead of the blob of glue-web intercepting the bar, the blob and cable hit an invisible barrier, rebounding in opposite directions. I dodged back and away from the blob's spatter, for a split second I wondered what had happened; then I thought, *Lensark.*

"As I much as I appreciate it, Lensark, you—" I said over the com-channel, but stopped to focus on Dragline's cable. What had been the frosty-gray spots on Dragline's cables were now white in the IR enhancement of my goggles. They had grown and merged to form a dappling all up and down their length. *Rust never sleeps,* I thought, and rather than trying to dodge the cables, I braced myself and stepped into their path.

"Watch out!" Lensark yelled.

I did my best to block the cables with my arms, but

they flailed past my guard to pummel me. Before Dragline could retract them, I gripped and pumped pneumatic power into my gauntlets, launching myself towards Dragline, the compressed air jets firing at max. When Dragline started reeling in the slack, I reversed direction. Hard. Half a second later the cables snapped taut, then parted, the two halves whipping back, one half catching and wrenching Dragline's arm back and around with enough force to snap the now-weakened boot cleats. As she staggered, I hit her with enough glue-web to hold her for at least a few minutes.

Lensark was holding his own against Wreckingbar, primarily by dint of TK-ing Chainsaw into the path of every attack that Wreckingbar threw at him. I looked around for Bang Galore, but before I located her I saw a darting motion of a silver-red blur looping around towards Lensark's back, and I felt an icy spike of dread spear up from my gut. At the same moment a proximity alarm blared and I braced myself as a miniature claymore mine on my backpack blew, spewing its load of quarter-inch-diameter ball bearings into the path of the flying bomb behind me. A second, much larger explosion sent me staggering forward, the power-assist pneumatics throbbing.

"Behind—!" I started to yell, but the flying bomblet had already attached itself between Lensark's shoulder blades, and I had visions of the raw, hamburger-like skin on Silver Archer's back. But I knew it wouldn't be that kind to Kinnison. I yelled, "Look out!" triggering my Lensark panic code. A multichanneled set of messages strobed, squealed, lased, and radioed out from my backpack.

In response, the Lensark suit swelled as dozens of tiny gas-propellent charges detonated at strategic locations around it. It inflated as if it were a balloon shoved onto a high-pressure tank of helium. A moment later Bang Galore's flitter-bomb blew, knocking the now-spherical green-and-gold Lensark into the ground, then rebounding up and away into the darkness.

"Unh—I think I'm—umph—going to be—urf—sick!" Lensark called over the com as he bounced.

"Not a good idea," Penny said.

Dragon's Teeth

The proximity sensor screamed in my ear again, and I ducked, but the side of a mountain slammed into my face.

While I had been focused on Lensark, Wrecking-bar had silently charged.

I jumped up on a blast of compressed air, the bar whistling below me. Through the haze of pain, I gritted, "Dragon's Teeth, Penny. Now." My reluctance to use Dragon's Teeth had disappeared with Lensark's bouncing departure. I palmed several wake-me-up patches.

"But—Okay, firing now. You know you've lost suit integrity, right?"

"Yeah. I've ordered all my vulnerable systems off-line," I said. The tear in my right side had opened a gap in the fine conductive mesh layer of the suit, reducing its effectiveness as a Faraday-cage. But with the electronic systems off-line, I was entirely under pneumatic control. While the suit would be sluggish, slower to respond to my movements, the electronic systems would have a much higher chance of surviving the—

I landed. There was a flash and bang thirty yards above my head as the missile Penny had fired from the stand-off drone blew. Moments later a rain of golf ball–sized bomblets showered down; where they struck, they stuck. Each bomblet blew with a firecracker–like snap, and nearly a hundred white-suited balloon duplicates of the Dispenser popped up, each in a different pose.

I turned. Wreckingbar had frozen, his systems momentarily overwhelmed by the EMP, and I moved quickly to slap the wake-me-up patches on his exposed cheeks. I didn't think the stun gas I carried would have any effect on him, but instead he would be vulnerable to a shock to his system that an overload of adrenaline would cause, particularly for a cyborg with a large portion of his original body mass replaced by machinery. I was also counting on the fact that his medical diagnostic systems had also been affected by the EMP, and would be slow to respond.

I only had a few seconds to locate and disable Bang Galore before she recovered. As I moved away from Wreckingbar, sliding—or, more accurately, lurching—my way through the balloon army, I unclipped the baton from my thigh and looked through the forest of white-suited figures for the red-and-silver-white harlequin-esque cyborg. And there she was, standing on a half-crushed car, frozen with her arms out, like she was about to dive into a pool.

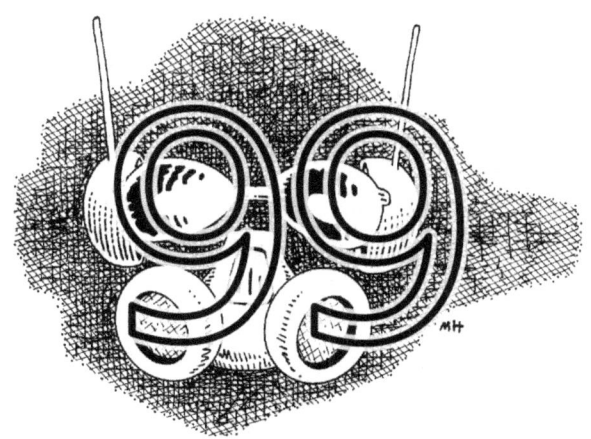

The Slippery Slope

I pointed the wand ten feet above her head and fired. It 'fumped' and a folded and compressed shroud arced out, weights spreading. From the corner of my eye I saw Wreckingbar spasm, his back arching; then he lashed out with his bar, clearing a swath through the balloon-duplicates like he was cutting a path through the jungle with a machete.

The shroud fell, engulfing Bang Galore. She jerked, and bomblets spat from the tubes above her hands. The bomblets 'thwipped' into the translucent mono-polymer sheet, which stretched like plastic wrap, but did not break. Their proximity sensors prevented them from detonating.

Wreckingbar had located me among the balloon army, and was bearing down on me. His face under the mask was a livid red, white foaming spittle spraying from his mouth and roaring "Ahhhh! I will crush you—" as he collapsed with a crashing metallic clatter, skidding to a stop nearly at my feet.

The airtight shroud began to shrink as Bang Galore

struggled, grasping at its surface, pulling and pushing with her fingers, but it wouldn't tear. Sealed off, she couldn't launch or detonate any of her bombs without endangering herself. Three down, leaving only my father's killer.

"You're cutting this close, Michael," Penny said. "Your reservoirs are empty except for webbing, and that's at eight percent."

"It'll be enough. I've got a gooey-grenade left. And a couple of the angel-wire projectors." Which would be more than enough to kill Chainsaw.

Chainsaw had struggled back to his feet and was slicing into balloon-duplicates with his right-arm chainsaw. Their popping was audible over the whirring buzz of his saw arm. To get his attention, I hit him with the last booger-bomb. With an angel-wire projector in each of my hands, we lurched at each other. Despite the drop in my backpack's weight, my right side was still slow and dragging. Smoke was spurting from Chainsaw's joint actuators and saw blade motors as he drove himself forward. I put all the power I could muster into a kick to his left knee as I blocked the overhand blow of his stuttering chainsaw-bladed right arm with my left. My power-assist pneumatics groaned and sputtered as my left arm went numb and the angel-wire projector dropped from my left hand. Only the composite boot cap prevented me from breaking my toe. I heard the crack of the armor on his knee—only possible because of the chemically in-duced decay—and he lurched again, the goo leaking into the gap, freezing his knee joint.

"You're going to stay dead this time," Chainsaw said as he drew his right arm back, the chainsaw blade starting to smoke, flicks of flame visible along its track as he fed it power to overcome the friction and burn away the last of the gooey-grenade goo.

The blades spiraling up Chainsaw's left arm were starting to chew their way through the suit as he leaned into me. I aimed my last angel-wire projector at his neck. One flick of the button and he would be a dead cyborg.

My thumb started to press; then I jerked the projector down, changing the target to just above his right elbow and fired. Taking his head off would be too quick. There was a crack, the hissing of the rockets at each end of the wire, and with a spurt of dark hydraulic fluid the chainsaw portion parted ways with the rest of his right arm.

I adjusted the catalytic mix on the webbing. Chainsaw stood, staring at the stump of his right arm. He opened his mouth and I sprayed the webbing in a swath across his exposed lower face and neck, an unhealthy dose going in his mouth. It stuck, and started contracting.

I watched with grim satisfaction as he clawed at the bands tightening around his face and neck with his left hand while his right arm waved. The chainsaw blade winding around his body fitfully jerked forward a few inches, then jammed in its track with a little whine for a stuttering second, before lurching forward another inch or so. His movements weakened. The blood flow to his brain was failing, choking off the flow of oxygen. Watching him die, my anger ebbed away. How could I betray my father's legacy like this? This wasn't the way it should end. I wouldn't let myself become like him or the rest of the Demolition Squad. I leaned forward and sprayed the detangler. I could dispense justice with mercy.

Judo and Kudos at the Black Lagoon

Saturday, December 8th, 1984
(13,822 days post Supernova 1947A)

It was a quarter to ten the next morning when I woke. Fifteen minutes to make it to the Black Lagoon. There had been no alerts to wake me, and I had let myself sleep in. Despite the rather prompt arrival of the police SCU and its armored Mobile Powers Containment Vehicle, it had taken the better part of an hour to detach myself from the police, and two hops of the jetpack, broken up by pauses to recharge the air tank, to make it back to the lab. Penny had remained at the command console, helping coordinate the clean up and making sure that Kinnison had made it home. She had left a little after two in the morning, and I had decided to sleep in the infirmary off the main lab rather than drag myself up to my room.

It was the aches from the night's combat that woke me. When I went to splash water on my face I found that my right eye had a ring-like bruise around it. *Oh, well,* I thought and shrugged. Which wasn't a good idea, as pain shot down my side from the cracked rib, despite the bandages that Penny had wrapped me in.

After I took some heavy duty painkillers, I checked my cellphone. There were dozens of emails and texts. I skimmed over them. One text from Cleo and half a dozen from Kinnison asking me if I was planning to make it to the Black Lagoon this morning. Most of the rest were from autonomous systems reporting their status. I answered the one from Cleo with a 'yes', and looked over the email. Increased activity on TheDispenser.hero website, starting at around 2:15, and one that, interestingly enough, looked like it was from Agent Sellers, which I saved for later.

I turned on my cellphone, thumbed the P2P mode, and said, "Mom? Are you up?"

I waited several seconds before she responded. "Yes, Michael." Her voice was dreamy.

"Do you need anything? I was planning on leaving for the Black Lagoon soon, but I wanted to make sure you are okay before I go."

"I'm fine. I had a dream about your father last night, you know."

"A dream? About Dad?"

To my surprise, Diana's voice came next. "I'm here, Michael. You don't need to worry about Liz. She's a little woozy from her meds, but otherwise fine." Then, slightly muffled she said, "Liz, would you be a dear and get me another slice of the coffee cake?"

"Certainly, Diana."

It must have been difficult, but Diana managed to lower her voice to say, "I heard about last night, Michael. You and Kim did good. Mike would have been proud of you. I only wish that Penny had taken a more active role."

I felt a knot forming in my throat, but I managed to say, "She was invaluable, Diana."

"Yes. Yes, of course," she said, but didn't sound all that convinced. Then her voice went back to its normal hearty volume. "Penny and Kim left together for the dojo about half an hour ago. If you leave now you won't be more than five or ten minutes late."

"Okay, I'll see you later." I closed the phone.

I checked the monitors, but there were still no alerts. I grabbed my spare workout bag and headed for the vehicle silo, only to retrace my steps to the lab when I was reminded of the ring-bruise around my right eye in my reflection off the glass wall separating the ready room and silo. I pulled out the first-aid kit, which was packed into a briefcase and included a rather extensive makeup section and mirror. The reason for their inclusion in the kit had taken me quite a while to work out.

After a quick application of foundation, I was driving the fastest of the electric carts through the tunnels, the lights blinking on ahead of me, the darkness closing in behind. My destination was the marina exit. It was a couple of Transit stops from the dojo. In fact, I thought, it might even be faster to fast-jog the last leg than to wait for a pod.

Something more than simple curiosity about Mom's dream chewed at me as I drove purring through the tunnels. What did it mean? Was this a sign that she was coming to terms with Dad's death? I'd have to talk to Doc Styx about it.

The jog through the crisp December air helped clear my head, the aches fading as my limbs pumped. A zen-like sense of calm overtook me. I was still alive. Kinnison was still alive. The Demolition Squad was sitting in a Powered Detention Center somewhere. I had successfully made lemonade from what life had handed me.

When I entered the dojo, all action stopped and heads turned in my direction despite my attempt at stealth.

"Ah, Michael," Sensei Fox said. "Good of you to join us."

"I'm sorry, Sensei."

"We were up late last night, Sensei," Kinnison said. He had a huge bruise on the left side of his face. "Uh, it was the Winter Wonderland Dance, and well..."

I briefly wondered how Kinnison had explained the bruise.

"No matter, Kim, we are all here now, so why don't we save a discussion of yesterday evening's events for afterward." And he gave me wink that left me with a thrill of acknowledgment. He knew about last night.

"Yes, Sensei," Kinnison said.

When I joined the line Penny gave me an almost smug look, making me think that there should be a small yellow feather dangling from the corner of her mouth. The twins were casting envious glances in my direction, and Cleo gave me a welcoming smile.

Kinnison spent nearly the entire training session looking like he was about to burst. Luckily, or, more likely, knowingly, Sensei Fox took it easy on the two of us, and my ribs thanked him for that mercy.

I Am Legion's Scoop

Sensei Fox's class dismissal was barely off his lips when Kinnison said, "Did you see I Am Legion's blog post, Gurick? It's all over the news!"

"I haven't had time to look at the news, Kinnison," I said. His bruise had turned a distinctive shade of purple. "Tell me you didn't go out looking like that, but no, you must have, because here you are."

"What?"

"Face-palm, Kinnison, face-palm is all I have to say."

He put up a hand, attempting to cover the bruise.

I sighed. "No, I meant I was the one that was face-palming, not you."

"Oh. Yeah, I guess I didn't think about it." Excitement returned to voice and face, "But it's all over the news!"

For some reason I felt like yanking Kinnison's chain, so I said in my most innocent voice, "What is? Your bruise?"

"No! Of course not. We—" Kinnison started to say,

then stopped, silent for several long moments as he tried to formulate what he wanted to say instead of the obvious.

"The Nova League defeated Doctor M's Robotic Horde again?" I prompted.

"No—Well, that yes, but, well, see for yourself." He pulled a tablet out of his bag and poked at it, then turned it to face me. I Am Legion's blog header read 'The Dispenser is Back!' Under it there was a sequence of photos, highlighting our fight with the Demolition Squad, and their subsequent loading into the MPCV, their arms and legs heavily shackled, and bulky power taps projecting from their backs, giving off the occasional spark as the cyborgs continually drained their internal Galactitech v-taps.

I took the tablet, paging my way down. The time of the post was 1:37 AM. I Am Legion's story was a scoop, both in breaking the news of the return the Dispenser, and in posting the first photos and video of the new superhero Lensark. There was something else about the Demolition Squad being part of a bigger conspiracy to plunge Galacticity into chaos by cutting the power at critical distribution points.

I looked up and caught Penny's eye. The smug smile was back. "Did you...?"

"I did," Penny said.

"You gave I Am Legion the videos?" Kinnison said.

"The major networks were all over the Robotic Horde story, so they were a little slow on picking up on the defeat of the Demolition Squad. So I thought I Am Legion should get it first."

Part of me was wondering if Penny might know, or at least have a strong idea about, who I Am Legion was. And if that had anything to do with her decision to hand the story to Legion.

"Well, that is interesting news."

"Speaking of news," Penny said, "Silver Archer wants to talk to the Dispenser about some weapon-smithing. What do you say, Hephaestus?"

I grimaced, then whispered, "With power—"

"—comes great responsibility," Kinnison and Cleo said together.

"I'll take that as a yes, then," Penny said.

The Last Message

When I got around to going through my email more thoroughly later that day, I was totally floored. What I had thought was from Agent Sellers wasn't. I could see where the assumption had come form. Under the 'Dad' label the real address had been agent-dad@GurickLabs.com, and I had made the obvious inference. But I felt a chill when I started to read it. When I was done with the brief message, I opened up the email header to confirm the delivery path. It had been sent from the lab computer system at 2:13, and had been immediately relayed to my cellphone, which I had turned off by then. I reread it to make sure I wasn't hallucinating or suffering from the blow to my head. It was addressed to me; instructed me to visit a web page on the lab web server via a secure link—emphasizing that I should be careful to visit the link using httpss, the super-secure http, not https—and was signed 'Love Dad'. I recognized the URL. It was for one of the instructional videos for the tunneling machinery that I had already visited, albeit only using the https protocol.

I pulled up a browser and fed it the link. The page loaded as I remembered it, and after a momentary delay, the video started streaming. But rather than a shot of the mole-machine controls, it was Dad sitting where I was sitting, the lab dark behind him.

"Michael, I have uttered many a cliché in my life, but this is the first time I have ever said this. If you are watching this then I'm dead.

"There. I've said it. Now I suspect you would like an explanation of how I was able to reach out from beyond the grave to send you this message, aren't you?"

"Yes. Yes, I am," I murmured.

"By now, I would expect you are familiar with software agents that filter the news feeds and maintain TheDispenser.hero web site, no? Well, one of the software agents I am leaving behind I call AgentDad. I've programmed it to monitor for news of my death or disappearance, then, after a suitably long period, the news of my reappearance, then email you the link to this steganographic video. Or, more accurately, your appearance as The Dispenser, because I know you are the only one who would, or could, become the Dispenser after I was gone. And how inexpressibly proud of you I am for putting on the Suit, for not letting the Dispenser die because I screwed up and got myself killed.

"It's a funny thing. Ever since I discovered your video camera in the mudroom, I knew you would become the Dispenser when I retired. I had just hoped my retirement wouldn't be forced.

"Your mother and I argued about whether or not to tell you about the Dispenser and our secret lives. She wanted you to have a chance to grow up without the

choice for your future being made for you. In the end I agreed and we told you nothing about the Dispenser. When you figured it out on your own, your mother refused to give in, and we all ignored the caped elephant in the room. Don't blame her for withholding our super-lives from you, Michael. She believes, and there is a truth in that belief, that your freedom to choose to become the Dispenser, untainted by legacy, is her second greatest gift to you.

"Oh, one last thing. You can trust Agent Sellers.

"I love you, Michael. I'm just sorry that it's been so hard for me to say that to you. And I'm even more sorry that you have to hear it this way."

And that was the last time I ever cried.

Epilogue [Checkmate of the Red Rook]

Saturday, February 2nd, 1985
(13,878 days post Supernova 1947A)

There is one last event I should relate to you, in part because it is a segue to the next narrator in this saga, and because it scared me as much as it did.

People go a little bonkers in Galacticity in the days leading up to Nova Genesis Day. The crazies come out, and the crime rate jumps right before February 3rd, the beginning of the celebration of our deliverance from Supernova 1947A.

Lensark and I had responded to a hold-up at a Star Dock convenience store that had turned into a hostage situation. Penny was sitting in the mobile command-center two blocks away. The MCC was still disguised as a pest exterminator's van, and I thought it reasonably invisible.

After I teamed up with Lensark, we had been forced to use the MCC—the 'Acme Pest Control' sign on its side still evoking a snigger from Kinnison every time he saw it—because Lensark's flight speed, and more importantly, range, was severely limited. So the three of us had been cruising the city and hoping we were within range to respond to any criminal activity when we got the alert.

Lensark and I were in the parking lot outside the Star Dock having a brief discussion as to whether I should just gas the place. Lensark was only picking up the thoughts of the hostages, nothing from the gunman.

"Send in a drone—" Penny was saying when there was a crash-bang over the radio link.

"What was that?" I radioed back.

"The MCC is under—" Penny started to reply when the radio link went dead.

"What's going on, Dispenser?" Lensark radioed. "I've lost contact with the MCC."

"Here," I unclipped a anesthetic gas grenade from my utility belt and handed it to Lensark. "I'm going to find out. You can handle this?"

"Yeah. Watch it, Dispenser—this could be a diversion."

"That's what I'm afraid of," I said as I rose on a stream of compressed air.

I couldn't help but curse myself for finally, after all those months, agreeing to play a pre-mission game of chess with Penny. And doubly so for using the very same red and blue chess set—she playing red like my Mom, and me playing blue—that my Mom and Dad had used before he had left her to fight super-criminals while she had manned the command-and-control center. The mission he hadn't returned from. Running tactical coordination like Penny was—had been doing. It was completely irrational, but I couldn't escape the feeling that when I had taken her red rook for a checkmate, that it had been some sort of sign.

I came up over the building, the compressed air of the jetpack roaring at my back, to find my worst fears confirmed. Where Lensark and I had left the mobile-command center van there was smashed and scattered wreckage. One forlorn piece of the van's side panel lay in the middle of the road, 'Acme Pest Co' still legible on its surface. Two bodies lay among the debris, limbs twisted, but it was obvious they weren't Penny's body. Smaller pieces of wreckage blew and skittered in the wash of my jetpack as I landed, sur-veying the scene for a sign, any sign, of Penny. It began to snow as I started my search.

I found Penny under a reinforced side panel of the van. Other than a gash across her forehead and tears in her eyes, she seemed to be in once piece. "Penny, are you okay?"

She gave a hiccuping sigh. "No, I'm not okay. I killed them."

I've gone on about myself for too long. Penny is perfectly capable of telling her story, so you are going to have to get it from her.

To be continued . . .

Penny takes up the Nova Genesis story in *The Red*

Rook available in print or ebook. See:

TheRedRookBook.com

or

FritzFreiheit.com/The_Red_Rook

If you've enjoyed *Dispensing Justice* (or feel strongly, one way or another), I encourage you to rate or like or even write a review on Amazon, Facebook, GoodReads, Google+, Twitter, or any other social media outlet. You can also leave a review or comment at DispensingJustice.com and NovaGenesisWorld.com

—Fritz Freiheit

#DispensingJustice

#NovaGenesisWorld

About the Author

My first memories are of watching the Lone Ranger and JFK's funeral on TV. I discovered Heinlein in my middle school library, and have been avidly consuming SF and fantasy, sometimes to the detriment of my grades and social life, since then. I graduated from East Lansing High School, Michigan, in 1977, but my taste in music didn't crystallize until 1985 when I found myself in Los Angeles, recruited to write a Japanese language parser after spending a year in Japan working for Sumitomo Electric. A decade after that I graduated from the University of Michigan with a Masters of Science in Artificial Intelligence and got married. It would be another decade before I finished my first novel. I live in Ann Arbor, Michigan where I irritate my wife and daughter by listening to 80's music. You can find Fritz on the web at:

www.FritzFreiheit.com

About the Artist

While best known as the creator of the "Those Annoying Post Bros." comic book series, Matt Howarth has many outlets for his twisted creativity: science fiction, fantasy, horror, numerous collaborations with musicians of international renown, and even commercial illustrations. You can check out his work at:

www.matthowarth.com

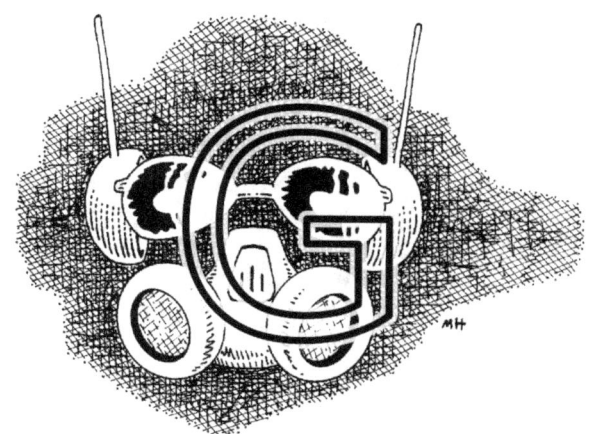

Glossary

This glossary is also available online:

http://www.NovaGenesisWorld.com/wiki/DJ_Glossary

1947
The year that the Nova Genesis alternate history branched from ours.

1947A
See Supernova 1947A.

Acme Pest Control
The name of the company on the side of the Dispenser's Mobile Command Center.

Aegis Team
A team of superheroes consisting of the Dispenser, Lady Lightning, Silver Archer, and Tsunami. It broke up in 1974 after the death of Lady Lightning.

Agent Psmith
A famous psionic secret agent movie character.

AI
An acronym for artificial intelligence.

alien
Someone or something not descended from Earth life.

American Super Football League (ASFL)
   A football league whose players are supers or near-supers.
android
   A robot with a humanoid shape.
Android Assassins vs. Kung Fu Clones
   A board game involving the invasion of a computer controlled fortress by martial arts clones.
angel-wire projector
   One of the Dispenser's weapons based on mono-molecular wire.
antigravity
   Galactitech that negates gravity.
Aqua Dome
   A Galacticity concert venue, partially submerged in Lake Michigan.
Archer
   See Silver Archer.
Arcobaleno Rex
   A super known for his garish costume.
arcology
   A self-contained city.
Arcology
   The Galactics' arcology, or self-contained city, dropped into southern Lake Michigan in 1948.
artificial intelligence (AI)
   An artificial intelligence, or AI, is machine or computer based intelligence approaching or surpassing human intelligence.
ASFL
   An acronym for the American Super Football League.
Astral Agent
   A member of the Astral Agents superhero group sponsored by the Galactics. Every Astral Agent has an Astral Orb through which the Agent derives his or her powers.
Astral Orb (or Orb)
   A Galactitech device issued/used by Astral Agents.
Atomic Jack's
   A restaurant in Galacticity.
Backslash
   A supervillain.

balloon-grenade
One of the Dispenser's weapons.

Bang Galore
A cyborg supervillain. She is a member of the Demolition Squad.

Baron Atom
A supervillain.

Bayside
A fusion-based electrical power plant run by Galacticity Metro Edison. Located in Southshore.

Black Lagoon Dojo
A martial arts training facility run by A.J. Fox. It is located in Galacticity not far from Lake Michigan.

Blowback
A supervillain.

booger-bomb
One of the Dispenser's weapons.

Brain Trust, The
A superhero. Member of the Galacticity Nova League.

brick
Superslang for a super who is tough and strong.

British Ballistics
A UK-based international transportation company.

Cape and Banter Improv
A comedy improvisation troop based in Galacticity.

cape tugger
Superslang for superhero fan.

Captain Fusion
A superhero.

Centurion High School (CHS)
The Galacticity high school that Michael, Penny, Kim, and Cleo attend.

Cerberus Defense Systems
One of Doc Styx's many corporations.

Chainsaw
A cyborg supervillain. He is a member of the Demolition Squad.

Charon Aerospace
One of Doc Styx's many corporations.

chimera
An animal or plant that is a genetically mixed with

another species of animal or plant.

CHS

An acronym for Centurion High School.

Cold fusion

Fusion that doesn't produce significant quantities of neutrons.

Cosmic Bowling (tm)

A kind of bowling similar to bumper bowling, but much more interactive. Reminiscent of old-style pinball.

Cosmic Bowling Station

A bowling alley in the suburbs of Galacticity. Known for its kid-friendly Cosmic Bowling.

Cowl, The

A bar notorious for catering to low-powered superheroes and supervillains.

Crash-Foam (tm)

A rapidly expanding foam that absorbs kinetic energy.

cryocapsule

A freezer container, usually used to store dead bodies or live ones in suspended animation.

cyber

Of or pertaining to computers.

Cyber City

A company that sells mass-market versions of superhero gear and gadgets, such as exoskeletons.

Cyberion

A retired superhero.

cyborg

A human-machine combination.

Demolition Squad (The Squad)

A supervillain team composed of the four cyborgs: Bang Galore, Chainsaw, Dragline, and Wreckingbar.

Dispenser, The

A superhero. He is a member of the Nova League. Former member of the Aegis Team.

Doc

Short for Doc Styx.

Doc Styx

Doc Styx, sometimes referred to simply as Doc, is a superhero and sole owner of Styx Enterprises. He is a founding member of the Nova League.

Doctor M

A supervillain. He is the most notorious nemesis of the Nova League.

Doctor M's Robotic Horde

An army of robots created and controlled by Doctor M.

doppelgänger

A duplicate of someone. May be a shapeshifter or a construct.

Dragline

A cyborg supervillain. She is a member of the Demolition Squad.

Dragon's Teeth

A code name for one of the Dispenser's defensive systems.

Dungeon Inglorious

The role-playing dungeon run by Max, a friend of Michael, Penny, and Kim.

Earth-Firster

A radical group seeking to oust the Galactics and return Earth to the humans.

Earth-tech

Technology whose lineage does not include Galactitech.

Electrode

A supervillain.

EMP

An acronym for 'electromagnetic pulse'.

Enhanced ERA

An amendment to the U.S. Constitution ensuring that all sentient citizens of the U.S. have equal rights.

Exoskeleton (X-K)

An external, power assisted skeleton. Exoskeletons are used to enhance an individual's strength, or allow someone to walk that would otherwise be wheelchair bound.

Family Protective Division (FPD)

A subdivision of the U.S. Government Secret Services, charged with protecting the spouses and children of superheroes.

First Bank of Terra

A bank established after the arrival of the Galactics.

First Generation

Superheroes born with powers or created directly after

Supernova 1947A.

FPD

An acronym for Family Protective Division.

G.I.D.

An acronym for a Galactics' ID. A Galactitech identification system, mostly used by superheroes to ensure their identity is not used by someone else.

Gadgeteer

A UPCS classification.

Galactic

An alien. Less frequently, someone with Galactic Citizenship.

Galactic Bounty Hunter 4 (tm)

A computer game.

Galactic Citizen

An alien or human with Galactic Citizenship.

Galactic Citizenship

The status of a citizen of the galaxy. Some supers have become Galactic Citizens in order to cut their ties with Earth governments.

Galactic Sentinel

A Galactic and superhero. Arrived on Earth in 1947.

Galacticity (GC)

Galacticity, or GC, is a city on the south eastern shores of Lake Michigan, established in 1948 shortly after the arrival of the Galactics' Arcology.

Galacticity Library

See Galacticity Nova Genesis Memorial Library.

Galacticity Metro Edison (GCME)

The primary (electrical) power production company in Galacticity.

Galacticity Nova Genesis Memorial Library

Galacticity's main library.

Galactics

The galaxy spanning culture composed of a diverse collection of aliens.

Galactitech

Technology from the Galactics.

GC

An abbreviation for Galacticity.

GCME

An acronym for Galacticity Metro Edison.

GCTV

An acronym for Galacticity Television.

Genetics, Transgenetics, and Molecular Research

A journal.

GME

An acronym for Galacticity Metro Edison.

Graviton

A supervillain, best known for his hijacking of the entire United Nations building, which he placed in Earth orbit while he held everyone inside hostage.

Heroes Weekly

A magazine.

Heroic Relations

A public relations firm specializing in superhero PR.

Hijacking, The

The the simultaneous hijacking of every major commercial aircraft in the world by Doctor M in 1970 that killed the demand for commercial flights.

HUD

An acronym for Heads Up Display.

hypernaut

A super who has the power of speed.

hypersense

A supersense.

I Am Legion

A blog.

IBS

An acronym for International Ballistic Shipping.

Ice Fall

The rain of comet ice containing the Galactics' repair nanites.

IFF

An acronym for Identify Friend or Foe.

International Ballistic Shipping (IBS)

A global shipping company.

inTouch (tm)

A popular model of cell phone with touch screen.

Iodine

A supervillain. She is currently incarcerated.

JASON

An acronym for Joint Authentication Superidentification Open Net.

jetpack

A strap-on rocket backpack.

Jetstream

A superhero.

JFK High School

A Galacticity high school.

Joint Authentication Superidentification Open Net (JASON)

An open standards identification system. It can interface with the G.I.D.

kata

A specific series of martial arts moves.

Kill Switch

A supervillain. He assassinated President John F. Kennedy in 1963.

Kinethis

A psionic superhero with telekinetic powers. He is a member of the Nova League.

Kingfisher

A supervillain.

Kissing Creek

A teen lovers' lane used by CHS students.

Lady Lightning

A superhero. Former member of the Aegis Team. Deceased.

League, The

Short for Nova League.

Lensark

A psionic superhero.

Leviathan-bot

A water-going member of Doctor M's Robotic Hordes.

levitate

To rise vertically or float in one location via telekinesis. A psionic power.

Light Fantastic

A superhero.

linear accelerator

A device that accelerates objects down a set of rails via electromagnetics.

Magician, The

A superhero. He is a member of the Nova League.

Magnetic Mistress

A superhero.

Mallet, The

A minor supervillain.

Man in Black

One of the Men in Black.

Mars Wars

A series of fantasy movies. The first, called Mars Wars, came out in 1977. It's darker, edgier sequel was released in 1983.

Master Mind

A UPCS classification.

MCC

An acronym for Mobile Command Center.

Megabot

A giant robot member of Doctor M's Robotic Hordes.

Men in Black

Agents of the U.S. government.

micro-mesh

A kind of armor composed of an extremely fine, extremely tough wire.

Mind Fire

A psionic superhero.

Mindspike

A psionic supervillain.

Mobile Command Center (MCC)

A mobile command center, or MCC, is a communications and control hub installed in a vehicle.

Mobile Powers Containment Vehicle

A Mobile Powers Containment Vehicle, or MPCV, is a vehicle designed to transport supers.

molecular edge

Molecular edge An edge a single molecule thick, thus extremely sharp.

monomolecular wire

A single molecular strand, extremely strong, and capable of cutting through extremely tough substances.

MPCV

Acronym for Mobile Powers Containment Vehicle.

nannite

The smallest unit of nanotechnology capable of independent action.

nanoborg

A cyborg created by Galactitech nanites. As with nearly all macro-scaled powered Galactitech, nanoborgs use v-taps for energy.

nanotech

Short for nanotechnology.

Neutrino

A superhero. She is a member of the Nova League.

Nexus War

A board game of strategic maneuvering and tactical spaceship combat.

Nova Day

February 3rd, the day commemorating Supernova 1947A.

Nova Genesis

A term used to refer to February 3rd, 1947, when Supernova 1947A impinged on Earth, or the milieu that followed.

Nova Genesis Day

February 3rd, the day commemorating Supernova 1947A.

Nova Genesis Memorial Plaza (Nova Genesis Plaza)

One of Galacticity's main plazas.

Nova Genesis Plaza

See Nova Genesis Memorial Plaza.

Nova League (The League)

The largest and most prominent superhero group on Earth. It operates predominantly in North America and its main headquarters are in Galacticity.

Nova League Tower

The main headquarters of the Nova League.

nunchaku

A weapon based on the Japanese rice flail. Two short pieces of wood or metal attached together by a short length of rope or chain. More of a danger to the wielder than the target for the untrained.

Orb

Short for Astral Orb.

Orpheus Information Systems (Orpheus IS)

One of Doc Styx's corporations.

Orpheus IS
Short for Orpheus Information Systems.

PICSEA
An acronym for Powers Investigation, Control, and Security Enforcement Agency.

PICSID
The PICSEA version of super identification. PICSID is an acronym for Powers Investigation, Control, and Security Identifier.

pixie
A derogatory, superslang term for a member of PICSEA, or Powers Investigation, Control, and Security Enforcement Agency.

pneumatic-pogo
A fire pole–like device that is a one-man elevator.

Popular Superscience
A magazine about the superscientists, their experiments, and gear.

power
A super ability or characteristic. Typically derived from a mutation, cyborg enhancement, Galactitech, or a great of deal of training.

power armor
A sealed suit of armor incorporating strength augmentation.

Power Registration Act
An early attempt to force all supers to register with the U.S. government.

power tap
A Galactitech device for diverting and/or storing energy generated via a v-tap.

Powered Detention Center
A prison for supers.

Powers Investigation, Control, and Security Enforcement Agency (PICSEA)
An arm of the U.S. government responsible for monitoring and tracking supers as well as peforming various law enforcement duties related to supers.

Powers Oversight Committee
A U.S. Senate committee focused on supers.

Proxima Drive

The street that Michael and Penny live on. It's located in the suburbs east of Galacticity.

Pscreamer

A psionic supervillain.

psi-scope

A device for measuring psionic abilities.

Psicorp

A corporation that manufactures psionic related gear.

psionic

A mental power or ability.

psionotropic

An active response to psionic energies. For example, some psionotropic materials glow in the presence of psionic activity.

purple piss

Superslang for a useless power.

Ragnarok City

A board game involving an AI-controlled supertank, the Ragnorak Machine, attacking a heavily defended city.

Ragnarok Machine

An AI supertank unit from the board game Ragnarok City.

retch gas

One of the Dispenser's weapons.

Robotic Horde

Short for Doctor M's Robotic Hordes.

Roswell

A town in New Mexico where the first recorded contact between Earth humans and Galactics occurred shortly after Supernova 1947A.

Rust Never Sleeps

A code name for one of the Dispenser's weapons.

S3PI

An acronym for Supplemental Strategic Super Powers Initiative.

SCU

An acronym for Supers Crime Unit.

shapeshifter

Someone who can alter his or her appearance.

Shield, The

The system constructed by the Galactics to block the Earth

from the effects of Supernova 1947A.

Silhouette and Supersuit Recognition Agent

A computer program capable of matching a silhouette or supersuit to a database in order to identify the super. Similar to face recognition software.

Silver Archer (The Archer)

A superhero and member of the Nova League. Former member of the Aegis Team. She is a brick.

SimOlympus (tm)

A computer game.

smartmask

An advanced form of mask capable of, among other things, mimicking the facial movements of the wearer.

SNN

An acronym for Superhero News Network.

Sociological Impact of Supernova 1947A, The

A non-fiction book by Dr. Jane Myers about the effects on society and culture of Supernova 1947A and the arrival of the Galactics.

Southshore

An industrial section of Galacticity.

Spungi (tm)

A spongy material used to make toys.

spy-ray

A terahertz-based scanner capable of penetrating many opaque substances.

spycam

A spy camera.

Squad, The

Short for the Demolition Squad.

star wisp

A kind of Galactics starship.

StarNet

The Galactics' interstellar communication network.

Strong Man (tm)

A line of exoskeletons sold by Cyber City.

Styx Enterprises

The top level Doc Styx corporation.

super

Someone with powers.

super-ID
Short for superidentity.

superhero
Someone with powers who fights crime.

Superhero News Network (SNN)
A cable TV news channel that focuses on the superhero world.

Superhero Vigilante Act (SVA)
A law enacted by U.S. congress to give, among other things, the legal basis for superhero crime fighting independent of the local police.

superhuman
A human with superpowers.

Superidentity (super-ID)
The persona, including supersuit, of a super. Legally recognized to be independent of any secret identity.

Supernova 1947A
The first supernova of 1947, whose wavefront reached Earth on February 3rd, 1947, and the event that branched the Nova Genesis alternate history from ours. 1947A occurred close enough to Earth to destroy all life, but due to the intervention of the Galactics, life on Earth was saved.

Superpeople
A magazine focused on gossip about superheroes and supervillains.

superpower
A power or ability not normally enjoyed by a human.

Supers Crime Unit (SCU)
An arm of law enforcement equipped and/or enable to operate against supers. Similar to SWAT.

Supers Registry
A list of supers and their known powers. Maintained by the Nova League.

superscientist
A scientist whose scientific abilities, at least in part, derive from their superpower.

superslang
Slang used by or about supers.

supersuit
The "costume" worn by a super. Also known as superwear.

supervillain

Someone with superpowers who commits crimes.

superwear

Another term for supersuit.

Supplemental Strategic Super Powers Initiative (S3PI)

An initiative to recruit and use supers for the strategic defense of the U.S. and NATO.

surujin

A weapon consisting of two weights separated by a length of rope or chain.

SVA

An acronym for Supers Vigilante Act.

syntheskin

A synthetic skin, commonly used in medical applications.

Tantalus Microdevices

One of Doc Styx's corporations.

telekinesis

Telekinesis, or TK, is the ability to move things with your mind. A psionic power.

telekinetic

Someone who has the power of telekinesis. A psionic power.

telepath

Someone who has the power of telepathy.

telepathy

The ability to read minds. A psionic power.

Telepathy blockers

A drug that blocks telepathic powers.

teleport

The ability to shift from one location to another without moving through the intervening space. A psionic power.

Things in the Saucer Tomb, The

A board game involving the exploration of a downed flying saucer in the Antarctic.

Titan, The

Usually short for Titanium Titan.

Titanium Titan (The Titan)

A superhero and member of the Nova League. He is classified as a Tool Master under the UPCS.

TK

An abbreviation for telekinesis.

Tool Master
A UPCS classification.

Tough Guy (tm)
The brand name of a type of armor sold by Cyber City.

transgenetic
Genetics that span species or are artificial in origin.

Transgenetica
A scientific journal specializing in transgenetics.

transit pod
A small, automated vehicle running on rails. Part of the mass transit system in Galacticity.

Tsunami
A superhero. He is a former member of the Aegis Team. Retired.

Turbocharger
A hypernaut superhero. Deceased.

Übermind
A psionic supervillain.

Unified Powers Classification System (UPCS)
A system established by the U.S. government to classify supers.

UPCS
An acronym for Unified Powers Classification System.

V-tap (vacuum-tap)
Galatitech that makes the universal vacuum energy available for use. A powerful energy source used by nanoborgs and most other macro-scale Galatitech devices that require power.

Vermillion
A superhero. She is an Astral Agent.

vocoder
An electronic voice transformation system. Often used to disguise a person's voice.

wake-me-up
A drug, similar in effect to a combination of caffein and adrenalin.

White Whirlwind
A retired superhero. He founded a very successful cleaning supplies company after retirement.

Witness
A member of a group (some would argue a religious in

nature) that considers the Galactics saviors of the human race and Earth who should be treated with the utmost respect.

Wolverine Dispatch and Security Services

A security and transport company operating in Galacticity.

Wreckingbar

A cyborg supervillain. He is the leader of the Demolition Squad.

X-K

Abbreviation for exoskeleton.

Zircon Man

A superhero. He works for Wolverine Dispatch and Security Services.